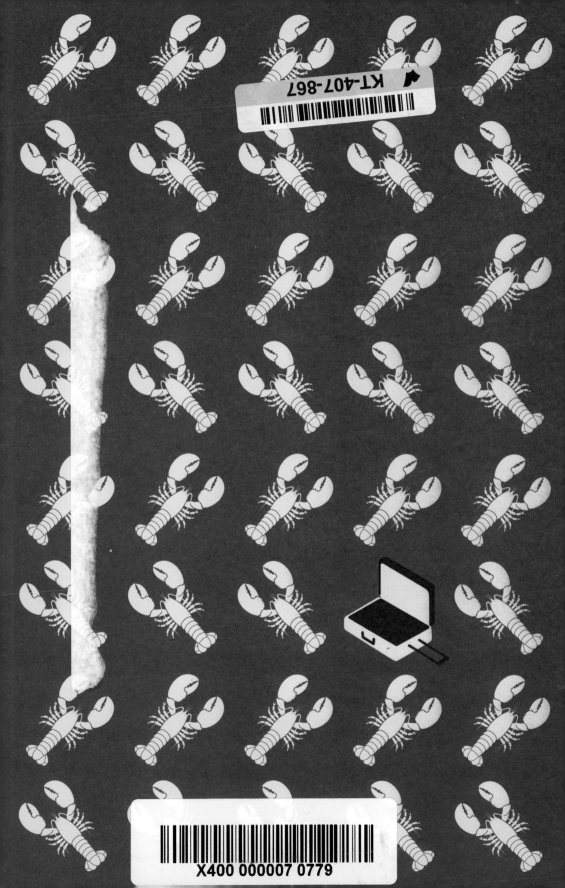

the
SUMMER
JOB

the SUMMER JOB

lizzy dent

VIKING
an imprint of
PENGUIN BOOKS

VIKING

UK | USA | Canada | Ireland | Australia
India | New Zealand | South Africa

Viking is part of the Penguin Random House group of companies
whose addresses can be found at global.penguinrandomhouse.com.

First published 2021
001

Copyright © Rebecca Denton, 2021

The moral right of the author has been asserted

Set in 12/14.75 pt Bembo Book MT Std
Typeset by Integra Software Services Pvt. Ltd, Pondicherry
Printed and bound in Great Britain by Clays Ltd, Elcograf S.p.A.

The authorized representative in the EEA is Penguin Random House,
Morrison Chambers, 32 Nassau Street, Dublin D02 YH68

A CIP catalogue record for this book is available from the British Library

HARDBACK ISBN: 978–0–241–47090–9
TRADE PAPERBACK ISBN: 978–0–241–99051–3

www.greenpenguin.co.uk

Penguin Random House is committed to a
sustainable future for our business, our readers
and our planet. This book is made from Forest
Stewardship Council® certified paper.

This book is dedicated to the entire Manson Clan.
With gratitude, love and a wee dram.

&

To my cousin Rachael Johns, the author who inspired me to write,
and continues to inspire me every day.

1.

May

'You here for a wedding?' the driver asks, his cheery eyes focused on me, and not on the tiny track we're careering up.

'No, no,' I reply, as my fingers begin to ache from all the seat-clenching they're having to do. He's got to be doing at least seventy.

'Aye, you're not dressed for a wedding,' he agrees.

I look down at my shirt, self-consciousness pushing away fear for a moment. I'd bought a white silk shirt for 60 per cent off from TK Maxx, but several hours into my journey I'd remembered that white silk shirts were only for rich people or anyone who liked doing laundry. The deal-clincher for me, when buying clothing, is whether or not it will come out of the dryer like it's been ironed.

The car takes a sharp turn, and the single lane thins to a ribbon, before the woods clear completely and we drive through a simple iron gate fixed to two old stone pillars. Vast lawns rise slowly upwards and, along the approach, rows of towering trees stretch their branches across to meet in a tunnel of crooked wood and leaves. Everything is sepia in the fog.

Ahead, the house comes into view, though in truth it looks more like a small castle. A grey and sandstone mother-ship, with pointed turrets flanking the sides and an enormous staircase leading from the circular drive to the entrance. It's far grander than I'd imagined, but strangely bleak. I text Tim immediately.

I'm in a fucking gothic novel

I'm pleased with my tone. Funny, irreverent, mysterious. I think about calling him to elaborate but I'm not entirely sure he'd get the joke. Tim isn't exactly well read.

The car tyres skid, jolting me back to the reality of the speeding vehicle. We are momentarily stuck as the tyres spin hopelessly in the mud and the driver revs the engine. He switches gears and we thrust forward.

'Round the back there's a short road to the stables and cottages. And then a small car park,' I say, double-checking the instructions on my phone.

'Staff entrance?' he questions, with a single raised eyebrow.

'Yup,' I say, nodding, then stare wistfully out of the window.

The back of the house is just as grand but arguably more beautiful than the front. The ground drops away from a pebbled courtyard and rose garden down to a river, which I can hear but not see. The stables sit about a hundred metres to the side of the house, and the car pulls to a halt between them and a trio of small stone cottages. I look back at the house, which is barely in view through a small grove of oaks.

The largest of the three cottages has wood smoke rising in pleasing spirals from the squat chimney, and there's a small slate-and-silver sign on the wooden door that I can just make out. *Staff Only.*

'This is it,' I say, getting out and handing the driver £200 in Scottish notes, trying not to wince as I say goodbye to all the money I had left in the world. 'Thanks for the ride. Who knew you could get to the west coast in under one and a half hours from Inverness? It must be a world record.'

He looks inordinately proud.

There are about a dozen cars in the car park, a white van, some four-wheel drives, a few of those big, black expensive-looking SUVs and a couple of golf carts – but still no humans. A dog barks once, far in the distance, the sound echoing ominously around the estate.

I feel my anxiety blossom into full nerves. This is it. The literal end of the road, and potentially the craziest thing I'd done since walking out on that stupid West End play. Right before my first line.

'Hope you enjoy Scotland, lass,' the driver says, then takes off with a screech of tyres on gravel.

I knock a few times on the wooden door. For late spring, it's far colder than I imagined, and my thin trenchcoat is proving a nonsense kind of cover-up for this weather.

My phone beeps and it's Tim.

What do you mean? 😊

I chuckle. He's so predictable.

There is still no sign of anyone. Crossing my arms to try and brace myself from the icy breeze, I look around the courtyard for some sign of life. I can hear the horses scuffing at the hay-covered stone floor in the barn, and I can sense the smell of mossy earth. I lean forward to look through the small window of the end cottage, and a small motion-light springs on, blinding me to my surroundings.

'Heather?'

I jump at the voice behind me – deep, with a thick but soft Scottish accent. I hold my hand up to my face and try to make out the figure emerging from behind the white van. He is tall, dressed in chef's whites underneath a dark coat that is open and flapping in the wind, with a dark woollen beanie pulled down over his forehead. *Tall, mysterious and can poach an egg.* I am instantly intrigued.

'Hello! Yes, I am. That's me,' I say, saluting him like a general, my nerves apparently turning me into a comedy idiot.

'We need you to start right away,' he says nervously, pulling up the collar on his coat.

'Right this minute?' I reply, desperate for a hot cup of tea and a shower.

'Our emergency cover fell into the River Ayr while taking a tinkle,' booms a posh English accent, as a much older, shorter man in a dark suit with a bulging belly arrives, dragging one of those fancy bellhop trollies behind him. The light shines onto his reddish face, which is heavily lined but jolly. 'Hospitalized with exposure.'

'Double exposure,' I reply, with a giggle – I can't resist – and he shoots me a wicked grin.

'I'm William. But everyone calls me Bill. And this is James, here to welcome you on behalf of the kitchen,' he continues, glancing down at my bag. 'Well, I won't need the trolley. You travel light. Goodness gracious me. You should have seen last night's late arrival – poor night porter had to make a dozen trips up and down the stairs. *And he's got a dicky leg.*'

'I don't like having more than I can manage on my own,' I say, smiling at him.

3

'Well, I hope you bought some wellies,' he says, glancing down at my shoes.

'No. I'll need to get some. And a coat. Didn't anyone notify Scotland it's May, for God's sake?' I say, clutching at my arms.

'Northerly. They're bitter, even in summer,' says Bill, as he sticks the key into the lock of the cottage, and it makes a heavy *thunk* as he turns the old lock. He pushes the door open, but instead of showing me in, he pops my suitcase just inside and pulls the door shut. 'Couldn't grow a Pinot in this wind-chill, eh?'

I stutter, then scramble for a quick reply. 'Yes. Certainly it needs to be warmer. Except when there's a frost. You also sometimes need frost.' He's staring at me, so obviously I continue my verbal drivel. 'For the grapes, because sometimes they need frost. To make the wine, er, better.'

'We need you to start tonight,' James says again, cutting through the chatter. He and his tense shoulders are looking back towards the main house as if he's left a pan of hot fat on full.

I start to feel a little panicked. 'I'm not dressed,' is all I can think to say. 'I thought there would be some kind of formal orientation first? Watch one of those *Welcome to the company* films. Spend hours getting your email set up? Meet the boss? Go for a welcome drink?'

'My kinda girl,' Bill chortles again.

'We've got you a uniform.' James furrows his heavy brow my way, then turns sharply away to do more brooding.

Bill turns to me with an apologetic smile. 'I'm sorry, this is all very sudden. But I'm sure you'll take to it just fine, with your incredible experience. Oh, don't look so sheepish – I was the one who hired you, remember? I've seen your CV.'

'Right. Of course. Okay, let's go,' I say, as confidently as I can. No need to discuss my CV in front of James, or anyone.

Bill jumps into the nearest golf cart and turns on the ignition. James offers an impatient smile and nods towards the passenger seat.

'Cheers,' I say as he jumps on a little platform on the back and hangs on.

'If James is edgy, it's because he needs to go over the menu with you, like *now*,' Bill whispers.

I'm going to have to be careful with everything I say. Play the new girl. With the amount of jobs I've had, that's one thing I can do.

We pull up at the entrance to the kitchen, and as the heavy modern door is pushed open, the light and noise spill out onto the courtyard, and suddenly a new set of senses comes fiercely alive.

The back kitchen is buzzing. There are three chefs in whites preparing for the evening service. Piles of small new potatoes are being scrubbed, and another chef has a great sheet of tiny herbs, which are being forensically picked through with what look like tweezers. There is a kind of rhythmical chorus as knives hit wood, pans slam on granite and my block-heels clip-clop across the stone floor.

'Hi, Chef,' says the youngest-looking of them. He's covered in blood splatters and holding a comically large butchering knife. James nods in approval at the young lad, who blushes and smiles shyly back at him. It's a cute exchange, and I warm a little to James.

Smells of lemon zest and rich, dark chocolate fill my nose as we pass the pastry counter. Then the sting of onions hits my eyes as we duck under a low doorway into the preparation area. There are two rows of stainless-steel cooking surfaces and large ovens, and another serious-looking young chef, her dark hair stuffed into a hairnet, is standing over a huge pot, carefully spooning in what seems to be an enormous ladle full of tiny lobsters.

'Oh my God, baby lobsters,' I whisper, aghast, but Bill has suddenly disappeared out through the swinging door into the restaurant. There's a glimpse of a dark, candle-lit room with accents of deep red and tartan.

'Langoustines, three minutes, fifteen seconds. Rolling boil,' the chef says to herself, as she starts a small timer. *Langoustines.* I blush at my stupidity and take a deep breath. *I won't last five minutes if I don't keep my mouth shut.*

'Heather?' James calls to me from the service area, where he is sorting through scribbled sheets of paper.

'Hey. Jamie for short, is it?'

'James actually,' he says abruptly, before glancing at the floor. 'Are you ready?'

'Sure,' I reply, painting on a face full of efficiency and confidence.

He waves a piece of paper at me. 'We've matches for the langoustine and hot-smoked salmon, but not the beetroot and pickled cabbage. We also need a pairing for the blade steak. I would have gone for a Cabernet, but there's the spring greens and turnip foam to consider in the balance. What do you think?'

James puts the paper down and looks up at me, and for the first time I see his full face in the light. He's definitely a looker, if you like that kind of accidentally handsome, full-lipped, furrowed-brow, forgot-to-shave-for-a-week kind of thing, which I most certainly do. Dark hair, chestnut eyes and cheeks flushed from the heat of the kitchen. And in those starched chef's whites too. I try hard not to stare.

Okay. I'm definitely staring.

Still staring.

'Heather?'

I shake myself out of my daze and back to the job at hand.

'Do you have any ideas what we could pair them with?'

'What do you usually pair them with?' I ask, hoping for a shortcut.

'The menu changes all the time, with the season, so this is a new dish, I'm afraid. There's normally something new needs pairing every day. As I said, we often pair the blade steak with the Cabernet, but I think the turnip . . .'

'*The menu changes all the time?*' I gulp.

James takes a breath. 'Sorry. I know this is a lot to take in. Before each service we sit and discuss the pairings for the degustation menu. The sommelier and me. Then I run it past Chef.'

'Chef? I thought you were the chef?'

'No,' he says, with a shy smile. 'Russell Brooks, our new executive chef, will check over everything tonight. It has to be right first time,' he says, somewhat apologetically.

'Russell Brooks,' I smile. 'Sounds like an electrical appliance.'

My gag hangs in the air for a moment, then withers and dies.

'He's got two Michelin stars,' James says, his eyes wide.

'Oh yes,' I say quickly.

Two Michelin stars? That doesn't make sense. I thought this place was meant to be stuck in the Dark Ages. I glance around the kitchen and realize the whole set-up does look rather too grand. 'Of course I know who he is. Everyone knows Russell Brook.'

'Brooks,' he corrects.

'Yes,' I nod quickly. 'Two Michelin stars.'

'Do you want a little time to familiarize yourself? I can give you thirty minutes, and then we have to get the draft ready for Chef.' He offers me the menu.

I study James's face for a moment. I can't tell if he is desperately begging for my help or angry that I'm not helping already. One thing is for sure: he is waiting for me to take control, and up until this point I've been trying to delay the inevitable. Time to bite the bullet.

'Where do you keep the wine list? And the wine? I'll need to see the cellar and maybe do some sampling,' I say, reaching for the food menu. Christ, it's complicated! This place is fancy as fuck. What the hell is smoked sea bacon? 'What did you say I need to match again?'

'The guinea fowl, the crab, the beetroot and fermented barley and the blade steak,' replies James, the raised vein on the side of his neck dissipating somewhat. 'The new wine list is here,' he says, dumping a large black leather folder into my arms. 'And the cellar is out back, the way you came in, and down the stone stairs by the deep freeze. I can show you?'

'No need. I'll be half an hour,' I say, nodding in determination, deciding the quiet of the wine cellar will be the safest place to panic. *New wine list?*

'One sec. Anis?' he calls to the baby-lobster boiler, who frowns at the disruption. She is carefully pouring deep-green oil into a blender with all the steady seriousness of an open-heart surgeon. 'Once you've finished the dill emulsion, make a tasting plate for Heather,' James commands.

'Yes, Chef,' she scowls and heads to the refrigerator.

And with that, James nods and almost smiles, before going back through to the kitchen. I breathe out for a moment, before remembering the clock is ticking and I have very little time to spare.

I walk quickly back through the preparation area and make my way down the gloriously romantic stone stairs to the cellar. I fish around for a light switch just as another bloody sensor-light flicks on, but this time it's a warm, dull yellow glow. My eyes adjust and, for a moment, I marvel at the space before me.

The cellar stretches out into the darkness, but it isn't only wine down here. Large rounds of cheese are stacked on modern steel shelving, and huge legs of cured hams and bacons hang from stainless-steel hooks in the ceiling. And beyond that, more cheese. God, I love cheese.

But there's no time to dither. I pull out my phone and lay the enormous wine list and the menu out on the shelf in front of me. Shit! This was certainly not the wine list I'd printed out from the website. The one I had stuffed in my bag back at the cottage had a dozen or so reds and whites, in varying degrees of cheap and less cheap.

The plan up until now – if you could call it a plan – was a crash course with my brand-new copy of *Wine for Newbies*, and Sir Google, as my tutors later this evening. Surface knowledge. A bluffable amount. Enough to blag my way through the summer at a crappy hotel in the middle of nowhere. Only the crusty, ramshackle, shithole Scottish hotel has not materialized, and instead I find myself in a fine-dining, luxury boutique property. This place is in need of a world-class sommelier to decipher the brand-new twenty-page wine list. Which I am definitely not.

It's time to call for help.

It's time to call the *real* Heather.

2.

Two weeks earlier

'So, are you all packed?' I asked, shaking my head as I looked around her bedroom for things I could 'borrow' while she was gone. I spied her T-bar heels poking out from under her chair, and her hair straighteners, for starters. Then I saw the bikinis laid out on the bed. Just how fancy was this Scottish hotel?

Heather had been my very best friend since primary school, arriving with her father in our home town of Plymouth not long after her mother had died. I could see right away how afraid she was, twisting and pulling on her curls, eyes permanently on the floor. It went round the playground like lightning about her mum. I knew immediately: this girl needed me.

I marched right up to her. 'Don't be scared. I'll show you round. I'm Elizabeth Finch and I'm already six.'

'Finch? Like the bird?' she whispered back. 'I have a pencil with little birds all over it. Do you want it?'

'Sure.' I marvelled at the bright little pictures and the beak-shaped eraser. I had never had a special pencil.

'Now it's yours. Can we be friends?'

'Sure, but you're going to need a lot more pencils,' I replied, grinning at her. Though of course it was never about the pencil.

From that day, we became inseparable. Me, her fierce protector, and Heather the kindest, most encouraging person in my life.

And little had changed. Here we were some twenty-five years later, and she had the London flat, the clothes, the make-up and a steady income that meant there was always milk for tea. And, following in her father's footsteps, she was now one of the brightest young wine experts in the country. Heather had found her way in the world. I still felt like the kid with no fancy pencils of her own.

She perched on the edge of her bed, taking a deep, steadying breath before looking at me nervously. 'Birdy, something big has happened. I'm fine, though. It's *all* good. Great, in fact.'

'Oh-kay, this sounds *exciting*,' I replied, a little tingle inside me at the thought of some high drama. I rested my butt on the edge of her dressing table and readied myself. 'Lucky for you I'm now officially unemployed again and so have time for *all* the drama, *all* the time. So do go on, I'm ready.'

'It's not drama,' she said, her large eyes narrowing on me, hurt.

'Shit! Sorry, I didn't mean to sound flippant. Please. What's going on?'

'I think I'm in love with Cristian,' she said as her mouth curved into a nervous smile.

'Oh,' I replied, trying to sound buoyant as my heart sank.

'I know, I know.' She was blushing and grinning, and I wanted to break something in half. *Not him. Cristian, the coked-up shoe guy.*

'Really?' I said, bracing myself. 'The cobbler?'

'The shoe designer – Cristian, yes,' she said, sighing. 'Anyway, I'm going to Rome for the summer with him, to see if it can be a thing.'

That explains the bikinis.

'He's going to break up with his girlfriend,' she said quickly. To reassure me, I suppose. And then she took a deep breath. 'Birdy, I think I might . . . I mean I think *we* might be in love. I think this is it.'

'Oh-kay,' I said, turning to inspect her bamboo-and-ceramic paddle brush, so I didn't have to look at her. I flicked my finger across the bristles and made a mental note to blow-dry my frizzy mess of a head more often. 'What about this job? You're not going to throw it up for Cristian, are you?'

I already knew the answer. This was her Achilles heel. Heather wanted Love. She jumped in boots first at the sniff of it. In the last two years alone there had been Vile Kyle, the forty-eight-year-old pet therapist who called her 'little kitten'; Kahlil the artisan baker, who couldn't get a rise in the bedroom and told Heather it was her fault; Woke Warren, the world's most sexist feminist; and now Cristian. Cristian with a girlfriend, whom he was apparently going to break up with, and a deep and lasting relationship with Class As. I'm no expert psychologist, but for a girl who lost her mum very young, and then her dad a few years later, there had to be some kind of connection between that and Heather's desperate need to be loved.

It was incredibly frustrating, because if anyone deserved to meet a really *fucking good* life-partner, it should be Heather. She was a really *fucking good* person.

'That was never my *dream* job.'

'What do you mean? You said you wanted to go *there*. Specifically, that very place. You spent ages waiting for a role to come up. Why would you just bail?'

'It was only a summer job,' she snapped.

Support her, Elizabeth Finch.

'Oh, okay,' I replied, nodding.

'And I only took it because I thought I should see Scotland at some point in my life because, well, I'm half-Scottish. It's a rundown old place in the middle of nowhere. But it was near Skye, and I wanted to see Skye. You know how I've always wanted to go to Skye. My mum was born there.'

'I know, I know,' I said quickly.

'Anyway, the place has terrible reviews on Tripadvisor. Honestly, they don't need a bloody sommelier, they need a total overhaul. But, Birdy, I have to find out if this thing with Cristian is something. Would you miss the chance for real, true love?' she asked me, her eyes big and round.

Don't get me wrong, I love a happy ending, but Cristian was not it. *Ugh.* I couldn't bear the thought of another undeserving arsehole taking up space in her good heart. And yet, I couldn't tell her that. I had learned, through bitter experience, that lecturing and intervention didn't work with Heather, when it came to *love*.

My job, as Heather's best friend, was to support her, despite all my reservations.

'*If* this is what you want, then go get the cobbler. Be in love!' I sighed.

'Oh, fuck off. You're taking the piss.'

'Sorry, I'm not. It's just a bit sudden,' I said. *Support her, Elizabeth Finch.* I looked her square in the eye. 'If it's what you *want*, then I'm happy.'

'You're happy for me?'

'Do you need me to be?'

'No. But it would help.'

'Well, obviously I'm a bit worried, because that would be normal, given the circumstances. But I'm happy for you, if it's really making you happy,' I said, my knee starting to jig. I didn't like this, not one bit, and I hated that I couldn't tell her how I felt.

'I just feel like I need to give this thing with Cristian a go. I know you think he's a bit of a good-time dude or whatever, but he's actually really sensitive. The sex is magic. Like we are so connected, and I've been really, properly sexually adventurous with him. When we make love . . .'

'Ugh, don't say "make love", it makes me itch.'

'Make *loooove*?' she said, all sexy.

'Yes. Yes, yes,' I jumped in. 'Okay, Italy. All the coffee and carbs. Can I visit, at least?'

'Of course! When I'm all settled, though,' she said sheepishly. 'Thank you, Birdy, it's a big relief to tell you.'

'Have you told *them*? The hotel?' I sighed, resigned to waiting an estimated three to four months before this whole thing caught fire and burned everyone to ashes, including Cristian's poor girlfriend. I would be there to pick up the pieces, of course. I always was.

'No. I'm not going to. I can't face it.'

She tried to wave away the conversation, and I paused for a moment. That wasn't like Heather. She was normally so professional. If I heard alarm bells before, now I heard air-raid sirens going off.

'Heather, don't be daft. You *have* to call them,' I said incredulously. 'Make up an excuse.'

'I can't lie. I've got enough on my plate.' Her voice was tight and high, and I felt my shoulders straighten as I readied myself to try and talk sense into her.

'Just tell them you were in a car crash. Or you have Ebola. Or you got stabbed, in a case of mistaken identity. Everyone's getting stabbed these days.'

'That's not funny,' she said sharply.

'What about you were stabbed through the rib outside an Internet café in Benidorm?' I said, on a roll.

'What?'

'No one would dare think you made it up. It's good. Trust me. You got stabbed in Benidorm. Is it Benidorm or *the* Benidorm?'

'Why was I stabbed? It sounds drug-related.'

'Randomly.'

'Why was I in Benidorm?'

'Studying.'

'Studying what?'

'Spanish wine, of course.'

'Spanish wine. Hmm. No. But it could be sherry. Wouldn't it make the papers?'

'No. People get stabbed all the time.'

'You need to stop reading those awful tabloids.'

'It's a little slice of my trashy childhood,' I said. And before she could protest and tell me I was not trash, I joked, 'Anyway, trust me. No one is going to search through Spanish local news to find out if some posh English girl was stabbed.'

'Did they catch the guy?'

'No.'

'He got away?'

'I mean, the police are still looking, obviously.'

'Well, that's a relief.'

There was a brief silence and then we both burst out laughing.

'You should tell them, Heather,' I said as the laughter subsided.

'It will be fine. It's only a summer placement, and they will replace me in a second. Paris in the autumn is my big next step. This was nothing. Well, mostly nothing. I'll probably never have to see or speak to them again . . .'

I couldn't let her do it. 'How about I call them for you? I won't pretend you got stabbed. I'll say something appropriate, okay?'

'Would you?' she said, eyes wide with pure, genuine relief.

'It's no problem.' It wasn't the first time I'd stepped in to do something for Heather when she was afraid.

'Okay,' she said, visibly relaxing. It was something I could easily do for her, unlike paying my share of the rent. 'I suppose I shouldn't risk any blemish on my track record.'

I cringed, thinking about the dumpster fire that was my career. That 'career' was essentially a series of dead-end jobs, the best of which was the latest – something with 'digital media' in the title – which, to be honest, I had blagged my way into, with my pointless knowledge of Instagram influencers. I got fired when they figured that out. Before that, there were a couple of attempts at acting, but I really couldn't bear the other actors; the bookshop job, which I quite liked but was made redundant from; the accountancy firm, awful; some bouts of unemployment; and two summers working in a bar on Tenerife that Heather had arranged for me. 'Just to tide you over until you figure out what's next. Find your calling,' she'd said.

But I'm now thirty-one, and no closer to that mythical *calling*.

'I'll make up a good, reputation-preserving excuse for you, okay? But you'll need to lie low. You can't pull out of a job and then be all over the Internet, sunning yourself on the Riviera.'

'Cristian actually wants me to lie low too, so no problem.'

I'm sure he does, I thought, my loathing of him redoubling.

'Leave it with me,' I said.

'Thanks, Birdy.' She let out a deep breath and there was a brief silence. 'I really wish I could afford to let you stay here, but you know I have to rent it out. You have sorted somewhere, haven't you? You don't have to go to your parents' house?'

'Don't worry, I'm going to try the cousin in Tooting,' I said. I couldn't bear to tell her he'd already said no.

'Your cousin the butcher?'

'Yes.'

'But he hates you.'

'No, I hate *him*. It'll be fine. I'll figure something out. You know me. Don't stress,' I said.

She frowned.

'Heather, relax. As soon as you go, I'll apply for a bunch of jobs and find something different that isn't in front of a computer. Something more practical. Something with my hands perhaps,' I said, injecting as much positivity as possible into my voice. 'I wish I had a passion like you.'

'You'll meet someone, Birdy.'

'I don't mean passion for a *dude* – I mean for a career. The wine thing, like you have. Anyway, in case you forgot, I've been kind of seeing Tim again.'

'Birdy,' she said, furrowing her brow. 'You can't get serious about someone you met on the night bus.'

I stiffened a little. I knew what Tim was, and chose to hang out with him anyway. Heather just didn't see Cristian for what he was, that was the difference.

'I'm doing Tim with my eyes wide open,' I said sharply. 'Well, not *literally*. If I did him with my eyes open, I wouldn't be able to think about Jason Momoa.'

'I just want you to be happy. He wouldn't even let you stay with him until you found a new place. And he's an insurance salesman, for goodness' sake!'

'Insurance Investigator,' I corrected. 'Not everyone wants the big Italian love story, Heather. You forget: I was once turned down by a guy who worked as a shopping-mall Santa. I don't have a lot of options,' I joked, wanting to spin the conversation quickly back to her and away from my catalogue of inadequacies.

'Love,' she began, and I knew I was going to get the lecture about how wonderful I am, if only I could see it. But then she sighed, and I felt even worse.

I put the hairbrush down to rest beside me, suddenly reluctant to do a long drawn-out goodbye. 'Hey, listen, Heather, you have to get a wriggle on.'

'Oh, you're right. Well, this is goodbye then,' she said, standing up and giving me a hug. 'But, Birdy, I won't enjoy myself if I know you're unhappy.'

'I'm happy. Really, this gives me a chance to sit back and write that book, *How to Avoid Responsibility for Almost Everything*, that I've been banging on about.'

'Only you could pen a self-help novel that devoid of action,' she said proudly. I tried to ignore the small twinge that her joke caused in my chest.

'Right?'

As our smiles gave way to the sadness of saying goodbye, Heather hugged me hard.

'Will you let me know when you've made the call? Could you do it today?'

'Will do.'

'Thank you. And let me know where you end up staying? I won't sleep if I know you've had to go back to that bloody house. I mean it, Birdy, your parents—'

'Yes, I will, I will,' I interrupted quickly. I didn't want to get into a conversation about my parents. We'd been there a million times, and talking about it didn't change the fact that they were, and always had been, completely shit.

'Oh, good,' she said, throwing herself back on her bed, breathing out with relief. I felt a stab in my heart again. I knew a part of me didn't want anything to work out for her with any man ever, if it meant losing her even a little bit. Heather and I may have been each other's family, but with every year that passed, I felt her cultivating a new life that was her very own, while I still flapped about, hoping that the answer to living and loving would somehow arrive on my lap.

I pushed away the tears that were beginning to form.

She suddenly sat up.

'I forgot to tell you. There's this black-tie thingy at the Ritz that I was supposed to go to tonight. My name is at the door – just do the usual and say you're me. No one will ask any questions. And it's free wine. Lots of handsome hospitality-types.'

'What's the event?'

'It's the British Wine Awards. Honestly, all you have to do is get in the door. There's no formal dinner or anything. Go! I'll leave the trapeze dress and the T-bar heels, okay? Oh, don't think I didn't see you eyeing them up!'

I grin. 'Sure, why not? Is there a plus one?'

'Yes, but you're definitely not taking Tim.'

3.

May

This is it. I'm ready.

I'm sitting at the edge of the bar, waiting for James and the famous Russell with my hastily scribbled notes, taken down during my emergency call to Heather. She was thrilled when I told her I was staying with my cousin, and even more thrilled when I told her I needed help choosing wine for a dinner party he was throwing.

'At last!' she'd squealed. 'Oh God, where do I begin?'

Big mistake, I'd thought, vowing not to call her again – at least not to talk about what I'm supposedly doing in London while she's away. I cannot be juggling more than one lie here. And I definitely don't want to lie to Heather more than I need to.

She reeled off a ton of suggestions, which I quickly cross-checked with the wine list, then gently told her I had to go because the wine shop was about to close.

I thought the call *had* calmed my anxiety somewhat, but when Bill appears like a jack-in-the-box from behind the bar, I jump. He's holding a bottle of red in one hand and some kind of spirit in the other, and his cheeks are redder than they were outside. I wonder if he's been sampling the offerings. And then I wonder how I can get in on that scam.

'You done?' he asks.

'Mostly. I went into the kitchen to show James, but Anis said I should wait here for Chef,' I say, staring longingly at the bottle of whisky in Bill's hand and wondering if this is the kind of place where the staff get wasted after work. All that booze, all these young waiters on seasonal placement. There must be a lot of sex at Loch Dorn.

'You're admiring this, aren't you?' Bill says, and I nod emphatically before I realize he doesn't mean the whisky in his right hand, but the wine in his left. 'It's a very, very old Châteauneuf-du-Pape.'

'Ooohh,' I reply. 'Can I take a look?'

'Of course,' he says, carefully presenting the bottle to me, label up.

'Bloody hell, it's older than me,' I say, blindly walking into amateur territory. 'I mean, it's, uh, such a good year . . .' My voice trails off.

'Not our oldest,' he replies proudly, as he turns to stack the liquor against the mirrored wall at the back of the bar. 'You can arrange tastings, you know. Just speak to Russell when he gets here. *You're* the sommelier. He won't mind.'

'James said something about a uniform?' I say, catching myself in the mirror as Bill moves a bottle of gin. My new chic, shaggy Heather-styled bob has morphed into a serious case of bed-head, and I know I am starting to smell. 'I don't feel especially fresh.'

'Oh, how rude of me.' Bill spins round, knocking a brandy balloon off the polished countertop in the process. I baulk, waiting for the smash, but there is nothing but silence, and he reaches down and picks it up off the floor behind the bar. 'Rubber mats,' he grins. 'After Russell is done with you, I'll take you out back and you can freshen up in the staff loos.'

I take a deep breath. I totally have this.

'What's with the music?' I ask him.

'It's traditional. Lyres and harps and suchlike.'

'Thank God no bagpipes, at least.'

'You're not a fan?'

'I don't think one is ever a *fan* of the bagpipes, are they? A bagpipe never headlined Glastonbury is all I'm saying.'

He laughs, glancing across to the door anxiously. We're both waiting for the famous Russell. Bill, I suppose, is feeling anxious to introduce his new hire, and I sit up a little straighter, finding myself wanting to make him proud.

'You're not how I pictured you,' he says quietly. 'And nothing like your Facebook picture.' My heart stops. I'd got a matching haircut, but it had done nothing to narrow the gorge between beautiful, elegant Heather and me.

'I'm very photogenic. It makes it hard to do online dating,' I reply to Bill, trying not to feel too miffed. 'Men are always disappointed when they see me in real life – my photos are so exceptional.'

'Oh, I didn't mean that,' he says, grinning. 'Your profile picture is a cat.'

For a moment I'm confused, and then I recall my advice to Heather. *Change your profile pictures to something nondescript.*

'Oh yes,' I say, thinking quickly. 'I really love cats.'

Don't go on to social media. Make all your feeds private. You need to be offline for most of the summer. And a cat picture will do. I can be into cats for three months.

I spin round on my leather bar stool and take in the dining room. Crisp white linen hangs across large square tables and over the chairs, where the fabric is pulled taut and tied in a bow at the back. It is a little twee, but super-cute.

Each table has a small candle on a short silver holder, with a tartan ribbon at the base. The huge curtains are swept to the side with matching tartan tiebacks. The walls are a deep burgundy, with some original stone brickwork exposed along the top. There are gilded paintings of men in tartan, with spaniels and guns. The room has a faint whiff of cigar smoke and all I can visualize is rotund men in their seventies drinking brandy and peering at old maps.

'This is the only room that hasn't been renovated yet,' Bill is saying.

'Renovated?' I say, confused.

'Oh, you won't have seen the rest of the place! We've done everything except this dining room. They're starting here next week, so we'll have a couple of slower weeks while they fit the new carpet and she gets a fresh lick of paint. Service in the bar area only, and a slimline menu. And then, come the first week of June, it's all on. Summer, new hotel, new restaurant. We're off!'

'Oh,' I say. A new head chef, a new wine list *and* renovations?

'See that old badger?' Bill says, pointing to a gilded painting on the wall. 'That's the great-grandfather of the current owner of the estate, Michael MacDonald.'

'Come on,' I say, grinning at Bill, who is now busy polishing a wine glass.

'It is. And his faithful hound, Duke. I do wonder what he'd make of all the changes around here.'

The kitchen is open and runs half the length of the far wall, adjacent to the bar. Now that I think about it, it did seem strange to have such a modern set-up in such an old-fashioned place. From most of the dining room you can see the serving area, with its stainless-steel heat lamps and solid oak frame. James is there, now sporting one of those fitted black bandana chef-hats, tasting something from a small silver jug with the end of a teaspoon. He makes tasting things look like a very serious business indeed.

He smiles as the kitchen door flies open and a huge bulk of bruising masculinity comes striding through. He is wearing a dusty blue tweed suit, including a waistcoat, with a pop of bright-yellow handkerchief in his top pocket. His hair is a mess of dark curls and his eyes are dark and bright at once. He is a forty-something supermodel, the kind you'd see in a luxury watch advert in *GQ*, rising out of the oak-clad cabin of a vintage sailboat, shirt casually open, reaching for a faceless woman in a gold bikini.

'Hello, Heather. Welcome,' he purrs in an unplaceable British accent, his voice like the burnt caramel atop a vanilla-bean gelato. He tosses a copy of *The Scotsman* on the bar top next to me.

'That's me,' I say.

'James!' he shouts as he looks me square in the face, pursing his lips ever so slightly. Handsome as he is, I have to say I find his Man Brand a total turn-off – any poor woman who married him would face a lifetime of bikini waxes, lunges and, in the worst-case scenario, vaginoplasty. It is less than a split second before the doors fly open again and James arrives, head down, examining his notes. Much more my type. If everything about Russell is hard and polished, everything about James is soft and easy. The way his hair looks like it smells of shampoo rather than expensive hair gel, for example. Good-looking, but not intimidatingly so, and far less likely to shave his balls.

'Welcome to our wee restaurant,' Russell continues, pushing back his sleeve to look at his enormous silver watch. 'We have just forty-five minutes to service, and I can see you need to get refreshed from your trip, right?'

'Yes, that would be good . . .' I reply, tucking my hands under my armpits to serve as a fume barrier.

'Good, then let's go through the list quickly,' he says, nodding.

I also nod, stealing a quick glance at James, who is biting his thumbnail. I mouth, *It's all cool* to him, but he looks confused and I make a mental note not to do that again.

I swing my stool in Russell's direction and pull out my notes. A deep breath, then I engage my ninth-form drama-class technique of speaking very loudly and clearly, with just a hint of Claire Foy from *The Crown* for authority.

'It's virtually impossible to make a perfect pairing without a thorough tasting of your cellar,' I say.

'Of course,' says Russell, nodding in agreement.

'And, obviously, I haven't tasted the dishes, so this is best-guess work.'

'You don't need to explain, Heather,' Russell says, touching my arm. 'I am simply glad you are here with us, and that Bill is no longer choosing the wine.'

Bill rolls his eyes and slides an espresso in front of Russell, who presses it sharply to his lips, downs it in one go and slides it back in Bill's direction with an approving nod.

'With the guinea fowl, you can see I've not gone for the usual Pinot Grigio. I have assumed,' I pause, glancing over my shoulder at James, 'that the celeriac is not roasted . . .'

'Yes, I've noted that on the final menu,' James replies quietly, as Russell purses his lips in his direction.

'Fabulous! Well, I definitely suggest the German Riesling. The dry. And for the blade steak, I disagree about the Cabernet – too heavy, with all the foams and whatnot. I think the Argentinian Pinot will fill the dish out well and,' I glance down at my notes, 'soften the savouriness with a hint of raspberry.'

'Good, good,' Russell nods his head, flicking his eyebrows up towards me, and a smile forges its way across his smooth face. 'And the crab?' *Shit, I forgot the crab.*

'Well, there's only one choice, right?' I say, freestyling. 'A Merlot?'

Russell's forehead creases and he looks over at James, whose mouth is slightly ajar. A silence hangs in the air, broken by the clang of a saucepan hitting the floor in the kitchen.

Behind me, Bill starts to giggle, and then a moment later Russell begins to chortle, and I join in with a round, deep cackle, eyeing everyone to assess the perfect moment to stop laughing.

'Kidding,' I say, tapping Russell on the hand. I vow never to guess again.

'She means the Chardonnay,' says Bill firmly, wagging his finger at me as his cheeks begin to redden. 'Oh, that's funny. The Merlot. Golly gosh, you really had me.'

'I'm sorry,' I say. 'Just keeping you guys on your toes.'

'Excellent work, Heather,' Russell says, wrapping things up.

'Oh, it's not that clever,' I reply, blushing. 'We're all winging it, aren't we?'

'Nonsense,' he says, touching my arm again, but this time he gives it a little squeeze. 'You are one of the youngest, brightest sommeliers in the country.'

I continue, 'I am the lucky one. To be under a chef with such an incredible reputation, it really is a dream come true.'

I can tell that Russell wants me to like him. To *respect* him. To fancy him. And the greatest thing about a deeply insecure and narcissistic man? Make them think you do, and you can get away with almost anything.

'I actually have a thought about tonight,' I say with some trepidation. 'I'd love to play more of an observation role, so I can get to know how you do things here.'

Russell looks at me, cocks his head and strokes his chin with his finger and thumb, before adjusting his pocket handkerchief.

'I suppose that makes sense. Of course you'll need to step in, if anyone goes off-menu. But yes, good idea.'

'I think it would be best,' I say simply, smiling up at Russell, relief washing over me. I start toying lightly with the collar of my shirt. It's such an obvious move and I hate myself for doing it, but I'm in survival mode, so I don't stop.

'Perhaps, Bill, we could show Heather where she can brief the staff on the wines, while James and I do the new plates, and then Heather can freshen up?' he says, more pointedly.

'Sure thing,' Bill replies, wiping his hands on his black apron and nodding towards a door at the end of the bar. 'If you could come with me, Heather?'

'Thank you, Russell,' I mumble, as I squeeze past him and a full hit of sandalwood and pepper tickles my nose. So much cologne, it almost makes me gag – although I can hardly complain about bad odours.

I give Bill a sheepish grin and we head down through the bar.

'Talk to me about the presentation of the damned dessert, and then we can talk about this fucking turbot dish,' Russell is saying to James, in a voice far less soothing than the one he used with me.

'God, he's fancy. I bet he has a summer *and* a winter duvet,' I whisper to Bill, glancing back to see James animatedly explaining the premise behind the balloon set of the chocolate casing on the ganache. James cracks it unceremoniously with a teaspoon, and Russell frowns. Then Anis appears with that sample plate I was supposed to get forty-five minutes ago.

I turn back to Bill, as he opens the door to the staffroom.

'Where is Irene? '

'You'll probably see her tomorrow. She said you were an absolute scream at the Wine Awards, by the way. What a coincidence that she met you there!' he added.

'Yes. A wonderful coincidence,' I reply. And then, realizing I should probably appear more dazzled by everything, I add, 'It's a real dream come true to be here.'

4.

Two weeks earlier

'Heather Jones,' I said confidently as Tim and I arrived at the Ritz's reception. 'We're here for the British Wine Awards?'

The doorman ran his finger down a guest list, and I watched as his pen struck through Heather's name.

I was wearing Heather's black trapeze dress, which fitted, but only because it's one of those dresses that you could smuggle a crate of beer under. Heather used to tie it round the middle with a pink sash, which I tried to do, but it made me look like two silk-organza rubbish bags instead of one. Tim was wearing black jeans and a velvet blazer that he borrowed from his favourite drinking buddy, Damon – or 'Damo', as he was known. He actually looked quite dashing.

'Welcome, Miss Jones. And could I take your name, sir? Apologies, we only have "plus one" written down here.' He glanced briefly my way, judging Heather for not RSVP-ing properly.

'The name is Tim,' Tim said, hamming it up with an uber-posh accent, his chin up and his lips ever so slightly pursed.

The man nodded, writing it down on something I couldn't see. 'And your last name?'

'Um,' Tim looked over at me, and I raised a warning eyebrow. 'McTimothy.'

'Tim McTimothy,' the man replied carefully, his unflappable manners standing firm in the face of common sense. 'Very good.'

And we were in, placards round our necks, making a beeline for the free bar and mini vegan canapés.

The Ritz's ballroom was rather more bland than I'd pictured in my dreams: big, though rather empty-feeling, with an only mildly ostentatious plaster ceiling. The guests were not the usual types that I'd meet at Heather's work functions – the opening of a swanky roof bar or a hip underground restaurant; this lot were stuffy and old-fashioned.

Perfect! Tim and I loved nothing more than chatting shit to strangers: double points if we could convince them we were someone else. Triple if I could get away with playing someone fancy or famous, or just more together than me. The last time we went out, it was to a British Film Industry event, where Tim sat in the corner in dark glasses and I spent the evening pointing him out to young actors, to see if any of them would bite: '*Oh my goodness, it's Jim Reeves. The director. You don't know him? Oh, he's prolific. And so talented. No, you won't find him online; he's notoriously private. I can't believe he's here.*'

'All right, I want to mingle.' Tim winked at me and I grinned. 'Together? Or alone and report back?'

'Alone and report back.'

Less than an hour later we were both riotously drunk and giggling in the corner about who we'd met.

'I've had conversations about Land Rovers, hyper-decanting, the length of merino-wool fibres and fucking jogging. I've even tried to keep up with some *cricket chat*.' I added dramatic emphasis to this one, since Tim is all about football. 'And someone called Bert had to excuse himself, as he wanted to catch tomorrow's shipping forecast. I've died and gone to some kind of Buckinghamshire hell.'

'I just had a conversation about trees,' Tim said, by way of agreement. And then burped.

'Come on, we may as well go and check out the winning wines. It's why we're here.'

In the centre of the ballroom there was a huge circular table, with about fifty-odd wines on display with various gold, silver and bronze awards stuck to them; and in the middle of that, an antique glass-and-brass centrepiece, made of wine glasses and ivy twisted about twenty feet into the air. It was stunning.

'Who knew the English made wine . . . It's like discovering a classy Australian,' Tim said, as he used one of the glasses set out for tasting to pour himself an enormous glassful, just a millimetre shy of the rim.

'Hey, go a *bit* easy there, my dude,' I said.

'Not gonna say no to freebies,' he replied, knocking back half in one go.

'Sav Blanc,' I said, picking up a bottle with a very modern-looking black label and an outline of the county of Kent. 'I don't mind a Sav Blanc, and this one's got an award. Look. Silver!'

I poured myself a more modest glass, but it was becoming hard to aim the bottle neck in the right direction.

'It's got the cat's wee on the nose, which I know we're all supposed to like, but with four tomcats at home, I can't stomach it,' said a woman's voice next to me. She wore a flared turquoise trouser suit that could only be made fashionable by someone like Alexa Chung.

'Cat's wee?' I said.

'Oh. Yes,' the woman replied, looking surprised. 'It's a tasting note?'

'Oh yes. Yes! Cat urine. Exquisite,' I replied, trying not to snigger into my glass, which suddenly did smell quite a lot like cat's wee. Tim roared with laughter and the woman frowned and inched a few feet away from us. How on earth Heather moved in these circles, I'd never quite understand.

'Okay, I don't know how much more of this I can stomach,' I said, looking at Tim with one eye closed, so that I didn't see two of him. 'I'm drunk, Tim. And I want a large stuffed-crust pizza with extra salami. And chilli. And a beer.'

'I'll drink to that,' he said, 'but first, where are the bogs?'

'Can you at least say "lavatory"? We're in the Ritz, for fuck's sake,' I shouted as he wandered off in the wrong direction.

'Heather Jones?' said a voice behind me. 'Well, isn't this a wonderful surprise. I didn't know you were coming, but, well, of course you would be. And then I saw your name at the door.'

I blinked for a moment, then glanced from her warm smile to her flowing mustard blouse and then down at her badge.

'It's Irene Reid, my dear. Bill must have mentioned me in your interview,' she said, beaming, her wild white hair flowing and her arms outstretched like a marble sculpture of the Virgin Mary. 'I'm so pleased to have you on my team.'

'Ahh, Irene,' I said, nodding my head and smiling along. *Who the hell was this?*

'Yes, yes,' she beamed. 'Oh, this is just wonderful. And, you know, Russell is here somewhere. At least he said he was coming, but I don't see him yet.'

Bill, Russell, Irene. Who the hell was this lady, and how quickly could I get away? And then, when my ears settled on her soft Scottish accent, I gasped. 'Irene!'

'Yes, dear,' she said, laughing now.

Oh shit!

I had not made the phone call yet. The very important call to tell the Scottish hotel that Heather was not coming to Scotland for the job. The call I was supposed to make that day. And then right there, hauling me in for an enormous hug, both arms fast around me, was Heather's soon-to-be new boss. And she thought *I* was Heather. Well, of course she did. It was printed in black ink around my neck.

I waited for a moment, until it wasn't rude to extract myself.

'Hi, Irene,' I said. *Could I explain the mistake?* I decided to try to buy myself some time while my drunk brain attempted to figure it out. 'Did you try the Silver Medal winner? It's quite good. Lots of cat's wee on the nose.'

'No, no, but thanks for the recommendation.' She winked at me, just as I saw Tim on his way back. I knew he would not be able to resist this situation – a delicious misunderstanding, which could be milked for maximum laughs when retold over a fourth pint of ale with Damo. I wanted to leave, but Irene was pouring herself a glass, and I didn't want Heather to appear rude by disappearing suddenly.

'Why, hello there, madam,' Tim said as he joined us. 'I'm Tim McTimothy. Like the badge says.'

I sort of giggled and snorted and watched in horror, unable to do anything.

'Irene Reid. I'm the manager of Loch Dorn, and we're so delighted to have Heather with us. Even if it's only for one summer.'

It took a moment. Tim cocked his head, puzzled, and as I very subtly and slowly shook my head at him, the penny dropped.

'Oh. I get it. Heather's new boss, right?' he said with a throaty laugh. He put his hand out to steady himself on the table, and I wished

I was close enough to do the same. 'Well, isn't this a massive fucking coincidence.'

I burst out into fake staccato laughter.

'Yes, it's wonderful. And it's very nice to meet you too, Tim. Is that the Sauvignon?' Irene asked as he downed the last third of his glass in one go.

'Uh. Irene?' My head started to spin as I tried to think of a way to level with her.

'Yes?' she said, as she took barely a sip of her own drink. 'Oh, isn't this so wonderful. It's great to put a face to the name I've been hearing so much about. Bill was absolutely effusive, and we're thrilled that you'll be joining us. What a summer we're going to have! You're going to love our little neck of the woods. It's stunning. But listen to me going on. What were you going to say?'

I looked square into her kind, excited eyes and didn't want to see the disappointment and condescension that would inevitably fill them when I told her who I really was. I felt the tingle of booze coursing through my veins. The look of pure excitement at meeting me – or, rather, Heather – that look was intoxicating. I couldn't resist. I couldn't stop myself rolling around in that feeling, at least for one night. I'd make good tomorrow, somehow.

'I can't remember. Did we, um, organize accommodation yet?'

'Oh yes. A spacious room in a lovely little cottage is available to all our staff. Bill must've gone over all of this?'

'Oh yes, of course he did,' I said, pointing to my glass. 'Better go easy on the cat's wee. I'll forget where Scotland is next.'

Irene laughed heartily and, before I knew it, I was professing my excitement at coming to Loch Dorn, while she regaled me with tales of horse-riding, fresh air and lobsters the size of my head.

It was a good thirty minutes before she finally glided off. 'I'll pop back and say goodbye – don't sneak off,' she said.

I turned to Tim, and the excitement morphed into panicked laughter. 'What the hell am I going to do now? I'm supposed to pull out of that job, for Heather. I was supposed to do it today!'

'That was fucking hilarious.'

'Yeah, but now what?'

'You know, you should just go and do it,' he said, putting his arm round me and yanking me in close.

'Don't be stupid,' I said, pulling away, irritated at the show of affection that always arrived after this much booze, but never when sober.

'Why not? You can't go back to your fucking parents. You said you don't even speak to them.'

'And I can't stay with you.'

'If I had the room—'

'You still wouldn't let me,' I said and, before Tim protested, I added, 'It's fine. No big deal.'

'Birdy, it's only a hospo job. You could easily do it. Didn't you work in a bar once? And you said yourself that Heather doesn't want it. She wasn't even going to call them, for fuck's sake.'

'That's true.'

'It's *free* accommodation. Probably *free* meals. Definitely free wine and whisky. Scotland, the summer – what the hell else are you going to do?'

I ruminated on the idea for a moment and it felt weirdly plausible. *Heather said it wasn't anything special. Just an old pub basically, a family-run place in the middle of nowhere. I've done a bit of bar and waitressing work. I'm not totally inept. It would be great to see some of Scotland . . .*

'If you don't do it, I will!' And as Tim said this, he threw his arms wide, knocking over a bottle of wine, which in turn knocked into the carefully balanced display of ivy-bound champagne glasses. A moment of teetering suspense, then they shattered one by one as they hit the table and scattered in great jagged shards across the carpet around us.

The room went silent.

Someone next to me gasped, 'Oh my word, that is vintage crystal.'

'And *that* is a vintage idiot,' I said, stepping back slightly as if I didn't know Tim. Catching the eye of Irene across the room, I did my best embarrassed face, trying to convey all in one look that while I was *with* Tim, I didn't endorse his actions in any way. Then the second the waiters bustled over to clear up, I did my thing. I grabbed Tim and we bolted.

5.

May

I'd rather be dead than this tired. The restaurant is full, it's midway through service, and I am doing an excellent job of hovering by the bar looking efficient, each step causing a searing pain on the balls of my feet. The uniform, supplied in Heather's size, was two sizes too small for me, but rather than have to explain that one, I squeezed myself into the dreary pencil skirt and white shirt. I have a long black linen apron, which is fixed with thick brown leather straps and does a good job of hiding the bulge at the waistband, but it won't help my ability to walk normally. The stupid skirt is so tight I'm sort of shuffling like an Eighties TV robot instead of walking.

The staff, whom I briefed as briefly as possible, are five serious young things, all ironed, polished and ready for service.

'Well, you've all been here longer, and therefore all know more than me,' I say, using vast swathes of flattery and very little else to keep them from suspecting I had no real idea what I was talking about. 'Tonight I'll be learning from you.'

A baby-faced red-head with a nose-stud looked at me with the kind of giddy excitement normally reserved for pop stars. She told me her name was Roxanne, but her friends call her Roxy, and gushed that she had been training to be a sommelier and would be thrilled to help me in any way she could. I wanted to hug Roxy for existing.

I can see her now, picking up a silver tray with two glasses of what I learn are Bellinis – champagne with a bit of mushed-up peach, at £18 a pop. She's the kind of gorgeous that comes with youth: perfect skin and long, lean limbs. Her vibrant red hair is pulled back in a tight ponytail.

The open kitchen gives me a direct view to Anis and, more interestingly, James, who seems to be getting progressively more vexed and sweaty as the service goes on.

'James doesn't actually do much cooking,' I say to Bill, who is polishing glasses behind the bar, as I watch James scold the dessert chef.

'Well, he makes sure everything is how Russell likes it. He's kind of the conductor of the orchestra. And Russell owns the orchestra,' Bill says with a wry smile, polishing yet another glass. 'But you know all about that. Listen to me. Telling *you* how a restaurant works.'

'Ha, yes,' I murmur, taking a moment to send Heather a quick thank-you message: *Thanks for the wine advice on the fancy dinner, I'll let you know how it goes.*

I'm really fucking sore, and really fucking tired, and although this charade is only a few hours into a three-month campaign, I am feeling too exhausted to keep it up.

'Bill,' I say, leaning across towards him, as a very tall Dutch waiter strides past me with two plates of what looks like some kind of overengineered chicken drumstick. 'What time do we usually wrap?'

'Wrap?'

'Wrap up this show.'

'Ah, I see,' he says, glancing at his watch. 'It's eight forty-five, so I guess – in three or four hours?'

I lie on the staffroom floor, my left foot on the wall, circling the ankle of my right foot and whimpering like a lame dog. The ridiculously too-small pencil skirt is hitched up to my hips and I've untucked the bulging cream polyester blouse and unbuttoned it enough to get some cool air onto my skin. The uniform isn't as fancy as the restaurant, that's for sure. I yawn and rub my eyes, caring little whether I've smeared black eyeliner down my face. I've been everything from freezing cold to roasting hot in one day. Every single cell in my body is ruined.

I think I did okay, though. Almost all the guests ordered off the pre-paired tasting menu, so there was little for me to do on the fly, although since the wine list had a couple of descriptions underneath each choice, I was ready enough to bluff, if I had to. But I found out quickly that most people just want you to take the decision away from them.

'I don't know about you, but I always say simplest is best,' I'd whispered to a nervous man who was clearly in near-cardiac arrest over the pricing – giving him permission to order a nice cheap Napa Valley Pinot.

'What kind of man doesn't buy his date the vintage champagne?' I said loudly to an elderly gent, who chuckled, glanced across at his smirking wife, folded up the wine list and replied, 'Well, I have to now, don't I?'

'I'm having the guinea fowl, with a glass of white,' a Very Confident American Tourist had said. 'Which would you recommend?'

'Oh gosh, I hate recommending wines,' I'd joked, scanning the list in a panic.

He chuckled. 'Sounds to me like you're in the wrong business.'

'*Quite*,' I quickly replied, grinning, as a memory of Heather complaining about how Americans only ever drink bloody Chardonnay flashed before me.

'Take the Chardonnay,' I said firmly.

'Oh, I love Chardonnay,' his partner said, in one of those perfect little Texan accents. 'Can I have an ice cube in that?'

'Yes. Yes, you can,' I confirmed, marching back to Bill, feeling jubilant.

'It's like they'll believe anything I say,' I blurted out. 'I'm the Donald Trump of wine.'

'Well, I agree we've not quite got the sophisticated clientele of Claridge's,' Bill said. 'They do need some guidance.'

'Quite,' I said again, resting once more on the word. I'm the kind of person who says 'quite' now, it seems.

After that, I mostly stood around looking very busy and important, which involved a lot of nodding at the junior staff and watching as they elegantly poured the wine, served gracefully and swiftly cleared. I also necked a couple of samples from Bill, 'for research purposes'.

As I stare up at the staffroom ceiling and wait for Bill to tidy the bar and show me my bed, I marvel that I'm actually here, in Scotland, and that I really did do this. In my delirious haze, I start to giggle to myself.

'Hi, Heather.' James looks confused by the state of me on the floor. And no wonder – I look a right mess. I pull down my skirt and re-adjust my blouse, but sitting up is beyond me, I'm so knackered.

'I haven't felt this exhausted since Ibiza, August 2014. No. That's a lie. The night I did a twenty-four-hour Nicolas Cage movie mar-athon. What's weird is, I barely even scratched the surface of his back-catalogue. He's prolific. I wonder how many hours of my life it would take to do every movie. *Con Air* was *long*. He doesn't do a lot of sub-two-hour films. I'm going to google it. Actually, fuck that – my fingers are too tired.'

Why am I still talking?

James actually laughs fully – at me or with me, I don't care – then removes his black hat and unbuttons his chef's jacket. A white T-shirt is underneath, everything stained. He sighs, and I get the sense that a great weight has been lifted from him.

'Glad you got an easyish first shift,' he says with a yawn. He must be kidding, although there are no signs of it. He moves towards his locker and pulls the door back to shield his body from view, though he needn't have bothered. I am far too tired to perv.

'Yeah, a total breeze,' I reply.

Finally, about three seconds later, the desire to perv overwhelms me, so I sneak a quick glance, but James has already changed into a black T-shirt. His shoulders are rolled forward as he spends a few moments on his phone. Then he leans over to pick up his bag, practic-ally waving his bum in my face. I can't help but notice how nice it is. It's not one of those little bums that disappear into a pair of sagging skinny jeans, but a good, rounded proper bum.

Mentally scolding myself, I focus again on my phone and wait for him to close the locker before I turn my head fully towards him. For the next three months James will be my closest work person, and I need to find a way to connect with things other than his very nice bum. I need to get him squarely on my side. If anyone is going to spot my shortcomings, it's him.

'So, how long have you worked here, James?' I ask, concealing a yawn. 'Sorry, a very long day. I was at St Pancras at the crack of dawn. Poor old Dawn. Everyone's always at her crack.'

He chuckles again, even though it's the lamest joke ever. His laugh is sweet – warm and from the belly. 'Yeah, of course,' he says, tossing his worn whites into a big laundry basket by the door. 'I've been here for ever.' He collapses into the chair opposite me, rubbing his face with a white towel. His dark hair falls forward across his face, hopelessly unruly once out of that hat, and slightly damp with sweat.

'Really?'

'Apart from a brief stint in Dunvegan.'

'Dunvegan?'

'Yes, you know – Dunvegan, on Skye.'

'Oh yeah, of course.' I make a mental note to check out a map of the area later. 'Are you from the west coast then?'

'Yes,' he says shortly, tossing the white towel into the laundry basket and flicking his head back to remove the hair from his eyes. 'Sorry. I'm not a good welcome party. Today was pretty long for me too. Russell needed . . . something.'

He stops himself and shakes his head. It's obvious he wanted to have a moan about the boss – something I could easily relate to. No one in history has moaned about bosses as much as me. I am the king of moaners actually. Almost every boss I've ever had has fallen short in every conceivable way and, as talented as he may be, Russell seems to be a bit of a classic prick.

James reaches his hands up to the back of his neck, and I admire his modestly toned arms; all he needs to do is run his hands through his hair and I will have a huge crush.

'Management always seem to come with the job,' I say.

'That's the truth,' he says, standing. 'Need a hand?' He stretches out his arm and offers it up.

'Thanks,' I say, feeling myself blush as he tugs me and I have to hastily rearrange my clothes, once I'm up. The burn on the pads of my feet is excruciating, and nothing can mask the funky stench coming from my armpits. 'Sorry, James, I'm a total mess. I'd like to say it gets better than this, but it really doesn't.'

He laughs. 'You look just fine.'

Delivered with that soft Scottish accent and quiet confidence, *You look just fine* is pretty much the best compliment I've ever received. I feel my cheeks burn with delight.

Bill comes bursting through the door with an open bottle of champagne in one hand and a red in the other. He staggers a little as he reaches for his coat, clumsily settling the wine down. 'Oh, my sweet Lord, let's get the fuck home. You'll need to drive the cart, James; I can barely stand. Overheard that golden-wedding couple on table nine have gone for a skinny dip in the loch, if anyone fancies a giggle,' he burps, then looks across and catches my amusement. 'Occupational hazard.'

James takes the red wine from Bill's hand. 'You should have left this one, Bill.'

'It's been open for days!' Bill says with a toothy grin.

As I slip my blazer on, I can feel James looking across at me. I turn to him while we wait for Bill to change, wondering if he has something more to say. I wait a moment and realize he's not going to speak.

'Wouldn't mind some of that,' I say, nodding towards the bottle in his hand.

'Sure.' His eyes are on the wine, before he slowly looks up at me and holds my gaze properly. 'Are you hungry?'

I sort of don't hear the words, because all I can see is his eyes. There is that unmistakable spark of connection between us.

I almost jump backwards with the shock of it, then tear myself from the invisible, fragile thread and it snaps. I catch my breath. He looks at the ceiling and then at the floor, and then I remember I'm supposed to answer.

'Oh, sure, yeah,' I reply, trying to be relaxed as my heart beats hard in my chest.

'I'm bloody starved,' Bill is saying, zipping up a grey hoodie, oblivious.

James has already pulled his coat on and is holding open the door by the time I get my shit together.

I follow them, my feet aching as we make our way outside to the cart, and James jumps in the driver's seat and turns the key.

'Get yourself in there, Bill, I'll ride at the back,' I say.

'Oh Christ, thank you,' he says, slumping down next to James, slapping him on the shoulder. 'Another stellar day, old boy. Amazing. You're really nailing it.'

'You need to get some sleep,' James replies.

The ride to the cottage is only a few moments, but it gives me enough time to gather my scattered thoughts into one place. This situation I am in here, in Scotland, pretending to be my best friend in a not-at-all-shitty hotel is already precarious. But it's containable as long as I work hard, keep everyone sweet and make it to the end of the summer. What I cannot afford is to have a crush. *Rein it in, Birdy!*

A crush would be a distraction, and I have to focus. Tonight the crash course must begin. Time to learn a million wines.

We pull up at the cottage, the motion light springs back on and while James dithers with the key, Bill finds his focus.

'I'll show you your room, and you can have a shower at last,' he says, holding his nose and coughing.

'Screw you,' I say, laughing. 'You stink worse than me.'

'I don't doubt it,' he replies, as the door creaks open. He picks up my suitcase and flicks on the hall light. 'Your room is down here, second on the right. All set up. I'm on the second floor, first door; and James is at the end with his own bathroom, the bastard. I'm about twenty years older than him, but that's nepotism for you.'

I sense a hint of something in his voice that isn't entirely jovial. I briefly glance over my shoulder as we make our way down the narrow corridor, and James is still standing by the entrance to the kitchen with the wine in his hand. His brow is in its naturally furrowed state and he looks like he wants to talk again.

'So, er, what are you making?' I ask him.

'Gruyere on sourdough,' he replies, though the lilt in his voice suggests it's more of a question.

'What?'

'Cheese on toast,' Bill calls out from the kitchen.

'Oh, bloody hell, yes please,' I reply with a grin and catch James's eyes brighten as I turn away.

The bathroom is small but clean, and after discovering I must have left my soap bag at the public toilets in Inverness, I rummage through the cupboards and borrow the newest-looking toothbrush I can find, the dregs of someone's Boots own-brand face-wash and plenty of body-wash named Power Clean Big Guy Wash or something.

I dress in the safety of the bathroom, since I now have male flat-mates for the first time ever. I pull on my flannel PJs and a sloppy old T-shirt and let my hair fall down around my shoulders. I like the lightness of it. I could definitely get used to having it shorter. With sleep in sight, I am feeling a little less stressed and suddenly very hungry. I pull out my phone, which I realize I haven't checked since I texted Heather hours ago. It's 12.15 a.m.

There are no messages. Of course. Tim will be drunk somewhere within a one-mile radius of his office. Perhaps he's already taken his suit off and jumped in the river, or started singing football songs with his equally drunk mates by the taxi rank outside. I wonder if he's told his friends what I'm doing. I wonder if he misses me at all. I wonder if I miss him, and for a moment think it would be nice to pine for a lover on the other side of the country. But I don't. I definitely don't pine for Tim.

I slip the phone back into my bag and open the bathroom door. I can hear Bill and James in the communal lounge, and the smell of toasted bread and cheese fills the corridor. I am ravenous, and happy to brave drunk Bill and shy James for the sake of a free meal.

'Hi,' I say simply, as I enter. Now it's me who feels a bit shy, which is slightly unusual for me, but drunk Bill looks so comically delighted to see me, and James offers a less uptight smile. I wish he wouldn't smile. It is a very, very nice smile.

The lounge is big enough. There is a small galley kitchen at the far end that clearly hasn't been updated since the Eighties – lots of veneer and Bakelite, overly customized for a generation that was no more. Tiny drawers for herbs, a terracotta brick floor and floral hand-painted fittings. There is also a microwave the size of a dishwasher. In front of me, a large leather chesterfield-esque sofa and two arm-chairs are positioned around a coffee table and a huge flat-screen TV is mounted up on the wall. There's a cork board on the far wall, with what looks like the staff roster pinned to it, alongside a few photos of people I don't recognize, and a flyer for something called 'The Wine Society Highland Fling'.

'What's this?' I ask, walking over and pulling it off its pin. 'Highland Fling? Sounds fun. Well, actually, it sounds like a swingers' club.'

Bill bellows with laughter, as he pulls three small wine goblets from the shelf and pours out a glass of red. 'It's the Glastonbury of west-coast hospitality.'

'Ooh, all-you-can-swallow haggis, with a side of ecstasy?'

'And rain,' says James, and I giggle, mostly out of shock that he's almost made a joke.

'Where's the champagne?' I ask. 'If that's still going, I'd love a fizz.'

This is about the most authentic my wine talk could get. I do love fizz. I love feeling posh when I drink it. I love cava and Prosecco and champagne at weddings. I love it with all my drunken, flirtatious heart.

'I just learned about champagne and Gruyere.' James appears from behind the counter. Now relaxed, he looks even more handsome, and I am surprised to see he is wearing reading glasses, which he swiftly takes off. 'Apparently it's a good match?'

'All right, nerd, I'm off-duty,' I say, smiling at him, and he returns the smile, ducking back down to inspect the grill.

'Come on, James, you don't always want to talk molecular foam of pig semen. Here you go – in a goblet, though, I'm afraid,' Bill says, pulling the silver stopper out of the bottle.

'Exactly,' I say, climbing up onto the stool next to Bill as James slides the tray of cheese toasties out of the oven. 'Christ, that smells incredible. What do you put in it?'

'Gruyere, mustard – whatever works,' he says, shrugging and seemingly blushing ever so slightly.

'Cooking is a mystery to me,' I say. 'I once tried to freestyle beef bourguignon using pork and lemonade.'

'They're not even remotely related,' James frowns. 'Though pork and Coke work surprisingly well. But neither of those things is beef bourguignon.'

'You have to wait for it to cool,' Bill is saying, ignoring his own advice and picking a slice up by the crust. 'So, if you don't mind me saying, Heather, you are not like other sommeliers. From your CV, I would have thought – well . . .' He trails off.

I don't want to think about where Bill is going with this, so I take another sip of my champagne, the bubbles dancing on my tongue. It's heavier and almost bitter, compared to the Proseccos I'd spent the winter drinking at the local pub where, conveniently, it came on tap.

Bill glances over at James. 'Don't *you* think, James?'

'What do you mean?' I reply, feigning indignation as I reach for a slice myself. It's just cool enough and I take a bite, and, unprepared for the nutty sweet-and-saltiness that envelops my tongue, I gasp. 'Jesus fucking Christ, this is better than—'

'Sex, yes, which is why I don't bother with it any more,' Bill says, nodding his head in agreement.

'I was going to say it's better than a Greggs toastie.'

James laughs like I'm joking, and so does Bill.

'See. That's what I mean. You're funny, which wine folk never are,' he says.

'Excuse me?' I say, laughing, since it is impossible to take offence at something that isn't technically directed at me. I take a big swig of my champagne, which I can just taste, thanks to the coating of cheesy fat in my mouth. And, my word, it's good.

'I dunno. You're obviously not a foodie. And you look like you work in a record store.'

'Bill,' James says seriously, 'don't say that.'

'What's wrong with working in a record store?' I ask James teasingly. I know he meant to be kind, but it's too good an opportunity to wrong-foot him and see if I can make him blush again.

I don't tell them that my third job after school was working at the local HMV, just before it went under. My entire record collection was formed from staff discounts during the final closing-down sale. My collection was enormous and varied, and probably the thing I was most proud of. Unfortunately, I sold the whole lot to a wedding DJ from Hull, to pay off my credit-card bill in 2015. I kind of own nothing.

'Sorry, I don't mean anything by that. It's just that most wine students are kind of posh, you know. It costs a lot of money to study wine and . . .' Bill stops himself, grins and bites his lip, looking sheepishly at the ground. 'I realize I've just walked perilously into a very deep hole and I can't climb out. Forgive me.'

He bows his head in faux shame, and I giggle, topping my glass up again.

'It's okay. I know I'm not the Heather you were expecting. Everyone thinks I'm going to be far more sophisticated, but at the end of the day I'm just a wino with a pay cheque.'

As Bill chortles again, I suddenly feel a bit grim. Even when I'm *playing* someone as accomplished as Heather, I fall short. I gaze down at my glass, feeling a sudden urge to sleep. James must have sensed my hurt, because he pushes the board of cheese toasties towards me.

'Have some more,' he says, turning to wash his hands at the sink behind him.

'But really, I mean it,' says Bill, like a dog with a bone. 'Like, think about Manuel, with his pinstripe suits and snobby bloody French accent . . .'

'Was it a snobby French accent, or just a normal French one that you think sounds snobby?' I say, toying with him.

'What?'

'Because one answer makes him a prick, and the other makes *you* one.' I take another swig of my wine, tossing my head back, feeling rather pleased.

'Ignore Bill, he's drunk . . .' James says, shooting him a glance.

'Look. All I'm saying, Heather m'dear,' continues Bill, ignoring him, 'is that I can tell already that you are a scream, and the other ones were not.' He slaps me on the back and almost slips off his stool in the process. 'I just can't imagine you as a Master of Wine – they're usually so stuffy. Don't you agree, James?'

James looks at me and, with the confidence of a couple of drinks, I can hold his gaze.

'I think you're a breath of fresh air,' James says, before looking down and wiping the blade of a cooking knife with a tartan tea towel. He turns the blade over in his hand to inspect it, and it catches the light above him. Then he unrolls a large knife bag and slips it into the empty slot in the middle. There is something undeniably hot and sexy-dangerous about his bag of knives, though I did just finish binge-ing *Dexter* on the train. James pauses to glance briefly at me, before sliding the knife bag back in the drawer.

A breath of fresh air.

I've been called many things in my life, but this is the first time I've ever been called *a breath of fresh air*. My mum used to call me *boisterous*. My dad called me *a little attention-seeker*. My first flatmate, an uptight cow who worked in HR, called me a *lying, thieving little cunt* because she thought I stole her MAC make-up pen. (I borrowed it and lost it, so I technically didn't steal it, but either way, she couldn't have known it was me.) I've been called a *fucking loser* enough times for it to feel normal. Heather mostly calls me *wonderful*, but then I have always saved the best of myself for Heather.

I look over at James and my heart flutters.

We both reach for the champagne. He gets there first and I deliber-ately 'accidentally' touch his fingers. I can't help myself. Even I can't have misread the signals. Plus, I'm this fancy protégée sommelier, and everybody knows *newness* is 80 per cent of attraction. Surely I am fanciable in this scenario?

I try to push the thought out of my head, suddenly embarrassed.

'Sorry,' I say, feeling a bit daft and pulling my fingers away. 'You pour.'

Bill finally slides off his stool and, using his free hand to steady himself, salutes James and slaps me gently on the back again. He burps, his eyes starting to lose their direction as he shakes his head and knocks his wine over onto the floor.

'That's my cue,' he says, tipping over to pick it up, catching himself on the bar before he falls too far forward. 'Goodnight, you guys. I'm pooped!'

'Pooped?' I say under my breath, suppressing a grin. 'Who says "pooped"?'

James tops up my glass and stands for a moment, looking at his own. He picks it up and then puts it down. Then he puts his hands on his hips and I realize he's feeling weird that we're alone in our kitchen together. New housemates. Colleagues of only a few hours. Consenting adults. The sexual tension rises. Or is that just me?

'I should go, too. I have some work to do tomorrow,' he explains. 'Sorry to leave you.'

'No need to explain,' I say, a little disappointed but equally relieved. 'I'm so tired I could sleep right here on this kitchen counter.'

'Oh, but your room is just down the hall?' he says, brow furrowed.

'I'm not really going to sleep here, James.'

'Of course,' he says, shaking his head. 'Hey – ah, sorry I was a bit, um, short with you when you got here.'

'It's okay; it was like, what, eight hours ago now. I'm over it.'

'It's just that everything is changing. And Russell is new, and his menu is new, and I don't want to make any mistakes, and I was worried that you . . .'

'Wouldn't be up to the task?'

'No, that *we* wouldn't have time to sort things.' He pauses for a moment, looking briefly at the floor. He rubs both his eyes with the palms of his hands and tries to conceal a big yawn. 'It's just – it's all quite serious as we bring in the new menu and the new look. It will settle.'

I want to reassure him that I'm not going to fuck up, and make a firm promise to myself to start my wine study tonight.

'It's definitely all new,' I say, suddenly fading fast from exhaustion and three glasses of hastily quaffed champagne. 'But don't worry. We won't fuck it up.'

I want to hug him. He reminds me of a tree. A nice, big, solid tree.

Go to your room, Birdy.

6.

'How's it going?' I say, yawning and rolling my shoulders back in circles to loosen them up.

That's the problem with ten hours of uninterrupted sleep – rigor mortis begins to set in. So much for brushing up on my wine knowledge; I could barely type the word 'wine' into Google, I was so exhausted.

'Sorry, what I mean is: hi, Irene, how are you? It's great to see you again.'

I grin, because if I've ever learned anything, it's that confidence is key.

Irene might be older than most of the staff here, but she's got the swagger of a bohemian French supermodel. She looks even more glamorous today than she did at the Wine Awards. Her wild white hair is tossed together in a ponytail, but her make-up is immaculate. She's wearing a long teal-green kimono over a crisp white shirt and wide bottle-green pants. I can't see her shoes, but I can hear them clip-clop on the pebbled path outside the cottages.

'And you too, darling. I'm so sorry I couldn't be here to greet you last night, but unfortunately the pigsty needed a big spring clear-out.'

I baulk, trying to imagine this elegant, majestic creature knee-deep in pig shit.

'It's okay, I've had a bath,' she smiles. 'We'll walk up, shall we? Such a lovely day.'

The mercury's at ten degrees, at an absolute push, and although I opted for a more casual look this morning – a grey sweatshirt and jeans – it's still woefully inadequate for this weather.

'It was so fortunate to meet you in London. What a wonderful coincidence. And we might never have known, if we'd not been forced to wear those insufferable name badges.'

'Yes, it was, er, a great night. Tim was so, um, embarrassed about those antique glasses.' *By the time he had relayed the story to Damo later that night, it was a whole champagne tower.*

Irene smiles at me and nods, like a lovely aunt might. It's a smile that says, *I didn't like him one bit, but I'm far too supportive of you to say anything, so I will remain silent.*

I speed up, as she's got a lot of pace in those heels. She's one of those people who walk effortlessly in stilettos, almost glides in fact. I'm grateful I'm wearing my running shoes, as my feet are swollen and showing no signs of calming down ahead of the next full service, which is in less than two hours.

'Yes, we're so lucky to have you,' Irene continues. 'I was telling Russell what a scream you are. You'll fit right in here, I'm sure.'

'Thank you. I'm so lucky to be here.' I want to make a joke about it being the only place that would take me, but I'm not sure how far I should push the *Heather is a riot* reputation.

'So, I want to show you around our little place,' she says. 'I know you have a mountain to climb to get up to speed in the kitchen and cellar, but I thought a quick tour would help orientate you. Bill seems to think you were unaware of the changes?'

'Ahh, yes. It was a surprise.'

We reach the rear of the house, but instead of entering through the kitchen door she takes me along the back, to a large set of French doors with an enormous pot plant on either side.

'This is the guest exit, though it's not used so much, except for guests going hiking or on horse treks. We try to keep all the traffic to the front of the house, where it's easier for cars to pull in and out.'

She pushes the door open and motions for me to go ahead.

I gasp. It's *stunning*.

Grey tiles lead down towards the glass front doors, which make what would once have been quite a dark little corridor airy and bright. There are vases filled with fresh flowers on either side by the door – great armfuls of pale pink peonies, my favourite.

'It's gorgeous,' I say honestly.

We make our way towards the glass front doors that sit inside the original carved wooden ones, which are fixed open. Two enormous staircases lead down to the drive area. I remember seeing them on my arrival but, up close, they are the most gorgeous original stone.

By the entrance an open, opulent lounging area sits to my right – comfy mismatched sofas and armchairs of leather and expensive patterned fabrics arranged under a wall of silver-plated deer antlers. It's so freshly decorated I can smell the paint. And it's extremely chic. 'The Library,' Irene says, although the books seem to be part of an art piece, glued to the wall in a huge spiral swirl.

'If you see a guest trying to take one down, do stop them. That thing cost us almost twenty thousand pounds. Can you imagine? Anyway, offer them one of our complimentary iPads, where they can download any book they like. Charged to their room, of course.'

'How modern,' I say. Is this what boutique hotels do now? Because it's definitely a departure from the whole *country getaway* vibe. I was expecting a couple of old boxes of Monopoly and Scrabble on a shelf among the literary classics and Dan Brown novels. It's not exactly cosy in here.

'The whole house was redone by Pardington's of London,' Irene says as though she can read my mind. 'Russell had them do his place in Edinburgh – the one that got the second star last year – so we are hopeful this will bring a new breed of guest to the hotel. Everything but the restaurant is left to do, as you will no doubt have seen last night.'

'It's incredibly swanky.'

'It's certainly brought us into the twenty-first century. You should have seen the place before. Oh, it was homely and quaint, but the roof of the library was leaking, everything was damp. We couldn't charge much for the rooms, in the state they were. It's been an absolutely colossal project, at colossal prices. Let's hope it does the job,' she says, clapping towards the ceiling, apparently to turn the light off, which it finally does. The place would truly be at home in Shoreditch. I mean, members only, and far too expensive. But right at home.

Heather used to go on and on about these private houses she went to. Babbadook House this or Hexleybarns-bloody-worth-Estate that, with all the awful ad-types and bankers standing around comparing hard-ons, with a punchy claret in one hand and a bubbly ad-exec in the other. *Upper-Middle Classholes*, she used to call them, even though Heather could fit right in with them, in a way I could not. Her dad gave her that. He was older – fifty-eight – when Heather was born, and a fairly noted wine dealer. Heather inherited his confidence and passion – and money too, of course. Not loads, but enough. A little part of me was always jealous when she swanned off to university, complete with a monthly 'allowance', while I had to work two shitty jobs to afford it. But to give her her due, Heather must've stood me about a million rounds, so it wasn't all bad.

In the corner of the library sits one guest: an older man in tan leather shoes, *sans* socks, and a bright-blue polo shirt.

'Good morning, Matthew,' Irene sings, in what is an expert mix of flirtatious and professional. 'Do you have everything you need?'

'Yes, Irene,' he replies, folding his paper and smiling at me. His icy-blue eyes and golden hair make him more Bond villain than gentleman. I half-expect a Russian accent.

'Our new sommelier, all the way from London,' Irene explains, nodding towards me. 'You can put her to the test another day.'

'I look forward to it,' he says, sitting back in his chair and lifting his foot up to rest on his knee. Classic power-move.

'You'd better bring your very best game, sir,' I shoot, automatically going into flirt mode.

'Well, now I'm *really* looking forward to it,' he says, folding his arms.

Irene turns to me, with the subtlest of head shakes, and leads me to the reception area across the hall, whispering, 'Mr Hunt is the President of the Highland Wine Society. But a word of warning: he's a regular guest *and* he's a dreadful drunk. He would try it on with a horse if he'd had enough single malt. Well, last year he very nearly did.'

I'm a bit shocked, but Irene is simply shaking her head as if she's seen it a hundred times.

'It's partly my job to look after you while you're here, and now you know what Mr Hunt is, you will be better equipped to handle him. Especially as you're a woman. Women in hospitality, as I'm sure you well know, must look after one another.'

Irene smiles so fondly at me, I feel sure she's going to pat me on the head. But then in an instant we're off again.

'You'll be curating the wine and menu with James for their next meet-up towards the end of the summer. We will need some ideas over the next few days, so we can get the orders across. The last theme was *Grape Expectations*. Bill chose a list of budget wines that were actually exceptional, and some supposedly exceptional wines that were very poor indeed.'

'Sounds cool,' I say, trying to hide my panic.

'Sweet girl, it's the Royal Ascot of Wine Society events.'

I try to look confident and nod earnestly.

'Over a hundred people from across the west coast and beyond. It's more than a wine event, it's fast become something of a cornerstone of the hospitality calendar here on the west coast. It's not just the stuffy old wine-bros that come, either. The key buyers, growers and producers come too. Full black-tie, a band, dancing and whisky until dawn. It's the pride of Loch Dorn, that event. And with the renovations, Russell and you, Heather, at the helm, we hope it will be the best ever.'

'Okay. Got it.'

Through the rising anxiety, I find myself feeling slightly irritated with Heather now, for pulling out of this job. Did she realize they were all counting on her this much? And now they're counting on me, which, frankly, is a disaster waiting to happen.

Irene turns and raises her arm to introduce the reception-space-cum-bar-area, which has some scattered seating and a door onto a small empty terrace. 'It's still a little cold for outside dining,' she explains. Again, the interior is stunning – more leather, polished brass and rich hues. At the far side of the room there is a door through to the restaurant and, behind the bar, a door to the kitchen.

'So, in the library room the guests can relax and enjoy coffee, tea, more or less anything they wish to eat or drink – we keep the music very low and the atmosphere very relaxed; but here, our bar and reception area, we keep a little more perky, for want of a better word. The bar is open twenty-four hours, of course, but not always manned – so you'd need to ring the bell if you want a brandy at three a.m. Probably. Sometimes, after dining, you can suggest they enjoy a whisky by the fireplace. Ah, and here's Bill.'

I am surprised to see him looking so sprightly after last night's drinking session. He grins at me and raises a glass that he's about to fill with something from a cocktail shaker. There is a wonderful whiff coming from a scented candle by the bar, a smell that's fresh and clean with a kick of liquorice.

'Don't let Irene mother you,' he says.

'Don't let William pour you a drink,' Irene retorts, but I can see there is an affection between them. I take both bits of advice as sage, and we continue on our tour.

'I'll take you up to see a couple of the guest rooms. It's not especially important that you see them, since there should be no reason for you to be on the first floor.'

Which is a shame because – holy shit! – the bedrooms are incredible. As we enter the first vacant suite, I am drawn to the rolled-edge wrought-iron tub, which is situated so very happily next to a large window overlooking an apple tree that is just starting to blossom. It's gorgeous.

The bed is an enormous super-king, finished with crisp linen and deep blue-and-gold cushions. There is no flat-screen TV on display – instead, a cherry-wood dresser, a large gilded mirror and a love-seat of royal-blue velvet.

'How the other half live, eh?' I say, losing myself in the moment.

'Well, so it would seem,' says Irene, opening the balcony doors to air the room. 'You should have seen this room three months ago. Dreary. I do love these linen curtains.'

As we make our way downstairs again, she finishes the routine with a little speech about how the staff of Loch Dorn behave with dignity and class, and uphold the traditions of a society that stretches back as far as . . . But I have trouble focusing, as Mr Hunt, who has been joined by his utterly fed-up-looking wife, is giving me the eye from the bar. *Poor Mrs Hunt.* His heel misses the footrest and he slips forward, almost knocking over the flowers, just as an Indian couple squeeze past us, rosy-cheeked and sheepish.

'Honeymooners,' Irene stops her monologue for a moment to inform me.

I feel like I've walked into an episode of *Love Highland*.

I refocus on Irene, who is preaching that Loch Dorn Estate is aiming for the gold standard in a country that prides itself on warm hospitality, and going the extra mile to make sure the customer's every need is met. She's using words like *satisfied, fulfilled* and *come again and again*, and soon I'm finding it very hard to keep a straight face.

'How *does* Russell fit into it all?' I ask, to try and stop myself from breaking down.

'He was brought in to help modernize,' she replies.

'Job done, I reckon,' I reply, as Irene claps at the light switch again.

'He's not here every day. He has other restaurants, so he's busy,' she starts explaining, as if this is a well-worn script. 'But he will expect his version of absolute perfection – which can be rather hard to anticipate, and therefore achieve, but achieve it we must! This hotel has been transformed by his name, at the owner's considerable expense and the staff's execution. We must ring in the changes. Get the job done! Rally behind it!'

I'm unconvinced she's behind it, despite all the positive-speak. It reminds me of Heather trying to make the best of one of my browned-until-burnt roast-dinner attempts.

'I just wondered, because last night Russell wasn't in the kitchen.'

Irene purses her lips slightly. 'Well, James does the day-to-day heavy lifting, but Russell is here to be the visionary and manage the bottom line, and we deliver that vision without question. And, with that in mind, you've got to get yourself ready for lunch service.'

'Got it,' I nod.

'By the way, did Bill say there's a staff meal available for breakfast, lunch and dinner? You can have it in the dining room, if it's empty, or the staffroom.'

'Oh, that's great.' I was expecting there would be, but Bill hadn't said, and I was beginning to think I'd need to go digging through the bins.

'And one last thing, sweet girl,' Irene says, holding my cheeks in her hands, with an ease of affection that makes me want to do her proud. 'That boyfriend of yours. The young man I met at the Wine Awards? Can we expect an appearance this summer?'

'Oh no. I mean, it's not serious enough for a weekend visit,' I say quickly.

'Well,' she says, dropping her hands with a sigh of relief, 'that's very good news indeed.'

7.

I've made a big mistake.

In the moment of silence before lunch, I stare into the dark abyss of the locker that says *Heather* in neat Sharpie on the front and face myself. I'm not in a forgiving mood. It's clear that, contrary to what Heather said, this place is a big deal. This *job* is a big deal.

What the hell were you expecting?

You've done some dumb things in your time, Birdy Finch, but this beats them all.

You're going to screw this up, and Heather will be furious. She was relying on you to get her out of this, reputation intact, and instead you're going to screw it up entirely.

What the fuck have you done?

I've made a big mistake.

When I decided to come up here, a large part of me was banking on this vision of me and Heather, huddled together by the fire at that tiny table at the Dog and Duck, giggling as I recounted my summer misadventure of playing sommelier at this crumbling Ye Olde Hotel. But suddenly this doesn't feel like a likely outcome.

Heather and I have only ever properly fallen out once. That dark, horrible summer. She'd finished a stint in Bordeaux at some fancy château and I was working at the ticket booth at a stand-up club in Soho. That year had been one Heather success after another. It felt like I'd spent a whole fucking house-deposit on balloons and bunting and Prosecco to celebrate endless new promotions, or her latest wine diploma. Of course I was proud of her, but I *had* to be her cheerleader. There was no one else. And sometimes it was exhausting.

I hadn't bothered to take down the last foil *Congratulations* balloon in our kitchen, and it had slumped halfway down the wall, deflated, and just read '*CON*'.

I stared at it as I held a final gas-bill notice in my hand. So I sublet her room.

Unfortunately, Comedy Courtney, twenty-one, from Margate, stole a bunch of Heather's clothes, burned her coffee pot and weed in her bed after a night on the Jägermeister.

Heather wasn't angry about the bed, or the missing clothes; she was angry that I'd hidden it from her. But instead of fessing up that I was skint, and saying sorry, all of my embarrassment and anger bubbled up and I shouted at her.

'You don't know what it's like to be completely broke! I have no fucking safety net. You have this inheritance, and you can go swanning off to France for the summer and study wine, just like Daddy, without debt; and get a fucking professional haircut from someone called Ashley!'

'I'd rather have a family than an inheritance.'

'I'd rather have an inheritance than my family. Families are not fucking everything.'

Three months of cold silence followed, before I turned up with a new coffee pot and half a bottle of whisky.

'I saw on Facebook you got into the Master of Wine course-thing,' I slurred. 'I told everyone on the Northern Line. And then there was this nurse on the way home from the hospital, who looked like she needed a drink. And then this builder called Raf joined in and, before I knew it, I was in Burnt Oak.'

'I'm still angry,' she said, swiping the whisky off me.

'I know,' I said, as she grabbed my free hand and yanked me inside.

'And I've already replaced the bloody coffee pot.'

'Heather, I'm so fucking sorry.'

'I know you are. Just,' she took a deep breath, 'just, please, try to get your shit together.'

'I'll try.' I nodded. 'When will you have enough of me?'

'Probably never, you fucking egg.'

But now, staring into her locker, I am wondering: is this it? Have I ruined our friendship?

How am I going to prove myself – or Heather, I should say – in a place with a Michelin-bloody-starred head chef? I can only surmise that she didn't know that the hotel was being completely revamped and injected with cash. She can't have known, because otherwise she would have been lying to me. And Heather doesn't lie to me.

I wonder whether I should up and leave. But I can't see how – it would be *Heather* running out on the job. The other obvious option is confess the whole truth to Bill or Irene and *then* run. But that would land Heather in the shit too. And then I picture Irene's face, the feel of her hands on my cheeks, and that look of such pride and determination. I have to find another way.

'Hello, you,' says a familiar voice.

'Hello,' I say to Bill, who has emerged from the adjacent bathroom.

'Russell's going to observe lunch,' says Bill, flipping his locker open.

'Oh?' I reply with a frown.

'Don't be nervous. You'll be fine. I've known him for years. He's all bark and no bite. The man only drinks Scotch anyway, so it's unlikely he'll know if you're doing a bad job.' Bill chuckles at this, but I cringe.

'Bill, I, um, haven't really had even five minutes to go through the list . . .'

'No one expects you to know the list yet,' he says, smoothing his thinning hair down around his ears.

I nod, deciding I might incriminate myself if I protest any further.

I make my way back into the dining room, with Bill following behind. There are only three lunchtime bookings today, apparently, and five tables this evening. But at lunch, Bill tells me, they rarely have the degustation, so I won't be saved by the pre-paired menu.

'Do you get many walk-ins?' I ask, staring wistfully out of the window at the endless lawns and woods in the distance.

'Maybe later in the summer,' Bill replies. 'But after the revamp, we're expecting at least a couple of weeks of steady bookings. We're already fully booked for the first Friday and Saturday nights.

'Fantastic,' I say, as I breathe deeply and reach for the wine list.

It hasn't got any easier to decipher. I scan quickly for anything familiar, beyond the few bottles I paired with Heather's help last night. I need to think fast.

What do I actually know about wine?

I know, from my limited waitressing experience, that you start a meal with champagne or Prosecco. At least generally. Or a cocktail perhaps – but I wonder if, as a sommelier, I should be pushing the wine?

I know that often a white wine accompanies the starter, and then on to a red, if you're having meat as a main. But that maybe you'd stick with white, if you are having fish or chicken as a main. But I also know it's far more complex than that. Heather, for example, could smell a glass and identify *notes*, which were things like butter (what?), peach blossom and grated lemon rind. Not just lemon – *grated lemon rind*, to be precise. I must have some Heather-expertise stored in my brain somewhere.

So yes, I can remember bits like that, but nothing useful – like what the wine that tasted like grated lemon rind *was*. I wish I'd paid more attention. All that knowledge I thought was nonsense is suddenly utterly critical.

But three tables? Can it really be that hard?

At the open kitchen, James and Anis are tasting a sauce from a silver jug with two tiny teaspoons. I watch for a moment as they share a satisfied grin. As she walks out of view, James looks up and catches my eye. And it's disarming, his smile. Shy but warm, with a small dimple on his right cheek.

I do a little over-eager wave his way. *Too much, Birdy, too much.*

He mouths, 'Good luck' to me in return and I'm instantly transported from sweet anxiety to the more sinister kind. I gulp and try to focus, but I'm not sure on what. Why has no one told me what to do? Is this what happens when you're really experienced – no one tells you what to do any more?

Irene swings through the double doors and places a plate of clear soup on the counter. She nods to Bill, who hands her a crisp napkin wrapped around a knife and fork.

'That's for Russell. He'll have a bar lunch while he observes.'

I must look nervous, because her face suddenly softens.

'You'll be fine,' she says, putting a calming hand on my arm. 'Bill says you're a real pro.'

I gulp, looking over at Bill, who is nodding supportively. No, I'm not confessing to these ridiculously kind people. Not now.

A waitress slides up beside me, with yet another open, warm face.

'Hi, I'm Bir—' I begin. *Fuck!* 'I mean, ah, I'm Heather. Heather is my name.'

'I'm Roxy,' she full-beams back at me and speaks in a very soft accent. She doesn't seem to have noticed the slip. 'We met last night?'

'Oh shit, of course,' I mutter. 'I was, like, train-lagged or something.'

'Are you okay? You look a bit hot,' she whispers gently.

Just then the doorway to the dining room is filled with two couples, easily in their seventies. Both men remove their flat caps as they enter, showing the way for the ladies. Irene moves at speed to greet them, arms outstretched, a wide smile on her face.

'Betty, Thomas, Shammi and . . . Govid, is it? A very good afternoon to you all,' she says warmly, extending her arm to the made-up table for four people situated by the large bay window. Roxy joins her, helping to remove jackets and scarves discreetly away to a coat rack. She's like a cat, the way she moves.

'Go,' says Bill, waving me towards the table.

'Go, what?' I say, my heart racing. 'Oh yes, right.' I turn and head to the table.

'Wait!' he says, and I spin round to see him holding four menus and a wine list out to me.

'Oh shit,' I say, unfortunately out loud, as my legs carry me towards the table. Irene beams at me as we pass, and then my eye catches Russell's as he appears through the kitchen doors to take his observational seating position at the bar. He's about ten feet from me now, and I can feel his presence like a spotlight. I turn my head back to the diners at the table, who are all facing me with expectant smiles. Everyone's eyes are on me.

'Who wants a wine then?' I blurt out.

I can feel Russell's eyes burning into the back of me, as the four pensioners cock their grey heads almost in unison.

'Can we see the list?' says the portly one, who I think is called Thomas.

'Sure,' I say, handing him the menu.

'That's the *lunch menu*,' Betty says through bleeding red lipstick, whilst pointing a long, wrinkly finger with very classy clear-polished nails at the big gold-embossed word *MENU* on the front.

'Right,' I nod, fumbling through the weighty folders in my arms before handing her the wine list. 'Thank God *someone's* paying attention. You want a job?'

She smiles tightly and hands the list across to Thomas, who expertly flicks it open at the same time flicking open his spectacles and sliding them onto his nose.

'We usually get the three-course set lunch. What are the wines available with that?' he asks.

'Um, definitely red and white,' I say confidently, before quickly adding, 'unless you want some champagne? Which, I guess, is also white. Technically. I mean who cares really; it all does the same thing – am I right?'

Oh God, shut up, Birdy.

The second lady at the table looks perky at the suggestion of champagne and, just as I'm hoping I've found a good angle, Betty-the-bore rebuffs my suggestion with a crisp, 'No champagne, thank you.'

'We'd just like to know which wines are on the Specials menu today,' Thomas repeats.

'Can you bear with me one moment? I'm so sorry – I'm new,' I explain as the heat rises in my cheeks.

'Oh, of course,' Betty says, softening.

I rush back to the bar and, unable to remember if I should know about the wine specials or not, I do what any incompetent professional does when they're caught out. I blame everyone else.

'Why has no one briefed me on the daily wine specials that go with the set lunch?' I say it loudly and directly to Bill, ignoring the gaze coming from Russell, who is seated opposite him.

'Ah, sorry. My bad,' Bill says. 'Here it is.'

He reaches across the bar, pulls a sheet of paper out from behind the cash register and hands it to me.

'It should have been in the front of the wine list,' he says, pointing to an empty plastic sleeve attached to the inside cover.

'Oh, thank you.'

'Make sure Heather is fully briefed, could you?' Russell says to Bill, shaking his head.

'Will do,' he replies, looking aghast.

'Sorry, I got a bit flustered there,' I whisper out of the side of my mouth to him, hoping Russell doesn't hear.

I head back to the table as Roxy arrives with some sparkling water, quiet and discreet as a mouse. With an elegant long arm outstretched, she tops up each of the small tumblers, before returning the water to a side-table away from the guests.

'Here's the daily wine specials,' I say.

Thomas jumps in right away. 'Betty will have the salmon and I'll have the venison. We'll both have the soup. And we'll decide on dessert afterwards.'

'Oh, that's great,' I say, scrambling around in my apron for a pad and paper. I didn't think I was supposed to take the food order. I look over my shoulder for Roxy, but she's not in the dining area. Must remember pen and paper. I engage my memory: *The salmon, venison and two soups*, I repeat in my head, and then look nervously towards the other couple. How am I going to remember all of this?

'We'll both have the venison, and the beetroot as a starter,' says the other gentleman with a polite smile. *Two beetroots, two soups, salmon, three venison. I've got this.*

'So what do you recommend?' Thomas asks pointedly.

I look down in dismay and realize the lunch-specials wine list has about a dozen wines on it. I could guess, I guess? Or I could . . .

'Ahh, one bottle or two?'

There's a very audible scoff from Betty.

'I mean, well, you're having fish and they're having meat, so . . .'

Thomas tuts loudly. 'Where's Irene?'

'Well, she's . . .' I stammer. 'Um.'

I look round and clock Bill, who immediately senses my distress and glides across the floor in seconds to rescue me.

'Hi, Thomas, how are the kids?' he says in a voice I've not heard before. It's so saccharine it gives me the creeps.

'Good, Bill. Good,' Thomas replies.

'What can I help with?'

'Well, so far your new sommelier has recommended a red or a white wine, two bottles of wine and a bottle of champagne. I was hoping for something a bit more specific from a new sommelier.'

I furrow my brow as if I'm agreeing with him that I've been rubbish.

'I see,' Bill replies with a reassuring smile. 'I'm ever so sorry, but it's her first shift here, so she's not really up to speed. Heather, here, used to work at the Wolseley, you know.'

Thomas looks up at me suspiciously, but the other three say 'Ahhh' in unison.

'I did,' I say quickly.

'Why don't you go and see to table three, and I'll look after these guys for now,' Bill says.

I scuttle off and I'm actually shaking as I reach the safety of the bar, but immediately notice that the guests at table three have their hands raised in my direction. I look for Roxy, who has returned from the coat rack and nods supportively to me. It's me: I have to go. I lick my dry lips and swallow a couple of times.

'Hello, how can I help you?' I ask the two sweet ladies, one of whom smells so overwhelmingly of a mandarin- or orange-based perfume that I have to take a small step backwards.

'Bill says you're a very good sommelier,' says one. 'We're ever so impressed. You've come all the way from London to be at our little local.'

'Ahh.' I blush. *Oh shit!*

'So, we were wondering, is the Picpoul any good? It's Margaret's birthday and we fancy getting a little . . . well, you know?'

Margaret reaches forward and touches her friend's hand and they both giggle in such a sweet way that my heart slows and I feel a sense of calm wash over me. Old friends. Old friends sharing a drink. Old best friends. And all these lovely ladies want from me is to know whether a wine is good or not. That I can easily pretend to do.

'Yes. It's the best,' I reply. 'Nothing like sharing a bottle with your best friend, is there?'

'That's right, dear,' Margaret nods.

As I head to the wine fridge behind the bar, I glance back at Margaret. She is giggling away at her friend, eyes full of delight, just like old girlfriends do. Old girlfriends like me and Heather. Another grim wave of guilt hits me as I think of her.

'Sorry about before,' whispers Bill as I limp up to the bar. 'I should have given you the list.'

'Oh, it's okay, forget it,' I say looking up. 'I need a bottle of, er, Pick Pool.'

'Picpoul?' he corrects me with the French pronunciation.

'Sorry, yes,' I say. 'Stage fright. You know.'

'Why don't I shadow you for the rest of the day and show you the ropes,' Bill says. 'It was a bit unfair to drop you in it like this. You've not had five minutes to get your head round things.'

'Thank you,' I say, quietly wanting to hug him. Tonight I will head back to the house and formulate a plan.

'And we can't have you sullying our reputation,' he says, a smile on his face as he slides a long dark-green bottle from the fridge. 'After all, I hired you.'

'Yeah,' I say, before forcing my broadest, most cheeky grin. 'What on earth were you thinking?'

8.

'Hurry up,' James says, waiting by the open front door.

'Five minutes!' I gasp, checking my phone for the time – 7.04 a.m. – and ignoring the three missed calls from Tim. I'd been awake when he rang, but that was at 1 a.m., 1.15 a.m. and 2 a.m., which could only mean one thing: he was so drunk he'd forgotten I was in Scotland, and he wanted a shag.

It *was* nice to feel wanted, though.

'I'm so sorry – I'm just exhausted.'

Bill had been true to his word and had taken the reins at dinner, while I did a bit more shadowing, *to see how we do things*. But it was all a blur; I don't think anything really sank in.

Afterwards I was, again, far too tired to go over the wine list, or unpack any of the wine books I'd brought with me. Instead I googled the 'Top Ten things you didn't know about wine', and then I went through Heather's now-private Instagram, with the same cat picture as her Facebook. She hadn't posted since she was in Italy, and I felt a deep stab of guilt as I scrolled through all the pictures of my dear friend.

Then I had lain awake, unable to sleep, trying to figure out my options. Leaving without a full confession would mean it was Heather running out on a job. (I mean, Heather actually *had* run out on this job, but still . . . 'She' was here now, so that option was off the table.) But leaving *with* a confession would also make her look bad. If I was going to leave, it needed to be as Heather, but with a cast-iron excuse. A death in the family was an option. But who could I kill off? She didn't have anyone left. No, it had to be something else. Something that left her reputation intact.

I look up and see James beaming at me from the end of the corridor.

Ugh! There has to be another way.

'We're late,' James says, shaking his head and handing me a large slice of generously buttered toast and a mug of tea.

'Oh God, thanks,' I reply, knocking back the lukewarm tea in one, and wedging the toast in my mouth as I zip up my hoodie with jittery fingers.

I chew on the toast, which is dry in my mouth. I feel a bit sick. I'm so far from being ready.

We're off 'foraging' at the crack of dawn – something I wasn't sure I could do, on the three hours of dream-filled sleep of angry old ladies, burning vines and crumbling corks. But Irene thought it would get me into the spirit of the restaurant, and that James and I could get to know each other a bit better.

'You two need to be a tight team,' she'd said.

'Got it,' I nodded. I was keen to be as enthusiastic as possible.

'But not too much of a team,' she said, with an eyebrow raised and a smile.

'Understood,' I replied. I liked Irene.

I wonder if working in an isolated hotel like this one is a bit like working on a cruise ship, where it's a *really* bad idea if any of the staff get together, in case they have a bad break-up. No escape.

But Irene doesn't need to worry about me. I'm not the boyfriend-at-work type. I'm not even really the boyfriend type. I've had three boyfriends, including Tim – none of whom unlocked any 'proper boyfriend' achievements, like meeting parents for dinner or going on weekends away to Whitstable. I also had a couple of very drunk one-night stands when I was at university for that one year. That was the year I nailed *Mario Kart*, watched all seven seasons of *Lost*, and discovered my flatmate had a hydroponic marijuana farm in the basement under my bedroom. Oh, and the year of *Dad's first and last attempt at sobriety*, which involved a lot of apologetic phone calls that were so emotionally exhausting I ended up leaving uni to backpack around Wales, to remove myself from it.

It's not that I don't want to have a normal boyfriend to cruise the aisles of Aldi with. I am just kind of happier single. It's easier. Plus, Heather is a walking, talking cautionary tale of romantic entanglement.

James is wearing thick tawny hiking boots and an almost stylish moss-green Barbour coat with a waxy finish. It's drizzling and still cold, but the fog has lifted and there is that smell of freshly cut grass in the air that everyone loves – especially, apparently, wine reviewers.

Anis is waiting outside in a fitted anorak, with a basket and an umbrella.

'Where does Anis live?' I whisper, pulling on my running shoes.

'In cottage four, with the rest of the younger ones.'

'Oh, does that mean we're the old ones?'

James laughs loudly, and Anis shoots me a suspicious look.

'I was just asking where everyone lives,' I explain, not wanting her to feel left out.

'Cottage four,' she replies in a thick Scottish accent, pushing her frankly incredible dark, glossy hair behind her ears. She's beautiful – petite and smooth-skinned, with the most gorgeous full eyebrows – and is sporting the cutest red Hunter boots. 'Are you wearing those shoes?' she says accusingly, looking to James and then back at my Converse.

'I'm afraid I didn't bring anything practical,' I say, shrugging. 'But perhaps I can go to town and pick up something next week?'

'Aye, you'll need to,' she replies, her brow furrowed, 'if you're going to do anything round here – work or otherwise. Those shoes are terrible.'

'You're so right,' I agree, shrugging off the offence. 'Fashion is pain, though, right?'

She doesn't smile, but rather looks at her basket and then over towards the horse stables and sighs dramatically. Like she's always having to sort people's shit out. In my experience, that kind of exasperated disapproval always comes from a good place. I smile to myself, vowing to win her over.

And so we head off in silence, a merry party of three, into the wilderness.

James leads the way down the bank towards the river at the back of the estate. The grounds are not kept like an English estate might be. There's the rose garden, but the rest is unrepentantly wild, with unkempt hedges, fruit trees, long grass and wildflowers in purples, yellows and deep pinks stretching up to meet the morning sun.

As we reach the swollen river we leave the sun for the canopy of oak, birch and beech trees, all that vivid green of freshly unfurled leaves. The cool air against my skin feels suddenly invigorating.

James directs us along a muddy path towards a footbridge.

'So, Anis . . .' I say. Wondering how to strike up conversation, I go with something outdoorsy. 'Do you like hiking?'

'I prefer hunting,' she replies.

'Right. Hunting,' I say. 'Like with a gun?'

'Aye, with a gun,' she replies. 'And a ten-inch blade, should I need it.'

I strategically slow my pace to fall behind her.

We walk for a few minutes while the sound of the river and occasional bird song fills the silence. Every now and then James pulls his phone out of his pocket and takes a picture of some bit of bright-green foliage or a bird perched on a branch. And once or twice he takes a photo of Anis pushing back bushes and pointing at things I can't make out. He tries to take one of me, and I shoot my hands to my face as fast as I can. 'Please, no close-ups,' I joke, and he's so polite he doesn't try again.

'What are we looking for, then?' I eventually ask. 'I've never worked at a restaurant that forages. What happens if we don't find anything?'

'Russell doesn't really *do* foraging, so it's just my and Anis's thing really. But he accommodates us,' James begins, pulling his beanie off and shaking out his thick dark hair. I try to suppress another swoon. 'We get the main things from local suppliers: you know, game birds, mackerel, salmon, Highland venison. But I try to forage some seasonal things like raspberries and mushrooms, and all the herbs, like wood sorrel, water mint, if we can find it – that kind of thing. I think it's fun for the guests to see *foraged mushrooms* on the menu, don't you think?'

'Okay, so we're not looking for Highland venison,' I say, 'unless you're concealing a shotgun in those trousers, James?' I joke.

I'm pleased to hear Anis give a deep, throaty laugh, but when I look over my shoulder, James appears mortified. *Too much.*

'No, not today. We have a really good supplier from Skye,' he says as he squeezes past me on the small path and pulls himself up towards some tiny white flowers. 'Few more days,' he says to Anis and she nods.

'And cuckooflower is great with our wild salmon. But the real prize is porcini, of course,' James says, grinning, 'I get a bit obsessed during mushroom season.'

'You have ceps here?' I say. Now porcini, I do know. Heather did an amazing pasta dish with them. But for some reason I thought they all came from Italy.

'Of course we do,' Anis says. 'James would get or grow everything local, like, if he could. And Russell would get everything shipped up from London, if he could.'

'Oh, do I sense a slight conflict here?' I say, smirking.

'No, no. He's the executive chef,' says James, not really answering the question.

'He's the executive prick,' Anis corrects, frowning in James's direction, 'but his attitude is that we need to make money, not friends.'

Kind of the opposite of hospitality, isn't it? I think.

'We've always worked at the source for some of the best produce,' James says, stopping for a moment and holding his hands out towards the forest around us. 'But flip everything you know about traditional restaurants on your head. If we need lemons for eighty covers? It's a three-day wait, so we have to be really organized. But we get lobster delivered fresh each day from about thirty miles away. It's the opposite of somewhere like London, where Russell's used to everything being consistently shipped in. Here, if there's a storm and the boats can't go out . . .'

'There's no lobster,' Anis finishes.

'Heaven forbid,' I say.

'Yes,' agrees James, shaking his head at the horror of it. 'But Russell's new system means we've got a consistent supply now, more or less. I've managed to keep some of the local ones, though. It's not a total takeover. Anyway, it's going to make us more profitable,' he says, shrugging.

'Well, that's something.'

I stop by a leaning oak with exposed roots that worm their way down the eroding bank towards a set of large rocks by the river. I slip almost immediately, and just manage to catch myself before I'm face-first into the water. It looks so fresh and clean as it glides across large boulders into one calm pool after the other. The smell of mud and wet stone is weirdly pleasing. I dip my fingers into one of the pools and pull them out immediately.

'Jesus fucking Christ,' I yelp, cupping my fingers in my hand and breathing warm air onto them. 'It's like ice.'

James grabs the arm of the oak and jumps expertly down towards me, leaping from rock to rock until he stops next to me. He dips his hands into the river and splashes some water on his face. 'Well, there's still a lot of snow-melt. I love it.'

'Can you drink it?'

'You can, but there's always a risk of dead livestock or something upstream,' he says. 'Do you fish?'

'Um, no,' I reply, wishing for a moment that I did, as I picture myself on a small boat in the middle of a loch with James. Maybe a parasol. No, actually, no parasol. 'I'd love to try, though.'

I look across and he is smiling at me. I'm not sure if he's smiling at the idea of me fishing, or because he'd like to go fishing with me, or because it seems absurd that I'd like to go fishing, but I'm leaning towards the last possibility.

'Wild garlic!' calls Anis from further down the path, stealing James's attention.

'That's our lamb main sorted. And no arguments from Russell, if it's free,' he says to me, as he drags himself up from the bank and rushes down the path to follow Anis. 'Come on!'

He's as light as a ten-year-old boy, and I have to move quickly to try to keep up. Unfortunately, my sneakers are not giving me quite the grip or support I need, and when my foot hits a wet, mossy rock, I slip again, this time to the side, and feel a shooting pain in my right ankle. 'Ah, fuck,' I murmur, steadying myself on the offending rock and waiting for the pain to subside.

'Heather,' he calls from the distance. 'Hurry up!'

'I'm coming!' I shout.

Ahead I can see them in a small clearing, both bent over. I take another few wobbly steps, cursing my luck. Imagine almost breaking my ankle two days into what was already a living nightmare. I bend over and roll down my sock and inspect the edge of my ankle, but mercifully, it looks totally normal.

As I limp closer, the pain begins to subside, but Anis catches my limp and her face drops. 'Are you okay?'

'Yeah, fine,' I reply, shaking out my ankle again.

'What happened?' She takes a few steps forward. 'Did you hurt your ankle?'

'It's nothing,' I say, shaking my head.

'It's those ridiculous shoes,' she says, frowning.

'It'll be fine. Did you find some wild garlic?'

'Oh yes,' she says, reaching into the high grass to pick up her basket, which is bursting with green. I'm confused for a moment as it appears to be full of thick grass, but I don't want to sound totally lacking in expertise here.

'Wow,' I say, 'so vibrant.' Then I get a whiff. Wow, it really does smell like garlic!

Her eyes narrow on me as she glances down at my foot again.

'I'm going to buy some hiking boots,' I find myself saying.

James strides across with an arm full of the same stuff that looks like grass and nothing like garlic. 'What's up? Heather, are you okay?'

'We've been away from the cottage for about thirty minutes and she's already got an injury,' says Anis accusingly.

'Can you put pressure on it?' James asks, looking genuinely worried.

And then it dawns on me. They're over-concerned because if I've injured myself, I won't be able to work. For a moment I feel really bad, but then I realize: this could work to my advantage.

'I didn't want to bother you guys . . .' I say, shooting out my lower lip and furrowing my brow.

'Don't be silly. Sit,' Anis says, bending down as she drops the basket. I lean on her for support and slowly lower myself to the ground.

66

It's damp, of course, and I can feel the cold wetness seeping through my jeans to my skin.

James tugs on my sneaker and, through a cloak of guilt, I fake a wince. I mean, it does hurt a bit.

'God, sorry.' He looks panicked.

'It's okay,' I say, and his shoulders drop with relief.

'Let me do it,' says Anis, pushing him out of the way. With the sock off, my foot looks fine, if in dire need of a pedicure.

'It's going to swell up terribly,' she says to James, 'like a hobbit's foot. Look, it already is.' She points to my chubby and slightly hairy big toe, and I try not to feel offended. 'It definitely looks like it's swollen—'

'Okay, thank you, Doctor,' I snap, pulling my foot back.

'We'd better get you back to the cottage,' James says, shaking his head.

'I'll stay and get what we need for lunch,' says Anis. 'You should tell Russell and Irene ASAP.'

'She can still do the menu pairings,' says James helpfully.

'Yeah, I guess,' Anis agrees through a frown. 'And Roxy can step up?'

'Let's try to get you up,' James says, leaning forward and threading his arm around my back, then swiftly pulling me to my feet. I'm uncomfortable with this whole damsel-in-distress act that's going on, but I decide to play along to maximize the potential extra time to get my head round everything that's going on: the wine list, the job, my life.

'Can you make it back like this?' he asks.

'I think so,' I reply.

'Anis, will you be okay?'

'Fine,' she replies, looking away from the two of us as we hobble down the path together. James is doing his best to support me as I walk, while simultaneously keeping his body politely as far away as possible.

'Thanks, James,' I say.

'It's okay. I'll get you into bed and we'll see if we can get you to a doctor, or get the doctor to come to you. Or Brett can take a look.'

'Brett?' I say, as I subtly lean closer to enjoy the feeling of James's body pressed gently up against mine.

'Yes, he tends to the animals. And tends the grounds.'

'Does he also tend to the ladies?' I say with a giggle, and James stiffens slightly and, for the briefest of moments, I fantasize that he just got a little jealous.

9.

News of my horrific injury travelled fast and when we returned to the cottage Irene was there, clutching two feather-filled guest pillows, insisting that my ankle was examined *immediately*.

Brett, the six-foot hulk of a groundskeeper/horse doctor, assesses my foot for breaks – none! – with an incredibly light touch, and is now moving it left and right and in gentle circles. I'm wincing as much as possible, without milking it too much.

James, who had gallantly but awkwardly supported me all the way home, had dashed back to the kitchen to get prep started. Bill had popped in with a shot of whisky, which I dutifully necked.

'So, where did Irene rescue you from then?' Brett asks, while gently wrapping the bandage around my foot with his huge horse-fixing hands.

'Eh?'

'Where are you from, lass?'

'Oh. Plymouth,' I say without thinking. 'And London.'

'Nobody's from two places.'

'I don't like being from Plymouth,' I say. 'Have you ever been there?'

'I thought Devon was supposed to be lovely,' Irene says.

'Sure, Devon is gorgeous. Plymouth is not really postcard-Devon. Plymouth is poverty with a port.'

'Hmm . . .' she says, and I decide to change the subject.

'How's it looking, Doc?'

'Honestly, I don't see why ye wouldn't be back at work tonight, lassy,' he says in the thickest Scottish accent yet. 'It's not even swollen. I thought it was at first, but look, both feet are the same size.'

'All right, Brett, that's enough,' I say.

'Oh, thank goodness. You poor thing,' Irene coos. 'So we don't need to take her to Fort William?'

'God, no. I think she'll be back on the horse in no time.'

'Thanks so much,' I say, shaking my head to show what a nuisance it all was. 'What a thing to happen, eh?'

'Well. Not to worry,' he says, grinning at me again as he packs up his emergency medical kit for animals and stands. 'Next time you'll have to lose a whole leg if you want to get out of work.' He winks at me, and for a split second I don't laugh, then I quickly do.

'Oh no. Why would I want to do that?' I say, flapping my arms at him.

'Heather, darling, I'll send James down in a few hours with the menu, and you can do the pairings, and then hopefully you'll be back with us for the evening service? No hurry, of course.'

'Uh-huh,' I reply, happily straightening the sheets on my bed. 'I'll do my very best to be back for dinner.'

And with that, Irene is out of the room and I am alone with my fake foot injury and the bottle of whisky left by Bill. I turn it round to read the label: *Oban, 18 years old*. I take a sniff of my empty glass and wonder how the hell whisky is made. Somewhere in the back of my mind, I think it's potatoes. Or is that gin?

I try to focus on the culinary mystery at hand. Wild garlic. I do a quick google on lamb with wild garlic, and find that yes, it does look a bit like grass. There are a couple of recommendations for wines, including a Côtes du Rhône, which I vaguely remember we might have on the menu. But mostly I sit there and feel tired from my lack of sleep, and the ibuprofen-and-whisky combo.

Perhaps I need another drink to perk me up.

I take another quick shot, enjoying the warm heat as it trails down my throat. But rather than perking me up, it drags me towards some sorely needed sleep. And just as I'm in that delicious state of sleepiness you only get from a midday nap, James ploughs into the room, clutching a sheet of paper.

'Shit, I should have knocked, sorry!' he says, panting as if he's been running. He stands over me, then looks as if he's going to sit. Then he sits down, and his weight tips me so that my body rolls into him a little; and then he stands in embarrassment and thrusts the menu at me. 'I did a really rough version early, so you could get on to it now.'

'You *can* sit down, you know,' I say, and he immediately does again. He's out of his hiking gear and in a pair of jeans, T-shirt and his chef's apron.

I glance down at the menu and am relieved to see some fairly similar dishes to the first night. But there is the inclusion of slow-roast lamb shoulder with wild-garlic velouté – *what the fuck is a velouté?* – spring vegetables and a Parmesan crisp, which is new.

'The Côtes du Rhône?' I try woozily, as the three shots of whisky and Nurofen plus codeine begin to weave their magic together.

'Too pricey for the degustation,' he says quickly. 'That's ninety-nine quid a bottle. Russell is all over the margins. How about a Grenache?'

'Tanks thas sexcellent,' I slur.

He smiles at me, but doesn't pull the menu away.

'Are you drunk?'

'Oh God, a little.'

'You should sleep.'

'I should definitely sleep. Did Anis get back okay?'

'Yes, with an armful of sweet cicely too, so she did well,' James says, lifting the paper up higher so that it's almost under my nose. I realize he's politely trying to give it to me, but the Scotch is impairing my judgement somewhat.

'Sorry,' I say, taking it from him. I look down at the menu and see the inclusion of chocolate-and-amaretti *délice* with Scottish wild-berry sorbet. God, I want to try it, whatever it is.

'God, I want to try that,' I say, closing my eyes and sighing.

'It's good. Has a thick mousse kind of texture, and the berry sorbet adds a lightness you have to try to believe,' James says with a big smile. 'It's Anis's invention.'

'I didn't know she did desserts.'

'She was a pastry chef, first.'

'Oh yes, but I didn't realize she did actual desserts too.'

James looks at me weirdly. 'We'll be finished in a couple of hours. If you can't do tonight, Roxy can stand in?'

'I'm sure I'll be better,' I say, suddenly wanting to be on shift with him again.

'Okay, great,' he says, sighing. 'What an absolute bugger of a thing to happen.'

'I'm daft. Who goes hiking in Converse? I'm just coming across as ridiculously city.'

'We'll break you in.'

'Goodness, James, we've only just met,' I tease.

He looks crushingly embarrassed and then loiters for a moment, gazing over at my case in the corner. 'You've not unpacked?'

'Not yet,' I say. 'Waiting to see if I like it before I commit. I can't even commit to a favourite ice-cream flavour, so don't hold your breath.'

'Same. Why do people try to make you choose? Vanilla? Chocolate? I want them both.'

I laugh at him. He's so endearingly earnest. And then I feel a little relief at buying myself a few hours. 'Hey, fanks muchly for your help. With the lifting me back, like some kind of lumberjack prince or something. And for getting hot Brett, the horse guy. And the menu prep. I really owe you.'

'Hot Brett?'

'It's just a fact,' I say with a shrug. 'And did you know that Brett is actually the nickname for a yeast. A yeast that gets into wine 'nd makes it taste like old sports socks and sticking plasters. Actually weirdly accurate, having smelled him up close.'

It was the one thing I remembered from the 'ten wine facts you probably don't know' googling I'd done last night.

'Brett?'

'Yes, Brett is a wine yeast infection,' I say earnestly. 'He shouldn't be around wine . . .'

'Okay,' James says and looks over at the empty glass next to me, and I can tell he thinks I shouldn't be around whisky.

'Thanks for everything, James. Can I call you Jamie, like the hot guy in *Outlander*?'

'What's *Outlander*?'

'Kilt porn. It's a whole genre.'

I love that it's so easy to make him blush. I watch his red cheeks slowly fade as he looks across at my ankle again and then back to me. 'See you later today, I hope.'

'Oh, I just wondered one thing . . .' I call out to him as he gets to the door. 'How does Irene fit into everything here?'

'Irene?' James says, surprised.

'Yes,' I say. 'Where is she from? I mean. Sorry, that sounds weird.'

'It's okay, she *is* pretty weird.'

'Isn't she?' I say, my eyes widening. 'I mean she's totally cool, but what's she doing *here*? She looks like she should be running an art gallery or a homeware shop, or the classy lingerie section of Harvey Nicks.'

'She's my mum,' he says, as though he's tired of the question.

'Wait! What?' I shout, and I can hear him laugh as he makes his way down the hall.

10.

I awake with a start and sit bolt upright in bed, confused.

Where am I? My eyes adjust to my little cottage room, and the still-packed suitcase in the corner, the whisky bottle on the side-table. The foot raised on a soft pillow.

My head throbs and a wave of memories from the last two days cascades over me like a frosty shower. I realize how tired I am. I'm completely wiped out. Not just from the medicinal whisky, but from everything – the train trip, the constant pressure to be somewhere or do something since I arrived. But, mostly, from anxiety.

I look at my phone. The time is 3.30 p.m. Shit! My power-nap has turned into a four-hour sleep. Sunday lunch service must be over, but dinner service is only a couple of hours away. I promised I'd be back for it and so, once again, there is bugger-all time to study.

I lie back in bed, looking up at the freshly painted ceiling and the plaster rose around the light fitting. It reminds me of my granny's house on Wolsdon Street in Plymouth. The one with the black fireplace with the little ornate rose-tiles around it, and the tiny little garden with the strawberry patch out the back. Granny was a hoarder, but a really organized one. You could still make your way around her house through the neatly stacked magazines and collections of glass bottles, but the lounge room eventually became uninhabitable. When she died we found newspapers dating back to 1945, eleven dinner sets, twenty-eight sterling-silver serving spoons, sixty-three silver-foil platters and seventeen garbage bags of clothes, including all of Grandpa's.

I'm the opposite of her, with my couple of suitcases of stuff, and my ability to shed whatever I'm surrounded with on a whim – including, apparently, my own identity.

My phone vibrates and it's Tim. *Tim*. I almost forgot about my other life.

'Hey,' I say, feeling an extra-strong throb in my right temple.

'Oh! Hey, babe,' he says in a loud whisper, his thick North London accent a punch of familiarity. 'I didn't think you'd answer.'

'Oh,' I reply, wondering why he's called. 'Well, it's good you called, because I need help. I need to come up with a good story.'

'What do you mean? Has it gone tits-up already?'

'I'm serious,' I say, rubbing my temple with my free hand. 'I need an out. Brain cancer might work – I have all the symptoms.'

'Uh-oh,' he says, laughing.

'Don't laugh,' I reply wearily.

'I knew you'd fuck it up,' he chortles. 'I've been telling Damo about it, and he thinks you're mad. He wants to know how you'll get paid? Like, which National Insurance number will you use?'

'I haven't thought about that yet . . .' I say, wishing now I hadn't answered the call that he didn't think I'd answer.

'Hey, I'm about to head to a meeting. We're starting legal action against a pensioner who might have set fire to her house accidentally. I really want to win this one, as I'll reach my target.'

'Inspiring stuff,' I say.

There's a moment's silence and then he chuckles. 'Come on. You'll be all right, Birdy.'

'I'm a bit scared,' I say.

'I bet.'

'*I bet?*' I say sharply, feeling really pissed off. 'Anything else to add? *You* thought it was a great idea, that night.'

'I *was* drunk *and* high,' he whispers.

'Fair enough,' I say feebly. 'But I need—'

'That was a fuckin' laugh, that night,' he interjects, like it's the most important detail.

'Yes, but I can't keep it up. The hotel is not a *shithole*, like I thought. It's really fucking fancy. And there's a brand-new fucking wine list, with page after page of nonsensical words, and years and grapes. Oh, and some of the wines don't even mention a grape! Like what the fuck are those ones? I'm totally out of my depth.'

'Right,' he says. 'Shit! That's not great.'

'No, it is not great.'

There is a long pause, when I hear the muffled sounds of office workers in the background, and then a deep sigh from Tim.

'You'll be all right,' he's saying, with a little impatience now. 'Just learn the wine list, be super-confident and you'll be sweet. And if you fuck it up, who gives a shit? It's just Scotland.'

'Thanks,' I spit, fishing round in my handbag for another ibuprofen.

'And don't get arrested or pulled over by a cop, or do anything you need ID for,' he says, slightly less jovially. 'Maybe ask to be paid in cash? I dunno. Do people still do that?'

'Not really,' I reply.

'I gotta go. You'll be fine. Take care, baby! Bye,' he says and hangs up abruptly.

Shit! The call with Tim has definitely not helped. I try to buoy myself up. *Come on! This is fun. You're always saying you want an interesting job.*

I roll over and flick open the first of the books I brought with me: *Wine for Newbies*:

Primarily, champagne is made from Pinot Noir, Pinot Meunier and Chardonnay, though sometimes varieties like Pinot Blanc and Pinot Gris are vinified.

What the hell? I flick open my five-year-old laptop, wait the whole three minutes it takes to boot up and google '*vinified*', which, it turns out, is just a word for 'making wine'. Bloody typical of wine snobs to have a pointless special word for making wine, just to give people like me another bloody barrier to overcome. I take a breath.

Then I google 'how many different wines are there?' The answer is ten thousand grape varieties. *TEN THOUSAND.*

I check my phone, and reread the text message from Heather that came through this morning, which I've been ignoring ever since. The photo shows her hot-dog legs on a bed of crushed white linen, with an ivy-framed window overlooking a stone balcony in the distance. It looks beautiful but, for some reason, slightly lonely.

Lazy Day. How are you? How's your cousin? xxxx

I check Apple's weather app and the report says seventeen degrees and raining in London. I climb out of bed and go over to the sash window and, no surprise, it's also raining here. I heave the heavy frame up, stick my phone out of the window and photograph a nasty-looking grey cloud. Nondescript enough. I swallow yet another wave of guilt and hit Send.

British springtime in full flight. Miss you. x

Almost immediately, she replies.

So bloody hot here. Nothing to do but eat, drink and shag. x

Hearing someone you've known since you were five talk about shagging will never not be gross. I ignore it, and flick the page of my wine book over to find out how the hell champagne can be made from Pinot Noir, even though it's white and every single Pinot Noir I've ever seen is red.

I can't do this.

I glance down at my phone again. *Fuck it! I'm going to tell her.*

I pace the 2.5-metre stretch of burnt-orange carpet between my door and one of those white Ikea dressers with the little black handles that everyone has. And then Heather answers.

'Hey, Birdy! God, it's so wonderful to hear from you.'

As soon as I hear her voice, I stop pacing.

'You have no idea how much I wish you were here,' she continues. 'You'd love it. Delicious pizza, sunshine, plenty of tourists to moan about.'

'Are they all taking selfies?'

'Yes. And slow-walking.'

'Infuriating.'

We both giggle and I melt into the warmth of her laughter – like a heavy blanket, it calms me. I can't tell her. I can't tell her *yet*.

'How was it?' Heather asks.

'What?'

'Your cousin's party?'

'Oh, right. Yes. Proper good. The wine pairings were spot-on – you should really do that for a living.'

'That's funny,' she replies, without actually laughing. 'It feels a bit weird not working.'

'Things going well with Cristian?'

'Oh, yes. Yes. Absolutely.'

Three confirmations. Not good.

'I hope he's showing you a nice time.'

'Yes,' she says quickly. 'It's basically been lots of lovely little romantic dinners on the balcony. The ivy is so thick and gorgeous right now.'

'Romantic dinners are good,' I say, treading carefully.

She perks up a bit. 'Oh, you wouldn't believe. A few nights ago we actually went *out* to dinner too. A trattoria, really, but the best courgette flower I've ever eaten.'

'Courgette flower?'

'Yes, stuffed with fresh cheese and honey. Battered as light as tempura.'

'Tempura?'

'Japanese method. Oh, really, Birdy, it's never any fun sharing foodie stuff with you.'

'Sorry,' I say, knowing I'm hamming it up somewhat. The truth is I'm utterly intrigued by food, but equally intimidated by it. A childhood of *fix-it-yourself* dinners will do that to you.

There is a pause, and Heather does a strategic direction change. 'Anyway, enough about me. How are you doing? Is staying with your cousin okay? The dinner party sounded fun?'

'I wanted to ask you a question actually,' I begin, really wanting to tell her all about Russell and the hotel, and posh, drunk Bill and Anis, and fabulous Irene.

'Shoot.'

'If a person was keen to learn more about wine, but really quickly – what would you say is the best way?'

'Oooh . . . you've got the bug! Finally,' she says, sounding genuinely thrilled.

I sit down on the edge of the bed, flicking through the *Newbies* book, willing Heather to give me a straight answer. I look down at my nails, bitten to the quick, and vow to try and grow them while I'm here. That is an achievable goal. I will go back to London with lovely long nails, and ten pounds lighter from all the walking up and down the hill to the house. Even if I do lose my best friend.

'Yes, I know I didn't show a lot of interest before, but I did kind of enjoy it the other night, and I thought I might learn some more.'

'Well, you have to drink and compare is the first thing,' she says, yawning lazily.

'Drink and compare?'

'Exactly. Like, if you're having a dinner party, get all the guests to bring, say, a Riesling or a Pinot or something, and then you can all sit and compare and learn. You can get some quite good practice that way. Does that help?'

'I was thinking of a more intensive programme. Like, say, a week?' I bite my lip.

She bursts out laughing.

'Well, you know, it being alcohol, you can't get *too* intensive. You'll die. They say the best way to learn is with a glass in hand – and it really is. You could go on a vineyard tour. Or visit my favourite little wine shop in Angel, next time you're up there. They do tastings every Thursday. Or surely there's a boutique wine shop or wine club in Tooting that you can ingratiate yourself with?'

'So what you're saying, essentially, is that I can't just swot up a bit and then wing it?'

'No,' she says, sounding vaguely offended. 'Wait? What's going on?'

'Well,' I say, suddenly having a genius idea. 'Donald has extended the butcher's a bit. He's including some deli food and a bit of wine, and I'm helping.'

'That sounds a bit unhygienic. Who wants to have a drink next to some big hunks of dead pig carcass?'

'He's paring down the butchering bit,' I say quickly.

'Who's doing the food?' she asked, and I realize this idea was not as genius as I thought.

'Ah, he has a new chef,' I say dismissively.

'A chef?' she says. 'Wow, must be an impressive deli.'

'Yes, well, it's a bit of an experiment.'

'What kind of chef is he, if he does deli food?'

'Oh, he's just a chef from up north,' I say, knowing it's the best way to shut any southerner up. Suddenly I'm struck by the surreal but pleasing image of working alongside James in a little London deli.

'Well, this all sounds rather intriguing.'

'I shouldn't have mentioned the chef really. It's irrelevant.'

'Why did you mention him then?'

Heather can be infuriating – I can't hide a thing from her.

'Okay,' I say, just going with it. 'He's very tall and good-looking. And a nice person, as it turns out. And not Tim nice, but, you know, ordinary human-male nice. A nice ordinary guy.'

'Oh, I knew one day you'd find someone ordinary,' she giggled.

'I know, right?' I can't help but giggle too.

'Well, what can I do to help?' she says, swooning.

Heather gives me a few ideas about doing some tastings at home, a few blogs I can read and, while we're chatting, I do a quick Google search and learn there is a great wine outlet about thirty minutes' drive away. But none of this is going to help in the short term.

I miss her. I wish we were back in London in her flat, eating two-minute noodles and drinking a fancy bottle of something Heather had swiped from her work.

'Oh, thanks for putting in the call to the Scottish job, by the way. I never heard from them, so I guess they found a replacement.'

'Oh. Yes,' I stammer.

'Birdy, you'd tell me if you need anything? I'm worried about you.'

'Yes, I promise.'

'Okay,' she says then, her voice dropping. 'Oh, that's Cristian, I have to go.'

She hangs up and, before I have a moment to think, there's a knock on *my* door.

'Heather?'

It's Bill. I slide *Wine for Newbies* under my duvet, straighten up my pyjamas and swing the door open.

'Hi.'

'Hiya. How's the foot?'

'Um, I think it's a tiny bit better. Hard to tell, with these internal injuries.'

'I brought you the wine list, so you can have a look through. Not the most riveting read, I know.'

'I already have one, but thank you.'

'It's pretty extensive, isn't it?'

'There's a lot to familiarize myself with,' I say carefully.

'A hundred and twenty-four different wines,' he says, nodding.

'All right, buddy. No need to rub it in,' I say, rolling my eyes with a grin.

But then I pause for thought. *A hundred and twenty-four.* Sure, it's a lot more than the old list, and feels daunting as hell. But a hundred and twenty-four isn't that many, really. It's considerably less than ten thousand. I wonder if I *can* learn the wine list and be done with it? *Just learn the wine list.* That's what Tim said. Surely if I learn what the wine is supposed to taste like, and add a little of my own lingo to the equation, I can do a pretty good job with the rest?

'See you for dinner service in a bit?' I say brightly. 'I might be a bit wobbly on the foot, of course.'

'Great. They're doing a new dish for tonight, a rip-off of the miso-salmon dish at The Pig & Whisky, which you'll need to pair.'

'What? I thought it was just the lamb and wild garlic?' My heart starts up again.

'Russell wants it included. Said the menu needed something with a bigger profit margin.'

'Oh.'

'Why don't you get up, head to the kitchen and sit with James and Anis while they test it. You could do a couple of on-the-spot tastings.'

'Wine-tastings?' I say, feeling bile rising in my throat.

'Yes, kill two birds,' he says, nodding at the wine list, and then at the bottle of whisky next to me. 'Hair of the dog?'

'Christ, this place is fucking relentless,' I say under my breath. 'Give me fifteen, Bill. Can you drive us up?'

11.

With my headache thankfully subsiding, I quickly pull myself off my bed. I put some pressure on the ankle and it's okay. I'm annoyed that I slept; annoyed that I missed a good three hours when I could have been working on the wine list. But perhaps there's a shortcut for this bloody new salmon dish.

I pull out my phone and quickly google The Pig & Whisky, and when I'm directed to somewhere in America, I swear very loudly, then add 'Scotland' to the search. And there it is. The Pig & Whisky menu and, by some stroke of divine intervention, a wine recommendation underneath the salmon dish:

> Complement this rich plate with the 2016 Gewürztraminer, the brighter but still gutsy Grüner Veltliner, or even the Lot 94 Pinot Noir — slightly chilled, of course!

'Fucking Bingo!' I shout, before throwing on my work clothes and half-fake limping my way to meet Bill by the golf cart.

I take a seat on a bar stool, groggy, mildly injured and smelling no doubt of whisky. But, despite everything, I'm fascinated by what's going on in the kitchen.

James is standing there, sleeves rolled up, his apron covered in a mix of green, red and brown smears, and his hair pushed back in a headband like David Beckham circa 2003. I realize that whenever he's around people he's a little shy, but whenever he's around food, that disappears entirely. He's focused and passionate, and it's sexy to watch.

He explains that he's preparing two differently cooked versions of the salmon dish to decide between. As Bill said, it's almost exactly the same as the dish on the Three Pigs website, and neither Anis nor James is happy about it. I caught them complaining about it when I hobbled in earlier: 'I mean of course we can do it. There's a version in every restaurant on the west coast,' James was saying.

'He's obviously been to The Pig & Whisky again,' Anis had moaned. 'He's obsessed. Wasabi and pea purée, pickled sea lettuce. Why doesn't he just re-create the menu *exactly*.'

'I sense some dissatisfaction here,' I'd joked.

James looked a bit embarrassed at being caught having a moan. 'It's just that we have the chance to be really original here, and it's a bit depressing to be copying the same dishes over and over.'

But he seems to have put that aside now, and is focusing on the different cooking methods to try to add a fresh spin to the dish.

'One is done in the water bath, and the other is pan-fried to medium rare,' he says. 'How do you like yours?'

'Fishcake?' I say.

And he laughs – finally! – as he expertly seasons the orange flesh, flips it and then rubs oil into the skin and sprinkles it with sea salt. Then he fries it; sizzling and spitting, it hits the fierce heat of the pan. After a couple of moments he slides it onto a small tray and slips it into the oven.

As he does this, I pull out my phone and remind myself of the recommended wines from the Three Pigs website. The only problem, I realize too late, is that I cannot pronounce them. *Gewürztraminer. Grüner Veltliner.* Shit!

'Have you decided on the wines?' James asks, as if sensing my panic, nodding to the open wine list on my lap.

'I think so. Can you grab us a glass of these two?' I ask Roxy as casually as possible, slipping my phone under my thigh and pointing to both names. 'Oh, and the bottles, please, so I can see the labels.'

'Ooh, I love the Gewürztraminer,' she says, before heading down to the cellar.

I'll never be able to say that word.

'Now to make the miso caramel glaze,' James is saying.

'It might be unoriginal, but it sounds delicious,' I remark, picking up a nearby plastic bottle with a green oil inside it, tipping a drop out onto my finger and popping it onto my tongue. Peppery, garlicky oil fills my mouth. 'Mmm. What's that?'

'Some of this morning's wild garlic,' says Anis, who arrives from out the back with a fillet of cooked salmon in a plastic bag. I presume this is the one that has been in the water bath. 'We normally use the extra to make an oil for the partridge, but Russell says no one eats partridge any more.'

She shrugs and hands James her salmon bag, which he swiftly slices open and slides onto a plate. He then takes the other fillet from the oven and slides that onto a plate, so the two sit side-by-side. The pan-fried one looks far more appetizing than the one cooked in the water bath, which seems a bit slimy.

'Now, we bring the mirin, miso and sugar to a boil,' says James, using what looks like a plastic spatula from my granny's kitchen (she had eleven). 'Then we stir until all of the sugar is dissolved.'

His stirring is frenzied, and he suddenly pulls the pan off the heat, slides it along the stainless-steel counter and plunges it into a bowl of ice.

'Plate up, Anis,' he commands in a voice that makes me sit up a little straighter. She adds some of the green purée to both dishes, and then some straggly-looking greens that must be the so-called sea let-tuce. James puts a pastry brush into the caramel sauce and brushes the top of the salmon, waits a moment and then brushes again.

Roxy returns with two glasses quarter-filled with white wine and two bottles in her hand. For a moment I panic, as I'm not sure which wine goes with which bottle, but she lines them up on the counter next to the salmon, so it's clear.

James is first to drive a fork into the pan-fried and roasted salmon and shovel a bit into his mouth. Anis follows, and I grab the third fork and do the same.

'You try too,' I say to Roxy, who beams with delight and grabs a fourth fork out of the jar on the countertop.

'Mmm . . .' James says, closing his eyes. He looks so sexy as he does so, I honestly have to cross my legs.

It flakes obligingly into perfect fork-sized bites with a crunchy, almost fried edge underneath the sweet, salty glaze. We all try the second salmon from the water bath, and it seems firmer, but almost falls apart in my mouth. The pickled sea lettuce is sour and crunchy, and I marvel at the contrast. Good God, it's divine.

'Tell us about the wine, Heather,' says James as he picks up the glass in front of the Gewürztraminer and takes a small sip, swirling it round in his mouth like a professional, but, importantly, not so much that he looks like a dick.

I follow his lead, taking a sip too. *Think, Birdy.* 'Um, well, we need something cool and crisp, but with enough guts to stand up to the salmon. I think both do that?'

It's a dangerously close mash-up of what was on The Pig & Whisky website, but no one even bats an eyelid.

'I like this one,' Anis says, spitting her mouthful into the sink.

'What do you think, Roxy?' I ask.

'I'd go with the Gewürztraminer actually,' she says shyly, as she swallows her mouthful, and I nod approvingly. Really, all this bloody spitting is gross. 'The sweetness really balances out the miso glaze,' she says, and I want to give her a secret high-five.

'Pan-fried or the boil-in-a-bag one?' I ask James, as if it will in any way at all affect my decision.

'Has to be the sous-vide,' Anis says.

'The what?' Roxy is as confused as I am.

'The water bath,' Anis says, 'the proper term is sous-vide.'

'Yeah, we should probably go with that; it will cut down prep time, and we're already pan-frying the cutlets.'

'Agreed,' replies Anis.

'Right, well, let's match with this one,' I say, pointing to the Gewürztraminer, because I'm still too nervous to attempt to say it out loud. 'Nice one, Roxy.'

I'm about to lower myself down from the stool when Russell arrives. He's wearing a khaki linen suit with a navy tie, and is reading something off his phone as he marches towards James. I watch as James's easiness instantly disappears, his shoulders stiffen and his face darkens.

'Is this it?' Russell asks the room, and Anis nods, sliding both plates of salmon in front of him.

He picks one up and sniffs it, hesitant, like a mum might sniff a nappy to check for a poo, and then, with his fingers, shoves a chunk into his mouth. He moves the flesh around in it, a bit like he's searching for bones, and then spits it into the sink.

'No,' he says.

'We all agree,' says James cautiously. 'We went for the other.'

'This one?' He points to the other plate, and we all take a collective deep breath as Russell does his disgusting tasting-thing again.

'Less salt,' he says, 'otherwise it's passable. And the wine?'

'We went with the German. Always best with Japanese.' I hope the over-confidence hides the fact that I'm a sommelier who can't pronounce wine names.

It works. He smiles at me and nods, before turning to James. 'Where is the lamb? I saw a photo on Instagram that looked . . . rustic.'

He says 'rustic' in the same way someone might say 'revolting'.

'Yes, Chef,' says James, and he hurries off to get it.

Now Russell turns to me.

'Your leg is okay? I hear you were hurt in the woods?'

'Yes, Chef,' I say, wondering if sommeliers are supposed to call him that.

'And Bill tells me you are familiarizing yourself with the wine list?'

'Yes, Chef,' I reply.

'Good. Then we need to discuss the Wine Society concept,' he says, smoothing his hair back.

'Perhaps James and I can discuss it once I'm up and, er, running?' I say, touching my foot to remind him that he needs to go easy on me because I'm injured.

'Well, you need to let the Society know your idea in the next week or two. They have to do their marketing materials.'

'Okay, I'll get on it.'

'Are you going to Skye in the morning?' Russell asks James as he arrives back with arms full of plastic containers.

'Wednesday,' James replies.

'Then maybe you can take Heather with you and discuss.'

'Okay,' James nods, and he drops his head. Does he look annoyed or shy?

86

'Anis, you can work on the venison this week. Try some different wood in the smoker this time,' Russell orders.

Anis lifts her chin a little, and although she's incredibly straight-faced, I can tell she's thrilled, by the twitch in her eyebrow.

'Yes, Chef,' she says with a sombreness that makes me laugh. I turn it into another *ouch!* and grab at my ankle again. Russell frowns at me, and I realize I'd better recover from my non-injury quickly.

'Well. That will do then, I suppose,' he says.

'Yes, Chef,' I say.

Irene is next to burst through the doors. She starts clapping her hands, and I half-expect a light to spring on. 'Heather, Roxy, we need you front of house now, please. Are you walking?' She looks at me.

'More or less,' I say meekly. She looks thrilled.

'Good. Roxy! Come, come.'

'James, we need to discuss orders, in the bar now,' Russell commands.

'The lamb,' James says, holding his hands up, 'you wanted to see it?'

'Bar. Now,' Russell repeats like a drill sergeant.

What an arsehole. As I lower myself down, I shoot James a smile of solidarity. He's clearly brilliant at his job – why is Russell such a knob to him?

In the dining area I edge over to stand by Roxy. I notice the apples of her cheeks have a slight dusty-rose shimmer to them. I remind myself to at least put some concealer on tomorrow.

'Can you help me out a bit tonight?' I say quietly. 'I don't want to worry Irene or Russell, but my foot hurts quite a bit, and it would be great if I could lean on you,' I say. 'Not literally. Well, maybe a bit literally.'

'Of course you can,' she replies. 'You know, the last sommelier we had was so rude to me. And he wasn't even a proper sommelier, like you. He was a waiter, but because he was French and knew a bit about wine, he got your job. I'm so glad you're here and you're a girl.'

'A girl,' I repeat, laughing.

'Yeah, it's inspiring. I want to be a sommelier so badly. Like ever since it was legal for me to drink – like three years or something – I've been hassling my parents to send me on a course. They're so expensive, though.'

'Yeah, they are. Do you get paid enough to save something?'

'Just about,' she says, nodding. 'And Irene has promised that she will help fund me, if we get through the summer. I'd love to learn from you. Just say the word.'

12.

It has not gone well.

It all started with those four Canadian men who were here on a college-reunion fishing trip and should have been drinking massive pints of ale, not sipping on vintage wine.

'Hi and welcome. Can I offer you the wine list?' I'd started confidently.

'We'll take your finest champagne,' said the roundest, glancing around at his table of friends, grinning.

'Are you sure about that? This place is really expensive,' I'd blurted out.

'Yes, mam,' he replied.

Feeling uneasy, I made a beeline for Bill.

'They want the *finest* champagne, and they don't want to see the menu.'

He smiled. 'Well, that makes your job easy.'

I nodded, flicking open the wine list. Dom Ruinart Blanc de Blancs 2004 seemed like it might be the finest – very old and £360 a bottle. I tried not to vomit.

Bill handed me the bottle and a white napkin, and Roxy followed me with a tray of crystal champagne flutes.

'Gentlemen,' I said, presenting the bottle label theatrically, as champagne glasses were placed, and everyone watched on in giddy anticipation. *I can do this.*

But the cork was stiff. *Really* stiff. I squeezed. I tried with both thumbs. I twisted it. I covered it in the napkin and pulled. It wouldn't budge.

'The one time you don't want something stiff between your legs,' I muttered to myself, as I stuck the bottle between my thighs and pulled again. It was ungraceful, but I was desperate.

'Do you want a hand?'

The round Canadian was being kind really, but I would not be defeated. I pulled the bottle out from between my legs, lifted it to my face to inspect the cork up close. It had moved a millimetre. And then, with an almighty boom, it flew out and hit me at almost point-blank range.

'Yes, she was hit by a cork,' Bill is explaining now, as I press a cold flannel to my eye. The dining room is empty, and Bill, Irene and I are sitting at the bar discussing what happened. A 'debrief' Irene had called it.

'She's a good shot, if nothing else,' Bill is saying.

'It was stuck far more than normal.'

'But you didn't point it at your face?' Irene says. 'Not really?'

Her voice trails off and she looks across at me, her face contorted with a mixture of concern and confusion. Concern, I think, that a human being in real life – and not in a black-and-white slapstick film – had pointed a bottle of champagne at her face while trying to loosen an extremely stubborn cork. And confusion as to how a world-class sommelier had made such a schoolboy error.

'You could have lost an eye, dear,' she says, 'but what was the issue with the McCluskys? He seemed very upset indeed.'

'Well,' Bill glances across at me, 'I think we should speak in private.'

'It's okay, I'll go,' I say, pushing back my stool. 'I'm really sorry again, Irene.'

'It's fine,' says Irene quickly. 'It's really fine. Please go and rest. I think perhaps we expected too much too quickly. It's the pressure of the relaunch and whatnot.'

'Yes, and she's had a lot of pressure since the moment her taxi pulled up – what, only three days ago,' Bill agrees.

'Sorry, Irene. I'm tired. The travel, and the new role, and a new wine list. I am feeling really like I need a moment to get my head around everything.'

Irene frowns a little more, but then her face softens. 'Of course. You get yourself to bed and rest. You have two days off now. And we're renovating the dining room, so everything will calm down for a couple of weeks and you'll have plenty of time to catch up.'

I smile meekly and nod, feeling the sting of tears beginning to form as I hobble out of the restaurant and into the staffroom.

Everyone else has gone home. I inspect my face in the staff bathroom and press on the small red bump above my right eye, which has started to retract. I'm pulling on what looks like an abandoned jacket from the coat rack and preparing to limp down to the cottage, when I hear Irene and Bill's raised voices coming from the bar.

I creep near the door and move my ear towards the gap.

'With the other table she just didn't do the tasting part,' Bill is saying.

'But it's Mark McClusky, Bill. He's friends with the MacDonalds. I'm mortified. I should have been here. Thank God Russell wasn't.'

'Look, in reality, all she forgot to do was to offer the taste.'

'It was a vintage claret, Bill!'

I feel the heat rising up my neck. It was a stupid, stupid mistake. I may not know the wine list, or anything about wines, but I know enough to know that I'm supposed to offer a taste to the person who orders it.

'I know, but we did a lot *by the glass* tonight . . .'

'She's a sommelier! Opening a *vintage* claret! You know what Mark is like. He's an absolute stickler for the old ways – he doesn't like what we've been trialling with the menu at all. He'll never be back. I'll lose this place, Bill.'

'It won't come to that! It was just one mistake.'

'It's been three in as many days, Bill.'

'Tonight was definitely off,' Bill is saying now, 'but she needs to . . .'

'Maggie said she suggested a two-hundred-pound bottle of Malbec to her earlier, and then suggested the house red, and finally plonked it down on the table without pouring a single glass. Really basic stuff, Bill.'

I froze. It was true. I had done that, but *Maggie*, the lovely lady from Stornoway, hadn't been annoyed. We even had a laugh about it.

'And overall she lacks confidence, Bill. Not only in the way she carries herself, but when she's on the floor. She's a totally different person from the one I met at the Wine Awards. She was so confident. I mean, I suppose she was quite tipsy. Did you really check her out thoroughly?'

'You saw her CV too, Irene,' Bill says, and there is a slightly dark edge to his voice. I recognize it. Blame-sharing.

'But in the Skype interview?'

'She was lovely, smart. I mean, she was perfect. Let's give her a few days, okay?'

Wait. Skype interview? Heather never mentioned an interview.

'I am under a great deal of pressure from all this, Bill. The renovations have ballooned in cost. Russell is great for the bottom line, but come on, Bill – he never speaks to our regulars. He's disengaged.'

'Russell is great,' Bill says.

'I know. I know,' Irene replies. 'But I'm feeling more than a little railroaded here. This isn't the Loch Dorn I know. New chefs, new sommeliers, new ruddy paint. And the regulars say nice things, but . . . You know, it's not them, is it? And James feels extremely downtrodden.'

'You love him,' Bill says more gently. 'But you know, deep down, he wasn't ready to do this.'

'Perhaps,' Irene replies.

Then there is a long silence and I realize the only sound I can hear is my heart thumping in my chest. I am glad I'm not the only problem, but I realize I am perilously close to disaster here. Could I get fired? What would that mean for Heather?

'I've pulled the press release,' Irene says, 'until she settles in.'

Press release. Jesus, there was going to be a *press release about Heather*?

'It's just teething problems,' says Bill, as I hear the clink of a glass. I imagine him pouring her a *wee dram* to calm her nerves.

'Three complaints in three days,' says Irene again. 'And she's not been properly tested. Imagine if we had a full restaurant?'

'That would be nice,' Bill says, and then I hear Irene let out a small laugh. 'Here's the facts,' Bill starts firmly. 'She's a long way from home. She's taken a tumble this morning and was obviously very tired and shaky during her first handful of services. Her CV is robust. James likes her a lot . . .'

James likes her a lot. A little thrill interrupts the horror, for a blessed moment.

'I hope I don't have to worry about James too,' Irene says. 'I couldn't bear to see him hurt again.'

'Don't stress. You leave Heather with me. I'll get her up to speed,' Bill says.

'Are you sure you can?'

'Irene, I vetted her. She's brilliant. I called all three of her references and they were absolutely glowing.'

'And I absolutely loved her, when I met her. There is no denying her charm. We just need to see her experience,' Irene agrees, her voice sounding softer.

'She'll be fine. She's got a couple of weeks of reduced service while we all get ready for the relaunch. And she's got two days off now, to regroup – hopefully to catch her breath and catch up. Let's get through the two weeks and then discuss? Deal?'

I hear the scrape of a stool on the floor, and I quickly slide back from the door and slip out into the courtyard. It's 12.03 a.m. and it's cold.

As I walk back to the cottage, I wonder about the Skype interview with Heather. Did they have one? They couldn't have, or Bill would have known straight away. In fact didn't he already comment that I didn't look like my cat picture?

I am too tired to make sense of it.

Besides, there is one thought that is so invasive, I keep returning to rest on it. James likes me. *A lot.*

I push open the door of my bedroom and see my suitcase, still unpacked, in the corner. The bottle of whisky is gone – I presume Bill has taken it back. I sit on the edge of the bed and can feel the stinging that has threatened for the last hour to burst into fully formed tears, which now begin to roll down my cheeks. I pick up my phone and scroll through the contacts list to find Heather – but then remember, for what feels like the millionth time, that I can't call her. I think about messaging Tim, but he doesn't really do *comforting*. Besides, our last chat made me realize this is no longer Project Birdy and Tim. He likes the egging-me-on bit of the misadventure, but now that I'm actually here doing it, he's lost interest.

Gasping through my tears as snot drips out of my nose, I look back across to my suitcase and imagine chucking everything in, maxing out my credit card to get back to London. Maybe I could call my cousin again? He might take me in? But this option leaves Heather open to a damaged reputation. I still haven't thought of an excuse that will save it. And now poor Bill and Irene are relying on me. Christ, this really *is* the worst thing I've ever done.

I pick up the wine list again and remind myself of my plan. *Learn the list. One hundred and twenty-four wines,* I scoff. As if they even sell that many.

Could I really learn a hundred and twenty-four wines? If not to taste, but enough about them to fake it? I managed the Periodic Table at high school; even if I had no idea what to do with beryllium or boron, I did know they were numbers four and five on the Table. I have a good memory, although I've never been dedicated enough to anything to put it to use.

Can I climb this mountain? I flick through page after page of what might as well be Chinese. Or at least French. A lot of it actually *is* French.

It's a mountain with only one hundred and twenty-four steps, I think as I turn to page one: champagne. While my laptop boots up, I sneak to the bathroom to wash my face and brush my teeth, happily noting that the mark from the cork is receding.

You can fucking do this, Birdy.

I jump on my bed with renewed vigour, open Google and type in the very first entry I find under 'champagne': *2010 Louis Roederer Brut, Reims.*

Smells of citrus, flowers, light minerals and white pulp fruits. And tastes of bread. Juicy, balanced, elegant, with a minty topnote.

Tastes of bread. Wankers!

I read the descriptor on the hotel wine list. *Bright and balanced; 20 per cent oaked, perfect with fish.* And next to it I add the notes: citrus, flowers, white fruit, juicy with a minty topnote.

Then I close my eyes and practise repeating it back. It takes about fifteen minutes and I've got it committed to memory.

Forty-eight hours until I'm back on the floor for reduced service. Including sleep and breaks, that's probably about twenty hours of hard study time. I do the maths: one or two wines an hour is reasonable, if I include distraction time and sleep and revisions. So I could be about one-third of the way through the list by the time I have to go back on the floor.

I can do this.

For Heather. For Irene. And for Bill and James, and everyone who is counting on me. I can do this.

One down, a hundred and twenty-three to go.

13.

My plan has given me a huge boost. That night I spent one hour and thirty-four straight minutes revising champagne and crémant (which is basically champagne made outside the region of Champagne) and then I curled up into bed and fell asleep. Properly asleep.

And for the last two days I have left my bedroom only to pick up food from the kitchen and use the bathroom. I have politely declined all invitations to go hiking, to get a to-die-for cream bun at a croft up the way, to go for a lobster lunch and even to go clubbing in Inverness with Roxy.

And I am starting to make some headway. I've made it through the French champagnes and the Italian sparkling wines, and am currently working my way through the confusing 'white Burgundies'. I'm at number forty-two.

I'm so dedicated, in fact, that this morning I woke at 6.15 a.m. and studied until James knocked on my door at 7.02 a.m. for our trip to Skye.

Leaving the estate has allowed me to exhale for the first time since I arrived. My wine-cramming stress has been replaced with a fleeting feeling of freedom as the car rolls alongside the water towards the Skye bridge.

We're in a big SUV, and I find that all I can do is stare out the window, stunned by the beauty of this place. At first it's all empty, green rolling hills and another loch. This one wider and longer than Loch Dorn. Then we get to the coast and head south. The road runs alongside it, and even at this speed I can see the tide lapping lazily at the tangle of fishing nets, boulders and seaweed by the water's edge. Across the ocean, green hills roll out of the dark-blue water in a spray of birch trees.

'What happened to your eye?' James breaks the peaceful silence.

'Champagne cork.'

'Oh, that actually *did* happen?'

'Yes.'

James had been in the kitchen when the incident occurred, but of course it wouldn't take long for rumours to start flying. It makes me feel grim to know that James's good opinion of me could be lost.

But then I catch him suppressing a giggle and, after a moment, I join in.

'Shame the sun isn't out for you,' he says, nodding towards the window, but I don't care – I am in love with this wild beauty, its greys and navies and muted greens. He is wrapped up in his waxed coat and a tartan scarf, and we're driving with the windows down, which, while cold, is exactly how I like it. I've borrowed an old coat from the hallway hook and stuffed my hair into a beanie, so it's not in my face.

I can feel the cold air slapping at me when I lean a little towards the window.

'I can put the heater on,' he says for the second time.

'I like it. The Scoootish air,' I say, attempting an accent, which comes out rather well.

'Are you from Finland?'

'Fuck off,' I say, laughing, and he shrugs and smiles at the road ahead.

James doesn't ask me questions, and it's nice. I don't think Irene has aired her concerns to him, at least not yet, and I'm glad.

I have finally accepted that I definitely have a crush on him. I don't *think* he has a girlfriend, as he hasn't mentioned anyone, but despite what Irene says, I'm definitely getting the friend-vibe from him. That's fine, though, I tell myself. Years of crushing on guys who don't like me back have taught me how to do that, without giving too much away. Or daring to hope.

Everyone says that Scotland is wild and rugged, but there is something about this Scottish west coast that feels extraordinary.

'It's beautiful.'

'You ever seen Eilean Donan?'

'Who?'

'It's a fantastic castle. A short detour. I'll show you.'

'Do we have time?' I say, looking down at my phone and noticing a message from Tim that wasn't there when we left an hour ago.

Hungover AF. Have you been arrested yet? Give me a call.

'Sure, it's only eight minutes,' he says. 'We can do a quick drive by.'

He spins the car round and we take a road inland as the landscape flattens and the west coast is behind us, and we travel down a two-lane road with small cottages dotted along the road, and every hundred metres or so a sign, like *MacKenzie's B&B* or *Three Seas Inn*.

'There's a croft coming up.'

'A what?'

'It's like a rental farm, I suppose. A smallholding for tenants to produce food. There!' he says, pointing to a small white stone cottage with a fenced-off garden. I am intrigued and wish we had time to stop, but we're nearing a bridge and a new stretch of water.

'Loch Long, Duich and Alsch. The meeting of the three seas,' he says as if he's reading my mind. 'And there ahead – see it, at the foot of the hill?'

'I see it,' I shout, and a stone castle with a beautiful arched bridge perched on the tiniest of islands comes clearly into view. 'Like something out of *Game of Thrones*.'

'I really must watch it,' he says as he pulls over to the side of the road for a closer look. 'When you work in hospo, sometimes it feels like you miss out on every cultural reference. Every summer, when the new staff arrive, is a reminder that I need to get out more.' He laughs and turns the car off, and we sit for a moment.

'Do I have time to go across?' I say.

'Next time,' he replies, glancing down at the dashboard to check the clock himself. 'We'd better get going or I'll be late for my first meeting.'

'So is Portree like the capital of Skye?'

'I guess you could call it that.' He laughs again. 'I go at the beginning of the season a few times,' he says, starting the car and doing a U-turn, and we're heading back towards the Skye bridge again. 'Although normally the company isn't . . .'

'As English?' I interrupt.

'As fun,' he says as he glances across at me. *Fun. Definitely friend-zone.*

I don't know what to say, so I say nothing. Even if I am in the friend-zone, who cares? It's just nice to spend time with a good, thoughtful, kind human man.

We park behind a nondescript building, and when I get out of the car it's like I've been slapped in the face by fish and fabulously expensive sea salt. I take a deep inhale and imagine what it must be like to smell this each day.

'Every day it smells different. Depends on the tide, the weather, what the oceans are doing, the wind,' says James.

'It's certainly pungent today,' I say. 'Gets right up the nose.'

We wander up the main drag – Quay Street – a glorious little strip of brightly painted terraced shops and restaurants overlooking the harbour, all named no-nonsense things like The Pier Hotel, The Pink Guest House, and Portree Fish and Chips. Dad had a fish-and-chip shop for most of my childhood, and a visceral memory of vinegar and fast-food fat and suntan lotion hits me.

The seagulls circle overhead, and a couple of dozen boats bob about in the harbour, but otherwise there is little action here this morning. I peer right into the fish-and-chip shop and think it's weird that I already feel more at home here than on Plymouth harbour, where Heather and I used to spend our time as kids. Me stealing Cokes from the fridge, and Heather half-heartedly chastising me for stealing, while we drank them on the edge of the pier.

But, like Plymouth, the sea air gets through your clothes and onto your skin, and within ten minutes I'm shivering.

James leans against the metal railing of the boat ramp, seemingly unaffected by the wind, and stares out towards one blue boat, piled high with bundles of nets, that's tracking its way through the moorings towards us. He's got that relaxed, carefree way about him that he had when we went foraging, and I can't stop looking at him. He has the beginnings of lines around his eyes where he smiles; and his dark hair, a little long, licks the edge of his ear in a way that is just begging to be brushed with gentle fingers.

I join him and we stand in silence for a moment. I look down at the water slowly reaching up to caress the stone edges of the ramp.

Then I look across at him and he's looking at me, but looks away when I catch him. Then there is a moment of silence that I compulsively need to fill.

'So, we're here to meet suppliers?' I ask.

'Yes. Here's one coming,' James says, nodding out into the port.

'Oh, right. He's literally coming right now on that very boat.' *Good work, Birdy.*

'Yep. That's Benji.'

As the boat nudges the edge of the port wall, a thin, wiry man with a high forehead leaps from it onto the ramp. He has a full, non-ironic bushy beard and, when he smiles to greet us, two of those little crest-shaped eyes, which sparkle and shine with all the kindness in the world. 'James, how's tricks, fella?'

He's English.

'Good, Benji. Good. This is Heather, our new wine lady.'

'Ahh, Heather, a good Scottish gal, eh? Hope you know your whiskies as well as your wines.'

'Better,' I reply – for once, truthfully – smiling as though it's a joke. 'Though I'm afraid I'm not Scottish.'

'Benji supplies our scallops. He's got a fully sustainable farm on the west coast – diver—'

'Diver-harvested,' Benji interrupts proudly. 'So they won't shrink up in the pan like a cock on a cold day.'

'Well, no one wants one of those in their mouth,' I say, and then immediately worry that I've misjudged the scene, but thankfully Benji belly-laughs, and James covers his face with his hands and shakes his head, laughing, so I'm pretty sure it's okay.

'Bet you're a handful,' Benji says, casting a quick glance at James.

'They're the best scallops in the west,' says James, as he pulls a rolled-up ledger book out of his back pocket.

'How does delivery work, then?'

'I'll let you take this one, mate,' Benji says, as he checks over whatever it is James has scribbled in his book.

'So the scallops are delivered fresh to the hotel from the morning pick, but I come across and meet Benji, Cal and Grant at the produce store, Kenny for sustainable fish . . .' James looks to the sky, 'Ella for flowers, Dennis and Denise for mussels, as often as I can. Weekly, at first. Then not as much, later in the season. Basically, I see all the local suppliers.'

'He's keeping an eye on us,' Benji cackled again.

James looks a little embarrassed and raises his hand in protest. 'No, no. That's not it. It's more to get an idea of where you're at, what's good; for the producers, it's anything new they've noticed, anything that might affect the next season.'

'A new bloody micro-herb or fancy seaweed sprinkle for that poncy fucking chef of yours,' Benji says, shaking his head as he rolls out the ledger. 'James just wants a hut on the west coast, but he can't tear himself away from the sniff of a Michelin star – or your mother – can you, mate?'

'That's not true,' James says, turning to me quickly.

'Bloody is,' Benji replies, handing a roll of paper to James as he turns to leave, tapping me on the shoulder and shaking his head at James. 'Lovely to meet you, Heather. Always nice to meet the new ladies of Loch Dorn.' And he's off, jumping over the railing and onto his boat, starting up the motor as we head back down Quay Street.

'I've known Benji for twenty years,' James begins, by way of explanation. 'Since I was, like, eleven.'

'Is it true? Do you want to leave?'

'Leave? No, not really. Maybe.' James shrugs as if it's nothing. 'All chefs dream of their own place. You want a coffee?'

'Oh my God, please.'

We push open the door to the little café and it makes a satisfying *Tring!* as it hits the bell. Inside, various booths and tables are filled with a surprising smattering of locals and tourists enjoying their fry-ups. James waves to a man in waders and a purple fleece; he's maybe mid-forties, with ginger curls and tight, lined skin. We navigate between the tightly packed tables to join him in the far booth, and a few minutes later he and James are discussing supply times, fishing quotas and the quality of line-caught sea bass over a pot of tea and my milky latte. I am struggling to keep up, but equally fascinated by the ins and outs of restaurant supply and the search for the perfect hake. The trick is, like all fish, the timing, apparently – but more so for hake, as it becomes soft and cottonwool-like, the longer it's out of the sea.

'It's not going to work, Fraser,' says James, 'looking at the time-lines, on any day but Wednesday.'

'Aye. Wednesday it is,' says Fraser, pouring himself another tea. 'How are ye taking to the west coast then, pet?'

'I'm liking it,' I reply, realizing that, for today at least, it's the truth.

Half an hour later we make our way out of the café and back onto the street, to find that the sun has pierced the clouds, and for the first time in a week I can feel it on my skin. I immediately slip off my coat and turn my face skywards.

'Sun,' I say. 'My dear old friend, how I've missed thee.'

'You've just had a bad first impression. You wait,' James says. 'Summer might only be three months long, but it's a stunning three months.'

'Three months,' I say, laughing. 'I couldn't live somewhere this cold.'

I didn't mean that. I said it because that's what people say. The truth is, I don't mind the cold. I was made for it really. I hate being too hot, and suntan on my pale skin is only patchy red blobs. Once I went to Madrid in high summer with Heather and spent three days in my room, with the blinds shut, binge-watching *Crazy Ex-Girlfriend*, venturing out only for breakfasts and sundowns. We never went on holiday together again after that.

'You get used to it,' James says, sounding a trifle hurt.

'People say you can get used to anything.' It tumbles out of my mouth. He doesn't reply and, in the absence of noise, I add, 'Do we see anyone else?'

'No, that's it, just those two this morning. Anyway, we need to get back for lunch service.'

His voice is a bit clipped, and I feel bad. I want to tell him I love the sun on my face when the air is cool, and I love Skye and the port, and the little castle with the arched bridge, but I'm not sure I can say it now and sound authentic.

'Okay,' I say and follow his lead back to the car.

I look back over my shoulder at Portree's colourful little port and take a deep inhale of that salty, fishy air. Then I stop, pull my phone out and take a couple of quick snaps of the harbour on the way out. It's a shame I can't put them on Instagram, but I'll have them as a memento, at any rate. I rush to catch up with James, who is already at the car.

'Sorry, just taking some snaps,' I say, laying my coat in the back.

'Can't be that bad then,' he says, looking right at me as if he's won an argument.

Then he does that thing: the searching of my eyes. I don't answer – I can't find any words – but I smile, then look at the ground.

After a moment he slams the boot shut and wanders round to the driver's side and we both get in and, almost in unison, buckle our belts.

On the drive back there is a strange tension in the car. It's the same tension as the first night, or is it? I can't be sure it's not all in my head. Does tension need two people to create it? Or is it something that can be categorically created in one's own head?

James leans forward to turn the car stereo on as we drive over the Skye bridge and head back on the main road towards the estate.

I don't want to talk about the restaurant, because as soon as we talk about it I have to be Heather again, but I remember we're supposed to discuss the Wine Society evening.

'The Wine Society,' I say quickly.

'Oh shit, yeah,' he replies. 'We're supposed to be thinking of a theme.'

'What about all-British wines?' I say, remembering the Wine Awards. It's literally the only thing I know about British wines: that there are awards and they're a bit of a *thing* now.

'British wines?'

'Yes, they're a thing now.'

'I know, I know,' he says, glancing quickly across at me, I think to confirm I'm actually being serious. 'Well, the menu would certainly be a doddle.'

'I know, I'm putting all the pressure on myself here. But it's a *great* idea, isn't it?' I say, thinking of what Irene stated about me lacking confidence. 'We could do a kind of street-party theme, you know?

Some cute bunting in the bar area. Gourmet-like sausage rolls, or whatever. Fancy-pants trifle for dessert?'

James laughs and I cringe. I've said something daft, but I'm not sure what.

'What?'

'It needs to be sophisticated,' he says slowly. 'But it could be fun, trying to do that. Make a street-party Michelin star-worthy. I mean, mostly we do like a Cabernet night or wines of the Wachau, or something like that,' he continues. 'But this idea is playful. Be fun to cater for, that's for sure.'

'You like the idea?'

'I think it's interesting.'

'What's the "but"?'

'It's Russell. He'll need to buy into it, and he definitely has his own ideas. About everything.'

'Leave Russell to me,' I say confidently. 'If you think it could work?'

'I think it could work. I think it's cool. It's very *you*,' he says.

'Me?' I am fishing. What does he think *me* is? I always like to know how other people see me, since I find it so hard to see myself.

'Well . . . unexpected,' he continues, and we drive in silence for a little longer as I bask in the pleasure of a compliment of sorts.

'I loved Skye,' I say.

'You did?' he replies, changing gears as we come out of a tight corner a little fast and he veers slightly out of the lane. I grab the hand-rest and try to conceal my fear by looking out of the window, but the car immediately slows.

'I did,' I say, breathing out.

'Perfect,' he says, and I sneak a look at his face and, even though we're on another bend, he steals a quick look at me before turning back to the road.

Then he looks again, and I'm totally blushing.

And just as I think he's nearly perfect, Phil Collins comes on the radio, and James turns it up. Though perhaps I can forgive him for that.

It's not quite midday when we turn down the windy little forest road towards the estate, but I don't want the drive to end. Silence is usually an uncomfortable place for me. I have this fear, if no one is speaking. This nervous apprehension that it's because something is coming. It's because they're thinking about something they don't want to talk about. And although I recognize this is entirely self-centred, I can't help but worry they're thinking about me. That's how it was, growing up; my mum was the master of ominous silence.

I knew it was a way to keep people out. Keep *me* out. Stop me from asking questions like 'Where has the television gone?' or 'Why is there a hole in the front fence?' The silence kept me away from the kitchen, where she pottered, clearing away evidence, hiding the truth.

'The silence is easier than explaining something bad happened, I guess,' twelve-year-old Heather had whispered to me, as we headed out for one of our curfew-free Saturdays, pockets stuffed with extra pocket money. Money that came in huge windfalls when Dad was particularly bad, or none at all when he was better. I called it my 'fuck-off allowance'.

But this — as we drive and I stare out at the rolling hills on one side, and the dark water on the other — this is a very different kind of silence.

14.

We pull in at the front of the cottage, but James keeps the car running.

'Out you get,' he says.

'Don't you need to get changed too?' I ask.

'Nah, my whites are in my locker. Anyway I've got to park this at the back of the house.' He smiles. 'You know it's a reduced service, right? So it'll be an easy week,' he says. 'Thanks for coming today.'

And then he reaches across and touches my hand. I feel it immediately, that wonderful energy of mutual attraction – and now I'm sure it wasn't in my head. He lingers there for a moment and we smile shyly at each other, then he pulls his hand back.

'Very fun,' I stammer, climbing out of the car, but before I get a chance to shut the door, he speaks again.

'Heather,' he says, looking at the handbrake and then up at me briefly, before looking away again. He's nervous, I think. 'Could we, on a day off or something, maybe go back to Skye for lunch or something? There's this seafood place on the far side of the island . . .'

A date? I think that's what he means. I feel weak at the knees. Like properly in the way people say you do, and giddy, and like I've lost all control of my bodily functions.

He's unsure, and is looking everywhere but at me and then past me, then back at his handbrake and then back to me. I don't mean to take my time to answer, and I don't mean to sound weird about it, but I'm in a bit of shock.

'Lunch?'

If it was Tim, I would have said something like 'What – are you too cheap for dinner?' or 'Do I have to be seen in public with you?' But I'm not sure James would find it funny, and also the question is *so* genuine that I feel like I need to reply in kind.

'Or something else.' He starts to look uncomfortable. 'I could take you fly-fishing? Or drive to Inverness. We could get a group, and all go out. I'm just thinking you're new to the area, and I know everywhere like the back of my hand. I mean, if you loved Skye, we could see more of it . . .'

His voice trails off and I wonder if that's the longest sentence he's ever said in his life. God, I like him. But I can't go on a date with James. Even if he is genuinely interested in me, he thinks I'm Heather. It's a disaster. *A disaster.*

Then it hits me: James has been living on the west coast of Scotland, and working in this remote hotel, for most of his adult life. He's not uncultured by any means, but he's also not been out and done much living. His interest in me is logical – I'm the only available woman this season. I mean, he really has no choice.

Yet as my mind wanders through those comfortable rooms called self-loathing and fear, I know that isn't true. He likes me. No one like James has ever liked me. If, by some miracle, they're still swimming around London single at thirty, they're looking for women who are as together as they are. I have zero to offer. No career. No money. No big family home in Sussex.

'If you went to London you'd get eaten alive,' I say under my breath.

'What?' he says, and now he looks fully stressed-out. I need to answer.

'Fishing sounds fun,' I say, pulling myself back into the reality before me. I like James. A lot. And he thinks that I'm Heather; and I'm lying to him and everyone here, and courting this flirtation really is a recipe for disaster. But fishing is casual. No sitting across from each other at a table, staring into each other's eyes.

'Oh. Okay,' he says, and then he looks up at me. 'Fishing it is. I'll be happy to take you.'

'Monday then?' I say.

'Monday,' he replies. 'See you in the kitchen for the team briefing.'

'See you in the kitchen.'

As he drives off, I feel like I'm gliding, and I fumble with the front-door keys just as it opens, and Bill is standing there, trying to keep himself upright on the door frame. He's drunk. I can smell the whisky coming off him so strongly it makes me want to gag. He looks like he's been crying, his eyes are so red and puffy. His fly is undone, and the tail of his white shirt is poking out through the zipper.

'We have to get you inside,' I say quickly, looking round to see if anyone has seen him, but the coast is mercifully clear.

'I have to go to work,' he says.

'You can't go to work.'

'I have to,' Bill says, as I try to push him down the hallway. I can barely budge him; he has that limp-limbed heaviness that makes him impossible to move.

'Come on,' I say quickly. 'Get up the fucking stairs.'

He stumbles forward and falls flat onto the floor, hitting the side of his head on the plaster skirting.

'Bill! Get the hell up,' I say, as he clambers onto his hands and knees. The picture is so stunningly similar to another that my heart starts to race. Dad on all fours in the kitchen, and Mum's high-pitched awkward laughter while she's ushering me out of the room, as if there's something terrible I might see, while at the same time insisting there is 'nothing to see here'.

I grab Bill's arm to help steady him as he pulls himself to his feet. His head is already going a dark purple where he bumped it.

'I have to go to work – it's opening week, next week, and the reviewer, Jason or Justin, is coming . . .' he tries to reason, but he's cross-eyed and can't really even focus on my face.

'You don't have to go. I can pour a fucking cocktail. I'll tell Irene you're sick.'

'I'm on my last warning,' he slurs, as he pulls himself up the stairs and round the bannister towards his room.

We take a couple of steps and I push open the first door.

'Don't open it,' says Bill and he tries to push me away, but I'm not having it. I duck under his arm, turn the knob and push it open.

The room is a mess. I mean a real mess. An empty bottle of wine in the bin. Clothes all over the floor. The bedspread is crumpled and the sheets are clearly unwashed. Next to the bed, without even an attempt to be discreet, is an open porn magazine (I can't help but notice it's got a light-bondage edge to it). A collection of glasses from the main house are scattered on every surface and the top drawer of his dresser is open, with nothing but a pair of tartan pyjama trousers hanging over the edge. The room stinks.

I walk straight to the window and throw it open and the cool breeze gushes in. I turn back to Bill, who looks shamefacedly at the ground and tries to hide the magazine with his feet, then subtly kick it under his bed.

'I've seen a porno before,' I say, as matter-of-factly as I can. 'You really ought to get a computer or watch some *Youporn* on your phone. Less chance of getting caught.'

He giggles, embarrassed. It's pitiful, and I quickly point to his sheets and tell him to get in.

'I'm humiliated,' Bill says with a sudden clarity, and plonks onto the edge of his bed, putting his head in his hands.

'My dad used to drink too much,' I say flatly. 'Does everyone know?'

'Irene knows.'

'You need to sober up and start again fresh tomorrow. Day one.'

'I'm not an alcoholic.'

'Yeah. Well, I've heard that before. Whatever is going on, tomorrow is a new day, and you can't drink like this at work.'

'I think I've run out of chances,' he says, smiling as he tries to focus on me.

'Don't be a dick.'

'I have a daughter your age. What are you: thirty? Eloise. Stupid name. I let *her* name them. I let her choose everything.'

'Well, that was very kind of you.'

'Who named you?' He belches, then covers his mouth. 'Sorry.'

'My, uh, mum,' I say, piling up some used plates and a mug of old tea.

'But you're not really Heather,' he says.

I stop what I'm doing and then put my hand to my mouth. My heart beats a little faster. *What did he say*? I'm not really *Heather*? Does he mean I don't suit the name? Bill's curled up now on the bed, his eyes starting to close. Did he say 'a' Heather? Or I'm not really *Heather*.

'Well, you can't pick your birth name,' I say, as he closes his eyes and mumbles something else I can't make out. 'What? What are you saying?'

'It's a mistake,' he mumbles again. 'There was some mistake.'

I think he's talking about my name, but I'm not sure. I lean down next to him and shake his shoulders. 'What are you saying?'

'No more wine,' he mutters and then his body goes limp.

'Close your eyes now,' I say, picking up some of the clothes from the floor and shoving them into a laundry basket. I turn round to look for what to do next to bring some chaos to his disorder, but the job needs a couple of hours, and I have to get to lunch service, and to Irene.

There goes any minute of wine study I'd hoped to cram in. It will have to wait.

'You're going to be okay,' I begin, but he's already snoring.

15.

I've traded in the Heather-sized uniform and now have one that fits me properly, and I feel quite smart. I didn't have time to do my make-up and perfect my hair, like the other staff seem to spend hours doing before service, but I managed to find time to slap on some tinted moisturizer at least. My hair is washed and left to dry naturally, which is the absolute best for my curls, though nothing can be done about the roots, which are starting to come through. The apron gives me a little bit of extra confidence, as it covers my slightly rounded tummy, and I know I look pretty good from behind.

I clutch my black notebook, which is easily tucked into the large front pocket of my apron, and make my way to the bar area to find Irene. She's sitting at the far end, with Russell, deep in a conversation that looks serious. I weigh up if losing Bill for a shift would trump whatever vexing thing they're working on, and opt to wait.

I find Roxy just inside the kitchen, going over the menu with James and the rest of the team, and I realize to my horror I've missed the team briefing. I totally forgot, with Bill and everything.

'Balls! Sorry,' I say, sliding behind Roxy.

'It's fine. I'm explaining the fish of the day; and some damned animal ate all the dill, so there's no dill emulsion. One of the junior staff is reprinting the menu now.'

'Oh, we could have got some in Portree,' I say.

'It's okay. Roxy says the wine match is still fine – do you want to check?'

'Honestly I think Roxy knows more than I do,' I say as she turns to me, looking a bit sheepish. 'It's fine. Go on. Keep going.'

'Sorry,' she mouths to me, and I pretend to be really offended, and that makes her smile.

'Try to sell dessert today. We're down on desserts,' booms Russell, as he and Irene join us in the kitchen. Irene looks weirdly ruffled for the first time since I've met her. She clutches a stack of invoices in her hands. 'As the renovations are ongoing, the menu is compact, but each dish will be from the new menu, so this is your fortnight to really focus and become experts. I want to see passion. Commitment. Perfection.'

'Bookings are not up as much as we were hoping,' Irene interjects, by way of explaining his ridiculous speech, I suppose. *It must be a blow to your ego to find you weren't the draw card everyone was hoping for, eh, Russell?*

Russell continues, 'Everyone has to leave this place ready to tell a friend, an uncle, their rich cousin or grandparent that Loch Dorn is the best restaurant on the west coast. That a Michelin star is only a season away. I've given you all the tools – now fucking use them.'

I snort and then, when Russell immediately catches my eye, pretend it was a cough.

'All right, eleven forty-five,' says Irene, looking at her cute little vintage gold watch, and the staff automatically disperse. 'Where's Bill? Is he stocking?'

'Oh yes, sort of,' I say. 'I need to speak to you about that.'

Irene looks at me, and I try to send her an *it's very important* face, as I don't want to say anything in front of Russell and James. She understands immediately.

'Very well, let's go into the dining room. Roxy can finish setting up.'

Irene is stressed. There is a deep line between her eyebrows that wasn't obvious a few days ago, and her voice is hoarse. The dining room has been cleared of furniture and the plans are laid out across the table, with swatches of fabric in shades of blue, silver and grey.

'Bill,' she begins, her voice dropping to a whisper. 'I assume he's been drinking?'

I flinch. *He's been drinking.* She sounds disappointed. No, gutted. She sounds absolutely gutted, and I no longer wonder if Bill was telling the truth when he says it's his last chance. I wonder if my dad had any *last* chances. He certainly had a lot of *chances*. There were months when he didn't drink, and those times always felt even more weirdly strained. Suddenly he took an interest in me and in things I was doing; and, honestly, I preferred being left alone. I could cope with the hour-long drunken rants about fluoride and chemtrails, but not the apologies and feeble attempts to bond. I felt a sense of relief when he drank again.

Last time I called home, about four years ago, he answered the phone, shouting and slurring, until Mum took the receiver off him, sounding panicked. 'Hello? Oh, goodness, Elizabeth, it's only you. No, no, your father's fine. Busy day at work.'

Dad had lost the fish-and-chip shop to creditors more than a decade ago. And I'm pretty sure he didn't have another job.

I flat-out challenged Mum. 'Um, Dad doesn't work. He's on sickness benefit.'

'That's enough of that talk, Elizabeth,' she said, her voice rising. 'How dare you—'

I hung up the phone and never called again. *No looking back*, I'd calmly told Heather, as I felt the last threads of a tattered safety net fall away beneath me.

'No, no,' I blurt now to Irene, falling easily into the role of my mother. 'Bill's got a stomach bug of some kind. Believe me, I just had to anti-bac the toilet.'

Irene doesn't look up from the two almost identical dove-grey fabric swatches she's holding. 'Okay,' she replies, and I can tell she knows I'm lying. 'Well, we must make sure no one else in the cottage catches it. Do I need to make up some rooms in the annexe for you?'

'No, that won't be necessary,' I say. 'I'm sure it's only something he ate.'

'It's better for us if it's stomach flu – in case word gets out. Food poisoning is bad for business.' Irene looks up at me and gives a soft smile, like she's grateful, but I suddenly feel uneasy about the charade.

'Who will do the bar?' I ask, more pointedly.

'I'll rope in Brett. He can manage,' she says, before looking back up at me, her immaculately pencilled brows knotted together. 'Will *you* manage without him? Perhaps you should take this as an opportunity to do the stocktake?'

I swallow down the rising guilt, remembering the concerns she raised with Bill, who is supposed to be keeping an eye on me so that I don't make any more embarrassing errors. I raise my hand instinctively to the bump on my eye, which has now more or less disappeared.

'I'll be fine,' I say quickly. 'Look, I know I've had a rough start. I'm so sorry. It's just, with the relocation . . .'

She waves her hand away and blushes slightly. 'I'm sure.'

'I promise to do my very best for you, Irene,' I say firmly. 'We're going to make the relaunch incredible, okay?'

She responds with a little smile, but her eyes are sad. 'The weight of everything is not on you, pet.'

I nod and feel a renewed determination to be the best I can be. 'We might have a theme for the Wine Society evening.'

Irene plasters on a huge smile now. 'Oh, fabulous, darling. And what are you thinking?'

'Okay, you have to go with me,' I say. 'James and I talked about it this morning and he's on board.'

'He is?'

'Yes, well, we thought we could do a British-wine event. Bunting and trifle, and posh Scotch eggs and whatnot.'

'Sounds rather English to me.'

'Well, we could find some Scottish wines too.'

Irene frowns. 'You must know that the first Scottish wine was a critical catastrophe. Did the breaking news "Fife will not be the next Loire Valley" not travel south of the border?'

'Uhh,' I stammer.

'And now another new attempt, this time from Château Glencove. You saw the owner at the awards night didn't you? Swanning around in his kilt, like a laird without a castle. An embarrassment to the whole industry. People need to choose that one thing they can do brilliantly and stick to it. And if you're Scottish, that means not growing ruddy grapes.'

'Sorry, Irene, I didn't think,' I begin, but she's on a roll.

'I don't have a problem with doing an *English* wine-night. I'm sure the Society will thoroughly enjoy picking as many holes in it as they can. Just don't call it "British". I'll speak to Russell and let him know.'

I glance over at the big, open kitchen and watch James arrange some things along counter, or the 'pass', as I know now it's called. I feel a warm flush as I remember our upcoming fishing trip/almost-date thing.

James looks across at me as if he knows I am staring and he smiles, and for a moment we're doing that teenage grinning-thing at each other, and I forget I'm being given a talking to by his mum. My crush is evolving, and it's been inexplicably complicated by the fact that James seems interested in me, in return.

'Come now, time to get ready for service.' Irene looks like she's pretending to disapprove.

Or maybe she does disapprove, I think, remembering her words to Bill the other night.

I shuffle off to catch up with Roxy, who is reading over the menu while arranging some bottles of champagne in the antique ice-box that sits decoratively at the end of the bar.

'Heather,' she says anxiously, nodding at the fresh printouts sitting on the counter. 'Are you happy with the pairings? I tweaked them a little, to keep it fresh.'

'All looks perfect to me,' I reply – not that I've had time to look. 'And great that it's the same menu for dinner, so we can busy ourselves getting ready for the relaunch.'

'I see you really did have an accident . . .' she says, her pretty face contorted with concern.

'Occupational hazard.' I wave it away. 'Not the first time.'

She laughs. I glance around the bar area. The small temporary tables are set more modestly than the tables in the main restaurant were.

'Six bookings today. Two for lunch and four for dinner,' Roxy is saying, following my gaze around the room.

Great, that's enough to learn more about serving, without being overwhelmed. And hopefully I'll get away in time after lunch to do some more revision.

'And Bill told me yesterday we need to stocktake. I can help with that?' she says. 'If you want the help, I mean.'

'Shit! Yes,' I reply. *The damned stocktake. It's relentless.*

'We only had a small cellar at my last place, around thirty-five wines, but I did the count and placed the orders. And of course I've helped out here before. But there were not as many wines to do then.'

'No, there were not,' I agree. Here goes. 'And can you do something else for me? Could you do the role of sommelier over lunch? I want to watch you, and take some notes.'

'I mean, sure,' she replies, her face flushing slightly. 'But I'm sure you . . .'

'Every place does it differently. Besides, no one is ever too experienced to learn something new, right? I want to see how you do a whole service.'

'I can do that, Heather.'

'But can we keep it on the down-low?' I say. 'Irene is really stressed, and I don't want her to worry that I'm not up to speed or whatever.'

'You got it!'

'Great, then we'll do the stocktake, and then I'll need to rest before dinner,' I say, looking at my phone. Lunch until 2 p.m., I'll allow two hours for the stocktake, then two hours hidden away in my room learning more of the wine list. And I've decided to change tactics. Two wines from each section this afternoon, so that I have a base knowledge across the whole thing. *I wish there were more hours in the day.* A new feeling for me; usually I wish the day was over.

'My dad says it's an incredible list, but a bit long,' Roxy is saying.

'Oh, it's absolutely ridiculous.'

16.

I watch Roxy intently.

Offer menu. Offer aperitif.

She knows I'm watching and looks nervously across at me. I write it down in my notebook. This is what I should have done that first bloody night, instead of chatting to Bill. And that other awful night, instead of half-knocking myself out with a champagne cork. I've seen it happen; I've been a customer eating and drinking with fancy service around me, but it isn't until you actually break it down that you realize there's a purpose to the order of every step.

Roxy suggests a glass of champagne as an aperitif to the first table. A Canadian couple. Honeymooners, I think. They decline.

She asks about water. Still or sparkling? Then the wine. They select a rosé – Whispering Angel. I know this one already: delicate and bone-dry through the finish. I'm not exactly sure what a 'bone-dry' wine will taste like, and I hope they might not finish the whole bottle, so I can find out.

As she passes me, Roxy tries to see what I'm writing down, and I have to pretend not to hide my notes while doing my best to hide them.

'I feel like I'm sitting a test.'

'So does the waitress normally do the water here, or the sommelier?'

'It depends on how busy we are. Russell is a bit more modern in his approach – we always offer it first, so there is at least something on the table.'

'Do you offer tap?'

'Russell says no.'

'And do you serve from the left, clear from the right? Do I have to help with any of that stuff too?' I don't mean it to come out as whiny as it sounds.

'Maybe sometimes. You know, it's not silver service. Irene says take the side that is more discreet. Like, don't clear a plate between two people who are talking.'

'Okay, well, that makes it easy.'

I watch her bring the wine to the table and turn the label round, to show the man, who nods. Roxy unscrews the lid – no corkscrew, lucky! – and pours a small amount for the man to taste. He does. He shrugs, giggling at his partner, and waves for Roxy to pour it. Roxy fills the woman's glass first. *Woman first*, I note down. Then she takes out her pad and notes down their orders.

When she returns, I watch her grab an ice bucket, fill it with ice and then grab a stand from the side of the bar, slide the bucket in, fold a white linen cloth neatly around the neck and tuck it discreetly by the back wall.

'I wouldn't always do that,' she whispers. 'But if it's just two of them over lunch we'll need to keep it chilled – they will likely drink slowly.'

As service wraps up two hours later, I head down to the cellar, telling Roxy I'll begin the stocktake while she sets up for dinner service. *I got this*. I've helped with a stocktake at a pub before: how hard can it be? Through the dark, that unmistakable smell of Stilton rounds hits my nose.

'Goodbye, darkness my old friend,' I whisper, pulling the light switch, only to find Anis there, sitting in the near pitch-black, hovering over a glass of red wine.

'Sprung,' she says flatly.

'Anis!' I shriek. 'Christ, sorry, I wasn't expecting anyone. Taking a break?'

'This isn't a usual thing, so don't go thinking it is,' she says sternly. 'I'm just a wee bitty jumped-up today.'

'Oh, I was going to start on the stocktake. Roxy will be down to help in a moment. So much to get my head round. A baptism of fire, as they say,' I smile.

'Yes, I heard you made a right twat of yourself the other night,' she says, making what I presume is a popping-cork gesture, but it comes off a bit like she's wanking.

'Well,' I say, frowning, 'I suppose I did. I'm a bit rusty.'

'Have you been out of work?' she asks, not missing a beat.

'No, no – you know, it's only an expression,' I mutter. 'I mean, I'm just getting up to speed.' *Christ, she's intimidating.*

'Well, get on then,' she says, nodding towards the huge rack on the far wall. I stare idiotically at the rack, feeling exposed all over again. Should I simply count them?

'You'll need that,' Anis says, nodding towards a big book with dog-eared pages and a biro slotted into its spiral binding.

'It's not done on a computer?' I ask, frowning. That would have been easier. *I wish Roxy would hurry up.* 'So, tell me,' I say, casually picking up the list, 'where are you from, where did you train, how did you end up here?'

'I'm from Glasgow,' Anis says, giving nothing more away. 'You?'

'Oh gawd. It's so boring,' I say with a wave and bury my head in the ledger as far as I can, wishing Roxy would appear. I peer across at Anis. She's sitting at a barrel that doubles as a table. She reaches for her glass and drains it, then grabs the bottle.

'Here,' she says, and it feels like an order, so I put down the list and join her, obediently filling a dusty glass from the shelf next to us and taking a sip of the wine, eyeing the label I don't recognize.

'It's from an outside catering job,' she says, nodding at a couple of cases in the corner. 'Paid-for leftovers.'

'Good to know,' I say, tipping my glass at her.

'You enjoy working with James?' she asks, and it feels weighted.

'Yes,' I reply. 'He's really lovely.'

'He is,' she says. 'He's sensitive. Had his heart broken by an Australian two summers ago. She treated him like part of her Scottish experience and left him cold. He took a long time to recover.'

It feels like a warning, and I decide not to reply and nod as if I've *really* heard her.

'Don't you have a boyfriend back home?' she then asks pointedly.

'Ahh, um, yes,' I say, thinking about Tim and realizing I've pined for my favourite buttermilk-fried chicken place in Soho more than him this week. 'Well, we've never explicitly called it that. I'm not sure he would say he was. So that probably says it all, really,' I blurt, almost involuntarily.

'So, what do you think of Bill?'

I try not to giggle. Is she gossiping? Am I being ordered to gossip?

'Ah, he's been super-friendly.'

'He's not gay,' she reports.

'Oh. Okay,' I say, really trying to swallow a laugh.

'He's just a posh English person,' she continues, as if that explains some *gay* trait that I might have noticed. 'He was one of the best barmen in London. He trained in New York with the Paxton Group and then he worked in London. That's how he's friends with Russell. He's up here because his wife left him.' Anis taps the edge of her wine glass.

She gives the impression that nothing is ever a secret around her, and if it was, it would be sensible to fess up straight away. She stands up and wanders over to the wine rack, reaches behind one of the bottles and pulls out a packet of Marlboro. 'They're communal,' she explains. Then she wanders right to the end of the cellar, flicks on another light and I can see a massive round metal thing that looks like an oven.

'What's that?' I ask.

'The old whisky distillery stuff. This is the copper boiler. Russell wants it removed and turned into a fireplace for the annexe,' she says, lighting her cigarette and holding it up to a tiny air vent in the ceiling. It's a gallant attempt, but absolutely not working.

I can't believe she's going to smoke amid all the hung meat and cheese rounds. I must be frowning, because she holds one towards me.

'Want one?'

'Ha! No. I haven't had a cigarette since I was nine,' I say, glancing at my watch. There are way not enough hours in the day. 'I didn't think chefs were supposed to smoke – doesn't it ruin the palate?'

'I have three a week,' Anis says.

'Must be hard, though, to be working for two dudes,' I offer, nearly gagging at the wine.

'Believe me, I can handle working for James and Russell,' she says. 'I'm a half-Malaysian woman who did four years in the British Army.'

'Ha, fair enough,' I reply.

We hear the door swing open and I'm relieved that Roxy is finally here. But the footsteps are too heavy for Roxy and I panic, trying to position my body in front of the wine, clutching the menu awkwardly, as Russell appears in bottle-green tweed plus-fours and a billowing white cotton shirt, almost as though we summoned him.

'Who the hell is smoking down here?'

Despite what she's just said, Anis looks utterly aghast.

'Me,' I say, raising my finger, painting on my most meek and submissive face, which I hate having to do, but brand-new-to-the-job-and-rules Heather can better absorb a ticking off.

'You can't smoke down here,' he snaps. 'This is not some Scottish spinster speakeasy. You should *both* know better.'

'I'm so sorry – we used to do it at my old work. In the cellar. Anis was just giving me what for.'

Russell studies my face, then looks across to Anis, whose head has dropped, and I realize even the army hasn't prepared her for Captain Cock.

'I'm sorry, Russell. A misstep. It won't happen again.'

'No, it won't,' he says. 'Tom is here, from Inveraray Wholesale – he wants to go through their buyer's list. I presume you're not too busy?' Then he notices the wine I've been trying to shield. 'Put the rest of those returns on the Specials list,' he snaps. 'And try to move them this week, please?'

'Oh, you want to sell them twice?' I say.

He narrows his eyes at me, and a deep crease tries to appear between his eyebrows. It's so odd that I forget what we're discussing for a moment and wonder if he's had Botox.

'Irene's just explained your idea for British wines for the Wine Society event. It's actually got a bit of merit. Why don't you find out if Tom can help source them for you?

'Oh, that's great. You liked the idea?'

'Now, please. Let's go,' he snaps, motioning to the stairs.

'Yes, Chef.'

We make our way into the kitchen and out towards the bar, and although I'm practically running I can't keep up with Russell. He stops to glare at me impatiently. *It's a marvel, really, how quickly I've got on the wrong side of the boss. Under a week! A Birdy record.*

Russell guides me towards a man who has his back to us, sitting at a small table surrounded by pamphlets and an open laptop that looks older than mine.

'Tom,' Russell says. 'You probably know Heather, of course?'

'Hi, Heather,' Tom says, a smile spreading across his face. He's kind of handsome, with shaggy blond hair and pink cheeks. *Wait, he knows me?*

'Hi, Tom.' My heart starts thumping in my chest as he kisses me on both cheeks. I smell very liberally applied body spray permeating from him, and I try not to recoil.

Then he pulls back and looks at my face, head cocked to the side. 'I thought we'd met, but I guess not,' he says with a smile. 'My bad.'

'I'm sorry, your face is not familiar to me, either,' I say, sitting down in the leather chair opposite him and grinning. 'I'd definitely remember it.' I know it's terribly flirtatious, but it's my only weapon here.

'I have to talk to Irene,' says Russell. 'I'll leave you both to it?'

'Thank you, Russell,' I say, relieved.

'Thanks, Russ,' Tom repeats, before looking back at me with a wide, expectant grin.

I quickly crane my neck over my shoulder to give the impression that I'm busy and have as little time as possible to chat. Because I don't. I made zero headway on the stocktake and now I'm sitting with a buyer, probably to order wines that we need, because *I should have done the stocktake.* And I desperately want to get back to the cottage to study. I turn back to Tom. My knee is jiggling.

'I totally thought we'd already met,' he says with a flirty grin. 'I feel a bit silly now.'

'Oh, don't,' I say, and then I lean forward and touch his hand. 'I'm afraid I have to make this quick. It's manic today.'

'Right. Of course,' he says, grinning. He smooths out the wrinkles in his trousers and points towards the brochure's first page. 'Well, the big news is natural wines, of course, and we've broadened our collection. They really appeal to people looking for more artisan wine-making, and of course buzzwords like "atmospheric yeast" and "minimum intervention" work really well as a point-of-sale to customers looking for something *now*.'

He stops for a moment and waits, as if I'm supposed to say something.

'Bloody hipsters, eh?' I say, nodding at him to go on, and he pauses before letting out a nervous kind of half-giggle. Then I remember Russell's suggestion. 'I'm looking for British wines, actually. You know. Stay local and all that.'

Just then I catch Roxy out of the corner of her eye and wave her over. *Thank God.* One thing I know very busy people do is delegate.

'Roxy,' I say warmly. 'Have you met Tom from Inveraray?'

'Yes, we've met,' she says, blushing slightly.

'Look, you know about the Wine Society night, right? We're going to do British wines. Do you reckon the two of you could come up with a shortlist of, like, a dozen?'

'Oh yeah. That's perfect,' Tom jumps in, sitting up slightly in his chair. 'We've got a deal on these from south-east England,' he says, running his finger along three whites with achingly modern minimalist labels, so small I can't read anything on them. But one of them is strangely familiar.

'Ah,' I say, focusing on one with delight. 'I tried this one a few weeks back. Sauvignon Blanc, right?'

'It won the—'

'Silver!' I say, thrilled that I have some knowledge to impart. 'Cat's wee.'

'Yes. That's for sure. Okay. Great,' Tom says, nodding at me.

'I'll leave you guys to it, okay?'

'Okay,' Roxy says, 'thanks so much, Heather.'

I put my hand on Roxy's shoulder as I go to leave and give it a little squeeze. Bless her, she genuinely sounds excited.

At breakneck speed, I sprint down the back path to the cottage, fling open the door to my bedroom and jump onto my bed. Laptop out. Phone out. I open my notebook. Forty-eight wines down, seventy-six to go. And so I make my way to the Loire Valley for a sprightly Sancerre.

As I'm staring down at the pen, a memory returns to me. School homework on the little table in our kitchen. One of those tables for really young kids that was hopelessly too small for me, but which I was still using at twelve. I was doing lines. Fifty lines. *I will not speak back to the teacher.* I remember taking my time to write each line out differently. One with flowers around the letter 'o'. One in full capitals. One upside down. One backwards. One line I used my mother's make-up mirror to write each letter in reverse. When I very proudly handed it to the teacher, she told me I had missed the point of the punishment and reprimanded me for being *cheeky*. Then she demanded that I do them again, properly. When I refused and pointed out the injustice of it, I was sent to the head teacher and my mother was called. I was a *defiant child*, apparently. I didn't get into trouble when we got home, though. Indifference would be a better way to describe the reaction from Mum. 'Can't you just do your lines and stop trying to stand out?'

For this situation at least, it was probably good advice.

I refocus on my task, jumping through to the reds, to begin on the Pinot Noirs. By 5.45 p.m. – about the time James, Anis, a thankfully sober Bill and Roxy are assembling in the staffroom for our evening service of four bookings – I am starting to feel like I can do this.

17.

There is a gentle knock on my door.

'Heather?'

I groan. I hate James calling me that. I consider asking him to call me Birdy, pretending it's a nickname, which isn't actually a lie, but it feels wrong. I look in the mirror. I look . . . kind of good. I've put on quite a lot more make-up than usual, but I'm hoping it's not too obvious. I wasn't sure blood-red lips were quite the right look for *fishing*, but I've gone for it anyway.

'Hi, come in!' I quickly scan my room but it's clear of anything incriminating. I've started keeping my studies between my mattress and base, so I'm pretty sure no one will find anything, even if I die in a boating accident today with James. It's rather strange living your lie to the extent that you're planning for an accidental death. But here I am.

He opens the door and he's ready to go – boots and everything. Same as the foraging day, in all the green wax-and-tweed clothing a man can muster.

'You look really . . .' He stops looking as soon as he mentions how I look, and then can't finish the sentence.

'Is the lippy too much? I don't want to frighten the fish,' I joke, but I feel a bit embarrassed now at the effort I've made. It was clearly too much. See, that's why I don't try at things; the opportunity for humiliation increases with every attempt to better yourself.

'No, it's good.'

I pull on my only sweatshirt to hide my blushing face and follow James out into the hall, where I pluck the same old man's jacket off the coat rack.

We get outside and it's clear he's been up for a while, as there is a four-wheel-drive jeep-type thing pulled up by the front door, and in the back some fishing rods, a tartan blanket and other green and/or tartan outdoorsy stuff.

'Let's go,' he says.

'Where are we going? I thought we'd be going out on Loch Dorn?'

'Nah,' James says, starting up the jeep. 'I'd like to get away from here, if you don't mind.'

'I don't mind,' I reply. I don't really want to go fishing, of course, but I love the packing of the car and the adventure of it all.

The car slowly moves forward and we take the main road from the hotel in the morning darkness. I reach over to play with the radio, but I can't get it to turn on.

'It doesn't work,' he says. 'Sorry. We have to take this one, as we're heading a bit off the beaten track. Anyway, you can't pick up a signal once we go down towards the river.'

'Thank God you're not a serial killer,' I say.

It isn't long before he turns up an almost invisible lane, which winds alongside a river. I grab the handle at the top of the car to steady myself as we are thrown left and right on the bumpy road.

'You're not comfortable in cars, are you? It won't be long.'

'I was in a minor accident when I was ten.'

'Oh shit! Really?'

'Oh, it's nothing, it was really minor. I backed into the carport.' I wait for the laugh. Most people really laugh when I tell that story, and James does too, but then asks, 'What were you doing, driving at ten?'

'Just being a naughty kid,' I say, finding myself wanting to tell the actual truth for the first time: that my dad had wanted me to drive him to work.

'I can imagine,' he says with a smile.

We pull up at what could loosely be called a *park*, in that it's the end of the hardly apparent road at the point where the non-road becomes a wood. I realize in abject horror that we will have to do the drive back up the lane in reverse.

James is out before me, pulling stuff from the back and laying it down along the river's edge and, as I make my way out, I check my phone to see it's still before 7 a.m. James is carefully checking the rods and laying them against the back of the car, and I wonder if it's too late to go to the movies or for a coffee somewhere.

'I don't have a clue what to do here – you know that, right?'

He grins as he hands me a rod, then flings a heavy backpack onto his back and nods towards a tiny path that I can just make out, about five metres from the car.

I oblige.

'You know, this is a weird thing to do on a day off,' I say. 'At this hour most normal people are in bed, binge-watching *Friends* with bacon, or still asleep on the night Tube.'

I look back at James, and he's doing that chuckle to himself that he's always doing.

'It only happened four times,' I say, squeezing another giggle from him.

'Keep going, you'll need to climb a little at the base – that's it – and down onto the bank.'

We're going to be fly-fishing I realize. And I'm annoyed, because in my fantasy we're on a boat in the loch with a parasol, and James pretends to tip the boat and I squeal and fall into his arms.

'Fly-fishing?'

'Yes. The one true fishing.'

'If you're trying to make a *Game of Thrones* gag, it doesn't work for this.'

He laughs and shakes his head at me. 'Come on,' he says and puts his hand out and takes mine. It's reassuringly strong, and I enjoy being led down the bank onto the rocks. It's cold. Cold and damp.

He pulls the rods out from his backpack and I sit back and watch him ready us for fishing. He must know I don't really care about it, but it doesn't seem to sully the mood. After all, he suggested lunch and I chose fishing.

'Heather,' he starts to talk, and I cringe again at the name, and James hands me a rod. I hold it in my hand and wait for him to take his own rod out, but he's rummaging through a plastic box for what look like tiny little bugs and flies. He chooses one and pulls the edge of my rod towards him and spends some time trying it on.

Suddenly a huge fish appears below us, jumping into the air. It's enormous and I scream. 'Oh my God, look!'

He laughs and pulls my rod back. 'It's just the salmon running,' he says. 'You know what they're doing, right?'

'Spawning,' I say. I know it, but I've never seen it and, as I speak, another jumps, higher than the first. 'Holy shit!'

James laughs and stops his prep for a moment.

'I don't like it,' I say. 'They're trying to make babies!'

'Don't worry, I'll make sure we throw any mamas back. Is it too much? You want to watch for a bit?'

'Yes,' I reply.

James is focused and he finishes setting up my rod and then does something similar to his own, and before I can say, *This is ethically dubious*, he's tossing his line into the water. The line lingers in the air, and what looks like plain fishing suddenly looks like dancing, as it never seems to do anything but skip about above the running water. I watch him move effortlessly between the rocks in his waders.

'James . . .'

'Shh,' he says. 'You can't shout when you're fishing.'

I take a place on the rock and observe for a while, as he throws the line out again. After about twenty minutes he stops and wanders back to his plastic container.

'Just going to change flies,' he says, leaning down. Then he looks up at me and he's totally vexed. 'Shit! Sorry, Heather, I am *so* into fishing.'

'Is there a bit where we drink tea?'

'Actually, yes. If I was here with Brett, we'd probably have a wee dram, but I did bring tea, as it happens.'

I feel a little disappointed at this and he catches my frown.

'All right, I brought both,' he says. 'But let's start with tea.'

Underneath the tartan rug is a picnic basket with a Thermos and some Tupperware containers from the kitchen.

'Is that lunch?' I ask.

'Well, you wouldn't let me take you to lunch, so I took it to you,' he says, kneeling down next to me. He pulls out the Thermos and pours me a cup, and I put it to my lips – it's milky and sweet, exactly as I like it.

'Mmm,' I say, feeling my throat warm as it gushes down.

'Tastes better in the outdoors,' James says, and he's staring at me. '*Everything* is better outdoors.'

I wonder if he's being flirty, because so far it's not really been his style, but I look across at him and he looks quickly away, like he's backed out of his flirtiness in a wave of fear or sudden regret. Then, in an instant, he looks back at me again and we catch each other's eyes. For a moment I let myself revel in that delicious thrill of pure, unadulterated chemistry, and then it's me who is crushed by unexpected shyness and looks quickly away.

'Do you miss London?' he says after a moment's silence.

'Sure. I miss *some things*,' I say, as I sip some more tea. James throws the rug on the ground next to me and motions for me to sit on it, which I do, and it's considerably more comfortable than the cold stone.

'Like what?'

'I like the South Bank in the mornings on the weekend. But really early morning – I'm talking five o'clock in summer. I miss the bustle of the markets in Borough. I was just thinking about them yesterday. You can get anything.'

'Anything?'

'Well, most things,' I say. 'Not chef-level anything, but civilian-foodie-level anything. You know, Jerusalem artichokes and porcini – that kind of thing. My flatmate, um, used to love it. I find it all a bit intimidating, actually. My dad had a fish-and-chip shop, for fuck's sake.'

'Nothing wrong with a chippy. Anyway, that can't be true. You can't work in wine and not know about food. All this joking aside.'

'Of course,' I say. I get this wave of disappointment as I realize I've got to be *on* at all times with James, or I risk giving too much away. 'I mean, I guess I know more than most. It's the cooking part I'm hopeless at.'

I look across at him, and he smiles at me, and I feel that little flutter in my stomach once more. I think of Tim, and it's hard not to compare them. If Tim is loud, manic and erratic, James is calm, considered and deliberate. And I like it. Why can't I just have a fling with James? He's a nice, decent guy with a full set of teeth. He knows I'm leaving in a couple of months. I'm not the first seasonal worker he's hooked up with. But for some reason it feels like a lie too far. And then I think of Anis saying that his heart was broken.

'But what about you? What's the story? Why haven't you left home?' I laugh, though if Irene was my mother, perhaps I'd never leave home. 'I know what I want to know! How come you're both working here – like, how did that happen?'

'She worked all over the west coast when I was little,' James begins.

'Where was your dad?'

He turns to me and laughs. 'Straight to the point?'

'Well, I'm fascinated is all.'

'He and Mum weren't together.'

'Where was he?'

'He was with someone else. Another woman, I think, though Mum never says this exactly.'

'What a creep,' I say, staring at a particularly spectacular beech tree with an almost-black trunk and bright-green leaves. 'I mean, I'm sorry, your dad's trash. So why'd you stay here anyway?'

'Well, Mum got a job at Loch Dorn. We used to live in the cottage we're in now. Mum was in your room actually. Then we moved to another cottage at the edge of the estate. That's where Mum is now. The owner, MacDonald, he looked after me a bit when I was little. But when his wife got ill, he started coming less and less, and the hotel got really rundown over the years. Then she died and he was going to sell, but Mum begged him to let her bring it into the twenty-first century. It's like home now.'

'Oh, so the renovations were her idea?'

'Yes, but Russell, the designers – all of that was not. She hoped MacDonald would let her do it, and he was going to, but he got some advice from his lawyer.' James pauses for a moment. 'And, well, it turns out that was Russell's lawyer too, so I guess he put them together? And of course Bill vouched for Russell, and so here we are.'

'How did the place get so rundown? It seems impossible to imagine it that way, when you look at it now.'

'Well, it was expensive to run. Expensive to maintain. And Mr MacDonald lost heart for it. I don't want you to think he's some arsehole. He's been really good to us. It's just if you don't invest and update, it's impossible to stay fresh. The people who come to Loch Dorn every summer are getting older. Rich, but older and older. And the outside catering jobs are drying up. There is one coming up, though.'

'What are the outside catering jobs?'

'Like, big parties, weddings. Film premieres. The one coming up is a film event, in fact.'

'Oh, now we're talking.'

'I have no idea what film it is, or who is in it, before you ask. But we've got to make it work – they pay way more than we'd take even in a month. Anyway, what I want to know is why *you* came here.'

'What do you mean?'

'Well, I saw your CV: you could have worked anywhere.'

I scramble my brain for something to say, and in the end just tell him the truth. 'I needed a radical change. My other life choices were not, um, satisfactory.'

'What's next?' he asks.

'France,' I say woefully, sliding back into Heather mode. Does he look disappointed? 'What do you think about Russell? Why did they bring in another head chef over you?'

'I've never been head chef. There was a guy called Peter Pierce before Russell, and another guy called Mick Williams before him. They never last long. Either their partners are unhappy here or they get bored. Russell is happy because he's been able to step back and executive-chef the restaurant, but live in Glasgow.'

'Holy shit! That's why he's never here.'

He laughs. 'Russell's okay. He's okay, really.'

'But you are *basically* the head chef, though.'

'Well,' with that he looks a bit sheepish, 'I mean, I guess so.'

'Do you want to run your own place?'

'Sure, but I don't really want to leave Mum. Not right now, at least.'

'Why?'

'I just couldn't,' he says as he reaches into the basket and pulls out a container filled with fresh strawberries. 'Want one?'

'Yeah,' I say, reaching for a plump, shiny berry. 'But everyone leaves home. It's normal, no matter what. Plus, dude, you're thirty. You don't have to move to China – maybe Edinburgh or something? *You* could go to France. Or Spain? Isn't the fanciest restaurant in the world in Spain?'

He laughs again and we sit in silence for a little longer, but I want to know more about him.

'Why did you start cooking, anyway?'

James looks up to the sky and moves his head to one side. 'Well, it's exciting. Tossing pots and pans in a busy kitchen is the closest I'll get to rock-'n'-roll dreams,' he laughs. 'I love the intensity of service. The creativity of working with food. But when it comes down to it, it's that *one* dish. Everything that's on that plate, from the sea salt to the squid ink, has taken time to get to that point. Someone's alarm went off at four a.m. to go out on the boats. The weather was just right. Someone else had to know the perfect soil, the right amount of water and sunlight, and how to prevent too much of both. And then, at the perfect moment, it comes down to me. And I take that bunch of kale, or mature scallop, and I have to show it that respect too.'

He folds his arms around his knees, and I'm hanging on his every word.

'And I get to transform it. Take its perfect natural state and warm it, or pickle it or dry it, you know? And sometimes I barely touch it. I kiss it with the pan, season it. Whatever. And then I plate it. And even though they're perfect strangers, cooking that meal for them is one of the most intimate things you can do. It's feeding someone. And knowing all the things that made them sit in that restaurant, that night, to eat local wilted buttery salsify, with that pan-fried scallop from Benji's sustainable farm, to celebrate life in some way. An engagement. An anniversary. An affair,' he adds, grinning. 'All of it is this long chain of creativity and passion. Of care. Of love, really.'

He shuffles a little in his place, and I want to disappear under this rock because I know what's coming.

'What about you? It must be the same for wine, right?'

'Wine . . .' I say, looking at the river again, as another salmon rises out of the pool and twists its body, leaping into the pool above. I'm not sure I really like fishing. 'What do they say? Find that thing you love and do it for a living. And I love drinking,' is all I think to say, and it comes out insincere, and I wish there was a way to answer him honestly.

'Come on. Wine is so . . . complex, and the details are tiny. I figure you have to be a bit nerdy to be into it.'

'I really liked that movie *Sideways*,' I say as the sun bursts from behind a tree and onto James's face. He looks so casual and handsome. Not model-handsome. Regular-person-handsome. Comfortable, thoughtful, handsome.

'You've been squirrelled away in your room between shifts prepping for the opening. We've all noticed how hard you work! That shows *some* dedication and passion.'

Avoidance of catastrophe is a great motivator.

'Well, I want to do a good job,' I say truthfully, then quickly switch the conversation back to him. 'But cooking – really, I wish I could cook. Every time I do, I get stressed and fuck it up. Even toast. I hate how you're controlled by it. It's like *Shit, this is burning* and *Fuck, this is splitting.* It won't succumb to my timetable. If I need a wee, or I get distracted by a text message or whatever, everything gets ruined. Basically, no matter what I do, it all turns to custard.'

'Well, actually,' he says, smiling, 'that's an achievement in itself.'

'Ha!' I say.

'The perfect custard is difficult,' he says, leaning forward in earnest. 'You can't rush it. It's ready when it's ready.'

'Well, that's probably the motto I need for my life. I'm seriously not yet ready for anything. Honestly, I don't know if I'll ever be. Did you know that some studies suggest female great white sharks take thirty-three years to hit maturity? That's nearly half their life.'

Another salmon jumps, and I feel mocked by its singular determination to do this one thing. Its mere biological urge. I wonder if James's cooking is a biological urge, or if Heather's passion for wine is in her DNA. I wonder if I just need to find *the thing*?

'I could teach you some basics,' he says, 'if you want to learn how to cook?'

'Oh, no,' I say, waving it away and laughing at the ridiculousness of the suggestion.

'I'd enjoy it,' he says.

'Oh, thanks, but I have enough on my plate. So to speak.'

I laugh and look over to James and, as I do, he reaches across to me and tucks a strand of hair behind my ear. It's so unexpected, and so intimate, I pull away from the shock.

'Sorry.'

'It's okay,' I say and I can't stop myself blushing.

'Is your hair naturally darker?'

'Yeah, it's dyed,' I say, feeling embarrassed.

'It's lovely.'

I take a deep breath. The attraction is so strong it feels overwhelming. This is dangerous.

'Ah, James,' I say. I need to call the situation. Lay it out. 'Look, you're like, so nice. And in some *Countryfile* version of my life, you would be very much my type. So far, all signs point to you not being weird. I mean, I'm sure, like most dudes, you've got some weird thing – and I'm not judging, we've all got them. And I'm ninety-nine per cent sure you've got a mother complex. And I'm *definitely* attracted to you? It's just . . .'

'What's the point, because you're moving on? We don't *have* to think about that,' he says, laughing.

We sit in silence for a moment and I try not to let the roar of the river drown my senses. There's a part of me that doesn't trust him. It's that deep, ever-present voice telling me that if he's interested in me, there has to be something wrong with him. But I'm also unable to stop myself from indulging in the undeniable pleasure of being next to him.

I reach over across the blanket and find his hand. I don't look at James, but I can see out of the corner of my eye that he isn't looking at me, either. His hand is warmer than mine as he's been holding the tea, and he must feel it too, because he slips his out from under mine and puts his on top, and then he wraps his fingers around my fingers.

I feel fifteen. It's so incredibly sweet. But a vision of Heather slips into my head and I quietly groan.

'What is it?' he says, as I pull my hand out from under his.

If this guy really is as wonderful as he seems, I can't lead him on like this. He thinks I'm Heather, and I need to find a way to put some distance between us.

'I'm sort of seeing someone,' I blurt out.

He looks mortified, rubbing his hands down his trouser legs as if trying to remove the evidence of our touch. 'Shit, I . . .'

'Your mum met him, actually,' I say, looking at the river so I can't see his face.

'Oh, right. She did mention that you were with someone that night, but she thought you . . .' His voice trails off.

'It's complicated,' I try to say more firmly. 'But I should have said something sooner.'

My throat chokes, as my mouth betrays my feelings, and I grit my teeth and try to keep going. 'I wasn't sure if this was a friend thing or I'd have mentioned it earlier . . .' My voice trails off. It's so unkind. I knew exactly what I was doing.

'Shit, I'm so embarrassed,' he says.

'No, no, don't be,' I say quickly. 'It's not exactly a concrete thing. How do I explain? Like, I've not met his parents or anything. I don't know where it's going really, but I felt like I should tell you.'

'Sure,' he smiles, but it's tight and he looks embarrassed. 'Well, shall we do some fishing? That's why we're here, after all.'

After a moment's hesitation James stands up and then offers his hand to help me up.

With one salmon in the boot and a blood-stripe down my temple, we're heading back to the cottage. I didn't really enjoy fishing. Those beautiful fish bounding up out of the water, only to be yanked out and prepared for a fish pie. Still, James seemed to enjoy it, and I could understand how, for someone like him, it was about being close to the land. After my awkward revelation about *the boyfriend*, he did finally relax again and I enjoyed watching him.

'The reopening,' he says, 'are you feeling ready?'

'I need to keep my head down and learn the wine list some more, then I hope I'm good to go,' I say.

'That sounds an awful lot like *passion* to me,' he says with a grin.

More like survival. 'Hey, thanks for today. I loved it.'

'No you didn't,' he laughs.

'I *did*,' I reply, wanting to tell him I loved it because of him.

'Do you remember I said to you that I once worked on Skye?'

'Yeah.'

'Well, I went there because one of Loch Dorn's old head chefs moved there and opened a little fresh seafood restaurant. I was going a bit crazy with Mum – you know what it's like at eighteen – and anyway he asked me to come, and I went.'

'You left your mum!' I gasp, grinning at this admission.

'Well, yes. But not for long. I was going to say that it was that summer that I fell in love with cooking properly. I met people from all over Skye on the supply lines and . . . I was hooked. If you'll excuse the fishing metaphor.'

'Oh, is this a pep talk?' I say, raising my brows in defiance.

'No, no.' He covers his mouth with his hand but he's still smiling with those eyes. 'I'm just saying that was the summer I found my true passion.'

'Maybe there's hope for me yet.'

18.

It's Friday lunch and four days until the relaunch, and I'm starting to feel good. I've done a load of shifts in the reduced-menu bar area and I'm no longer secretly shadowing Roxy. I'm well over halfway through the list, and so far I've only really been tested a few times, but nothing I couldn't get through without an off-the-cuff suggestion or a 'give me one moment and I'll come back with a recommendation'.

The older folks who seem to make up the bulk of the clientele are what I categorize as unadventurous as fuck. I've met Amandeep Singh, a gentle retiree from Aberdeen, and his wife Yasmine, a whippet who likes to smoke cigarillos and dine on clear broth and a wedge of a lemon. And the inevitable 'Scottish' Americans in their cotton and khaki, with booming voices and generous tips.

Only six covers tonight. Easy, right?

Then in walks the elderly Mr John and the not-so-elderly Izzy Cardiff, visiting from their weekend home fifteen minutes' drive away. She has all the bombastic confidence of a woman schooled at Fettes College, with winter holidays in Lech – swathed in cashmere and drowning in entitlement. He, on the other hand, looks like a retired chemistry teacher, in his moss-green heavy-knit wool sweater and mustard slacks. Old Scottish money.

Izzy Cardiff is soon putting me through my paces.

'Darling, please can you exchange this Sancerre for something a little less aggressive?'

'Aggressive?' I say, pulling the bottle from the ice-bucket. 'Not again. I'm constantly having to reprimand the Sancerre. Would you like me to exchange it for something more amiable?' Oops, quick swerve needed. 'Perhaps something from New Zealand? Everyone loves New Zealand.'

'To be frank, darling, I'd prefer a gin. At least then I will be able to drive. Yes, bring me a gin.'

'Does everyone round here drink and drive?' I ask Bill as I arrive at the bar with the aggressive Sancerre. 'Like, are there separate government-recommended guidelines for what makes you too drunk to drive a Bentley?'

Bill has been on the straight and narrow since last week, as far as I can tell, although I know better than to hope it was the last time. I wonder once again why Irene would let him work the bar.

'Oh yes. And don't forget the farmers,' says Bill. 'So no walking along the hedgerows at dawn or dusk. Here, try.'

He pours the last of the Sancerre into a glass and I taste the tiniest amount. It has what I can only describe as bracing acidity. My notes say gooseberry but, frankly, it tastes like that wine you left in the fridge for a week.

'It's going well, isn't it?' says Roxy sliding up next to us, handing Bill an empty bottle of sparkling water, nodding that she needs another. 'We're nearly out of the sherry.'

'Oh, but the duck!'

'I know, we'll just have to pair something different while we wait for a new delivery.'

She looks at me, waiting, and I swiftly reply, 'Well, get on it. What do you recommend?'

Roxy beams. 'I'll come back to you before evening service tomorrow.'

One of the younger waiters wanders past with a large black tray to deliver the main course for table four. My tongue rolls out of my mouth at the smell. Venison, three ways, with porcini and barley. I must remember to ask Anis what the foamy white stuff is on top of the loin. My stomach rumbles.

I so want to learn to cook this stuff. Even just one or two of the dishes, to roll out for a hot date or to impress Heather.

'Do you mind if I go into the kitchen and watch for a bit?' I say, longing to find out how they get that blackened crust to cling to the outside of that lean burgundy flesh. 'Tables four and five are done.

Oh, balls, a gin and a splash of tonic for Mrs Cardiff. She had an alter-cation with the Sancerre.'

I point to the almost-empty bottle on the bar and raise my eye-brows.

'I can take it from here,' says Roxy, pulling at her ponytail to tighten it. Her equivalent of cracking one's knuckles.

In the kitchen, James is mid-service and looking deliciously sweaty and pink-cheeked. I head over to Anis, who is overseeing a very young chef (young enough still to have teenage acne) putting together a very delicate lavender ice-cream dessert. His hands are shaking, bless him, and every time Anis barks an order, he shrinks further into his oversized whites. *He won't masturbate for a week*, I think.

Anis turns to me and nods in recognition. There is no smile, but I'm realizing that is not the telltale for warmth or approval with her.

'How's it going?'

'Good. Everyone seems to be loving the venison. Think it's going to be a winner when we open properly.'

'Too many things on that bloody plate,' she replies. 'And as for the fucking foam . . .'

'Can I ask a favour?'

'I don't do favours,' she says, before her eyes narrow. 'But what?'

'Could you show me how you make it?'

She straightens up and her brows descend to meet her suspicious eyes. 'Why?'

I look left and right and step closer, my voice dropping to a whis-per. 'I'm a terrible cook.'

'Bit fiddly for home cooking,' she replies, straight-faced. 'Do you really have the patience to tend simmering bones for several hours, just to make the jus?'

'In one of those big witch's cauldrons you're always stirring?'

'Yes.'

'Perhaps not,' I agree with her, 'but I'd like to try at least.'

'That'll do. Send it,' Anis says to the young chef, who scurries off in relief.

'What are you two whispering about?' James asks, sidling up to us and leaning casually against the service area, undoing the top two buttons of his top to let the air in.

'Heather here wants to learn how to cook.'

James looks amused, but nods his head in approval. 'Yes, I know. Sounds like quite a challenge too.'

'What's the challenge? Are we doing another challenge?' Roxy walks in, removing her apron and grabbing one of Russell's tiny artisan dinner rolls from the service area and downing it almost in one. 'Last summer we had a challenge to grow something edible in the garden. Brett won with his massive cucumber.'

'Everyone loves a massive cucumber,' I say, nodding my head in approval.

'James was very upset it beat his carrot,' Roxy teases. 'But worst off was poor old Bill, who couldn't get anything to grow.'

'What are you doing all crowded in the kitchen? This is not a house party,' says Irene, clapping. 'Table two are awaiting that dessert, Anis!'

'Heather wants to learn how to cook,' explains James.

'Okay, everyone. Calm down. I just want to make that one venison dish.'

'Well, you can't make that venison at home,' Anis continues, obviously still concerned. 'If it's home cooking you're after, you'll want a good ragu for spaghetti or a nice spicy curry.'

'Who do you want to cook for?' James chips in.

'No one,' I snap. 'This is ridiculous, I simply wanted to learn a bloody recipe.'

'Is it true you can't cook?' says Bill, who has strolled in to join the commotion.

'Fuck this!' I say, laughing now.

'You must be able to cook something. I don't buy that you could know that much about wine and not be able to cook at least a spaghetti bolognese,' says Bill. 'Let's start with the basics. Can you open a tin can?'

Everyone is laughing now, and normally in such a situation I would feel a bit prickly, but there's a warmth to the ribbing.

'Can you boil an egg?' Roxy asks.

'I can make fish and chips,' I say.

'Oh, I mean that's not the easiest. You need to do a batter, and at least twice-cook the chips. There's *some* method,' Anis says generously, and I decide not to explain that I actually meant I could open a plastic bag of frozen pre-battered cod.

There's a huge gust of wind through the kitchen, and bright sunlight spills onto the floor as a hulking frame fills the doorway. Brett has arrived, rugged and windswept, and yet carrying a very delicate basket filled with what looks like large clover. It's quite a contrasting sight.

'Wood sorrel,' he says, gently placing the basket on the counter.

'Maybe I should learn to forage for food instead,' I say.

'Get Anis to take you – no one knows these banks as well as she does,' he says, and Anis rolls her eyes, but I'm fairly sure I see a little red in her cheeks.

'I already have to teach her how to bloody cook,' Anis says.

'Now, Heather, you know I've already offered,' says James, flicking a tea towel casually over his shoulder. I look over at him and feel a sweet thrill at being teased by him. I don't answer right away, but a big smile spreads across my face.

'Thank fuck for that,' Anis says, as she picks up the wood sorrel and takes it to the sink to clean. 'I'm busy enough.'

'All right everyone, time to get cleaned down,' Irene says, and our little party disperses. But as I go to leave, she grabs me by the arm.

'Darling, I really need you to sort out your bank details, so we can set you up on the system.'

'Absolutely. I'll get on to it next week,' I say, nodding. She's asked me about this a couple of times in the last few days, and I still have no idea what to do about it. I was hoping that three months of rent-free work would mean I could leave with a bit of cash to pay back Heather for the room. Maybe a deposit to rent a flat of my own. But it's no good if I can't give her any bank details.

'Well, let me know, or I can pay you in cash,' she says. 'We sometimes pay the European staff in cash; it's just easier and quicker than getting them set up for a few months over the summer.'

'Oh well. I mean, if it's easier,' I say, feeling the tightening in my chest relax.

'Great. In the meantime, I know you're supposed to be having a rest before evening service, but could I trouble you for some advice?'

'Sure.'

As we walk through the bar area I see Roxy cleaning the table of a very wobbly Izzy Cardiff. She look like she's had a right knees-up, whereas her husband looks like he might fall asleep at any moment. There is another couple by the window, the lady in a wheelchair, her younger gentleman friend feeding her the lavender ice-cream dish with a spoon.

'That's Zelda and Charles,' Irene whispers. 'A lovely couple. She *can* eat perfectly well herself, don't be fooled.'

I follow her through, but we are stopped in the hallway by a fidgety German woman in at least her fifties. '*Die Toiletten*?' she barks, as she dances from foot to foot like a toddler.

'Down the hall to the left, Ms Schneider,' Irene replies loudly, as if Ms Schneider is both foreign *and* hearing-impaired.

'So,' she says, taking a seat at the little round table by the window, 'I've asked all the staff this, but as someone who has worked in London, I figure you will have some ideas.'

'Shoot,' I say, plonking down next to her. God, I hope she doesn't ask me something about wine.

'With the renovations more or less tied up, we're looking for ways to attract younger people here,' she says, sliding her glasses on and looking at me expectantly, her little leather notebook open on the table and a pen in her hand.

I nod earnestly.

'I wondered if you have any ideas?'

This I can do. 'Off the top of my head, you definitely need a new website.'

'Oh, that will be finished next week. Russell has a company he uses.'

'Oh, good. Yes, your old website was very out of date. People would be quite shocked when they arrived – they're two entirely different propositions,' I say, sounding rather more irritated than I mean to be, but I'm speaking from personal experience here.

'Well, I hope it would be a *good* surprise?' Irene says, frowning.

'But regardless, that is taken care of. Do you have any other thoughts? I just . . . well . . . with all your experience, I thought you might know what places like the Dorchester, or somewhere more fashionable like the Soho House group, do to help attract clients.'

'Umm . . . are you guys on social networks?'

'James does Instagram, but it's a personal account. Russell of course has his own accounts, I believe.'

'Well, you need the restaurant to be on those channels. Could you ask him? And why don't you contact some PR people in London and invite some influencers up to stay for free?'

'Influencers? Like critics?'

I suppress a giggle. 'Ah, not quite. More like young people that other young people aspire to be.'

'Famous people then.'

'Well, not exactly. Sort of Internet-famous. Like instead of being pop stars or something, they are kind of famous for being themselves.'

'Really?'

'It's a whole ridiculous thing,' I say, 'but it really does work. Those people have tons of followers and can really give you a boost.'

'Internet-famous,' she nods, writing it down. 'And to stay for free?' She nods again. 'To what end?'

'Well, they might post on their own accounts, so in the end it's advertising.'

Bluffing my way into that digital media job might have had its uses, after all. It's great to feel like I have something to offer here.

'And can I be super-honest?'

'Please. It's for the hotel.'

'I just think . . . the food: it's amazing, but have you considered a more casual approach – for the bar and terrace, for example? Especially for the tourists who only want a warming bowl of Cullen skink, or maybe kippers for breakfast. I mean, on the train I was looking up Scottish food, and those were the things I was looking forward to.'

'No, no, that will never do. Alongside his vision for the interiors, Russell's menu was *the* big improvement,' she says. 'What with the Michelin stars and whatnot. And Mr MacDonald insisted on Russell.'

'Oh, okay.'

'We want this place to be . . . ah, modern luxury, but we need more of a mix of people here. Mrs Cardiff's wine consumption won't pay all our bills. Most of our bills. But not all.'

'Well, I can keep thinking,' I say, hands on the table, ready to stand.

'Please do, Heather,' she says with a smile. 'It's all finally happening now. After a lot of planning, we're ready to go. We just need a good review from *The Scotsman*, and for word to get out. I'm confident.'

'That's great.'

'Bill tells me you're really finding your feet here?'

'Getting my head around things, yes.'

'Good, good. Now, Heather,' she says, a little more seriously. She takes off her glasses and folds them up. 'Will you be taking James up on his offer of cooking lessons?'

I shuffle in my seat a bit, feeling embarrassed. 'Well, I mean if he's busy and if you don't think it's a good idea . . .'

'I don't mind the idea as such,' she says, pausing to look down at a ring on her little finger, which she spins as she continues. She is uncomfortable for the first time since I met her. Then I realize. She's worried about James.

'Oh, Irene, you don't need to worry . . .' I begin to formulate a response in my head, but I'm stuck. She's worried that I might hurt him. And isn't she right to worry?

'Why don't you do it at my house?' she suggests. 'I have a proper home kitchen, and you can't do it at that cottage. James says the oven only works on grill . . .'

I nod, not sure what to say. It's almost like James is still a teenager and needs to be protected. But it will keep us both on the straight and narrow, I suppose, and I really do want to learn how to cook.

'That sounds like a great idea,' I say enthusiastically, and she looks relieved.

'Okay. Well, let's leave it until after the relaunch, though. How does that sound? So Monday week?'

'Perfect! This placement is basically going to be the finishing school I never had. All I need is to learn Scottish, and how to play the lute, and I'll return to England ready to marry a barrister.'

'Yes, dear,' says Irene, passing zero visible judgement.

19.

June

It's Sunday afternoon and the last shift before the big launch on Tuesday night. Everyone is either working in the kitchen or deep-cleaning the dining area. Roxy and I have just finished the stocktake, and she has arranged to meet Tom later in the week to go over the shortlist for the Wine Society event. News came back that President Matthew Hunt was thrilled with the 'English wine' idea, so now Russell and Irene are fully on board too.

'What will you do with your days off?' Roxy asks now.

'Well, tomorrow and Tuesday I'm going to chill and make sure I'm a hundred per cent across the list, but from next Monday, James is going to teach me to cook,' I say, trying not to beam too much.

'Oooh, you're going to learn,' says Roxy.

'Though, honestly, I feel like I don't deserve any days off yet,' I say. And it's weird, but for the first time ever I really do feel like that.

'I'm sure you'll have your nose in that notebook, as per usual,' she teases, as I quickly slip it back into my jeans pocket.

'How else do you remember?' I ask her, feeling a little defensive. 'There are over ten thousand wines, you know. Nearly a hundred and thirty at this restaurant alone.'

'Oh, sorry,' she says, and bites her lip. 'I was just being silly. I'm sorry.'

'Stop saying "sorry". You haven't done anything wrong,' I say with a sigh.

'Sorry,' she says and then covers her mouth, her eyes wide.

I laugh at her. She's so fucking fresh.

'What do you think makes a good sommelier?' I say, as casually as possible.

'Um,' she looks at me, and then to the wine rack behind me. 'I guess a good sommelier should be able to recommend wines that go with each dish. Maybe a couple of choices? Perhaps a slightly unusual one, for adventurous diners. They shouldn't assume anyone's budget – instead, they should guide people to price options they are comfortable with.' She pauses, looking to the floor. 'That's what I've seen you do really well.'

I feel all warm inside at this compliment. It is true I do try to put people at ease – but not because I am good at my job, more because I know what it's like to feel intimidated.

'Well, it sucks to feel poor,' I reply. 'Sucks even worse to *actually* be poor, I might add. No one who comes here is truly poor.'

'How can you read people so well?'

'What do you mean?'

'You seem to have that intuition. Irene has it too. Like, have you seen her predict a diner? You'll have to ask her one day,' she says, picking up her phone and putting the stocktaking book back on the shelf.

'What does she do?'

'When people arrive she will predict, to within ten pounds, what they will spend. How much they will drink. Where they're from. Why they're dining with us. It's incredible. Bill tries to trip her up by upselling, but he hardly ever manages.'

'Well, that *is* impressive.'

'Are you sure you want to chill tomorrow?' she asks again, and I can tell she wants to suggest something.

'Yeah. I need to get my head round everything. Catch my breath.'

'You should go out on the horses – have you met Brett properly?'

'Yes, he treated my sprained ankle,' I reply, following her up the stairs to the kitchen.

'He's really nice. I couldn't believe it when I was told he was in prison.'

'No! What for?'

'It was when he was, like, eighteen – he robbed a shop in Glasgow. I mean, so the rumour goes.'

'Good God.'

'Oh, don't be scared. He's the nicest person I know. Like most of the staff, he got a job here at Last-Chance Saloon. That's what Anis calls it.'

'Why?'

'Because most people here are on the run, or at the end of the road. Irene collects strays.'

'Are you a stray?'

'Not yet,' she says with a grin. 'Seriously, go riding! Get Brett to take you out on one of the horses. There's an amazing trek right along the loch. He should have time.'

'Oh shit, no. I'm too scared,' I reply.

'Don't be scared. He'll put you on one of the old ones, you'll be fine. Do it!' she says, grinning. 'I promise you'll love it.'

'Okay, Roxy,' I say, humouring her.

Then she's gone. Almost skipping down the hill to the cottages.

The sun is more powerful this afternoon, *almost* warming. I shrug my trench off and toss it over my shoulder, as the ground below me becomes more sodden and muddy.

I pull out my phone and there's a message from Tim.

It's shit in London. Damo isn't drinking this week and they've shut down the Rose and Crown for the new rail line.

Nothing to do in London when his favourite pub is closed is *so* Tim. If I was there, we would have been moaning about it together and moping along to the Market Porter, to try to make do with a substandard pale ale at tourist prices for Tim, and rancid white-wine spritzers for me. I miss the markets in Borough, though. Our favourite haunt: me and Heather. Mooching around on a Saturday morning was great, but we most liked to go after work on a Friday night. Heather knew the staff at several of the restaurants, so there was always somewhere to pull up a pew and get drunk.

Tim only ever went to the Rose and Crown, though. And without fail he would end up doing something hilarious, like swimming naked in the Thames, being photographed by tourists who had accidentally strayed south of Tower Bridge and were astonished to learn that not all English people are from Downton Abbey, or Mary Poppins.

I wander downwards and come to what has to be the now thoroughly overgrown kitchen garden, a fenced-off rectangle on a slope, with a half-dozen terraces joined by little well-trodden walkways.

From here, the house is mostly obscured by the bank. Two horses lazily eat grass behind the stables, and I can just make out the top of one of the cottages.

I decide to keep walking down the bank.

The valley hits the river upstream from where I started the walk with James the other day, so I know there is a path I can follow. I struggle through some waist-high bushes and tumble out onto it. I decide to walk in the opposite direction, downstream, to see where it comes out. I know there is a loch here, but I've not seen it yet. The windy path has been neatly cleared for hikers. Then it takes a sharper turn downwards, but the roots of the trees have formed natural little stairs and I can easily make my way down.

As the trees ahead start to thin, the stony river spreads to a wide, low stream, cutting ribbons through the pebbles as it races to join the mass of cool, dark-blue water ahead. I pick up speed and chase the river out onto the bank, and gasp.

A beautiful lake – loch – dark and wild, with bare grey-and-green hills rising up on all sides. The wind blows gently around my ankles and up my body in little gusts. Above, sheets of grey-and-white clouds blow slowly across the sky, obscuring the sun and plunging the temperature down momentarily. I spot a large, flat rock to my right and decide to sit and take in the view. There is something about this kind of beauty that reflects back to us the best we can be.

I feel, for a moment, absolutely at peace.

My mind wanders back to London and sitting on the pier in Wapping by the Prospect of Whitby with Heather, staring out across the Thames. She had just turned eighteen and had finally received the inheritance her father had left her. It was a weird, bittersweet moment.

She had wanted to drink and talk about her dad. It was one of those strange, disconnected conversations where I struggled to find true empathy. I couldn't imagine losing my dad, but I also couldn't imagine truly caring about it. How do you care about losing someone who believes, like *really* believes, that 5G and Bill Gates are the greatest threats to humans since vaccines? But for Heather, it was like she had lost her handsome prince. Her absolute everything.

After his heart attack, Heather had stayed on in Plymouth with her stepmother, who was kind enough, but not really good at parenting and pretty openly resented inheriting a daughter. Since neither of us had boundaries or curfews or rules, like other children, we became utterly inseparable.

Then she was sent off to board at thirteen, and our friendship briefly faltered. I remember Heather came back that first year with pink nails, and I teased her mercilessly until she took the polish off. And then I felt guilty, and stole money from my mum to buy some more pink nail polish so we could both have pink nails.

Heather helped me make sense of my parents. It was easy to understand Dad, he was a drunk. But Mum was confusing. It wasn't just her obsession with bat-shit conspiracy theories, she lived a different reality from the one I could see in front of me, and it made me feel . . . unsure.

'Your mum only told the teacher it was your fault you were late again because she doesn't want them to call social services,' she'd tell me. I was never sure what social services would do, but it always sounded infinitely scarier than having a dad who was sometimes very drunk. Besides, I had a roof over my head. Food on the table. I wasn't *neglected*.

And when Heather took her report cards home and pinned them to the fridge, only to have them tidied away by her stepmother, I would celebrate her results with her. We were family. It was just her and me, plugging the gaps in each other's lives wherever we could.

It didn't matter how much her life changed, and the successes she made for herself, she always came back to me. And no wonder. I wasn't going anywhere – literally or figuratively.

I think Heather should have come here. I think it might have connected her to her mother, and I wonder why she so abruptly bailed out of this gig. Was Cristian really the whole reason? It was so strangely out of character. Had I missed something?

I throw a stone out into the water and it makes a heavy, musical sound before it sinks to the invisible deep.

I have a moment of new regret that I may have taken that from Heather. It always feels like I am the one of us who needs shoring up – after all, I have the dreadful parents. But Heather is alone in a different way. I think back to our conversation at her house over a month ago now, when I watched her telling me about Cristian. The nervous hope on her face that this guy could be the one who would replace that unconditional love she so desperately missed.

I didn't intervene because whenever I'd tried to in the past, Heather would get distant and withdrawn – and I'd made a decision to support her always. That way, whatever happened, she knew she could always come back. A bit like I think a parent should.

I think about calling her, but I know I cannot hear her voice right now.

Shaking off my thoughts, I pull myself up and take off my filthy sneakers, roll my trousers up and tiptoe to the water's edge, standing just far enough back that the water needs to come to me.

'That's the wrong place to dive in,' says a voice. It's Bill.

'Hi!' I say, a little disappointed at the interruption.

'I still haven't had a chance to thank you.' He looks ahead to the horizon on the loch. 'For the other day.'

'Don't mention it,' I say, not really wanting to talk about it with him. I already knew what he was going to say anyway. *Sorry—*

'Sorry,' he says.

'Bill. It doesn't matter,' I say, shooting him a dismissive look.

'You are really coming on,' he says, after some time.

'I'm feeling confident,' I reply quickly.

'It's like you're a whole new woman . . .'

'Okay, okay,' I say, crossing my arms. 'I'm sorry about my shitty first week. But I'm on top of things now. I won't let you or Irene down. I promise.'

He nods seriously, as though to say 'I have no doubt', then leans down to pick up a rock. He tries to skim it, but it only jumps twice. I remember again the conversation I overheard between him and Irene, and turn to him and smile.

'What?' he asks.

'Nothing. Just,' I pick up a stone myself, and run my finger along the smooth oval edge, 'thanks for backing me up.'

'I don't want you to fail,' he says.

I sigh and look out to the water. The loch is spectacular – open, exposed and wild. 'I think I might love it here,' I say wistfully. I toss the stone forward into the lake. It skips once, twice, three, four, five times.

'Most people who come to the west coast for work are running away or hiding from something, or both.'

'Most people on the west coast, or most people here?' I ask, looking across at him. 'Roxy tells me this is the Last-Chance Saloon. Irene's home for lost souls.'

Bill laughs. 'Well, it's true in a way, I suppose. She likes to help people who have nowhere else to go.'

'Is that right?' I say, looking around for my socks and shoes. It's getting cold.

'Why did you come here?'

'What?' I say. 'To the loch?'

'To this job? Really, why did you come?' Bill says as he buttons up his coat. I shiver and shove my feet into my sneakers.

I turn to him. I don't know what he wants from me. 'For some peace?' I say lightly, and I shoot him a smile as I take off up the path.

20.

A weird calmness comes over me as I think about the service ahead
today. I've done as much as I can to prepare. The two weeks of renovations have bought me enough time to cram all the information on the
wine list that I can, writing everything down in my little notebook so
that I have a reminder if I forget while on shift; and Roxy's eagerness
to learn means that I have another person to lean on. Bill has been as
good as his word, 'shadowing' me at every moment he could spare,
gently pointing out wine suggestions if he sensed even a moment's
hesitation from me. It feels vaguely like he's watching me, which I
suppose he is. But his tone is never unkind or impatient. It feels, bless
him, like he's truly trying to help me.

The weird thing is how people just *believe*. They believe I'm Heather,
and they believe I'm a wine expert. They don't see Elizabeth Finch –
Birdy to her friends – thirty-one years old, a girl lacking in credentials
and experience, owner of a CV filled with a million different jobs, a
risk-taker, liar, gobshite, daughter of conspiracy theorists. They see
Heather. Or maybe a bit of both of us, I allow myself.

Irene is ushering all the staff into the new-look dining area.

'Everyone, gather round!' she is saying. 'Welcome to our proper
launch! Doesn't the room look fabulous?'

There is a muted round of applause. I don't know Irene that well,
but it seems to me she doesn't think it's *that* fabulous. It's okay,
though – as masculine-looking as before, but less twee, more modern. Gone are the linen-covered chairs and tables, replaced with dark
wood and leather. I'm happy to see Mr MacDonald's portrait still in
pride of place on the far wall.

'And so the summer is nearly upon us. We have several big
moments this season. Obviously the Highland Wine Society will be

the big test. And we have the film-premiere wrap party coming up. Lots of major players attending, who will be looking at how well the new Loch Dorn can throw a world-class event.'

There is a murmur of excitement from the younger staff.

'Settle down, settle down,' she says, grinning. 'Most importantly, we have had word that a very special guest will be dining here in the next few weeks, though we're not entirely sure which night.'

'Last time she said that, it was Tom Hardy and his wife,' whispered Roxy.

'Oh God, he's my undoing,' I reply.

'Too old,' Roxy replies. 'I'm more of a Noah Centineo type of girl.'

'Too wet,' I reply, shaking my head.

'Yes, I would be,' she replies, before bursting into a giggle, which gets her a frown from Irene. I feign outrage at her filthy mouth.

'With the renovations complete, and the restaurant ready for its relaunch under the brilliant work of our new executive head chef, Russell, it should come as no surprise that we're getting a visit from one Josh Rippon, writing for *The Scotsman*. As you know, he's notoriously difficult to please . . .'

'I didn't catch that,' I whisper to Roxy. 'Who did she say?'

'Josh Rippon – you know him, he's like the funniest restaurant critic ever. But also the most brutal. Ugh! Every single service will be a drag until he's been. He needs to hurry up and come.'

'Oh Christ,' I say.

'You must have had a million reviewers before.'

'Oh, I've *had* reviewers,' I joke.

But seriously. A reviewer now? I only just finished memorizing the wine list, and I've not really been tested.

'Oh my God, Heather, you're too much,' Roxy says, giggling.

Irene sends us another frown. 'So, everyone, tonight: be nice, don't fuss – and move the venison.' She stops talking and waits for Roxy to stop giggling. 'Ladies! Are you all caught up?'

I mouth *Sorry* to her.

'Josh Rippon,' says Roxy confidently. 'Be nice, don't fuss – try to move the lamb?'

'The venison.'

'Sorry,' says Roxy, giving Irene the thumbs up.

'That's all. See you back here at six sharp.'

She claps her hands and the small group disperses, as Roxy grabs my arm. 'Do you want to hang out?'

'I have to do a final check on the wines,' I say.

'Can I come with you to the cellar and help?'

'I also need to make a call,' I say, pulling a disappointed face.

I have not spoken to Heather in days. We've been on WhatsApp, but suddenly I have an urgent need to speak to her. I'm sure something's going on with Cristian. She hasn't said so, but I can always tell with Heather.

I make my way to the cellar. The fourth step is the best one to get coverage, so I sit on the cold stone and dial her number. She answers on the third ring.

'Birdy,' she says breathlessly, and I feel a rush of love at her voice, and the sound of my very own name.

'How are you doing?'

'Oh, great,' she says, and I'm surprised to hear her sounding like I've woken her up. It's six p.m.

'Are you tired?' I say.

'I was taking a nap,' she replies. 'Sorry. How are you?'

'There is absolutely nothing to report, but I want to hear about you, and the big romance. How is it all going? You've seemed a bit flat?'

'No, no. It's okay. I've realized that my Italian wine knowledge is a bit lacking, so I've been practising that, and my Italian. I've got the time, which is a wonderful luxury.'

'You've got good Italian,' I say.

'I have restaurant Italian, which basically means I can order food,' she laughs. 'You think anyone who says hello in an Irish accent is bilingual.'

I laugh. She's right. I'm absolutely hopeless at languages. Learning to pronounce the names of the various European wines has been one of the biggest parts of the challenge.

'I just wanted to check in seriously that you're okay,' I say. 'It's a big thing going to Italy with someone you're getting to know – even if it's only temporary or whatever. Especially with the girlfriend complication.'

'Yes,' she agrees, but stops short of revealing whether Cristian's still got a girlfriend or not, and I don't want to push her.

'Okay, so you're great, Cristian is great and you love Italy?' I say.

'Well, of course it's not *all* great,' she sighs. 'There are lots of challenges, but Cristian is looking after me well. I see him most days.'

'Well, that's good. But I have to say something, and can you please listen? I'll feel like a shit friend if I don't say it, okay?'

'Um, okay.'

'I know you feel very strongly about Cristian, and I *know* you made the best decision for you in that moment,' I say, 'but I want you to know that if you have any doubts, or need anything from me – like, ever – call me and I will jump on a plane if I can, okay?'

Silence on the line from Heather, and I hope I haven't overstepped the mark. I hope it's both supportive of her decision and offers the safety net she needs, just in case.

'I had to say it,' I say quickly.

'Okay,' she says quietly. 'I'll let you know. I promise.'

I breathe out a bit, and then ask the question that has been playing on my mind since that afternoon by the loch.

'I wanted to ask you something that I was thinking about . . . like, um, randomly. That job – the one in Scotland that you didn't want.'

'Loch Dorn,' she says. 'I never thanked you for calling them.'

'Well, yes, but I wanted to ask you why?'

'Why what?'

'Why you wanted to go there? And then why you suddenly didn't? I mean, other than Cristian, of course.'

Heather sighs and there's another long silence down the line.

'I dunno. Do you ever want to go somewhere and simply start all over again?'

'Um, yeah. All the time,' I laugh. 'It's me, remember.'

'I wanted to see if I could make it work . . .' Her voice trails off, and I'm not sure if she's talking about Scotland or about taking off to Italy. 'I think I'm lonely, Birdy. Like a big part of me is missing.'

Bloody Cristian again.

'We all want to be loved,' I say.

'Yeah, and someone to be proud of us.'

'I'm proud of you,' I say. 'I can't believe all you've achieved.'

'I know,' she says, but I can hear in her voice it is not enough. It's her father and her mother that she wants to be proud of her.

'Well, if you mean your mum and dad, I'm sure they are beyond proud of everything you've done with your life,' I try. 'If there is a heaven, they would be that dull couple forcing everyone to watch home videos of you.'

'It's a nice thought. Better to have loved and lost, and all that . . .'

I'm not sure if we're talking about Cristian now or her parents, or what.

'You'll never lose me.'

'Well, *that* I know,' she replies, sighing. 'Sorry, I've just woken up and I'm feeling a bit morose. Must be coming on. How are you?'

'Oh. Me? Don't worry about me,' I say, as I try to squash down the rising guilt. 'My latest and possibly worst fuck-up is a story for another day.'

'God, what's happened?' Heather says quickly.

'It's a story for over a pint, in London, or wherever we next see each other, okay?'

'Okay,' she says. 'I think I need that promise.'

'I absolutely promise,' I say, determined to tell her the entire story. Once I've made a success of it, obviously. Then perhaps she'll be able to forgive me.

'I love you,' she says.

'Me too,' I reply. 'Oh, fuck!' I say, hearing the cellar door open as Roxy appears in the doorway above me.

'First table is about to arrive,' she whispers.

'I have to go!'

'Okay,' Heather says warmly. 'Speak soon.'

I spring up the stairs two at a time and straighten my shirt. I stand up straight, shoulders back, and push through the kitchen doors, pausing momentarily to smile at James as he nods back at me. I'm trying to ignore the building excitement I'm feeling about our looming cooking lesson, but it's hard when every time we catch each other's eye I see James's excitement too. Except today. Today, we've got other things to focus on.

Here we go.

I watch as Irene takes the table of four to their little table at the bay window. She glides across the floor towards me and whispers into my ear, 'A bottle of champagne – could you please recommend one for them?'

'On my way,' I say, walking towards the table.

It's a slightly younger party than I'm used to seeing, which means a far more relaxed expectation of service, and I feel immediately at ease. Jeans, beards, denim shirts, trainers on the men, the girls dolled up in midi-dresses, with those perfect brows that look almost like they've been applied with a thick black felt-tip pen. I think of my own brows, which I sometimes lovingly refer to as my 'face bush', and wonder if it's time for a wax.

'Champagne?' I ask the guy to my right, who nods across at his partner.

'Yes, please,' she answers.

'It's a little pricier,' I say, opening the list to the first page and running my finger down, 'but can I recommend the Ruinart Brut Rosé. It's absolutely luscious. And peachy-pink.'

'Ooh, that sounds lovely,' she coos.

'Fabulous,' I smile. 'And I do really suggest you go for the degustation. Your choice of five or seven courses. Fresh scallops from Skye, hauled in off the boats this morning by a guy called Benji. The venison is to *die* for. Although, the poor doe might not agree with that assessment . . .'

They all laugh, and I bask in the warm glow of it.

'I'll go and get your champagne, and your waiter will be along to take your food order. And if you need any recommendations, please ask.'

I walk back to the bar and straight to Bill, who is smiling and nodding at me.

'Look at you! On fire, young lady.'

'As long as everyone keeps ordering champagne,' I grin.

'Need a hand with the cork?' he says teasingly, sliding it across the counter to me, as Irene joins me and pats me gently on the back.

'You've got a good way with people,' she says. 'A natural host.'

'This doesn't feel chilled,' I say to Bill, arching an eyebrow. 'Can you grab one from the back of the fridge?'

'Very well,' he says, glancing across at Irene, who bites her lip and beams with delight, gliding off to meet the next table.

We nailed it.

Even Russell, who arrived about an hour into service, nit-picking at everyone, seems thrilled with our performance.

We gather round the bar for a drink, and Irene pours out several modestly filled glasses of Prosecco, as the kitchen staff, all sweaty and red-faced, shuffle through to join us. She is jubilant and raises her glass into the air.

'Well done, everyone. That was absolutely brilliant, for our opening service. I'm proud of all of you.' She looks over to me and nods as if she's especially proud of me, and I feel a thrill of pride in return.

'To the all-new Loch Dorn,' she says.

'To the all-new Loch Dorn,' we all repeat, clinking our glasses. I give Roxy a hug and then Irene.

'May we pay off the creditors and piss off the competitors,' I say, and everyone laughs. I catch James's eye and, as I wonder if it would be normal to give him a hug, I realize he's already moving my way. He throws his arms around me and whispers, 'Well done' in my ear, and the warmth of his breath on my neck makes me pull away, feeling instantly shy.

'Well done to you, too!' I say, sipping on my glass, feeling my cheeks burn.

'Didn't she do great?' says Bill, grinning as he slaps me gently on the back. 'Good for you – you only went and aced it.' I'm thrilled to notice that Bill is not sharing in the celebratory Prosecco.

'Thanks for all your help, Bill,' I reply.

I look round the room and I feel a real sense of something new. Happiness certainly, but it's something else too. I want to say 'belonging', but that's not quite it. I look over at Irene, who is almost crumpled over the bar with relief, and tear myself from the magnetic pull of James.

'How are you feeling?' I ask gently. 'Want a top-up?'

'Oh yes, go on then,' Irene says, smiling. 'If everyone can bring this energy to the film-wrap party next Tuesday evening, we might just come through this.'

'That gig is important, isn't it?'

'Crucial. Once you have the best event of the summer, people hear about it and then you start getting the big weddings and other events booked in for next year. It's a huge income-stream for us.'

'I'm sure we'll nail it,' I say.

'Oh, I think you won't be going, so don't worry. We don't usually need a sommelier, as it's a very short wine list. Plus you'll need to be on here.'

'Well, I'm sure they'll do great.'

'I know. I know. I am so proud of everyone I could cry, really I could. They've all worked so hard and come so far. They had only basic experience, some of them. Just local kids, really. And look at them now! It's a miracle, it really is.'

'It's brilliant,' I reply, filling her glass. 'Everyone has done an amazing job.'

Everyone, including me, I think to myself, a little grin creeping slowly across my face.

And then I realize the feeling that is filling my heart is not only a sense of belonging. Or feeling like part of a team. It's pride in myself. Quiet, personal pride.

And it feels good.

21.

Irene's cottage is everything I expected: eccentric, with its jewel-toned soft furnishings and odd little Art Nouveau pieces; welcoming, with its lambskins and cashmere throws; and practical, with heavy, hardwood furniture and floors. It was an easy drive in James's car – a mere eight minutes to get to it – but I know that Irene stays at the hotel for much of the week, and I find it a bit sad the place must be left empty so often.

James is in jeans and a black T-shirt, with a blue-and-white striped apron tied round his waist.

'You're very brave, wearing white,' he says.

'I'm hoping it shows up the blood,' I say, pulling a large butcher's knife out of the wooden block next to me. Thankfully, he laughs. And then I feel my cheeks burn red and look quickly away.

'So, all joking aside, where are you at, with cooking?'

'I know how to burn toast,' I reply, and he shakes his head.

'I just don't believe it. You work in restaurants! What do you do when you're at home, back in London?'

'Ready meals. And my friend . . . ah, flatmate, she likes to cook.'

'Seriously? What about your boyfriend?'

'Oh.' I feel my cheeks redden. 'Well, he's more of your kebab-on-the-way-home type of foodie.'

Which is frankly being generous. The last time we ate together was at our regular greasy spoon in Bermondsey. Tim had, as always, menu number one: two eggs, two bacon, two sausages, tomato, mushrooms, fried toast and black pudding, which he never touched. I had baked beans on toast with a cup of sweet tea. The mood was hangover-grim, and Tim was smelly, sweaty and snappy.

'Okay, okay, okay,' I say, pushing Tim's grey complexion out of my mind. 'I can put a roast chicken in the oven, and follow instructions on how to roast it. I can peel potatoes and carrots. But, like, the chicken skin never crisps, and the breasts are dry. I can't seem to whisk egg whites properly. And I'm not sure what all the settings on an oven are. Like what's the fan with the circle versus the fan without? And honestly, with ready meals, I know it's not too fattening and I get a nice variety. Curry one day, bangers-and-mash the next.'

'God, that's depressing,' James says, shaking his head. 'I can't make you love cooking, Heather, but I am going to fucking try.'

Then he announces that he is dropping me right into the hot fat and teaching me how to make a soufflé.

'Did you hear my monologue before? I can't make a soufflé,' I remind him.

'You *can* make a soufflé,' he says, tossing me an apron.

'Ah, I don't even know what a soufflé is exactly, except that it's fancy. And literally no human in this day and age whips up a soufflé for dinner.'

'Can you crack an egg?'

'Yes.'

'Can you stir something over the heat?'

'Yes.'

'Can you read the time, and listen for an alarm?'

'Um, yes?'

'Then you can make a soufflé. Put that butter in a small saucepan.'

He's suddenly turned very bossy, and I like it.

I reach down below the stove and pull out a pan that I consider to be small, but he gently takes it out of my hand and passes me something small but very heavy, good for a couple of glasses of milk and no more.

'Sorry.'

'It's okay,' he says, biting his bottom lip to stop himself laughing. He's enjoying this. And I'm enjoying James enjoying it. He's given me a novelty apron, the kind you might get for Christmas; it's a cow with all the butcher's lines on it: Fore Quarter, Sirloin, Rump.

'How do I turn this thing on?' I say, playing the fool.

He leans over me, his forearm touching my shoulder as he presses down the gas knob and waits for it to spark. I feel the heat on my shoulder where his arm was, and now want to put other body parts in his way. I'm so distracted by being close to him that it's hard to concentrate.

'These are definitely not optimum soufflé-making conditions,' I mutter.

'Remove it from the heat and stir in the flour. That's right. Like that. This is called a roux.'

'Is it looking rouxly?'

'Concentrate,' he commands. 'Now return the pan to a low heat and cook for two minutes, whisking continuously. No, that's not whisking, that's stirring. You have to really give it some muscle. Like this.'

He takes the whisk off me, our fingers touching in the process. The mixture of stress and sexual chemistry is kind of overwhelming and I want to suggest a drink to calm my nerves, but I'm not sure it's wise.

He whisks, and it's like proper, strong whisking. I notice the slightest flex in his arms and decide that arms are now officially my thing.

James makes his way over to the large stainless-steel fridge, pulling out some smoked haddock and unwrapping it from its waxed paper.

'What time will your mum be back?'

'Later. Hours.'

'Oh, I thought she was going to be here.'

'She was, but I asked her to leave us to it. Does it smell like biscuits?'

'No, more like smoked fish?'

'No, the roux? In the saucepan.'

'Oh yes, I think so. Kind of? It's gone a pale browny kind of colour.'

'Cool! Now the milk.' He hands me a small stainless-steel jug, and I tip the whole lot into the saucepan.

'Ahh . . . we need to start again,' he says, taking the saucepan out of my hand. 'You're supposed to add it slowly.'

'Oh. Balls! Sorry.'

He tips my lumpy roux down the drain, wipes it clean and hands the saucepan back to me. I fall into the role of hopeless student, with a full pout and my best flirty eyes.

'Don't,' he says, shaking his head, trying to suppress his amusement. 'What?

'You're here to cook,' he says, picking up my arm and thrusting the saucepan back into my hand. 'Butter,' he barks, and I bite my lip in delight.

But then I turn to the stove top and remember that I actually want to cook – to learn something here. I pick up the block of butter and look back to the tin of flour and realize I've completely forgotten what I just did.

'Ugh,' I say turning to him. 'I don't remember how much flour. I'm hopeless.'

'Don't say that. Once you have the base-rules down, you'll be able to cook anything. I know a soufflé seems super-stuffy, but you'll learn a heap of different techniques from it.'

I nod emphatically and start again, and this time when I get to the milk I pause to ask him how to tip it in.

'A little at a time, until it is completely whisked in. We want a thick, glossy white sauce.'

'Okay,' I say, wanting to pretend I can't do it, so that he has to show me again.

'Time to focus – it's turning,' James says, and I turn my full attention to the pan.

'Is this nearly right?' I ask, and I am amazed to see exactly what he described appear in my pan. Thick, glossy white sauce. He dips a dessert spoon into it, and the sauce hugs the back of the spoon. I stick a finger in and lick the sauce off my finger, slowly, trying to figure out what it tastes of – but it doesn't taste of much, apart perhaps from a mildly cheesy, thick milk drink. I lick my lips.

'Don't do that again,' James says, taking the pan off me.

'Sorry – unhygienic,' I say rinsing my finger under the tap.

'Well, there's that too,' he says, shaking his head. 'Congratulations, Heather. The roux is one of the mother-sauces. It's the basis of béchamel, espagnole and velouté, and will thicken any soup or stew.'

'A mother-sauce?' I repeat.

'Yes.'

'Ooh, so versatile,' I swoon. 'It's like the Madonna of sauces.'

'Only far less saucy,' James says, without missing a beat.

'Very good bantering, James,' I say, teasing.

'I'll give you some recipes to take back, so you can practise.'

We leave the pan on a granite work surface 'to cool', then I am ordered to crack some eggs and beat the yolk into our slightly cooled roux. Some salt and pepper later, and apparently I'm on the home straight.

'Bit fancier than fish and chips, but easier than I thought,' I say, washing my hands and drying them on the front of my apron.

Then we are interrupted by Brett, who comes barrelling through the door with two small cocker spaniels; he is dressed in plaid breeks and olive wellingtons. Chaos ensues as the dogs scramble up our legs, looking for treats and ear scratches.

'Out! Bobby and Jaxon, out!' James orders, gently kicking away the jet-black dog as the other golden one sniffs at my crotch. I giggle and push him away, but he's as persistent as hell.

'What gorgeous dogs!'

'They're good boys,' Brett replies, nodding towards James as the dogs continue to pant and jump and bark in excitement. 'You learning how to rattle the pans, lass?' he says, stealing an apple from the basket by the door.

'Hi, Brett,' I say, tipping the pan and very nearly spilling its contents. 'Yes, look! I made a roux!'

'Good for you, lass,' Brett says, before turning to James. 'I've cut down the two remaining ash, but they weren't infected.'

'Well, better to get rid of them at least.'

'Aye,' he nods. 'I'll prepare them for the woodshed.'

James nods, and Brett lets out a piercing whistle and the dogs start to bark again and run madly in circles around the tiny kitchen.

'Out!' James shouts once more, and Brett is back out the door with a dog by the collar in each hand, and a whole apple jammed between his teeth.

'Does Brett help out round here too?' I ask, as the door shuts and the room falls happily back into silence.

'Only very occasionally,' James says. 'He's an all-rounder. Does Mum's roses.'

Then he snaps back into hot chef-mode and is on at me to butter some little ramekins. And poach the haddock. And I'm finding myself in a state of happy anticipation as I wait for my next instruction. I tuck my hair behind my ears and focus.

'That's it, now lower the fish into the simmering cream.'

I'm surprised by how satisfying this all is, as I marvel at the pan of bubbling haddock, and expertly sprinkle some grated Comté (a fancy French cheese) around the edge of the ramekins.

'It's kind of nutty and earthy,' James says, feeding me a small slither from the edge of a knife.

'Everything has so much fat,' I say, shaking my head. 'Butter, cream, cheese. My mum would have a heart attack. She wouldn't eat again for a week after one of these.'

'You can have a soufflé now and then!' he says, gasping. 'God, I hate the thought of someone dieting a soufflé out of their life.'

I laugh, but I'm also vaguely irritated. 'Everyone says that,' I scoff. '"You just have to eat properly." What do you mean by "properly"? Do you mean bone-broth and paleo, or vegan and plant-based? Do you mean low-fat, high-fat or intermittent fasting or super-low-calorie? Believe me, I've heard them all. My mum was on a diet my entire life. Every. Single. Day. It was probably a reaction to Dad's job. I didn't eat anything that wasn't part of one of her diets.'

'Don't think like that,' he finally says, after staring at me for a couple of beats. 'About food. You'll never enjoy it.'

'You're not a woman.'

He shakes his head and moves beside me to check on the fish, and we are hip-to-hip, the heat of the stove starting to make me sweat. I reach up with a tea towel and wipe my brow.

'I just hate the thought of all that deprivation,' James says quietly. 'It's, like, imagine you were a painter and people made rules not to use the colour yellow.'

I bite my lip, trying not to laugh, nodding, 'Mm-hmm.'

James looks vaguely mortified and I curse myself for teasing him. It's mean.

'You need to flake the haddock and whisk the egg whites now,' he says, back to business, and I oblige, draining the fishy cream into a saucepan and pulling the haddock gently apart with a fork. Once I'm done, he hands me a whisk. 'I don't think I'm really like a painter,' he says quietly, shaking his head. He's embarrassed, and it's all I can do not to throw my arms around him to soothe him. He shouldn't be embarrassed about being passionate about something. I'm making him unsure about himself, and I hate it.

'You *are* like a painter,' I say turning round. 'An artist. It's, like, totally art, innit?'

Why am I so allergic to being earnest? But he studies my face for a moment and then nods and smiles. It's enough.

'Soft peaks!'

He's pointing to the egg whites, and I lift out my whisk and the peaks do indeed gently fold over. I think about my mum and wonder if diets are why she is so joyless, but I suspect it mostly had to do with Dad. And perhaps the dieting was more about keeping up those appearances. Seeming to be together and in control.

He reaches his arms round me from behind and begins to fold everything in the bowl together gently. I can feel his chest brushing my back, but he's careful not to step too close.

I lean very gently back against his chest. My head sits right at his neck and I close my eyes, taking in the warmth from his firm chest on my back. We are still for a moment, as I enjoy the feel of the heat of James's body against mine. Everything suddenly disappears – the sounds, the smells – and the only feeling left is the heat between us.

He lifts his hand as if he's going to put it on my shoulder, and then stops and drops his hand to his side. Nearly. He *nearly* touched me. His breath is so very close to my ear and it is slow, deep and steady. Mine is not.

And then we hear the sound of the front door and the heavy squeak of hinges.

'James? Are you both still here?' calls Irene from the hallway.

I step away immediately, turning to face James.

'It's your mum,' I say breathlessly.

'It's okay, he says, reaching forward to touch my hand, but I jump back.

'No,' I say, tearing my eyes away from his, looking at the floor, the cheese-covered ramekins, the folded, fishy batter, and I squeeze my eyes shut.

'Hello, Heather!' Irene says, beaming at me as she hoists a basket filled with vegetables onto the counter. She looks at James and then over to me, studying our faces for evidence of something. This must be what it's like to be a teenager with parents who care what you're doing. 'How's the lesson going?'

'We're just about to put the soufflé in the oven,' James says. 'Heather has been very studious.'

'I have. We've hardly stopped for a moment. We've been cooking up a storm, as they say.' I employ as much reassurance in my tone as I can.

'Oooh, well that sounds good,' she says, sounding approving. Then she walks to a glass cabinet and removes a large bottle of gin and three crystal tumblers from the shelf. She looks at her watch. 'Brett can drive you back.'

James suddenly springs into action, filling the ramekins and sliding them into the oven, then setting a black egg-shaped timer on the counter, which clicks loudly.

'I've just been to Kindorn Castle to check out the set-up for the film-wrap party,' Irene says, as she pours a very large double gin and tops it with San Pellegrino, sliced cucumber, lemon and some small purple flowers from her basket. 'It's going to make a great venue since they've added the toilets, and we don't have to bring in those horrible Portaloos. The set-up is looking fantastic. Fingers crossed.'

'Oh, that's good news,' I say.

'I'm really counting on us pulling this off,' Irene says.

She looks grim, then shakes herself out of it, turning to me. 'Sorry, who needs to hear this, on your day off? How are you enjoying Scotland, Heather?'

And then it's like the spell is broken, and I'm back as Heather, among strangers, trying to keep up.

'I love it,' I nod.

I look across at Irene, this warm, kind, wonderful woman, and back to James, her sensitive and kind son, and wish I had always been

167

here. That my small family had even half the warmth and honesty of this one. That my mother had the gentle easiness of Irene – a mother who asked questions, enjoyed my company. A father who didn't tease me for showing an interest in things, who made me feel important. And then I wish Heather was here with me too.

'You're really settling in,' she says, taking a tiny sip of her gin and then adding more lemon to all three glasses.

'At last,' I say, minimizing the compliment.

'It's behind us,' Irene says, waving her hand. 'And this must be our welcome drink! I can't believe we've not had one yet. So, what will the toast be? Let me see. I've got it. "To Heather".'

She raises her glass and beams.

'To Heather,' says James softly.

22.

I wake with a gasp and a fuzzy head. I pull at the flimsy curtains but it's still dark outside.

My mouth tastes like juniper berries, and I giggle at my memory of Brett arriving in the tractor to bring me and James home to the cottage.

'Your chariot awaits, my lady,' Brett had said, as I tried and failed to climb up into the passenger seat. In the end James had to push me from behind. And so there I was, squashed between hot Brett and even hotter James as we careered across the banks of the loch, back to the cottage – not a road in sight.

'I'm terrified in cars. But it turns out, with enough gin, I'm totally cool in tractors!' I'd yelled, as we rocked over uneven hills and even across a small stream.

'Hold on,' Brett had shouted, as the water shot up and soaked us through.

I ate my first soufflé yesterday, which I can't believe I almost totally cooked myself. It was divine. Salty, fishy, melt-in-the-mouth fluffy with a crusty top. Absolute heaven! James served it with a peppery salad, whipped up somewhere off-set, while I nattered with his mum about the merits of a good hair conditioner. I vow never to return to over-chilled salad boxes and bun-less burgers.

I close my eyes and think about James for a moment, and wonder, through the haze of my hangover, if I need to shut it down. If Irene had not walked in, I don't know what would have happened. My attraction to James is now so potent I would struggle to stop it.

When we got home, it took all my resolve to tear myself away from him and into bed. Though Bill's presence helped. He was sitting in the lounge when we stumbled back in, and engaged me in unmemorable chit-chat while my drunken giddiness subsided and I began to yawn. And, before long, I was able to force myself away and into the safety of my room.

James is so different from Tim. There's no bravado, no posturing, no talk of pubs and fags and drugs. He's gentle and strong, all at once. Unsure and confident at the same time. He's perfectly balanced. Like the Blanc de Blancs – crisp, peppery and sweet all at once. *Get me, with my wine knowledge.*

I look up at the ceiling again. He's up there, perhaps directly above me, lying on a bed I haven't seen, in a room I've never been in.

I imagine him coming down in the night, tapping gently on my door, as he did a few mornings back, and calling my name.

'Birdy,' he would say as he opens the door. He knows my real name, in this version. He knows me. Perhaps he knows what I've done and wants me anyway. He puts his full weight on top of me, crushing me into the too-soft mattress. I want to be crushed. 'I don't care who you are,' he'd whisper in my ear, as his hand runs down my neck to my breast. I wouldn't stop him. I'd let him take me exactly as he wanted.

'But,' I'd protest, 'what about Tim?'

'You don't care about Tim,' he'd say, breathing into my ear.

You cannot fall in love with James. You have a job to do here. Learn the wine list, Birdy. Do a good job. Focus on getting out of here without further incident. Sort your fucking life out. You cannot fall for James.

Besides. He thinks you're Heather.

A wave of adrenaline rushes through me, and I have to get up and do something. I pull on my trainers and make my way sleepily into the kitchen, flick on the light and make myself a cuppa.

I grab a hideous-looking jacket from the entrance. It's orange and man-sized, but I don't care. I balance the tea in one hand, turn the handle of the front door with the other and slip out into the darkness. There is no fog any more, but it's still what one might call brisk. I clutch at the mug in my hands, feeling its comforting warmth.

I sneak past the stables. A dim light is visible through the far window, and the occasional sound of scuffing is the only break from the eerie silence.

The gentle breeze is cleansing. And before long I find myself at the bottom of the bank and down at the river that leads to the loch.

I am moving towards it, the loch, without really knowing why. In the blue-black of the light, under the canopy by the river, I step carefully over knotted roots and slippery rocks. The path is treacherous in this minimal visibility, but I am not afraid of slipping any more. I duck as I feel something pass overhead, and hear the hoot of an owl as it flutters to rest on a branch above me.

As I emerge on the shore of the loch, I look left and right, choosing the less obvious path that leads away from the estate and meets a small foot-track that heads all the way to the far side. I misstep and my feet sink into thick, cloying mud. My sneakers nearly pull off as I haul them free – spraying mud up my legs. I like it. I like the mud clinging to me; it feels good to be dirty and earthy, after years of London's polished concrete and glass.

The sky is now hinting at morning, but the stars above still spray out in a fan, mirroring the direction of the loch and leading me on. I sip the tea, which I find is beginning to cool, so I knock the whole thing back and shove the mug into the deep pockets of my jacket. I want to feel nothing but this silence.

A large rabbit – perhaps a hare – scoots in front of me, the white rounded tail illuminated by the full moon, which has emerged low in the sky from behind a cloud. I gasp as its reflection stretches across the water, like a silver path to my feet.

I stop, the sound of my footsteps disappearing into the noises of the morning. Birds beginning to wake. Crickets beginning to sleep. Occasional unexplained splashes, coming from the surface of the loch below.

My phone beeps in my pocket, and I feel a sting of resentment as I slide it out of my pocket. The bright light of it shocks my senses and dims the twilight back to darkness.

A message from Tim, whom I have not spoken to or messaged in days. Out of sight, out of mind.

Late night. Where you been? Radio silence. How's it going?

And then I notice a message from Heather, which must have come through in the night.

Just thinking about us maybe planning a little weekend together somewhere . . . on me. Would you like that? We could meet in Madrid or something?

I stare at the message, wanting to say yes, knowing that it would be impossible.

But I feel some sense of hope this morning: that perhaps I can get through this. Perhaps I will be able to tell Heather what happened, over that beer.

I put my hand down to check how damp the earth is – a little – and decide to sit and watch the sunrise.

Across the loch, the sun starts to make its presence known, low cloud picking up the blood-red and then orange as it rises. I make a little coo sound, and hear it echo round the loch, bouncing off the hills and back to me. And then silence.

I coo louder, and listen again. My voice like a stone, skimming off the mountains.

It's June – we're still a couple of weeks from the solstice and there is precious little dark night, this far north – and it must be around 5 a.m. when the first ray of sunshine bursts over the hill and hits my face. It is welcome, as the ground is cold and I am suddenly shivering.

I decide to take a walk all the way round the loch and back to the hotel. As I stand, I feel a damp patch on my bum. I remember someone saying it is a popular guest trail and passes the ruins of some stone houses, somewhere. I take in the entirety of the loch and, guessing it can't be more than two hours all the way round, decide to go for it.

I set off slowly at first, then my pace begins to pick up and suddenly I'm running. I run and I run. And I don't stop until I'm on the far side of the loch, looking back towards the estate. As my heart pounds in my chest and the sun shines on my face, warming my skin, I feel alive.

I double over, breathless, panting, and as my breath subsides, I spot something that looks for all the world like mint, poking out of a rock in a bunch. Is there such a thing as wild mint? I pluck the small top leaves off and sniff them, and just as I'm about to taste the little edge of one, I hear the clop-clop of horses' hooves behind me.

'Heather?'

I hadn't heard them before. I didn't expect anyone to be up. And I certainly didn't expect to see James again so soon. The horse Brett is riding is enormous. A stallion that is in no mood to stop. It leans its long neck towards me, then kicks a little when Brett tugs him back.

'Hi there,' I say, standing up. I must look a sight: red-faced and sweaty. I swipe the sweat away with the back of my sleeve.

James pulls on his reins, forcing his slightly less enormous chestnut horse back round in a circle, before coming to a stop facing me.

'You're not going to eat that, are you?' he asks, his forehead creased with concern, as his mare kicks into a canter to run the length of the fence before settling back again. Part of me is glad to see he's not the ace at horse-riding he seems to be at everything else.

'No,' I say, tossing the stem to the ground, before feeling a deep burning sensation on my fingers.

'Well, good. Because they're stinging nettles. Were you foraging?'

'Maybe.'

'Well, it's a beautiful morning for it,' he says, grinning.

'Aye, the red sky was a picture earlier. Did you catch the sunrise?' Brett asks.

'Yes,' I say, feeling suddenly a little woozy. The sun has some heat in it and I am thirsty.

'You need a ride back? You look a little peaky.'

'No.' I fold my arms in defiance.

'You should have water with you,' James says, dismounting from his horse. He leads it to the side of the path and it immediately goes for some longish shrubs. Then he unstraps a flask of water from his saddle. I salivate.

'Thanks. I didn't mean to get this far,' I say, taking the flask from him and gulping half down in one go. With the slight hangover and my impromptu run, I'm gagging for it. The ice-cold water runs down my throat and I almost groan in ecstasy.

'You sure you don't want a ride back?' he replies, placing one of his leather riding boots on a nearby tree stump to wrestle out an irritating bunch in his socks. Then he looks across at me, and the valley falls silent as his dazzling eyes catch the morning sun. He reaches up to shield them and takes another step closer.

'I thought I'd do some more foraging on the way back.'

'Yeah?' He looks suspicious.

'Yeah.'

It must be nearly six. James is still looking at me and I imagine for a moment what he must be seeing. I'm hungover and sweaty and pink, and covered in mud. Is that sexy? I'm not so sure. It sounds a bit like how you might describe a pig.

I can feel my underpants halfway up my bum, and have a sudden urge to tweak them out, but with a superhuman effort I don't. Instead I hand back the flask.

'How's your head?'

'*You* and your mother are responsible for this hungover hot mess you see before you.'

'Come on, lass – let us take you back. You don't want another minor foot injury,' Brett says, grinning, as he leans down to stroke the horse's long, thick neck.

James motions towards his horse and I look at the saddle, trying to figure out where I am supposed to go.

'Unless you want to go with Brett?' he says.

And so I slip my foot into the stirrup and he helps to guide me up, as he steadies the horse. I imagine what my huge bum must look like as I teeter between falling and hoisting myself up. Why are horses so bloody *tall*?

'Sit forward,' he says, and then in one swift motion he is up, sitting behind me, his arms round me, holding on to the reins, and we begin to ride back.

If I wanted to do anything to dampen my crush on James, I should not have got on this horse. It is almost comically sexy – a large horse between my legs, James's steady arms around me, his chest barely touching my back, and the rhythmical swaying as we traverse the path. He occasionally points out a bird: *an osprey circling* or *a kite* or *a golden eagle*. And I make as much small talk as I can, so as not to focus on the deliciousness of being so achingly, intimately and feverishly close to this man.

*

When we pull into the stables, I am exhausted. My thighs hurt and I just want to crawl back into bed and rest up before service later that night.

James helps me dismount and I make a joke about how I must stink, and he shakes his head. 'I couldn't tell if it was you or the horse.'

'Is that supposed to be a joke or are you serious?'

He laughs, and I feel a buzz in my back pocket. I pull it out to find I've missed four calls from Irene. Four calls. It has to be serious.

'James, has your mum called you?' I say, hitting the dial icon and waiting for it to ring. He checks his phone and nods, as Irene picks up.

'Heather. Oh, thank goodness. I'm sick, dear. Sick,' she says, coughing as soon as she splutters the words out.

'Well, same here, Irene. I mean, double G'n'Ts will do that to you.'

'No, it's not that. It's some kind of flu or something. I've a temperature.'

'Oh. Shit!' I say. 'Do you need anything?' I cover the receiver and mouth to James, *Your mum is sick*. He frowns.

'Can you come to the cottage? I'll need to brief you on everything for tonight.'

'Tonight?'

'The film party, Heather. You'll have to manage it. I can't trust Bill to do it.'

'Manage it?'

'Yes. There is a lot to know. Can you come now?'

23.

I didn't get any rest, but who the hell needs it, when you're on a drug called adrenaline?

I have my apron fixed over a less formal, though starched-to-a-crisp white T-shirt, for the film-wrap party. We're at the venue, Kindorn Castle. The grand, grey ruin has been elegantly adorned with great wreaths of ivory lilies, English ivy and massive white candles for lighting as the evening approaches.

It's bench-style dining, with a spit-roast suckling pig, crushed new potatoes, Loch Dorn's candied-apple sauce and wilted greens. There are two wines, which were inexplicably chosen by Russell on this occasion – both, Bill said, from Russell's mate's supplier. The wine is not to be poured, but placed on the long oak tables for self-serving. More ivy climbs up the marquee pillars, while heather, pine and thistles decorate the rustic tables.

It's gorgeous.

I can see now why outdoor catering events like these are not usually ones for the sommelier to attend. But I can also see why Irene needs someone to manage it. There's a lot to coordinate. It's bloody frantic.

Bill is managing the bar and is helping me open the wine bottles, while several casual waiting staff are scurrying round, helping with final touches.

'They're arriving at six,' I say, slipping my phone out of my apron to check the time.

'Yes, you've told me several times,' Bill replies, easing a cork out of a bottle of the red and then gently fixing it back in. 'It's all looking good – you can relax now.'

'Is anyone famous coming, do you know?'

'Andy Murray's mum is definitely coming. And all the other usual Scottish celebrities.'

'Ooh, I'd love to meet Andy Murray's mum. What's the film?'

'It's a historical thriller, apparently. The lead is from one of those small-town detective series. I can't remember which one.'

'That could be literally any actor in Britain. Male or female. Anyone else?'

'Honestly, I don't know,' he says, shrugging.

'You're useless. There's got to be a few famous faces,' I say, rubbing my hands together.

'I wish it was a wedding,' Bill replies. 'Much more fun.'

'I do love a wedding. It's hard not to get wrapped up in it all. All that promise . . .'

'I'm with you,' he says. 'All that promise of what's going to happen later on that night.'

'Ew,' I reply. 'Don't sully it!'

'Oh dear, Heather, I wouldn't have had you pegged as a romantic.'

We head back to the storage area behind the tent, and I stare longingly across at the gravlax being prepped by Anis. James is back at the hotel, but it's probably just as well he isn't here to distract me.

'Well, I shouldn't be a classic romantic,' I say, shaking my head free of thoughts of James. 'My parents' marriage was fucking awful. Dad had . . . his problems, and Mum fannied around, pretending there was nothing wrong. It was like she lived in an alternate universe. *What's happened to my clarinet, Mum? Oh, you must have lost it. It's your fault. Because there is no way I could admit that your father sold it this morning to pay off a fucking debt. Because that would mean I would have to admit that he has a massive fucking drinking problem, or whatever. No, no. It's easier to gaslight my nine-year-old and insist that she lost it.*'

Bill stops and furrows his brow, looking absolutely horrified.

'Really?'

'Yes, I used to play the clarinet,' I say. I've made this joke before.

'No, your mum. Did she do that?'

'She did,' I say, although today there is little of the pleasure I usually take in shocking people with this story. For reasons I cannot entirely fathom, I feel rather more exposed, after telling Bill. I look up at him, and he's still frowning.

'I'm sorry that happened to you,' he says, and it stings a little. I shake my head and wave my hand.

'Come on,' I say, 'let's get this done.'

I run a box-cutter down the tape on the next case of wine, make a mental note of how many we have left, and we make our way back out of the prep area into the marquee, where I see a huddle of the casual waiting staff by the head table, mucking about.

I frown and turn to Bill. 'I'll see what's going on.'

As I approach, I notice one of the young waiters is holding a large roll of kitchen paper stained red to his nose, while the others are loitering around, hands in pockets, one filming the chap with the nosebleed on his phone and another rolling a cigarette.

'What's going on?'

The one rolling the cigarette looks up at me with a toothy grin. 'Fraser lost a bet,' he says, smirking in a way that makes me want to grab him by the scruff of his neck and toss him into the moat that circles the castle. Yes, there is a moat.

'What do you mean?' I ask, hands on my hips.

They look at each other, shuffling back and forth. Oh, this is going to be good.

'What happened?' I say more plainly.

'I said he couldn't take a selfie of his butt-hole,' snorts one, 'and so he actually fucking tried. Pants down, he fell forward right onto the table leg.'

The one with the bleeding nose looks mortified.

I want to laugh. I mean, I should laugh. It's funny. But it also pisses me off a bit, which is an unusual reaction for me. My mind is on Irene, at home with a high fever and high anxiety at not being here to watch over every little thing. I know there is no time at all for mucking about. Tonight is really fucking serious for Loch Dorn, and I can't have these halfwits ruining it for her. For us.

'Guys, you know you're here to work, right?' I say.

'Yeah,' says the one on his phone, and he slides it away into his apron pocket.

'Aye, we're just having a bit of fun, like,' says Toothy Grin.

'Have some fun later, eh? In your own time.' I stare hard at him. I know his type. I turn to the waiter with the nosebleed. 'Go to the van and clean yourself up.'

'All right,' says Nosebleed, looking sheepish.

'And don't be fucking dicks,' I say sharply. 'Do you want to get paid?'

'Aye,' Toothy Grin says, looking far less pleased with himself. 'Sorry, mam.'

They disperse quickly, but I feel a slight sense of concern as I return to help Bill open another case of white wine.

'Where are the staff from?'

'Wherever we can get them,' Bill says with a laugh. 'They only need to clear tables and stay out of trouble.'

'That might be a tough brief for this lot,' I reply, frowning.

'They're all local,' Bill says, reassuring me. 'There's not a lot of work round here, and Irene . . .'

'Say no more,' I say, nodding and suddenly understanding the situation. Of course Irene would employ some local kids to help out. And of course they're a bit rough round the edges. And usually Irene would be here to keep them in line. I look over at them and vow to be more compassionate. But also watchful like a hawk, and ready to step in with firm authority, if they put any of this at risk.

Within seconds I spot an older gent in a kilt, sporran and formal black jacket at the doors of the marquee. They're here.

Instinctively I clap. Just like Irene.

'Places, everyone,' I whisper to the lads by the door. 'Be discreet, thoughtful and, above all, manners, please.'

Toothy Grin gives me a reassuring nod.

I wait by the door, nodding and smiling at the guests as they walk in. I guide some to their tables, if they can't make sense of the seating plan, and help others with their jackets. I make sure everyone has a glass of champagne or orange juice or sparkling water. I fuss over a couple of children, David and Alva, who are each accompanied by a nervous-looking parent. Neither can be more than eight years old.

'We were burned alive as revenge for our father killing the king's only son,' says David proudly.

'That's my mum over there,' Alva says, pointing to a beautiful blonde in a shimmering silver gown. 'She was bludgeoned to death in front of me.'

'How exciting for you both,' I say, showing them to a seat and offering them both some freshly pressed apple juice.

Then, to the sound of bagpipes, the main cast arrives, shuffling in slowly.

'That's the lead actress,' Bill confirms, whispering in my ear as she passes. 'The director, Bob Someone-or-other, to her right; and that guy on the left is the one from that dancing show.'

'Christ, you're hopeless at this,' I say to Bill, laughing.

The actress is exquisite-looking, and I'm sure I know her from something, but I can't place it. Her hair is left loose, tumbling around her face and down her back, with a crown of tiny white flowers. Her dress is midnight-blue and elegantly decorated, with a cap-sleeve made from lace and a small, tasteful fishtail, which glides behind her as she walks. She is glowing.

I feel very ordinary, suddenly, in my apron and T-shirt, and with my dry, dyed hair, as I guide her to her seat. I can smell her perfume and hairspray, and I reach my hand up to my own hair and wonder if I can get it fixed. And maybe paint my toenails.

The lead actor is handsome, his hair unkempt and his sharp tuxedo styled with the bow 'undone', like a Vegas crooner on his last song. He also smiles in that same saccharine way.

As dinner begins, the tempo and volume of the room increase. The band, who I'm told also performed a scene in the show, is playing modern songs in the style of a sixteenth-century tavern band. Currently it's 'Poker Face' by Lady Gaga, with the accordion taking the place of the vocals. It's completely surreal, but I like it.

The waiters are behaving themselves. Nosebleed is being relatively efficient with his clearing and definitely knows how to open a bottle of wine. But the guests are going through it – the wine. I head to the back of the marquee, where Bill has a small whisky bar set up. I catch him taking a shot with his back turned, as I approach. *Oh, Bill, not again.* I curse myself for believing he might be getting better. I should know better.

'Heather!' he says, trying subtly to wipe his face.

'I saw you – don't bother,' I scowl.

'Well, it's all free, isn't it?' he winks.

'No, *they* paid for it,' I counter.

'Come on,' he says, his eyes flickering with shame. 'Perks of the job.'

'Just don't get drunk,' I say sharply. 'So, where are we keeping the rest of the wine? They can drink, this lot.'

'It should be all out by the catering tent.'

'Well, there's like one case of white left,' I say. 'There must be more. How many did Russell order?'

Bill frowns. 'Gosh, I don't know.'

'They can't run out of wine, can they? They can't. Irene wouldn't let them run out of wine.'

'It has happened before,' Bill says, as he starts to clear away some empties.

'Ugh!' I sigh, rushing back through the tent, the darkness now having fully descended. I clock each table as I pass. There's plenty of red everywhere, but it looks like the white is what everyone's going for. It's no surprise really, since they're eating pork. Why did no one check the orders? Should I have checked the orders?

Back in the catering tent, Anis is finishing packing up.

'What do we do if we run out of white wine, Anis?'

'Fuck! What? It's not even nine p.m.' Anis stands up straight.

'I know. I asked Bill, but he thinks it must've all been drunk. I mean, they are really going for it.'

Right then Toothy Grin comes racing through the doors.

'Are we out of white?' he says, shifting from side to side. 'That famous guy wants another bottle for his table, and he's asked for the manager. Also, I just met Andy Murray's mum.'

'Shit. Shit. Shit!' I say, biting my lip.

I look at Anis, who is rubbing her hands on her chef's whites and pulls a set of car keys out of her pocket. 'I can't leave. I have to get the dessert out.'

'How far away is the nearest town?'

'Fort William? I don't know, twenty minutes?'

'Will anything be open?'

'Go to a pub called the Thistle and Crown,' she says, looking at her watch. 'It's closer than Fort William. Tell them Anis from Loch Dorn sent you. And we'll settle with them tomorrow. In fact I'll call them now, tell them you're coming.'

'Okay, then.' I nod at Anis, before turning to Toothy Grin. 'Reckon you can keep everyone happy until I get back?'

His face reddens and he looks terrified.

'Why don't I go for the wine?' he says. 'I know the roads, like. And I know the Thistle and Crown. It's my local.'

I look at him and back to Anis, unsure.

'I'll do it,' he insists. 'I'll get the wine. What, like, half a dozen cases?'

'That should do it. Just get the house-wine. This deal is all in, so we shouldn't have run out, but we can't afford to supply something expensive.'

'Oh, they only have house-wine anyway,' says Anis. 'I mean, it's the Thistle and Crown, not The Pig & Whisky.'

'Right. Well, off you go,' I say, nodding to Toothy. 'Thank you so much. I'll go and keep the Very Important Men satisfied for as long as I can.'

'What are you going to do?' Anis asks me.

'I have a plan,' I say, looking across at the still-unopened box of spirits.

With six tumblers, ice and a bottle of still water, I head to the main table. As I approach, they appear to be role-playing an angry king in want of a pitcher of wine.

'Where is my wine, boy!' the Vegas crooner is saying in a mock ye-olde-English accent, to the roars of laughter around him. It's a total men's club, this table, and I can't help but glance across at his co-star, who appears to be taking time to speak with the two children's parents, over on the table by the toilets.

Each man is nondescript, like a bad photocopy of the one before. If there is a film-industry look, they've all been to the same stylist and ordered it. Blindingly white teeth, slightly messy greying hair, shirts straining against bulging bellies.

I set the tumblers on the table: one for him and for each of the five seated with him. The men all stop talking and watch me in silence. The band has chosen this exact moment to stop playing, and while the room is filled with nothing but the clinking of cutlery and the boisterous sounds of tipsy folk, I steel myself.

'Who's ready for a real drink?' I say, slapping a bottle of eighteen-year-old Oban on the table.

The men all look at each other for a moment and I hold my breath. If they are anything like most of the men I know, they won't be able to resist. Even if they don't want a whisky, they're going to have to have one, if just one of the table says yes. That's how it works.

'I'd love a Scotch,' says the eldest man, in a deep American drawl. 'You must've read my mind, young lady.'

'Well, as the only Scot at the table, I'd better have one too,' says the Vegas crooner, putting his wine glass aside. 'But if anyone ruins it with that ice, we're going to have to have words.'

'I take mine straight,' says another.

'You gotta have some water,' another insists while practically fondling his massive man balls, as I walk slowly back from the table and take a moment to rest against an ivy-wrapped pole.

'Thistle and Crown are going to meet us halfway with the wine,' whispers Anis in my ear. 'You did it. Well fucking done!'

I did it. I, Birdy Finch, did it. I was calm under pressure and I pulled it off. I feel absolutely giddy with relief and pride. And as the band kicks in with a medieval version of 'Wonderwall', I finally breathe out.

24.

I've been getting comfortable and falling into a routine. That's what happens in life, isn't it? Everything eventually becomes routine, even in extraordinary circumstances.

I shower and dress in my uniform. I go over the menu with Roxy and James and Anis. We agree on the pairings. This is the only part that I still find intensely challenging, but I make sure they give me a couple of hours' notice, so I can do some thorough research before we discuss. Sometimes I get it wrong, but I have learned this is okay. In the world of wine-tasting, some things still come down to personal taste. And as long as I can keep up the pretence that my choices are sometimes 'bold' or 'unexpected', rather than plain wrong, I'm doing fine.

Roxy has taken over the dreaded stocktaking under my supervision, much to her delight and my relief. Though today she's taken the day off to see the doctor in Inverness.

And then there's Bill, always checking in: *Have you done the stocktake, Don't forget to offer water . . .*

There is something going on with him that I can't put my finger on. It's not the drinking; he's mostly functioning at work, and the last time I saw him drunk was at the film party, although he could be hiding it from me. I was quite sharp with him then. But what am I supposed to do? I'm not his therapist. I've got my own shit going on here.

Each day I do my shift, safe in the knowledge that all the pairings have been agreed with the rest of the team. I keep my little notebook close, ready for last-minute requests or those wanker alpha-male types who want to impress their friend or lover with something 'unexpected'.

With each shift my confidence has grown, and – a weird side-effect – I think I'm actually starting to know a few things about wine. At least the wines at the restaurant.

And I'm enjoying it. I enjoy meeting the guests, and I enjoy feeling like an expert. I like making them laugh and I feel at ease. I like the creativity of putting the menu together, and I love the way people leave happy.

James.

James.

James and I have not been fishing again, or on any kind of date-like activity. Since my disclosure about Tim, he's definitely keeping a respectful distance. But he's still attentive, kind and always finds a reason to spend time with me, though sometimes we catch each other's eye and the spark is there. But then he looks away; or I do. He never mentions Tim, and I never bring him up either, but he is present: a small barrier that keeps us from crossing any lines and betraying anyone, even though Tim and I have barely been in touch these last four weeks.

At Irene's suggestion, our cooking lessons have moved to the morning – perhaps to avoid an inevitable once-a-week booze-up, and keep James and me safe from making any mistakes? Irene is often in and out, so there's certainly no opportunity to flirt, but I look forward to it so much that I spend most of the week wishing the days away. And I can tell James looks forward to it too.

He's taught me how to make chocolate mousse, prawn cocktail and a proper boeuf bourguignon. Look at me, Elizabeth Finch, getting all above my station in life with knowledge about what makes a good bowl of chowder, and which white wine goes best with crayfish.

The Monday just past we sat out in the garden, drinking peppermint tea with his mum for hours while she talked about the early days of Loch Dorn – James laughing as we rabbited on together.

I now like to hike. HIKE! Extraordinary. I have become a kind of Renaissance Birdy.

I even found an old book in the cottage called *Edible Scotland*, fully annotated by James, I think, which I carry with me in the hope that I will eventually find something to forage. James talks about the mushroom season with Anis all the time. I have a fantasy about stumbling upon armfuls of porcini poking out of the damp earth in late summer. The key to separating them from others that look almost identical is, according to the book, the net-like webbing on their stems. If they're out before I leave, I'm determined to find one.

Everything is working. It's working, and I can hardly believe I'm pulling it off. The only thing that is getting me down is Loch Dorn itself. The relaunch seemed to go well at first, but as the days have passed there haven't been enough bookings, and there is an oppressive worry slowly cloaking the spirits of everyone at the hotel.

Today in the kitchen Anis is stressing out in the corner, plating up the last desserts, and James is in the deep freeze counting artichokes, while the other two chefs are clearing down the surfaces.

'Can I help, Anis?' I ask.

'Get the chantilly,' she snaps.

'Roger that, Chef,' I reply, and fish around in the fridge for the container and hand it to her. Chantilly: *vanilla and sugar and whipped cream.*

'Busy shift?'

'Ish,' she says, looking irritated as she gently places toasted hazelnuts on the plate. 'I just wish the word would get out about the relaunch.'

'Any day, I'm sure,' I reply. 'Want a cuppa?'

'Yep,' she nods.

James comes in, his chef's whites unbuttoned, and he's got that slightly stressed flush to his cheeks.

'I'm going to head off. See you back here at four?'

I grin at him and he holds my gaze, but something in his look is different from usual. He holds it firmly, with serious eyes, and I narrow mine in return.

'Can we speak?' he says in a lower voice.

'Sure,' I say. 'Just making a cuppa.'

'It's important,' he replies, and motions towards the back of the kitchen.

He does look *very* serious, and it makes me anxious. Has something happened? Does he know? I haven't felt a wave of panic in days, and here it is, as potent as ever.

I nod at him and rub my shaking hands on my apron, then follow him towards the cellar door, but when we're alone in the back-prep area, he stops. I am momentarily disappointed we're not going to be alone in the cellar, but try to remain focused.

'The reviewer, Josh Rippon. It's tonight,' he says sharply.

'Oh shit,' I reply and then, 'Oh SHIT!' I almost shout, realizing Roxy isn't here to help me. 'Do I need to do anything?'

'I'm not sure. Mum is going to stay on between shifts and deep-clean the dining room, and I'm going to rest for an hour and then come back up and double-check every little thing in the kitchen.'

'Okay,' I nod, wondering what a sommelier would do to make sure a special guest was catered for, without making too much of a fuss.

'Well, I guess I'd better prep myself too?'

'Okay,' he breathes out. 'This is it! I'm super-nervous.'

'You're going to be great,' I say, and I reach across and grab his hand in mine. 'Really. You're totally awesome. Russell has hardly even been here this week – he must totally trust you now.'

'He'll never make it here in time. He's fuming, apparently.'

'You can do without the pressure. You've totally got this.'

He looks at my hand and slowly runs his thumb along my knuckles. He looks at me as though asking if it's okay. *It's okay, James, I love it,* I think, allowing him to squeeze my hand a little, before I pull it away with a mix of heartache and shame.

'Heather,' he says tentatively.

I hold my breath for a moment, but he stops talking and his eyes drop to the floor.

'Not now,' I say gently.

He looks up at me and purses his lips. 'Yeah. Not now,' he agrees, before glancing back at my lips and murmuring, 'but soon.'

'What?' I say, catching my breath.

'Soon.' He pulls back, turns and then he's gone.

'Bill?' I say, knocking on the staffroom toilet. I know he's in there, and it's urgent. I knock again.

'Heather!' he replies. 'I'm on the loo, love.'

'I'm sorry. I'm being really rude. I'll wait.'

'Are you going to wait right there?'

'Yes.'

'Right.'

I pace back and forth the length of the room until finally I hear the toilet flush, the tap run and then a moment later Bill comes out and grimaces at me. There is a warmth to his skin tone, and his eyes are much brighter. A good day. And that's a relief, because today I need him.

'What the Dickens is going on?'

'The reviewer is coming tonight and Roxy isn't here, and I need someone to go over the wine list with me, to make sure I don't fuck it up,' I say. 'For Irene and James, and for everyone.'

He looks at me for a moment, and I see something flash across his face and I'm not sure what it was. Pity? I think it might have been.

'Calm down,' he says and motions me to the seat in the corner of the staffroom.

I thrust the wine list out to him. 'Test me. Ask me about any wine on the list.'

'Memorizing the wine list is one thing, but that's not what you need to be confident about. You just need to do your thing. Charm him,' Bill says, shaking his head at me. He sits and tries again to get me to do the same, by patting the seat next to me.

'I can't sit down. Please test me. Start anywhere.'

He takes the list off me and flicks it open. 'Well, okay, I can do it if it makes you feel more prepared.'

'It will,' I say, because I can feel my heart beating hard and my chest begin to tighten.

'The 2014 Perricone del Core,' he says and I start to pace back and forth.

'Intense,' I reply, biting on the edge of my thumbnail. 'Rich, thick, with white pepper on the palate.'

'Yes, it *is* all those things,' he says. 'It doesn't say that here in the wine list, though.'

'We need to cross-reference with my notes,' I say. Then I panic as my hands reach the notebook in my apron. Will the contents look suspicious? They won't, will they? Won't it just look like I'm really prepared? Fuck it! I toss the book towards him. 'Everything is in the same order as the wine list. Can you check I got it right?'

'Heather,' he says, shaking his head at me. 'Keep it brief, you'll be fine.'

'Check, please,' I say, trying to steady my breathing.

'Okay.' He flicks through the notebook and finds the matching wine. 'You said white pepper? Intense? That's correct. Also says here it goes well with game, because of the berry notes.'

'Yes, I knew that. Game,' I nod. 'Okay, next one.'

'The 2016 Pinot Gris, Man o' War, from New Zealand,' he says.

'Waiheke Island, technically. Ginger and citrus fruits. Thirst-quenching. Delicious,' I say. 'Is that right? Serve with anything spicy, probably. Chilli and seafood works. Have you got it yet?'

'Hang on, love,' says Bill as he flicks through my notebook again, then nods. 'You know it.'

'Heather should know about more than simply the wine. Ask me some pairing questions, as if you were a reviewer,' I say, glancing up at Bill as I realize the mistake I just made, and he looks back at me with deep concern etched across his forehead and mouth. 'Sorry for the third person. I'm in the zone,' I say quickly. 'Come on, ask me.'

'Okay, well, tonight we have lobster and summer leaves: what would you recommend? I don't like the Meursault it's been paired with on the tasting menu.'

'Good. Good question,' I say, nodding furiously. 'May I suggest a glass of one of our vintage champagnes?'

'I don't like the Chardonnay grape at all. But I do want something equally fabulous.'

I nod at Bill, to let him know I'm very pleased with the second test, and stop to breathe out slowly and fully, before recalling, 'Our rosé from Provence then. Can I recommend the Bastide de la Ciselette 2016? It's rich and elegant.'

'With a long finish,' Bill says, as he finds my notes. 'And it says here these need drinking right now.'

'Yep, I knew that,' I say. 'Another. Go on.'

'Even the best sommelier in the world doesn't know everything there is to know about wine. I promise you, even *Heather Jones* is not expected to know everything.'

I breathe out a little, but I feel light-headed and Bill is right – I need to calm down.

'It's two forty-five,' I say. 'Can you go over it with me for a bit longer?' I hold my hand up to stop his protests. 'And then I promise to sit down and do some meditative deep breathing or yoga, or whatever the fuck.'

25.

Irene is clip-clopping about with purpose, making sure everything is perfect for this bloody reviewer, whom I absolutely hate, even though I've not even met him.

Bill and I practised for almost an hour and I was near-perfect. I've studied this list more than I've ever studied anything before. I feel proud and quietly confident.

'Chop, chop!' Irene says, clapping at the younger staff, who jump like deer every time they think they're in trouble. I doubt it would be possible to be truly scared of Irene. But, when you're twenty, all bosses are intimidating, even the ones as sweet and motherly as she is.

'I want the windows cleaned too, please. Where are you going, Heather?'

'I want to speak quickly with James, to make sure he's happy with everything.'

'Leave the kitchen be, please. They're stressed enough!'

I nod, even though I know it's clearly Irene who is the most stressed.

'The reviewer will likely be dining with a friend,' she calls out to everyone, just as a vase is toppled off the bar and the intricate summer bouquet spills across the floor. 'Damn it, Bill!'

I decide the best thing for me to do is double-check that the stock is all perfectly chilled or close to hand, and that I look presentable.

'Fifteen minutes until our first reservation!' Irene shrills, and her hysterics are actually making me feel less nervous. I even have to stifle a giggle as I watch her move from table to table, making minute changes to napkins and glasses, despite the fact that she did it five minutes ago.

As I push through the door into the staffroom to check my face, I can hear her telling Bill to 'turn the bloody pop music off and find something bloody adult.'

And then I do laugh. I make my way into the staffroom and push open the bathroom door and run straight into James, who is drying his hands. For a moment we just stare at each other, and then I can't help it: I reach up and put my arms round him and swiftly pull him in for a hug, resting my face in his neck.

It's the closest we've been since we rode the horse together, and I can feel the beating of my heart against his ribs, the smell of lemons and rosemary permeating his clothes, and the acidic topnotes of sweat. I could roll around in it.

'You're going to do great,' I say, as I squeeze him hard.

And as I'm about to pull away, James puts his arms round my shoulders and pulls me closer. He doesn't say anything, but moves his head slightly and brushes his lips across my forehead and plants a gentle kiss. Like everything with James, it's sweet. I turn my face up to him and he looks down at my lips for a fleeting moment and then stops himself.

'Sorry,' he whispers, before pulling back. 'Good luck.'

'You too,' I reply as he hurries towards the kitchen. I allow myself a little moment to close my eyes and remember the kiss in every beautiful detail. Then I shake my head and look into the mirror. As I do so, my phone rings. A number I don't recognize.

'Hello?'

'Is that Heather?' says a girl's voice, and for a moment I scramble my brain. Who is this? Why are they calling me Heather?

'Roxy?'

'Hi. Yes, it's me.'

'How's it going?'

'Oh, everything's fine. I just heard that the reviewer is coming tonight, and I wanted to apologize. I can't believe it's happening tonight. I'm driving back in an hour or so, but I'll never make it!'

'Oh, don't give it another thought, Roxy.'

'Oh, thank you, Heather. I felt so bad!'

I turn to look in the mirror and realize I definitely look a bit rough and in need of a freshen-up before service.

'Good luck! Not that you need it – you're going to be amazing. I was telling Mum how awesome you are.'

'You're sweet,' I say, wanting to hang up in embarrassment.

'Oh, oh, oh, oh. One other thing. I just Friend-requested you on Facebook. Sorry if it's a bit presumptuous, but I thought I'd do it anyway.'

For a moment I'm annoyed that she's still talking, as I need to put on my make-up. But then it sinks in. *YOU DID WHAT?*

'What?'

'Ah, like I said, I'm sorry. I know you probably want to keep work and whatever separate – I know Anis does . . . please ignore it, if so. Oh God, I'm so embarrassed.'

I am silent for a moment as I start to feel my chest tighten again and I mouth 'Fuck!' at the ceiling.

'I have to go, Roxy,' I say and then, as brightly as I can, I add, 'see you tomorrow.'

I hang up my phone and as I do so, notice there is a message from Heather from four hours earlier.

Missing you. Getting a bit bored here TBH. Let's book in a chat tomorrow – it's been ages.

I call her immediately, and she picks up after a couple of rings.

'Hi, Heather,' I say. 'What are you up to?'

'ELIZABETH,' she replies, all perky and not at all bored-sounding. She sounds like she's out, as I can hear music. 'How the bloody devil are you? Let me turn the radio down.'

'What are you up to?' I repeat, desperate to conceal the panic in my voice.

'You got my message then?'

'Yes, yes.' I realize I'm sweating under the armpits, and unbutton my shirt to try to get some air in. I gently close the bathroom door to make sure no one can hear me.

'I can't talk for long – just wanted to check in with you. It's been so long.'

'Are you okay?'

'I'm okay. After I sent that message, Cristian whisked me off for the evening. He's here with me now. Driving. Right next to me.'

That was a clear sign that I shouldn't talk to her now, and I don't even know what I'm going to say. I can't mention the Friend request.

'Oh, lovely. Make sure you get some pictures. But don't post them on social media,' I add quickly, wondering if I'm starting to sound like a weirdo with all my instructions.

'I won't. I've absolutely promised Cristian, but regardless, the job is long gone now. I'm sure some other person jumped at the chance.'

'Jumped at the chance?' I repeat back to her. It makes me feel sick that I'm policing her life almost as much as Cristian is at the moment.

'Are you okay, Birdy? You sound a bit tense?'

'Yeah, I guess.'

'Are you sure?'

'Sorry, you know – I'm just worrying about your . . .' I cringe and pray to the gods for forgiveness, 'reputation.'

'Can you give me a call back tomorrow or something? We're driving, and Cristian is putting the roof down. Plus you keep cutting out,' she says. Right at that moment there is a sharp knock on the door.

'Heather! You have to come now. The first diners are here!' It's Bill.

'Who was that? Did they say my name?' Heather asks in my ear, and she's shouting now over the sound of traffic in the background.

'No one!' I reply. 'Only my cousin!'

And I hang up and open the door to Bill, who is standing there looking concerned. 'What's going on?'

'Don't ask. Can I have one minute to clean myself up?'

'Hurry. If Rippon arrives and we don't have a sommelier, that will *definitely* make the review.'

I scrape my hair into a bun and splash water onto my face. I rush over to my locker and pull out a fresh shirt and clean apron, and smear a little tinted moisturizer across my cheeks. There is no time for anything else, but at least I don't look like I might die.

I take a deep breath and set off to meet my doom.

The dining room is quieter than usual and I think Irene, desperate not to let the music be too loud, has made it far too soft. I can hear the clinking of the glass on table three and the entire conversation on table five.

'Turn the music up a little,' I whisper to Bill, who sneakily leans under the bar and raises the volume just enough to fill the room with atmosphere, but no more.

'Okay, I'm good,' I say, although inside I'm an absolute wreck. The conversation with Heather has made me unaccountably jumpy, although on the surface she sounded fine. And the Friend request. I have to speak to Roxy as soon as possible.

'He's here,' says Irene in a sing-songy voice as she walks past me and Bill. 'The moment of truth!'

Bill immediately heads to the other end of the bar and picks up a brandy balloon to polish. I realize, as I watch him shining it aggressively, that this is his nervous tic.

I stand to attention and smile as a man enters the dining room, glancing round at the new decor, straight-faced and utterly unreadable. I turn to Bill for confirmation it's Josh Rippon, and Bill discreetly nods back.

Josh's dinner guest is a long, thin-faced bald man, round in the belly, grey and almost powdery, like he's been dug out of a collapsed whisky cellar. Josh himself is sort of handsome, in a short and ruddy intellectual kind of way, with his black-rimmed glasses and brown rollneck.

'Okay, I'm up,' I mutter to myself, as Irene shows them to their table. As I approach, I try to push away all thoughts of Heather and this ridiculous situation. I feel my stomach gurgle and my chest tighten, and I summon all that is ballsy and brave within me and arrive at the table with my biggest smile.

'Welcome, gentlemen. Can I offer you an aperitif?'

'Oh yes,' says the older gent, who keeps wriggling his nose like he's got something stuck up it.

'Can I recommend a Gimlet, sir?' I say, knowing that Bill can knock it out of the park. He spent most of yesterday making fresh lime cordial.

'I'll just take some sparkling water,' says Josh, 'and the menu?'

Shit! I'd forgotten to offer both.

'The Highland Quarry sparkling or the Maldon Superior?' I say, desperately attempting to rectify the situation by dazzling him with our sparkling-water selection. He's not responding, but instead is looking at me curiously.

'I don't mind,' he says eventually, extremely politely.

'No worries,' I say, and I slip back to the bar to pick up the two leather menu cards and ask Bill for a bottle of sparkling water.

'I forgot to do the water,' I say. 'Shit balls! Roxy's been doing this tag-team thing with me, and I just fucking forgot.'

'Don't worry,' he says. 'It's only nerves. He'll have seen it a million times. You can recover.'

'And the menu,' I say grimly.

'Deep breath,' Bill says. 'You can do this. You've simply got to give them a fantastic wine choice, pour a glass and then you're done. Irene can take care of the rest.'

I nod at him and head back to the table, moving round to the right of Josh and pouring his water into the correct glass, before moving across to his guest to do the same.

'I'll take a Gimlet,' his guest says, smiling warmly at me. I can tell he can sense my nerves, and I'm grateful for the look of solidarity.

'Excellent. Your waiter will be with you shortly,' I say. 'In the meantime the degustation menu is at the front, paired with a selection of wines. I'll happily talk you through anything. I'll be back in a moment.'

'Could you talk through them now?' says Josh.

'What – all of them?'

'No the wines in the degustation,' he sighs dramatically, adding an eye-roll in his friend's direction. 'You know what? Give us a moment and we will get back to you.'

I scurry off like a frightened chambermaid.

And then I'm annoyed. Seething actually. And I can't stem the flow of fury, and I keep thinking how stabbing Josh with his fish knife would feel really good.

I make my way back through the kitchen door and push maybe a little hard on the doors, so that they bang loudly, and James is standing there with an expectant, almost excited look on his face. That makes me angry too. His stupid, childish face smiling at me, wanting to know how it's going. I can hear the sounds of chopping and frying and boiling, and Anis looks like she's plating up the quail and haggis starter, and I fantasize about dropping it on Josh's head.

'He's like a constipated tortoise, in that polo neck,' I say to James, as I walk into the back area and pace back and forth, trying to get my breath. James is now preoccupied with getting the starters out, but keeps looking over at me and I can tell I'm distracting him. I don't want to knock him off his game too.

'Heather?' says Bill, coming in. I try to stand up straight and shake off the anger.

'Yes?'

'He wants talking through the wine list.'

'Jesus fucking Christ, this guy,' I scowl.

'You can do this,' he says, but I realize now that he looks as unsure as I feel. He doesn't trust me, either.

'I'm coming,' I reply and march back through to the front of the kitchen, where James is gawping now, then I push through the doors. But something pulls me back into the moment. It's Irene, standing by the bar, clutching the menu and looking to me for reassurance. It's sobering, and I realize suddenly how high the stakes actually are. Not for me, but for them.

I close my eyes and breathe slowly out to the floor of my stomach. I can pull this back.

I walk slowly over to Josh, ready to recover from my mistake. It's only a little misstep, I tell myself. Anyone could have made it. It's nerves – you're a bit nervous.

'Hi, I understand you want talking through the tasting menu?' I say, and I'm impressed by how relaxed I make it sound.

'Well, the wine list actually,' Josh says.

I look at him, his smug little face filled with haughty, well-bred superiority, and I hate him. The flood of anger comes rushing back.

'We'd like some additional options for the degustation? I'm not a Riesling fan, and Holland here doesn't fancy anything white at all.'

He doesn't like me. He just doesn't fucking like me, and so here we are. I've been here before. My voice. The way I hold myself. These people can almost smell the class permeating from you. I'm not in the club.

I take a breath and dig deep. I try not to think of James and Irene, and I try to find the right words. 'Maybe I can suggest the Grüner Veltliner instead of the Riesling? And we have plenty of rosés.'

'I'm happy with a Grüner Veltliner, if that's all you've got,' says Josh.

'And how can we do this, if I'm only for red?' asks Holland.

'Well, you're absolutely screwed, because three of the seven courses in that absolutely divine tasting menu would be drowned by red.'

It just jumps out, and I wish I could shove it back in. It's sneery and sarcastic and not playful and witty, and I feel like the Birdy of a couple of months ago once again, with the weight of a lifetime of failure and disappointment heavy on my shoulders. Pissed off at the world for not being more awesome towards me.

Holland roars with laughter, but it's a mixture of shock and embarrassment, I think, and then I clock Josh, who looks like he's the cat who got the fucking cream. Like he's caught out the place for the crappy sham it is and will enjoy crafting a nasty little eight-hundred-word article about how the west coast of Scotland is unrefined and boorish. I've fucked it.

'Do you think the Beaujolais is light enough to suffice?' Josh suggests, because apparently he's now doing my job.

'Sounds like you have all the answers?' I snap, unable to stop myself now.

What am I doing? Why is it that sometimes I try so hard, and then at the last minute I fail? And at the first sign of it, I double-down?

Bill arrives with the Gimlet and eyes me across the table. He's trying to get me to calm down, but honestly it's just more pressure. I wait until he's finished, racking my brain to think of a way to deal with this arsehole.

'Yes, I'll go with the Beaujolais,' Holland says, and I have no idea how long I've been standing there, but nothing is normal any more and I'm starting to get the tunnel vision that means an anxiety attack is imminent. 'Josh is going to take the pairings, with the Riesling swapped for the Grüner Veltliner – is that right, Josh?'

'Yes, exactly. Perfect,' he says, handing the menu back to me. Something has changed in his tone – is it pity?

I try really hard to take it from him normally and smile. 'Thank you.'

And then I turn on my heel and head to the bar, where Irene is hovering nervously. I look at her and I feel grim and nauseous.

'I have to go,' I say. 'I'm going to be sick.'

I walk through the doors into the staffroom and burst into tears.

26.

I may have exhausted Irene's inexhaustible patience.

In she came, throwing her long, maternal arms around me, but her hug held rather less of a squeeze than usual. She insisted it would all work itself out, but that she needed to go and focus on finishing the evening. *If I could not.*

'If you're not up to it, then take the night off,' she said. 'What's done is done.'

I blinked up at her through my tears, and her tone softened a little.

'We've all been there. Sometimes nerves get the better of us. You just head back to the cottage and get yourself a hot shower and bed. Okay?'

I nodded and then, when she was gone, untucked my shirt, tossed my apron – notebook and all – into the laundry basket, vowing that, no matter what, I was going to resign and leave them all to it.

But I can't. So now I sit with my head in my hands, unable to move. And as I begin to calm down, I look at my watch and guess that James is probably on the dessert. James!

Then I hear the door open. Anis comes in and sits down next to me.

'What happened?' she says.

'I lost my temper with the reviewer.'

'Oh,' she says, nodding her head. 'Impressive.'

I don't laugh, but reach down and pull off my shoes. I can't look her in the eyes, so I try to pretend my shoes are really fascinating, closely inspecting the heel.

'It wasn't that bad, was it?'

'Everyone was counting on me, and I fucked up.'

'Oh, for Christ's sake,' she says. 'Once, Roxy had to serve Nicola Sturgeon and dropped a gravy boat right in her lap. And Ines from

Portugal, who was here last summer – she got caught shagging a guest, by one of the house maids. That guest was a real weirdo. He got very obsessed with Ines. Brett caught him the next night trying to climb into the cottage through the top window, and he broke his leg.'

'What?' I said, sniffing. 'Brett broke his leg?'

'No, Brett broke the guy's nose, and then he broke his leg falling off the windowsill,' she says, cracking both her knuckles loudly. 'After I pushed him.'

'Sounds like an eventful evening,' I say, sniffing again.

'It was. This thing – hospitality – it's a team game, okay? Like the army. You can't have the best front-of-house in the world and serve soggy bread. And you can't serve haute-fucking-cuisine on a hub cap.'

'I feel like I'm the hub cap,' I say quietly, as a half-smile creeps across my face.

We look at each other and Anis smiles grimly, patting me on the shoulder. An Anis hug.

'You shouldn't take this whole thing so to heart. I'm sure James has nailed it. And even if there is a review all about the crazy, weird sommelier who lost her shit at the guests, which I'm sure there won't be, but even if there is – you never know, it might even bring in more guests to meet the crazy sommelier?'

I half-smile. 'I just spun out. He was so—'

'I know,' she cuts in. 'A royal prick. Don't worry. I'm sure it's not as bad as you think. I hope it isn't. We really need this.'

But I know in my heart that it was.

Anis sits for a moment longer and then places her hand gently on my leg one last time and gives me a squeeze.

Over the next hour the rest of the staff finish up, most of them moving quietly around me, unaware of exactly what has gone down, but knowing that obviously *things did not go well*. Everything goes silent, and still I sit. I think about texting Roxy, but I feel like I need to speak to her to her face. I check my phone and there's another message from Tim.

Call me!

Why is he suddenly so bloody eager?

I hit the Close-screen button and slip the phone into my pocket, and wonder if James is still in the kitchen and if it would be stalker-like to go and say hello. I decide not. After all, I need to say sorry. I pull myself up and head into the kitchen, but he's not there.

I find him at the bar, having a beer. It's dark, with only the night lamp on. He's alone. He must have got changed somewhere else, because he's in a black T-shirt and looks as if maybe he's even had a shower. He's also eating some leftovers from the kitchen – looks like the polenta or maybe the truffle mash.

'James?' I say meekly as I walk towards him. I stop just short of sitting down.

'Hey,' he says, smiling at me. 'Are you feeling better? Mum wouldn't tell me what was going on, and I didn't want to disturb you.'

'Ah yes,' I say. He's the same as usual. He's not angry – probably because he doesn't know how much I messed up – but I want to say something anyway. 'I'm sorry about the reviewer.'

'What happened?'

'I said some stupid things. I got overwhelmed,' I say truthfully.

'Everyone did. Mum managed to drop an entire bottle of claret on the floor.'

'Oh God.'

'And I fucked up too,' he says, shaking his head.

'You did?'

'Yeah, overcooked sea bream. The pigeon was tough. I totally choked.'

There is a comfort in the camaraderie, but I don't expect James's shortcomings are as bad as he claims. 'I doubt you did,' I say, wondering if I should sit down or if he wants to be alone.

'I did,' he shrugs and spins round on his stool to face me, and I am standing there holding my shoes, feeling as vulnerable as hell. James is different, like a tension in him has dispelled and although he's definitely pensive, he's not guarded. It's almost as though his disappointment in himself has relaxed him somehow. It's a lesson in how to take failure, I think.

'James?' I say quietly as he looks up and holds my gaze.

'Yes?' he asks and he's not looking away, for once.

I close my eyes and then look down at my bare feet. *This is not the time. Not the time. Not the time. I'm too anxious. This is a disaster.*

'My feet ache all the time,' I say, trying to deflect, wriggling my toes and wincing with embarrassment.

'Come here,' he says, and I look up and he's holding his fork out to me.

'I don't want any, thanks. I couldn't eat.'

'Do I have to come to you?' he says with the softest of smiles. His voice is low and soft, his eyes not leaving mine.

'Yes,' I reply.

We hear the back door shut, and I guess it's probably Irene leaving the office for the night, but to be sure we're alone I walk slowly into the kitchen. I can feel James following me. There is only the buzz of the fridge and the smell of industrial soap in the air, as he walks silently across the kitchen until he's only inches from me. I let out a small gasp at the closeness and shut my eyes for a moment, and James stays silent for as long as it takes for me to get the courage to open them. He's making sure I'm present.

'Are we going to have a meeting about the sinewy pigeon or are you going to kiss me?' *What are you doing, Birdy?*

But James's face breaks into a smile and his hands swing forward enough to brush past mine, and there is a surge of excitement as our fingers barely touch and I feel completely, breathlessly on edge.

'You know, when I think about it, it's probably just as well I fucked up the wine and you fucked up the food, because at least it's both of our faults,' I say to him. 'No one's going to fire you, and if they don't fire you, they won't fire me. And that would be a relief. You know, you should make a decision about what's happening here, because I'm no good at reading people.'

'*I* should make a decision?' he says, and then his fingertips trail up my arm, all along my shoulder, gently up my neck – all the while his gaze fixed to mine. 'You're the one who—'

'We broke up,' I say quickly. 'I mean, we haven't talked about it, but I can text him now? Where's my phone? I'll do it right now. James, Tim is a terrible boyfriend. He was never really a boyfriend even. We've hardly spoken the last few weeks.'

'If it's over . . .' he says, searching my eyes for reassurance.

'It's over. Right now. It's over.' I feel my heart thumping in my chest, every single part of my body tingling with anticipation. And it's true — in my heart it's true.

'Well, if it's definitely over . . .' he says again.

And then it happens and my eyes are still open when it does, I'm in such shock. His lips are gently on mine, and I can feel the light brush of his nose on my cheek. I drop my shoes. It's a softer kiss than I thought it would be. Soft, but determined. My brain is racing and I wonder why I can't just enjoy being kissed without analysing every moment of it.

Then James's arms are round me and his hand traces down my back to the base of my spine and he pulls me in closer. Then the kiss gets a little harder, and his mouth opens wider and I shut my eyes and let myself go, reaching my hands up to his neck.

He steps back and nods at the door. 'Let's go.'

Moments later we're at the back of the building and I'm walking barefoot along the cold pebbles. I'm in front of him, pulling him by the hand. He's walking slowly, watching me walk with this funny smile on his face, and I start to feel even more exposed and vulnerable in the relentless silence.

'It's cold,' I say, as I slow myself down to his pace and we walk alongside each other, me holding James's hand. 'Why are you so slow?'

'We've got time, haven't we?' he says.

'I don't like waiting,' I say. Thoughts are trying to get into my head: horrible thoughts about what he'll think of me naked; if I'd have to be on top; if I'd even enjoy it. 'Delayed gratification makes me anxious.'

He stops walking and pulls me into him and kisses me one more time, and I wonder if he wants this because it's only got a shelf life of one summer, or if he wants it because it's only one night. But I try to push my fears away and enjoy being kissed, and kissing him in return.

Now James is leading me. His hands are warm and clammy and I can't quite make out whose lights are on at the cottage in the distance. The oak leaves waving in the night breeze look small and fragile against the thick, old trunks. I feel a sudden affinity with those leaves.

With everything around me, finding warmth and sun. Beginning to really grow.

We creep into the hallway, but the house is deathly quiet. James leads me up the stairs, putting his finger to his lips to keep me from making any noise as we inch down the hall past Bill's room. I realize I've never seen James's room, and then I have a minor panic that it's too tidy, or weirdly decorated with posters of some strange obsession, like Oasis or a crappy local football team. Then, as we near his door, anxiety washes over me and I don't want to think about why – but it's not about posters.

James unlocks the door as gently as he can and pushes it open, and his room is the perfect mix of clean and surface-mess. Definitely boy-ish, down to the navy-blue pinstripe duvet, classic M&S, with only one matching square cushion that came free with the set. There's an acoustic guitar in the corner, and some books, including what looks like a novel *with a bookmark* by his bed. Impressive. Mercifully, there are no posters on the wall.

He looks a bit embarrassed as he shakes his duvet out and closes his laundry basket. 'I wasn't expecting guests,' he says, his cheeks a mar-vellously sweet shade of pink. 'Most of my stuff isn't here anyway.'

'I'm nervous,' I blurt.

Immediately I regret it, but it's the truth. The ten minutes or so between the kitchen and his bedroom have cooled me somewhat, and I suddenly feel a new pressure to do the *thing*. I mean, I like the rush of someone fancying you on a night out, and that exciting bit as you tear each other's clothes off, but then it's almost always a bit disappointing. Some chad watching his own biceps, while I wriggle around trying to find some satisfaction. For me, it's the bits you do between the sex that I *really* want. The intimacy. Eating takeaway in a guy's T-shirt and having him bring me a coffee. I don't have much of a chance to think about it any further, because James is removing his T-shirt.

I'm staring, I know I am. He doesn't drop his T-shirt, just holds it in front of him, and for a moment he looks a bit lost. I take a step towards him, because making him feel comfortable is more impor-tant to me than making myself feel comfortable. I want him to know that he's got permission to keep going, even if I'm not sure I want to join in. But he senses my conflict and stops. I feel that stab of worry; without the promise of sex, he's trapped in his room with me. I don't know how to negotiate this situation.

'Sorry, we should have stayed in the kitchen. I'm not good when I have to think about something too much.'

'Heather,' James tosses his T-shirt to the side and walks over to me, then picks up my hand and puts it in his. I cringe at the name and pull back slightly.

'Don't,' I say, and he immediately obliges, dropping my hand and pulling out of my space. I look at his pale collarbone and thick, round shoulder and imagine running my mouth along it, in some super-sexy manner that might make him groan. I want to throw myself into it, but I can't.

'Fancy sticking on a film?' he suggests.

'A film?'

'Netflix?'

'And we can just hang?' I search his face to see if he's disappointed.

I think about Peter Faulkner, who I fancied for about six months when I was twenty-three. But when he came on to me at a party in Croydon, I got nervous and asked if we could simply talk for a bit. He reluctantly agreed and suggested we go get a kebab at the only place open down by the Tube station. When I collected my chicken doner from the man behind the counter, Peter had already called himself an Uber and didn't even say goodbye properly. *You're on the Northern Line, right? There's one in six minutes*, he said, with a bright but dismissive smile.

'Yep. We can just hang,' James replies.

I'm not one hundred per cent sure he means it, but I'm relieved.

'Okay,' I say and feel the tension disperse. 'A film would be good.'

He nods and, with a smile, walks to the cupboard and pulls open the doors. There's a massive flat-screen TV hidden behind it, and a couple of remotes on the shelf. He turns to me and, although his bare chest makes me nervous, I grin.

'You have to let me choose,' I say. 'Can I get in?' I nod to his bed.

'Please,' he says. 'Shall I make us a cuppa? Or a wine?'

'I'm sick of wine,' I say with a laugh.

'Tea it is, then.'

He slips his T-shirt back on and disappears downstairs to the kitchen. After battling with myself for a moment, I peel off my skirt and shirt, laying them carefully over his laundry basket, and jump between his sheets, wearing nothing but a tank top and knickers. I switch on the television, flick through the Netflix offerings and wonder if he would sit through my third-favourite film of all time, *Die Hard*. All men like *Die Hard*, don't they?

Moments later James comes back, balancing two ginger biscuits on top of two mugs, and closes the door quietly.

'Did you choose *Die Hard*?' he says.

'You sound surprised,' I reply. 'It never fails to entertain. And it's got Alan Rickman.'

'I trust you,' he says, stripping to his boxers and climbing into bed next to me. I move across to make room.

'You've never seen *Die Hard*?'

'Nope,' he says, laughing. 'Honestly, I usually fall asleep when I'm watching TV. I'm always so tired.'

'But *everyone* has seen *Die Hard*,' I say, hitting Play and settling into one of his massive pillows to watch.

An hour later I'm snuggled into James's shoulder and he's asleep. As I listen to his slow sleep-breathing, I feel a wave of tiredness and for a moment think about creeping out of his bed and downstairs into my own. But then I close my eyes.

27.

My phone wakes me in the middle of the night. I'm not sure how long it's been buzzing, but I leap out of bed and fumble around in the dark until I find it. My brain is racing. Who is it? I must have been dreaming about my dad, because he's the first person I think of. Or is it Heather? Did Roxy and Heather talk? I know I'm tired and confused, and I almost feel sick as I pull the phone out from my bag.

But then I see it's only Tim, so I quickly put my phone on silent. Okay. He's not going away. I'm going to have to deal directly with it at some point. Especially now that I've promised James I will. Later today I will speak to Roxy about the Facebook request and pull my shit together, put my head down and finish off this summer without fucking anything else up. For a moment I think about leaving early again. I could call a taxi right now and be gone before anyone wakes up.

But I can't do it.

I look over at James just as he stirs and then rolls over, and I can hear his breath fall back to a slow, deep rhythm. I watch his chest move up and down for a moment, wanting to feel its comforting rise and fall.

I look down at my phone and decide I'd better message Tim. I need to get him to stop hassling me until I'm ready to deal with him for real. Tim can be a bit of a wild card, and he's the only person who knows I'm here as Heather.

Hi, what's up? Sorry, been super-busy here.

He replies immediately.

Birdy! Thought u drank 2 much whisky & got eaten by the Loch Ness Monster.

I roll my eyes – the Scottish jokes got tired a while ago.

Ha. Not exactly. Been working v hard. It's good here.

Do they still believe you're Heather?

It's all working out so far.

Fucking awesome. 👌, 🍆, 💥 and 👰

Did you have news?

Yes! We've got this wedding to go to in Glasgow, so I'm coming to see you!

I freeze. Fuckitty-fuck.

A wedding?

Yeah, we thought we'd swing by for a night and say hi, and then head on to the wedding.

Who's 'we', I wonder? And a previous Birdy wonders if Tim's going to invite me as his plus one.

Whose wedding?

The little speech bubbles appear and disappear, and then finally: No one you know. Distant cousin.

Cousin? So, his family will be there. And looks like I'm definitely not invited. Not that I'd want to go, but still.

Then I hear James's breathing pause and I close my phone down, so the room fills with darkness again. He rolls over, then starts deep breathing again, and I gaze at the outline of him for a moment before pulling my phone out again.

I won't be able to see you. It's busy here. And you can't stay here – it's high summer.

I wait, but there's no immediate reply.

So, don't come. We could meet in the middle somewhere? If I can get Tim to meet me somewhere else, maybe I can avoid the disaster that would be Tim at Loch Dorn.

I wait another few minutes.

What do you think?

Finally he replies.

We're coming. We're so into it. We'll come undercover.

CHRIST! Oh my God. I can't think of what to say, so I try to lay it out for him honestly.

Tim. No. Absolutely not.

I wait in the dark, my heart thumping. Shit. No. Shit!

No. You shouldn't come. It's a bad idea.

I hear James cough in the dark and then stir again. 'Heather?' he says, and I feel a deep sense of panic. 'Are you okay? You're not sneaking off, are you?'

'No, no. Just got a message,' I say, and I look down at my phone. Tim still hasn't replied. 'Sorry, my mum got in touch and I was worried,' I say, cursing myself for lying.

I hear him shuffle a little. 'Everything okay?'

'Yes, yes. We're all good,' I say, my heart thumping hard in my chest.

I slip my phone away and wander over to James and stand by the bed. The blinds are open, and a particularly bright moon means I can see his face and he can see mine. He looks sleepy and warm, while I feel a chill around my bare shoulders. He smiles at me and reaches up to hold my hand, our fingers intertwine and he reaches his other hand up and touches my thigh. I want to stop him, but I also don't. There is something intoxicating about the distraction. Everything else is pushed into the background while I feel his fingers on my leg, and his thumb gently stroking my hand.

He runs his hand upwards, so it's on the waistband of my knickers, and he tugs me towards him gently. I can feel his curled fingers pressed into my lower belly, and the waves of pleasure and anxiety are so intertwined I cannot think clearly.

I climb onto the bed, so I'm on top of him, and lay myself down across his body, keeping just enough weight on my arms so he doesn't take all of it. He reaches up and puts his hand on my face and kisses me gently on my cheek. I feel desperately nervous and I'm scared how it's coming across to him.

'Are you okay?' he whispers, as his hands stop short of my lower back.

'I don't want to crush you,' I say.

'You're not,' he says, reaching up to touch my hair.

'I don't know if this is a good idea . . .'

'It's probably not,' he says with a laugh.

And then I think, *Fuck it*. It's easier to do this than not. I want to, and don't want to, so equally that I can't make out the truth of my feelings any more. I close my eyes and relax my body and decide I'll deal with everything tomorrow. James kisses the side of my neck and his breath is on my ear, and the pleasure is so great I want to cry out.

He moves his hand up across my tank top until his palm is flat against my nipple, and then he gently kisses my chest, so I can feel the pound of my heart against his lips.

'You smell so good,' he says into my skin, as his hands roughly tug on my tank top and he pulls it over my head. I sense the heat rising in my cheeks as I feel his naked chest against me.

It's almost too much. Like the feeling of desire is swamping me and I cannot catch my breath. I pull back, trying to steady myself, and James waits until I am back with him.

But I let myself go further, and suddenly the pace picks up.

His hands move slowly, but with clear determination. Down my back, gliding across my skin, his mouth exploring my face and neck. We are listening to each other, our breathing guiding us. Wherever I go, he follows.

When I can't bear to wait any longer, his fingers move inside me, and I like them there. His cock is pressing into my stomach. I can hear him now, on that precipice. Just holding on. Like at any moment I might bite his ear and he would lose control completely. I feel a surge of power in that instant and it drives me crazy.

'You're so fucking hot, I feel like I'm in a dream,' I say.

'So are you.'

Then we are rolling over and he is on top, pushing into me, and everything falls away.

28.

There are two pressing issues, I think, as I look out of James's bed-room window at the sky – deep blue, with stretches of red-and-purple clouds as it wakes. One is Tim, my 'boyfriend'. He thinks he's coming to Loch Dorn en route to a family wedding, and I need to tell him he can't, and that whatever we have is over. I promised James last night, and yet the idea that Tim might ask me as his date momentar-ily engaged me. What is it with Tim? The reality is, he's crap. I'm not even sure if we're meant to be exclusive. But there is something about his lack of commitment that feels . . . somehow safe. Or perhaps I mean normal?

What does romantic love actually feel like? I wonder, not for the first time in my life.

I sigh. I definitely need to end whatever it is, properly. Not with a flippant text or voicemail. A total pulling off a plaster, no question the-deed-is-done kind of clarity, rather than just ghosting him: my hitherto preferred method. But Tim's not answering his phone. And I definitely don't want to do this face-to-face.

In every scenario in which I imagine him visiting the estate, it ends badly. It's like a 'Choose your own adventure', which finishes with me either being arrested for fraud or the hotel looking like that scene from *The Hangover*. And in all options, I can see the look on James's face and it makes me ache.

I look at my phone again. It's time to head up to the restaurant and see if Roxy is back. And that's the second issue.

I haven't fully decided on a good way to ask her to delete the Face-book request – all I know is she has to. It's already breakfast time in Italy, and Heather will surely be online soon, checking her messages and ignoring her partner over coffee, like every normal person.

If Heather blindly accepts a request from a stranger, which is totally on-brand for her, Roxy will have access to all her photos; and, maybe worse, Heather will wonder why a waitress from Loch Dorn has suddenly Friended her and started chatting, as though they're besties. I curse myself for not asking Roxy to delete the request then and there on the phone last night. I *need* her onside. Roxy has proved completely indispensable. Also, I like her. A lot. I need to shut this down, but carefully.

I unhook James's heavy arm from where it rests on my chest and gently place it beside him. At some point he must have put pyjama bottoms on, which is a relief. There's something about seeing a dick flailing about in its natural state that is just *too much* for 8 a.m. But then, for a moment, as I sit there looking down at him, last night washes over me, clear and fresh like it was captured on 70mm film. Or first-press vinyl. I settle into the delicious memory, the smells and feelings. The touch of skin.

What do you want?

All of it.

I shiver at the memory. I allow myself to gently touch James's arm, the soft brush of hair along his forearm, and run my finger down one of the many tiny scars across his hands.

I revel in the memory of that moment between the first and the second time, where we talked like lovers do. Disclosing the best parts of ourselves, coy and practised.

I briefly went to university.

I've always wanted to go to Morocco.

I could inhale you.

I want to eat your shoulder.

What do you like most about wine?

And then we'd played, turning it into one of those silly games you'd die of embarrassment for someone else to overhear.

Lovely open texture.

Luscious and juicy.

Impressive length, becomes fleshier with each taste.

Beautiful body with plenty of elegance.

Refined and muscular.

Surprising length.
Lingering finish.

In the distance, I can hear Brett's dogs barking, which means that he is up and with the horses. I have to go. It feels like I'm stuck with thick, resistant Velcro as I tear myself from the bed.

I creep as quietly as I can. Pull my clothes on. James doesn't stir. Before I shut the door, I take one last look at him and my heart lurches. I want to run back, crawl into bed and stay there for ever. I want to lie across his chest like women do in films, and take sneaky sniffs of his armpit. I whisper, *Bye, James* as I shut the door, and wonder if last night will ever happen again. I hope so.

As soon as I'm out, I creep down the hall, desperate not to wake Bill. His bedroom door is slightly ajar, and as I tiptoe past I see he's passed out, snoring, face-down and still in his uniform. And then I see them: the cases of wine from the film premiere. I'm sure it's them, stacked at the bottom of his wardrobe, door ajar. There must be a dozen bottles in the distinctive red and black boxes. I frown. There has to be some explanation. But it has to wait.

I stop in my bedroom to throw on a T-shirt and slip on my now completely filthy white trainers. I hope Irene doesn't see me, because she wouldn't approve of staff schlepping about the place looking like I do right now.

Focus, Birdy. Roxy! I can't waste any time, and breakfast will be starting to pick up. I race up to the back of the house and crash into the kitchen area, where I see Anis, who shoots me a wry smile. Does she know what happened last night? Has Roxy already discovered my secret? My heart is pounding as I push the kitchen door slightly open and spot her in the dining area.

'Hey,' I mouth to her, pointing towards the staffroom.

Roxy sees me and shoots a big smile, which swiftly changes into a wide-eyed look of worry as she finishes de-crumbing table four with one of those little sterling-silver scrapers. It seems a bit much, clearing breakfast crumbs, and I think, not for the first time, that they should toss this whole high-class service shit out of the window and do something more relaxed.

As we both slip into the staffroom unnoticed, I feel my heart beating a little faster in my chest. Roxy looks nervous too.

'Is this about the reviewer? Or the incident with the Chablis? Anis said there was a review on Tripadvisor about it. I already told James and Irene that it was *my* suggestion. It was corked, and I just don't know why he didn't return it. I would have replaced it – you know I would!'

I have no idea what she's talking about, and frankly it's the least of my concerns.

'No, no,' I say, waving away her concern. 'It's okay, it was definitely not your fault. Sometimes wine is bad, but the customer doesn't return it because they're arseholes who are trying to impress their friends and don't know anything at all about wine. Like me.'

She giggles, thinking I'm being self-effacing when I'm being honest. The Heather I presented at the start of this gig is slowly but surely melting away.

Focus, Birdy. Focus on the clean-up.

'Oh, thank goodness, I've been so worried,' she replies, visibly relaxing. 'How was last night? No one will tell me.'

'Well, not great actually,' I say, shaking my head. 'It was all a bit of a comedy of errors in the end. James thinks he overcooked the pigeon, and I offended the reviewer.'

'Oh no!'

'It will be fine. Fine. Don't worry about that,' I say quickly. 'It's not about that.'

'Oh. Okay? What is it then?'

Here goes.

'Look, it's about the Facebook thing,' I begin, feeling my cheeks burn. 'It's just that I really try not to mix my work and friendships, you know?'

'I totally understand,' Roxy replies quickly, her cheeks turning a deep crimson in return and her eyes dropping to the floor. 'Please ignore the request – I'm so embarrassed.'

But it isn't enough to give her an explanation of why I don't want to accept it, because that damned alert will still be on Heather's account. The request needs to be gone.

'This will sound kind of rude, but can you delete the request?'

'Sure,' she says, with a sort of forced smile. I realize she's hurt, but I have to suck it up and push forward and focus on the trouble at hand.

'Now?' I say.

'Now?'

'Yes, if you wouldn't mind,' I say, smiling apologetically and trying to behave like this is a normal and not-at-all-rude request.

Her eyes are up and right on me, but she's not angry or suspicious or any of the things that would make me more nervous. Rather she looks completely humiliated.

'Okay, sorry,' she says, walking over to her locker. I watch as she fumbles with the lock, spins the dial left and right, then pulls the lock down to open it. She finds her phone, looks briefly up at me and then clicks a few times.

'I know this is a bit weird,' I say, wanting to soften the blow.

'It's fine,' she interjects, and then tosses her phone back in the locker and slams it shut, the only hint that her embarrassment is turning to anger. 'I'm sorry I bothered you.'

'It's not a bother – I'm just trying to stay professional. That means no Friending, fighting or fucking,' I say, forcing a grin.

'Okay, Heather,' Roxy says with a deflated smile. And then she goes to leave and I feel so bad. I want to grab her wrist and tell her I adore her, and that we will be friends for ever, but I can't.

I still have to sort out bloody Tim.

I pull my phone out of my back pocket as Roxy lets the door shut behind her. Still nothing from Tim. I try to call, but it goes straight to voicemail. I also see the battery is at only 4 per cent. Shit!

I decide to head back down to the cottage, charge my phone, have a coffee, wait for Tim to turn his phone on and try to relax.

29.

Back in the quiet safety of my bedroom I boot up my computer. It's started to sound like a helicopter trying to take off, so I'm pretty sure it's on its last legs. I plug my phone quickly into the side and check it's charging. I think about a shower, but I can't bear to wash away the night before. In the mirror, I see a girl who needs sleep. I inspect the new lines around my eyes and vow to at least wash my face and put on some make-up later. I squeeze out the last of my moisturizer and rub it into my wind-blown skin, and run Heather's bamboo paddle brush through my hair, feeling guilt with every stroke. I need to speak to her. I need to make sure she didn't see that damned request. I send her a quick message.

Heather, are you there?

I am suddenly famished and realize I've not eaten and should have grabbed something from the hotel kitchen. I'll have to make do with what's in the cottage. I open the fridge, which has the rind of some cheese, some milk, an empty carton of eggs, the usual assortment of condiments – soy sauce, mayonnaise, tomato sauce and half a jar of capers. All those cooking lessons and there's nothing I can utilize my fledgling skills on. Thinking of James makes me feel giddy and vaguely sick. I ignore it. Hunger is the next task.

Then I check the cupboard and find a tin of M&S chicken korma at the back. *Bingo!* I fish around for a saucepan and dump it into the pan.

Then I put my laptop up on the counter and open Facebook. I check Heather's page and am relieved to see she's not posted at all, and my anxiety eases somewhat. She probably hasn't been on it in days. I pull out my phone, and there's a message from her.

Yep, I can talk.

I call her while I'm stirring my chicken korma.

'Hey, babe,' she says lazily.

'How's Italy?' I ask, speaking quietly, though I'm pretty sure James and Bill are both still asleep.

'Well,' she says, taking a breath, 'it's been okay. It was nice last night, but Cristian left this morning before I woke up. Probably work or something.'

'Oh,' I reply, biting my tongue. I hate this guy.

'But things are okay, I guess, in other ways. I don't know. What's up with you?' she asks. 'Any luck with Mr Chef? Have you seen him again? And are you still staying with your cousin? Really, we've not caught up in ages!'

She doesn't mention any Facebook request, and I'm pretty sure she would have, right off the bat. I relax. I want to tell her about James and the cooking lessons. And last night. I want to tell her everything about it.

I'm totally into him. He's sweet and shy and kind of naïve, and absolutely nothing like other guys I've dated. He moves at a slow pace. He doesn't get distracted. He's dedicated to his work, and he's so clever, but he doesn't have the confidence to go out on his own. He likes power ballads, and he's never seen Die Hard. *He's kind and gentle, but deeply passionate when you get to know him. And even occasionally funny, though admittedly mostly unintentionally. He's really handsome, but he doesn't pluck his eyebrows or have hundreds of bloody tattoos. He makes me feel calm and comfortable and giddy and anxious all at once. You would love him, Heather. LOVE HIM. And I am waiting for him to learn the truth: that I'm no good.*

But I can't, so I say the other part of the truth. The part that can't be avoided. 'Well, it doesn't really have a future.'

'What do you mean?'

'Nothing, it's just that it can't really go anywhere.'

'Does he have a girlfriend? Why wouldn't you pursue it?'

'Heather, not everything in life revolves around dudes.'

The line goes quiet and I silently panic that I've upset her.

'I miss you,' I say truthfully.

'Same, Birdy, same,' she says in a tone that is almost woeful.

I want to ask her more about Cristian, and my sense is that she wants to share, but I don't have the time right now.

'I'm about to . . . er . . . head out. Can we book in time for a proper catch-up?'

'Yeah, sure, Birdy. Any time. I'm always free.'

I deflate further. I called her to find out if she had a bloody Friend request on Facebook, but what she actually needs right now is a real friend. My phone beeps. I can see it's Tim calling.

'Hey, I better go, that's the other line.' Part of me is relieved – if I find out how bad things are with Cristian right now, I won't be able to stop myself telling her to come home. *Birdy, you really are the worst.*

'K. Speak soon,' Heather says, sounding a little upset, and as I hang up the phone I feel bad. But there's no time for feelings.

'Hi, Tim. Thank God,' I say, feeling relief washing over me.

'What's up?'

'Look, I don't want to be an arsehole, but you can't come here.'

A very delicate problem suddenly occurs to me. How do you break up with someone that you're not actually in a confirmed relationship with? What if he laughs at me?

'Ah, come on. It'll be awesome.'

'It won't. I'm totally stressed all the time. I nearly got found out today – someone bloody Friend-requested Heather.'

'Oh shit,' Tim says, laughing loudly. 'You need to create some fake profiles, so if they search for her, they'll find you.'

Damn, why didn't I think of that?

'You *so* need me. Come on, I'll call you Heather, and Damo can crack on to one of the waitresses. Are there hot waitresses there? He's asking me right now.'

'Yes,' I reply, thinking of Roxy. 'But she's too . . .'

'What? Too fancy for Damo?'

'No, no. She's like nineteen. Tim, sorry. I feel like a bitch, but I just think it's better if you don't come.' Deep breath. 'I think that we should stop seeing each other. In Scotland or London.'

'What about Wales?'

'Tim, I'm serious.'

'Okay, okay. We won't come, bloody hell.'

'Thank you.'

'It would have been so much fun,' he says, with an exaggerated sigh. Does he actually sound pissed off? 'Damo will not be happy.'

'You were taking Damo as your plus one? To a family wedding?'

'So?' he replies.

I would laugh if it wasn't so infuriating. I want to get off the phone now.

'Tim, don't come. I'll call you, okay?'

'Fine, fine, speak soon,' he replies and hangs up.

I check my phone – it's nearly 9 a.m. I feel a rush of exhilaration that I've put both fires out and I've still got a couple of hours to get my head back in the game before service.

'Hello,' I hear a sleepy voice, and I feel my tummy tingle as James comes through the archway between the lounge and the kitchen. 'I missed you this morning.'

He comes straight over. There's no nerves about possible mistakes or uncertainty about his feelings. He's completely clear on what this is. He puts his arms round me, pulls the wooden spoon out of my hand and pulls me close.

'You can't eat that.'

'Are you going to start telling me what to eat?'

'It's likely,' he says, glancing across at the pot.

I bite my lip.

'What time is your shift?' he asks.

'Eleven-thirty.'

'Good,' he replies and pulls me by the hand, turning off the curry as I give in. 'I know a place.'

We get to the hall and James pulls the keys to the SUV off the hook and hands them to me. 'Go get the car, I'll be outside in one minute.'

I obey. It takes me a few minutes to figure out the car and its weird button ignition system, but when I drive down the path to the house, James is there, holding his coat and a pint of milk, looking deliciously unwashed.

'Get in,' I say as I pull up, stalling the car almost immediately.

'Are you sure you don't want me to drive?'

'No, let me,' I say. 'It's not far, is it?'

'Just twenty minutes. Follow the main road out of town – same way as if we're going to Skye, but turn right at the main intersection instead.'

'You'll have to show me, I can't remember.'

'Okay. How are you feeling about last night?'

'You mean . . .'

'Oh, I know how you felt about *that*.' He grins. 'I meant the constipated . . . turtle? Was that what you called him?'

'Tortoise,' I say, a new wave of regret washing over me, which I swiftly shove down.

'Let's not talk about that now.'

'Fair enough.'

'Heather,' he says, and I can tell by his tone that he wants to say something serious.

'Can you not call me by my full name any more?' I say on the spur of the moment. 'Reminds me of my mother.'

'Okay . . . what should I call you?'

'My close friends call me Birdy,' I say, changing gears, crunching the gearbox in the process. Fuck it! I want him to call me by my name. Just for these last few weeks.

'Birdy? Cute,' he says and looks out the window at Brett, who is leading two guests along the garden path.

'What were you going to say?'

'I was going to tell you that you look pretty.'

I gulp, crunching the gears harder than the first time as we whizz out of the grounds of Loch Dorn and onto the windy single-track road.

'Well,' I say, 'don't let me stop you. Jesus Christ, I have no idea if another car is coming. This is worse than Cornwall.'

I look across and we meet eyes and grin at each other, and then I narrowly miss a tree stump, swerving at the very last minute. 'I'd better concentrate. Where are we going, by the way?

'My house,' he says, and I can hear the pride in his voice. 'Left here.'

'*Your* house?' He can't mean his mum's – that's in the other direction.

'There!' he says, pointing to another almost-invisible lane amongst the trees.

'What is it with all the damned roads in this place?' I say, slamming on the brakes, then reversing backwards and turning off down the little lane. It's actually quite a pretty lane – and is properly cleared of trees and not too bumpy, now that we're on it.

'See that collection of oaks over there?'

'Yep.'

'That's where I found my bounty of porcini last year.'

'Oooh,' I say, 'when do they come?'

'August, usually. Okay, down there,' he says, directing me along another lane.

'So, wait. *Your house?*'

'Yeah. I bought it a while back, but it's still a bit of a mess. Well, you'll see.'

Suddenly the trees clear and we follow the lane alongside a farm, where a few sheep are lazily eating grass in small fields. We head down a steep road, until the land completely opens up and we're driving towards a stony inlet.

'Is that the sea?'

'Yep,' he says.

The road takes a final sharp turn, and at the end of a crumbling stone drive sits an also crumbling stone house without a roof; and then, further on, a bigger stone house built right out of the rocky cliff, complete with a very decrepit old boat-launch. I pull the car to a stop.

For a moment I sit there, gaping.

'Well, it's a bit of a fixer-upper, but a hell of a view,' I say, gazing out across the deep-blue bay. There is a sudden singing in my heart at the emptiness and peace of it all.

'Come on,' James says, and he jumps out of the car and pulls a set of keys out of his back pocket. The sea air hits me, and I have a brief flash of Plymouth and happy days by the seaside, with hire-by-the-hour striped deckchairs, candyfloss and crowds. I can't quite place the memory, but Heather is definitely there.

Then seagulls break the silence, squawking as they circle the hilltop above the cottage.

I gasp as he opens the door. We go directly into the lounge area, and it's stunning. The cottage was obviously falling apart, but instead of rebuilding and restoring it, James seems to be creating something completely modern out of the shell.

'That wall came off about eighty years ago. Just crumbled into the sea,' he says. 'So I got that glass plate and oak frame cut, to fit the hole exactly. I love how you can see where it's falling apart, but obviously now it's airtight,' he laughs. 'But it's cool, because sometimes the tide comes right up – almost to the window.'

It's incredible. A huge glass wall makes up the sea-view side of the house, giving it an openness and lightness you wouldn't expect from a cottage of this age. But because it's glass and wood, it looks completely at home against the old stone.

'I've only done that wall so far,' he says, as I swing round and see that he's putting coffee on an old gas stove top and pulling eggs out of the fridge. 'It's expensive. And it takes time to get it right, you know?'

'It's amazing. It's like the perfect mix of old and new,' I say, turning back to the view.

'There's heaps to do,' he says. 'I just do bits and pieces when I have the time. But it's got power now, and gas. And last year we got a septic tank installed, so the toilets are not as gross as they were.'

'Do you want to live here one day?'

'That's the plan, Birdy.'

I close my eyes and listen to him call me *Birdy* on repeat in my head.

The sun spills suddenly into the room via a small skylight. I look up and cover my eyes. 'Was that a hole once, too?'

'Yep. Good place for it, though – makes the perfect skylight. Have a seat, let me make you breakfast.'

I take a seat on the old sofa that faces the view. I sink into it. It feels like a feather bed. It's deep enough to pull both my feet up and cross my legs, and I drag a soft woollen blanket across me. There are a bunch of cookbooks – an old copy of Nigella's *How to Be a Domestic Goddess* and *Jamie's 15-Minute Meals* – on a little upturned apple crate, I note with amusement. There are also two framed photos: one of

Irene and James (he looks about an awkward eighteen), and another of a man with enormous sideburns and a mousy brown mass of curls. He looks familiar.

'Is that your dad?'

'Yeah.'

'Wow, great sideburns.'

'I know. It's the only photo I have. And will ever have, I suppose.'

'I feel bad that I said he was a creep, when we went fishing.'

'I didn't know him,' James says with a shrug. 'Mum gave me that photo, and it felt like I should stick it in a frame. Not sure I'll leave it out, but she didn't want it at the cottage.'

It isn't long before he's prepared a tray with French toast and a couple of mugs of coffee made with warm milk. The toast is lightly dusted with icing sugar, but we don't get very far through it before the tension starts to build again. It's the squeezy honey's fault. As he swirls it around the toast, I am finding it ludicrously erotic, which makes me giggle.

James puts his hand on my waist.

'I stink,' I tell him. 'I haven't had a shower and I'm still wearing yesterday's knickers. Oh, and in this light, I'd better warn you, there will be some disappointments. My nipples, for example, are too big and the wrong colour for my skin tone. I have a scar that runs down my right thigh, from when I slid down a bannister drunk and there was a nail sticking out of the railing. My stomach is only flat if I'm lying down *and* breathing in. Then it looks quite good, I think. But it's at the expense of my boobs, which will start to disappear under my armpits.'

And then he's kissing me again. I think to shut me up, and I think it was probably a wise idea, because it looked like I was going to continue listing all my imperfections like some sort of pre-shag disclosure agreement.

'Birdy?' James says moments later, as we lie across his sofa in a haze of sweat.

'Yes,' I say, soaking up the sound of my own name coming out of his mouth, playing with his smattering of chest hair.

'I don't want you to go.'

It's the most beautiful, and the most sobering, sentence I've ever heard. I can't look at him, but I can feel his eyes scanning my face, looking for reassurance. I feel the same. But I don't look up; instead I stare out onto the water, watching it ripple along the bay, lapping at the black stones of the shore.

'Me too,' I say in the end, because it's the truth.

30.

'Hi, Russell,' I say, with as much swagger as I can manage.

He's sitting at the bar, looking furious, and I have to assume he's been filled in on the other night's reviewer disaster. I've been avoiding him as best I can since then, and admittedly I have been distracted by the delicious haze of fresh lust with James. James in the cellar. James in our cottage. James in his cottage. Even James, unsuccessfully, in the chiller. 'It's just a bit cold,' we'd agreed.

I shrink into myself momentarily, before deciding I am comfortable hating Russell from here on in.

'Hello, Heather,' he says.

'Listen, about the other night . . .'

'We'll do a debrief later,' Russell says dismissively, 'but in the meantime an order's come in. It's by the back door.'

'Thank you,' I say. And then I have a memory of the wines in Bill's wardrobe. I haven't thought about it again. That day, with Roxy, the Facebook request, my first night with James . . . it just slipped my mind. 'I wanted to ask you,' I say, pausing to make sure I word it carefully. 'The wine orders for the film premiere, who put them in?'

'Is this a joke?' he replies.

'Um, no . . .' I say carefully.

'Surely you put the fucking order in? It's your job?'

'Oh,' I say, confused. What the hell is going on? Bill told me that Russell got the order in from a friend. I have a sinking feeling in the pit of my stomach as the puzzle begins to come together. It's one thing to take the odd nip at the bar or an after-work pint — it's a bit of a perk on the side. It's quite another to siphon off a few cases of wine. I am relieved, somewhat, that Bill has not taken wine from the main cellar. But he has seen an opportunity and taken it. I wonder if I should speak with Irene and James about it at some point, or just let it go.

I glance over at James in the kitchen and we smile at each other. In that look, a thousand million secrets scroll between us. The cottage. The coffee. The seagulls diving for fish. Fishing. French toast.

'The Wallaces are wanting to see the manager in reception. Heather, can you go? We can't find Irene,' Anis says, sticking her head out of the kitchen.

'Christ, what now?' says Russell, slamming his hand on the bar.

'No problem,' I say quickly. There is a large man, at least in his fifties, gesticulating furiously in his dressing gown, which is on the precipice of spilling open. His wife — I guess — is standing in front of him, wrapped in a towel with her hands over her mouth, looking terrified.

'Hello, sir, madam. Whatever seems to be the matter?' I ask, genuinely nervous. Have they been fighting? Why are they naked? Why are his legs covered in mud and grass stains?'

'There's a deer in our room! A big deer with big horns,' cries Mrs Wallace.

'Antlers,' Mr Wallace interjects, as if he's already corrected her a dozen times.

'Okay, well—' I start to respond.

'Antlers! On our anniversary we like to have a bath, with champagne, together. We've always done it.'

'Everyone loves a good, relaxing soak,' I say, looking round and hoping Irene will appear soon.

'It pushed open the door of the bathroom!' Mrs Wallace says, her voice starting to rise again. 'We both ran, and then the door to the annexe closed behind us.'

'I didn't run,' Mr Wallace corrects.

'Yes, you did. You ran right out and down that muddy bank. You didn't look back to see if I was even alive! Look at the mud up your leg, you absolute coward.'

'I beg your pardon, Karen, I don't think that's quite what happened.'

'Off he went. Like Forrest Gump.'

'That's quite enough,' he says, eyes darting towards me. 'I was clearly running for help.'

Mercifully, this is when Irene arrives.

'Hello, Karen. Gregory. As I understand it, a stag has wandered into your room?' Irene says calmly. I marvel at the way her soothing tone quietens them. 'I'm sure we can get that fixed right away. Heather, could you call Brett, dear, and have him come up with the shotgun?'

'A shotgun?' I say, gulping.

Irene turns to me and gives me a reassuring nod. 'Yes, Brett will know exactly what to do. Now, Mr Wallace, can I get you something stiff to drink? We'll have this taken care of immediately, and of course there will be no charge on your room this evening.'

'Christ, how did a deer get into their bedroom?' I whisper to her, as she ushers the couple towards the library, handing Mrs Wallace a throw blanket.

'Can I get you something, Mrs Wallace, a whisky perhaps – you look like you could do with it?' Irene continues loudly.

I yank up the reception phone and Brett answers in three rings. 'Irene says you need to come with your shotgun,' I whisper, before quickly clarifying, 'because of a deer in a bedroom. You're not going to kill it, are you?'

'Don't worry,' he says plainly and hangs up.

'He pulled my handbag off the bed,' Mrs Wallace is saying now, pitifully. 'He was going through it with his nose. I hope he doesn't find my Xanax.'

'It will all be over soon. We'll have you moved to the main house,' soothes Irene.

'Do you need anything else from me?' I ask her.

She shakes her head and I catch a hint of an eye-roll. 'No, dear, just get yourself ready for service.'

When I return to the restaurant, everyone is huddled around a laptop and Russell is reading something out to the gathered team. He looks up briefly and there it is, right on his face: the review. The review has been published, and the review is dreadful.

228

'Ah, Heather, let me start again, so you can hear it from the beginning,' he says. James is pale.

'No one wants to write a takedown piece on a place as iconic as Loch Dorn, but sometimes the entire experience is so woefully lacking that one must be completely honest.

'I arrive at Loch Dorn, recently renovated – although for whom, I cannot be sure. Every shade of grey has been displayed, to dull effect, giving the immediate impression that no one here wanted to take a single chance to be brilliant.

'Upon arrival at our table, the so-called sommelier, a perky, sharp-tongued Englishwoman, forgot the water and appeared completely out of her depth when we asked to change out a wine. I wonder if she'd tasted the chemically enhanced Gimlet served as an aperitif? The small shot of nuclear waste would be more at home cleansing a sink than a palate. The sea bream arrives and it is a tired, overworked slice of chewy sponge, sitting on – credit where it's due – some spectacular locally grown salsify.'

I glance up at Bill, who looks mortified; and then across to Anis, who looks like she might cry. Wow! We're *all* getting crucified.
It's the most part of a team I've ever felt.
'But here is my favourite part,' says Russell:

'I long for something dark and punchy to go with my divine venison, but the maître d', who has spent five courses hovering like a police helicopter, drops the bottle all over the dreary carpet.

'It's all I can do to keep from screaming for the old place, where the haggis, neeps and tatties came with a huge side of relaxed Scottish charm.

'Quite what Loch Dorn is aiming for, with its watery foams and exhausting wine list, one can only try to imagine. Has that recluse Michael MacDonald seen what's become of his once-grand old place? Does he even care?

'Desperate to end on a good note, I eventually find it, in the generous glass of local whisky I receive just before I call for the bill, which, at £265, is the final steak knife in the eyeball of this tasteless embarrassment to Scottish tourism.'

It's so bad, I can't help but giggle, then quickly bite my lip, because Russell isn't laughing and neither is anyone else.
'Well, it could not have gone worse,' says Russell, frowning, and the circle of staff all drop their heads in shame.

Roxy, who returned just in time to hear about the dropped wine bottle, is the only one who looks vaguely amused. *Fair enough*, I think. Truth is, she would have done a better job than me.

'I turned down a fucking judge's spot on *Iron Chef* for this. What a fucking joke! This place is a fucking joke. You're ALL A FUCK-ING JOKE.' Russell's so angry he's panting. 'Where the *hell* is Irene?' he says, craning his neck.

'She's dealing with a deer running amok in the annexe,' I reply, and then I really do have to work hard not to giggle.

Russell doesn't even justify that with a reply. He turns to James.

'We need to sit down and rethink the menu. Perhaps we need to rethink the entire set-up of this place. Some people have been a little distracted lately, haven't they? We'll talk later.'

James looks at the ground, as Russell slips on his glasses and stomps out through the swinging kitchen doors. *Damn it. Was it that obvious?*

I look round at the staff, but no one is looking at us. They're all still staring at their feet, with faces like they've been stabbed through the heart.

'Come on,' I say, trying to bolster the mood. 'Look, it's just one review. And I arguably came off the worst. And I'm sorry about that – I should never have let him get to me. But you're all amazing. Who gives a flying fuck what some floppy-haired tosser thinks?'

'Everybody! Fucking everybody does,' shouts Anis – and then, showing an unexpected degree of raw emotion, her eyes turn glassy and she storms into the kitchen while the others shuffle about on their spots.

Right at that moment an almighty BANG! comes from outside and everyone jumps, including me.

I decide to ignore it and power on. 'All that actually died here is a *strategy*. And *strategy* is just a bunch of words sewn together on a dodgy PowerPoint, with pictures no one bought the copyright for. What those bastards don't own is the bones of this place. We've still got pots and pans big enough for a king crab, and a cellar big enough for a serial killer. We've got talented chefs, and a mostly trained front-of-house. What we lack in skill, we make up for in false bravado. We can pull this back!'

I wait, hoping for some kind of cheer, but there is only silence and a cough.

'Back to work, everyone,' James says quietly to his kitchen staff, and off they shuffle.

The waiting staff begin to peel off too, moving slowly and wearily. Defeated.

And so we get on with lunch. Or, rather, we get through it, serving up the menu that we all had such investment in a few days ago, to guests who seem to like it fine – all the while knowing that we fell hopelessly short in every single way.

31.

At the end of service, I can't get out of there quick enough. James disappeared before the desserts went out, and I want to see him, see if he's all right. I'm relieved, of course, that it wasn't just me who got a pasting – but it's hard to believe that my dreadful performance at the start of the meal didn't have a knock-on effect on everyone else.

As I get ready to leave I see Irene in the bar area with a large glass of red wine – an immediate red flag, since I've never seen her drink at work. She's got changed into a flamboyant pink, green and gold trouser suit, which is the fashion equivalent of getting drunk to mask your pain.

'Irene?' I say, creeping over towards her as she tucks a bunch of paperwork under a magazine and pats the chair next to her. A dreadful attempt at hiding what was clearly *the books*.

'Heather, dear. I want to square up your back-pay, so I'm clear on the books. You never did give me your National Insurance number and whatnot.'

She fishes out a little envelope and hands it to me. It's cash and I want to hug her.

'Oh, thank you.'

She rattles her bangles down around her wrist, and I wonder why she's not saying anything about the review. Surely she's read it? Though she has been dealing with the deer situation. I wonder if it's a bad idea to bring it up, but I'm only happy when I have the complete lie of the land, so I plunge in.

'So is the deer, er . . . dead?'

'No. The shot was only for show. Brett opened the door and it walked right out,' she says, looking up with a wry smile. 'Christ knows, it walked into the wrong bedroom. Can you imagine being locked up with those two?'

'No, thank you,' I say. 'Um, Irene, I'm sorry about the review.'

'Well, yes. Quite. We all are.' I can see she can't even bear to mention her own faux pas.

'What are you going to do?'

'I don't know.'

'Russell's just left.'

'I know.' She smiles wearily.

'Where did he go?'

'I assume he's gone to see Mr MacDonald.'

'Oh. Do you think he'll get fired? I mean, it was all his vision, wasn't it?' You can hope, right?

'Oh, I'm sure Russell doesn't think this is his fault, and in truth it isn't. It's all our faults. It's mine for not standing up and speaking what was in my heart. Loch Dorn was never supposed to be this,' she says, waving her hands around at the pristine new paint job and fancy interiors. 'But it doesn't belong to me,' she says with a practical smile. 'It's Mr MacDonald's.'

'Can't you buy it?'

She laughs sadly. 'Oh dear, no. I'm a single woman of limited means, as Jane Austen would put it.'

'You have such excellent cultural references.' I try to make her laugh.

'We are where we are in life, for better or worse. I've done my best.' And she looks at me through her glasses, in the way a bank clerk might when studying a person's face upon receipt of their ID.

'Can't you go and see Mr MacDonald too, and tell him your vision? It wouldn't take much to give the place a more authentic feel. We just take down that dreadful hotel art, and some of the more ridiculously ostentatious things, like that book art and the sterling-silver stag's head over the fireplace. Oh God, and those ridiculous driftwood placemats – I mean, Jesus, those things are seriously stupid. People don't want to climb a tree to get to their rainbow chard.'

My voice wavers as I realize how emotionally attached I feel. I frown, looking to the ground.

'It's less than a month until the Wine Society event. If we can hang on until then, there is a chance we can turn it around.'

I nod, feeling a weary pressure, as I remember all the preparation I need to make for that event. And then I feel my phone vibrating in my pocket. I pull it out clumsily, and it falls to the ground and lands with a thud, face up. I rush to collect it from the floor. It's Heather.

'I have to take this,' I say.

'Go, go,' Irene nods.

I try to ignore the knot that is tightening in my stomach, and answer my phone.

'Hi.'

'Birdy, can you talk?'

'Of course,' I say. My search for James will have to wait. I head out of the chaos of the restaurant towards the cottage.

'I think I've made a huge mistake, Birdy,' Heather says.

'Oh no. Tell me,' I reply. The sun bursts out from behind a cloud, and the afternoon is suddenly bathed in light. I want to go down to the loch and regroup in the peace of that view. 'What's going on?'

'There's so much going on.'

I sigh. I'm going to have to extract it from Heather slowly.

'Right, give me two secs, I need to change my shoes.'

'Okay,' she says meekly. 'Where are you?'

'Just got home.'

I push open the door and race up the stairs to James's bedroom, where the door is wide open. His whites are dumped on the bed, not in the staffroom where they should be. He left in a hurry. I rush back downstairs, grab my sneakers and slip off my stupid work heels, then head down past the kitchen garden to the loch path.

'All right, shoot,' I say, once I'm clear of the cottages.

'Well. God, I don't know where to start.'

'Are you okay?'

'Not really.'

'How are . . . things with Cristian?'

'Well. To be truthful, we've started bickering a lot.'

'It must be stressful, if he's still sneaking around with you and hasn't told his girlfriend. Still.'

Birdy, stay calm.

'Yes,' she jumps in. 'That's exactly it. He's not left her, and it's been, what? Over two months now. Nearly three.'

Shit! She's really angry.

'Do you think he will?'

'Who knows?' she says, like she's had this conversation a hundred times in her own head. 'And, honestly, I don't want him to. I want to come home.'

There it is.

'I don't love him. I'm not sure I ever did. I think *everything* is fucking love. I clearly have no clue what it is or I wouldn't be so terrible at identifying it.' She pauses, her breath catching. 'He turned out to be a not-very-honest person,' she whispers.

'Do you think he ever had any intention of leaving his girlfriend?'

'I don't know. In the beginning maybe, but then the excuses started. She had some kind of minor surgery. And then her mum was ill. It just seemed like bullshit in the end.'

'Ugh! Piece of absolute shit.'

'Well. Yes.'

'It's great that you fall in love so readily, Heather. It's nice,' I continue softly. 'Better than being unable to do it at all.'

'I wish I was more protective of myself, like you,' she sighs. 'Anyway, I'm coming home.'

'Oh, really? What will you do?' I say, hearing the sharpness in my voice. 'I mean, how long until the Paris job happens? Will you go back into your flat? Isn't it Airbnb'd or something?'

'Well, I can fix that,' she sighs. 'I'm just humiliated.'

'Don't be,' I say, ducking through the long grass and onto the little path by the stream. 'Listen, if I lose you in the next few minutes, I'll call you right back – the coverage is bad here.'

'In Tooting?'

'No, no – I've kind of gone somewhere,' I say, scrambling.

'What are you doing?'

'I'm going for a walk.'

'A what?'

'Am I cutting out?'

'Maybe. It sounded like you said you were going for a *walk*.'

'Oh yes, that's right, I am.'

'What?'

'Sorry, am I losing you, Heather?'

'No!' she shouts. 'I'm just dying of shock!'

I can't help but burst out laughing. 'Oh yes, I know. This summer has been quite transformative.'

'I can't wait to hear about it. Could it be a certain chef you've mentioned?'

'Hmm,' I say, and think, for the millionth time, about James and the inevitable end of our romance. And in that moment, speaking to my best friend who I've been lying to for weeks now, I realize I'm one sob away from everything coming out.

'I can't talk about it now. But I will have to tell you what's been going on.' I feel the tears forming, getting ready to spill.

'Jeez, Birdy, you let me go on and on, and you're upset! What's happened? What did the chef do?'

But I stop, swallow and focus on my friend. 'Nothing. It's not him. It's my fault, but it's all going to work out. Somehow it will.'

'Are you sure you're okay?'

'I'm totally fine. Never been better. That's what so grim about it all.'

'You can tell me anything. *Anything!*' she says softly. 'We're family, remember.'

'Family,' I repeat and the line is quiet for a moment.

'Birdy?'

'I'll tell you everything when I see you. I don't want to talk about it right this second,' I say. 'Look, don't feel shit about Cristian. You took a chance. It's better than never taking a chance, isn't it?'

'Well, it wasn't really about him. I ran away.'

'With him.'

'No, I mean I ran away from more than that.'

'Look, chalk it up to a long holiday. Heather, get on a plane. Get back to London. I'll come down to your place as soon as I can.'

'Up.'

'Yes, I mean up. And we can get you ready for Paris. Who knows, maybe I'll come too?' I say, tossing the idea out there.

Heather lets out a big sigh and repeats herself, 'It's more than that, though, Birdy.'

'What is it? You fell for the wrong guy. It's okay, we've all been there. And you didn't want to go and take that summer job, did you? So, you went to Italy instead. Relax. It's not that big a deal. Any of it.'

I gulp. That sounded far harsher than it was meant to.

'Sorry, I don't want you to spiral. It'll be okay. Book a Ryanair flight and get yourself home as soon as you can.'

'You're right,' she says and then she starts crying. 'I'm just so embarrassed. And I'm angry with myself. I should have gone to Scotland.'

'I'm sure that wasn't the career move you really needed.'

'My career wasn't the whole reason for going.'

What does she mean?

I stop as the river widens and the loch comes into view, taking my breath away as it always does, though this time it is tinged with sadness. If Heather is coming home, I have to go back too. Sooner than I want to.

'What do you mean?' I ask, picking up a stone for skimming, and balancing the phone between my chin and shoulder.

'I wanted that job for other reasons.'

'Like what?' I say. 'Visiting your Scottish roots?'

'Ah, it's too much to get into over the phone. I'll tell you over a wine, okay?'

'Sounds like we both need a big chat in person as soon as possible. With whisky. Are you okay tonight?'

'Cristian is at his girlfriend's. For talks. But he has been for the last few nights, and he stays there, so . . .'

'See, Heather, relationships always start with these giddy highs and inevitably let you down. And *this* is why Tim is the perfect guy. Completely, dependably . . .'

'Crap,' she finishes and we both burst into laughter.

I hear a sound behind me on the pebbly shore. I turn round to discover James; wind-swept hair, beautiful eyes staring at me.

'Fuck! I have to go,' I say to Heather. 'Let's catch up again later today or tomorrow?'

'What's wrong?'

'Nothing's wrong.'

'Are you okay, you sound stressed?'

'I have to go. See ya.'

I hang up my phone and slip it back into my pocket.

'Hey,' I say, as brightly as I can. 'I was actually looking for you.'

'Hello,' he says flatly, narrowing his eyes ever so slightly at me. 'Your friend's name is Heather too?'

'I know. Funny, right?' I reply, uneasily. 'Are you on a break? I didn't see you leave.'

'I snuck out. Wanted to think about everything,' he says. It's the first time he's ever been a bit off. Is it what I said about Tim? Or is this about the review? Either way, I want to reassure him. Soothe him. Make him smile.

'Yes, same,' I say, looking at him and then out to the water. 'Can I join you? Can we think together?'

'Sure,' he says, without looking, and we sit together on the pebbled shore. It's cold on my bum, but the sun is intensely warming and it feels for all the world like summer at last. James looks out pensively over the water, and I want to ask him if he heard everything I said, but this could also be about the review, so I decide to start there.

'Are you okay about the review?'

'Of course not. But what can you do?'

'I spoke to your mum and she sounded, I don't know, kind of defeated?'

'Well, we gave it everything Russell asked for, and we weren't good enough, I suppose.'

'But don't you think the real heart of that review was that they didn't like all the pomp and fanciness? Isn't that how you feel too?'

'I guess.'

'Well, you can't honestly feel like you failed, if you didn't agree with the test.'

'Yes, it's true this isn't my kind of food. But I thought I was good enough to deliver it.'

I can hear the deflation in his voice and I want to touch him, but I'm terrified it will instigate a conversation about what he's heard, and right now I can't do that.

'You *are* totally good enough. You're an amazing cook.'

'*Cook* – exactly.'

'What do you mean?'

'Ah, nothing. You *really* don't know much about food, do you? It's weird.' He shuffles up on his elbows and looks me in the eye. 'A cook is not what you call a chef. I don't work in a camp kitchen. Anyway, it doesn't matter.'

I feel tired suddenly. I don't need another person on my case right now.

'Are you angry with me?'

'Everyone was called out for something, even Mum,' he says, and then he bites the inside of his cheek. 'I'm not angry about that, no.'

About that. Great. Here we go.

He pulls himself up and dusts the stones off his jeans. He looks down at me, sitting there. 'I need to be on my own for a bit. To think.'

'Sure,' I say.

James looks at me for a moment, and then to the sky and then back to me. It's coming. He wants to know . . .

'Have you not broken up with . . . *him*?' he says at last.

This is what you call an opportune moment. I can use Tim to cool the relationship with James, which needs to end anyway. I can say that Tim begged me not to leave him. I can say that the last few nights were a big mistake.

'Tim is not important,' I say, sighing.

James nods calmly.

'Is he *not important* or is he still your boyfriend?'

'He's not my boyfriend. Jesus Christ! I already told him that we should stop seeing each other,' I say, and scowl at myself for being so blunt. 'I was just joking around with my mate on the phone.'

And now my anger and frustration are rising, fast. And when James doesn't acknowledge my explanation, I feel it rise further.

'Were you,' he says finally, 'just joking around with a friend?'

'Yes, I was.'

'I don't know if I believe you,' he says. 'You could easily tell me that. I'd never know.'

'What do you want? A written statement of intent? Because my intent is to leave here in five weeks.'

He looks shocked. He puts his hands up to his head and rubs his face. Then he shakes his head.

'Right, so it doesn't matter either way? Is that what you're saying?'

'Stop hauling me over the fucking coals. It's not like this is going to go anywhere anyway. You know it, and I know it.'

'Why are you being like this?'

'Like what? This is me. Here I am. It's BIRDY. Want your money back, James?'

He looks at me, and his shock is turning to defeat. His eyes narrow and he shakes his head. 'Something's off here.'

'I think that was your pigeon.'

He turns to look out across the loch, shaking his head again. My heart is thumping and I can feel the surge of heat up my neck, all the way to my ears. And then, as he takes a step backwards from me, my instinct is to reach out and pull him in. But I can't. I have to let him go. It should never, ever have gone this far.

'James,' I say, desperate to – I don't know what. 'James,' I say again, 'I . . .' But my voice trails off into silence, and there is nothing but the wind and the water lapping against the shore as he walks away. I want to grab him by the shoulders, look into his eyes and explain it all, but it's too difficult. How do I explain anything?

Then I feel irritated.

Irritated that he's being sensitive, and irritated he's upset. Irritated by having to feel bad about something. Annoyed, actually, that I've been caught and am losing control of this situation. Annoyed at Roxy. Annoyed at Bill. Annoyed at James. Annoyed at stupid me.

'There's a whole world out there you know,' I say, on a true Birdy-shaped roll, 'not that you've ever seen it. You've never been outside Scotland, for fuck's sake.'

'Yes,' he says, and offers up a small smile. 'You're right.'

And then he looks down at my muddy, hopelessly trashed sneakers and a flash of something painfully sweet crosses his face. In all of this, he cares about my feet.

And then he's gone. He disappears up the path, sure-footed in his sturdy boots, at home on the earth below him.

As he leaves, I'm almost pleasantly angry. Like a huge weight has been lifted. It's for the best, I think. I can't actually fall in love with the guy. There are so many roadblocks, it's better if everyone simply gets on with things.

Yes. The best way forward is to put my head down, get to the end of my time here and get the hell out. No more stupid mistakes. No more surprises. Just work hard, play the game and get out of here.

32.

James cancelled our last two cooking lessons, no surprise. And he's taken this morning off and gone with his mum to see Mr MacDonald again. Irene's been horribly quiet with me too, and I wonder if James has told her what happened between us. She gave me the morning off, to work on the Wine Society event, she said.

I feel like everything at Loch Dorn is hanging in the balance and I wish they would talk to me about it.

Instead I'm left alone, to feel such deep guilt about everything, it's unbearable.

I pick up the keys to the SUV. Once I'm out of the driveway I pause for a moment, wondering where to go, before turning down the road towards Skye and Portree.

I switch off the stereo and roll down the windows as I drive, and put my right arm out the window to feel the cool air rushing between my fingers. The roads are quiet, even though it's mid-morning. When I cross the bridge onto the Isle of Skye, the spectacular view makes my heart lurch.

Bright-green fields rise out of the pebbled, craggy shore. Sheep grazing too close to the road take off up the rising hills as the sound of my car nears.

James once told me the name was Norse: *Ski* meaning cloud and *Ey* meaning Island. Cloud Island, owing to the mist that often clings to its saw-toothed mountains. When I came here with James the first time, that certainly fitted, but today everything is that heart-lifting, soul-cleansing summer blue. The blue of joy and hope. Sunshine and laughter.

In Portree I make my way to the edge of the pier with an arm full of newspaper-wrapped, piping-hot fish and chips, which I eat with unbridled pleasure and not a single ounce of regret – the greasy, salty fat running freely down my fingers, the cold can of Coke washing it down with fizzy sweetness. I'm sure Dad's chips never tasted like this.

I toss my leftovers to the gulls, watching them clamour and fight mid-air, as I throw each handful higher.

I look down into the water as it laps against the pier, the same way it did on that first trip with James.

Would it be possible to come clean? I examine the outcomes over and over again in my head. The sound of the words 'I did something really stupid' forming in my mouth as I look at his face. I try to picture James smiling and saying he understands, as he vows to work through it with me, but it feels a ridiculous fantasy.

Heather, too – I imagine telling her. The story I had told myself about coming to Scotland, pretending to be her, and how it would all end up as a great big joke that we would giggle about, over a beer, stopped sounding convincing a long time ago. Heather was never going to take this whole thing on the chin. She'd be devastated that I lied, and heartbroken that I would be so reckless.

I pull myself up from the pier and decide to take a walk along the coast. I pass a little store near to the café we visited last time, and I see hiking boots in the window. Why not? I have all this cash now, with nothing to spend it on.

A few minutes later I'm lacing up my £100 tan hiking boots and tossing my old trainers in the nearest dustbin. I may as well spend my hard-earned cash on something useful.

I spot a sign that gives me the option to climb 'The Lump' or take the Scorrybreac circuit path. Three kilometres – God knows how long that will take. The sun is high in the sky now and the air is getting hot.

All this worrying about what to do with James is wasted, I tell myself as I meander along the tarmac path by the wooded shore. It's over, and he'll survive, move on. It may have felt like a summer romance, but in reality we were together for under a week. After a few minutes I stop and look back towards Portree harbour, which is sparkling in the sunlight. There's a stone tower peeking out of the woods, which I seem to remember someone telling me was a sign for ships that there was medical assistance in the town.

I want to speak to Heather, who arrived back in London yesterday. We have been speaking every couple of days and I have made a firm decision to keep everything I've done up here at Loch Dorn quiet until I am sitting with her, face-to-face. I have the feeling she has something she needs to get off her chest as well, and so our conversations are future-facing and mostly bright, if a little flat. Neither of us wants to engage fully until we are ready.

I'll come see you soon, I'd said in my last text.

After this bloody wine-night. My plan is to put on the best Wine Society Highland Fling the west coast has ever seen. I want to recover some of the losses I helped to create with that shitty review, but I also want to prove something to myself, I guess. I may not be the best wine expert in Scotland, but I know how to show people a good time.

I want to do the wine-night, then be gone. Perhaps I should leave directly afterwards? I could book a car back to Inverness, and then fly to London. Perhaps I could leave a little note on the bar counter for Bill and Irene. Something that says: *Family crisis to attend to – so sorry to dash off a little earlier than intended.* Yes, that feels right. I'd be leaving, hopefully, on a high, and only running out on the last couple of weeks of the high season. They can manage without me.

The path passes a little boathouse and a sign that reads *Urras Clann MhicNeacail* (Gaelic, I guess), and I wonder about the history of this edge of the island: the bloody clan battles on the foreshore, the harsh winters, the warm fires and whisky. And there I am, thinking of James again, as the path turns to gravel and begins to ascend to a little bench, with glorious views of the hills across the loch. I sit for a while, staring out, feeling a deep aching in my heart.

And now I cry. At first it's a few tears that slip out and roll gently down my cheeks, but after a few moments it becomes a deep, visceral wail. A cathartic exorcism of grief and anger and self-loathing. I look down at my hands, nails bitten to the quick. And I bury my face in my hands, switching between feeling fascinated by how much liquid my eyes can produce and wondering if there is any way back to the place where I made my choices – but this time I make them right.

And then I think of all the things I would have missed out on, if I had.

I want to stay. Who knew that coming here, for little more than the sake of a yarn at the pub, would end up touching me in the heart this way? This ramshackle family hotel, which was trying so desperately to be grander and more magnificent than it was. This imperfect place, filled with imperfect people, all muddling along together with their ridiculous flaws and gigantic hearts. This place. I want to stay, desperately, and help rebuild it. And I want Roxy to be the youngest sommelier in the country. I want to sit on the stainless-steel counter with James and Anis and plan menus. I want James to be the head chef, making real, good food from the heart. Food that people are not intimidated by, but comforted and delighted by.

And as James comes to mind, he arrives in full Technicolor, blinding my senses to anything but the pain in my heart.

But pain – even the worst heartbreak – can never be felt at its most intense for too long. There's something in us that wants to survive. Finally the tears start to slow, and I let the sun dry my cheeks.

33.

As I pull into Loch Dorn and back into mobile coverage, my phone springs to life with three missed calls. It's Tim. What does he want? Just as I ponder ignoring it, it rings again.

'What's going on?' I say tightly.

'Birdy!' he practically yells down the phone. He must be pissed.

'Three missed calls? It's the wrong time of the day for a booty call.'

'Yeah, I wanted to find out if you know where we can get a phone charger around here, but we asked reception.'

'Reception?' I feel a chill through my body. 'What do you mean?'

'We're here, Birdy! We're in our room and I need to charge my phone,' he replies, as if he's been very clear on this already. 'Lovely view of a tree out one window, and the car park out the other. Bloody isolated, though – nearest pub is eighteen minutes away. We timed it. I don't know how you cope.'

'Oh my God, you're here,' I reply, feeling sick to my stomach.

'Yeah, baby. We're really excited. I'm wearing Damo's velvet blazer, like I did at the Wine Awards, for continuity.'

'Oh, good Christ.'

'Damo's already been at the bar.'

'I told you not to fucking come. I told you we weren't seeing each other any more.'

He bursts out laughing as if this is the funniest thing I've ever said. 'Yeah, yeah, I've heard all that before.' And I guess, to be fair, I have told Tim I didn't want to see him before, and then ended up sleeping with him again.

'SURPRISE!' yells Damo in the background.

'What the hell?'

246

I hear the floorboards creak as James moves about on the second floor, and realize I need to get up to the main house and shut this down as soon as possible.

'How the hell could you turn up?' I say as loudly as I can, while hurrying up the path towards the house. 'Tim, this isn't funny.'

'I thought the whole point *was* that it's funny?' he retorts.

'Well, yes, but things are more serious now. I can't have you ruin this.'

'Calm down.'

Can I fix this? My mind is racing. Can I get Tim in and out without a scene? Oh Jesus, I told James that Tim wasn't important, and now he's visiting? FUUUUCK!

'I just saw your boss, Irene, again. She checked me in, and she seemed fine. Lovely lady. Damo thinks she's hot, but you know he likes a mature lady,' Tim says, laughing.

'She checked you in?' I say, gasping.

'Yep. She was a little confused about the one double bed, but don't worry, I didn't say I'd be staying with you,' he says. Then I hear Damo roaring with laughter again in the background and I cringe. Oh God, this is a fucking nightmare.

I begin to race back up towards the main house. *He can't talk to anyone. He can't talk to anyone. He can't talk to anyone.*

I try to sound calm. 'I'm only just keeping my shit together and, with you here, everything could fall apart. You can have dinner at the restaurant, you can spend a few hours in the library room with the whisky and then tomorrow, right after breakfast, you have to go.'

I swing open the staff entrance and run – tits first – into Roxy.

'Hi,' I squeak. 'Christ, sorry. Are you okay?'

She gives me the sharp *Hello, Heather* attitude, with the purse-lipped smile I've been getting of late. I deserve it, but it still hurts.

'All right, all right,' Tim is saying calmly. 'Christ, calm down, Birdy.'

'Sorry to interrupt, Heather,' Roxy says. 'Just letting you know I've set up for the ladies' Auxiliary Club tonight. They're having the special set meal: it's fifty-five a head for the budget wine-flight and three courses, but I've put all the information in the staffroom. They're really nice, but, you know, no tips.'

'Okay, thanks,' I say, smiling meekly.

I slip past Roxy, wait for the door to close behind me and whisper as angrily as I can, 'You called me "Birdy", for fuck's sake. You're going to fuck this up. What's my name?'

'Mate. Calm down.'

'What's my name?'

'Heather. Jesus, you're so fucking highly strung. What's happened to you? Why don't we head out, go back to that pub – can you throw a sickie and join us?'

'I can't throw a sickie! They need me!'

He scoffs and I prickle. *They DO need me.*

'What's got into you?' Tim says, and I am stunned to hear that he sounds vaguely hurt. 'I thought I'd surprise you. I thought you'd think it was a right laugh.'

'I have to work,' I say in a heavy whisper as I arrive at reception. Bill is standing there grinning, and I give him a little salute.

'To pour fucking wine? Fuck, Birdy, I kinda wish I hadn't come now. I thought we were going to get on it and, you know, I'd sneak into the ol' staff lodgings and we'd make a night of it. It's been over two months.'

I die a little bit more inside. I'm not going to be able to get rid of him without a scene. I can see that now. I'm going to have to work with this, get Tim in and out with minimal disruption.

'Tim. It's a small place. Everyone is going to know you're here.'

'Fine. Fine. I wouldn't have come, if I'd known you'd be so fucking uptight about it.'

As I rush back through the kitchen, I'm invaded by images of James kissing me in here. So vivid I can feel an impression on my neck where he pressed his lips. The knot in my stomach tightens. What the hell is James going to say now?

I have to think. Tim is here. There is nothing I can do about that. How can I fix this? 'Look. Stay there, I'll come up. What room are you in?'

'Damo, what room number is it?'

'Six,' he says after a moment.

'Okay, wait there. WAIT. THERE,' I repeat, like I'm talking to a dog.

'All right,' he replies. 'But there is one other thing.'

'What?'

'We were kinda hoping you could get us a deal on the room.'

'How much of a deal,' I sigh.

'The best deal you can think of?' Tim laughs, and Damo shouts *free* in the background, and I'm suddenly angry as hell.

34.

'Call you Heather – we get it,' says Tim, who looks completely ridiculous in his T-shirt and velvet blazer, perched on the edge of the dove-blue crushed-linen duvet covers. He couldn't look more out of place. Damo is wearing a Millwall T-shirt and his boxer shorts, his thick dark thighs bulging as he leans on the windowsill to smoke a cigarette out the window.

I decide not to pick that battle.

'It's particularly important in front of Bill, Irene or Roxy . . .' I continue. They are unlikely to run into anyone from the kitchen.

'Roxy – that's the young girl with the big boobs,' says Damo, and I try not to throw the blown-glass vase filled with powder-pink roses at his head. 'What?' he says, like he doesn't know I'm appalled.

'Don't say that.'

'That's how *you* described her!' he says accusingly.

'Please, Tim,' I say turning my head, and pleading with him to take this seriously.

'I'll give you a snog and make sure I call you Heather,' he says, grinning.

'Don't snog me,' I say, trying very hard not to think of James and how he would feel if he saw that. 'It's inappropriate at work. Please, as I said, make sure you call me "Heather" in front of her. Please. All I ask is that you leave here without blowing my cover and making too much of a scene.'

'Okay,' says Tim, already looking bored with the plan. 'You look sunburnt.'

'I was out walking. And don't take the piss.'

'I won't. Walking is . . .' he scratches his chin, 'necessary?' Then he examines my face, narrowing his eyes. 'But it's not just the sun. You look kind of healthy.'

'Are you giving me a compliment?'

'I'm not sure,' he replies, reaching out to hold my hand, which I let him do for long enough so it seems like I want him to. His hand is clammy. I know if I look down I'll see the signet ring on his pinky finger, which I have a dreadful flashback of sucking on, during a particularly drunken fantasy role-play attempt.

'What is there to do around here?' Damo asks, leaning as far as possible out of the window as he can without falling.

'You could take a walk around the loch.'

'Enough with the walking,' Tim moans, as if I've killed fun for ever.

'You could go for a horse-ride—'

'Boring!' Tim bellows.

'There's not even a television in here,' Damo complains.

I stand up and open the cupboard to reveal the forty-two-inch TV and speak directly to Damo.

'Why don't you order room service? Have a bath?' I try to ignore Tim's eyes boring into my head, and continue, 'The food is absolutely fantastic. Like, amazing. You can have something a bit like chicken, or a massive steak; they will deliver a whole bottle of whisky, if you want that.'

'That room-service menu doesn't sound very fancy,' Damo says abruptly, his heavy brow furrowed. 'I was hoping we were going to have some game. Pheasant, partridge? Plus, I want a proper flight of wine. That's what you've been doing, right? There's a fabulous Picpoul on the menu. Isn't this a Russell Brooks restaurant?'

I pause for a moment to let that settle in. Damo is a foodie.

'We're at least coming to the restaurant,' Tim says. 'Non-negotiable.'

'Fine, fine,' I relent, 'but please don't draw too much attention to yourselves. Like, please. It's super-posh and full of older folk here, and if you start swearing and jumping on tables . . .'

'How much is the degustation menu?' Damo asks.

'I mean, with wine, it could be a hundred and fifty quid each,' I warn, 'maybe more.' My last possible chance to get them to reconsider.

'Come on,' Tim frowns, 'surely you can get us a free dinner?'

'Tim, please.' I am resorting to full begging now, as I raise my hands in the prayer position. 'If you promise to be sensible, I will buy you both dinner.'

'Then it's settled. Damo and I have a date,' Tim says.

'Okay. Dinner. In the restaurant. At seven p.m. sharp,' I say, looking at him now. 'We'll need the table back at nine, probably. So, early night! Don't drink too much, please. And for fuck's sake . . . Call. Me. Heather.'

Two hours later and I'm standing nervously at the bar next to Bill, who is showing Brett how to make a Cosmopolitan. Roxy is Tim and Damo's waitress, and so far they're playing it perfectly.

I've seated them on the table that is least visible from the pass. I'm sure James knows by now that Tim is here, but at least I can stop them from meeting. Irene has been offsite with Mr MacDonald again, and I'm not looking forward to her returning. We are on the fourth course now, and although Tim is starting to show signs of being happy-drunk, there haven't been any incidents. I take a deep breath. *Can I please get through this?*

'So . . . he just turned up, eh?' says Bill as he pours the pink liquid into an elegant long-stemmed Martini glass.

'Yes,' I say, glaring at Bill. 'He has a wedding near Glasgow.'

'And you're not going with him?'

'No,' I whisper quietly, 'we're not together any more, Bill, and honestly I don't know why he's here. I want him in and out with minimal incident.'

'And how long were you together?' Bill asks, as Brett looks across at me and furrows his brow, then slowly shakes his head in silence. I get the distinct impression they don't believe me. And I admit it looks bad – Tim travels from London to Loch Dorn to see an ex? I don't know if I'd buy that.

'How long?' I say with a sigh, focusing on Roxy, who is trying to deliver one large pint of beer and what appears to be a glass of our most expensive tasting wine, the Bordeaux, to their table, without wobbling the small silver tray. Damo checks out her arse as she bends to deliver the drinks, and I stiffen protectively.

'Yes, how long?' Bill says again.

'Not long. It's complicated,' I mutter, looking across at Brett.

'Heather!' I hear from across the room, and I glare at Tim to remind him to keep his voice down. As Roxy passes me on the floor, she gives me a little half-smile. 'Hey, Heather,' he says again too loudly, and I glance quickly at the tables closer to me, bringing a finger to my lips to remind him to behave. 'I was just telling your waitress friend all about you,' he says with a big wink.

He motions me to come closer, and although now is not the time for this conversation, I am so petrified of pissing him off that I oblige.

'I said you were my girlfriend.' Tim flashes a grin, and underneath the 'just joking' veneer, I can see a glint of steel.

'Jesus! Why? Please don't say anything at all,' I say, grinning as best I can, glancing back to Damo, who is swirling his Bordeaux in his mouth and groaning with pleasure.

'Well, why else would I come and visit you?' Tim says playfully, putting his hand on my thigh. I take a step backwards and shake my head. Is this some kind of revenge for trying to break up with him, or is he really, really stupid?

I glance round the room and spot one older lady at table three in a floral tea-dress and fascinator practically winking at Damo, and the entirety of table two – the ladies' Auxiliary Club from Fort William – all giggling into their sherry. I mean, it has to be the first time there have been two strapping young men dining in this place, so it's unsurprising they've caused a stir.

This whole thing is playing out to a soundtrack of traditional Celtic folk songs, and the clatter of pots and pans being aggressively tossed about in the kitchen.

James, for sure, knows Tim is here.

'So is this what you do then? Every day?'

'Yes,' I say, steeling myself for a ribbing, but we're interrupted by Irene, who puts a firm hand on my shoulder from behind. I spin round and feel myself turn red. 'I'm sorry,' I mouth, shrugging at her.

'Hello, gentlemen,' Irene says, with a large, pleasant smile. 'If I could borrow our sommelier for a moment.'

'Sure, we just had some questions about the wine,' Tim replies, relaxing back in his chair. Oh no, Tim doesn't like people looking down on him, and Irene is very much giving off a stern-teacher vibe.

'No problem, sir,' Irene replies. 'But if I may have Brett here help you? I really must borrow Heather for a moment.'

Brett now appears, with his dark and stormy Heathcliff looks, and leans menacingly across the table. He looks part bouncer, part barman, but definitely not like a waiter.

'Good evening, lads,' Brett says with velvety warning.

'Fucking love this red.' Oblivious, Damo has a mouth full of pigeon and wine. 'You're not even eating it, Tim, you dickhead. It's fucking epic.'

It's so disarming a comment from Damo that Brett softens his stance.

'Wait till you try the raspberry parfait,' he says in his baritone west-coast drawl, 'it's as delicate and soft as ye like.'

As Irene leads me away from the table, I take a glance up to the pass and see James glaring at me, furious. Like I've never seen him so furious, and I close my eyes and bite my lip. *It's not your fault, Birdy. Not your fault. You can explain it later.* But any explanation feels so far away from this precise moment, when I simply have to get through this nightmare.

'I trust everything will remain under control here. I have to leave early, and they're both already drunk,' Irene snaps as we enter the kitchen. She stops abruptly when she sees James, and I can see a look of motherly concern on her face.

'I'm sorry – I didn't know he was coming. I promise. I told him not to. We're not together any more . . .' I whisper, stepping backwards so that we're out of earshot of James.

'I remember his behaviour at the Wine Awards, and you promised me, dear, that this wouldn't be a problem,' she says. She doesn't believe me.

'I'm sorry. Really,' I reply, feeling James's eyes on me.

'I think we'd better retire you for the night, and we'll get Brett to see them through their meal. I don't want any scenes here.'

'I appreciate that, but I really think the best approach is for me to keep an eye on Tim,' I say quickly, imploring her to listen. I can't leave. I need to watch his every move, in case he does something stupid.

'Is that yah *boyfriend*?' Anis asks accusingly, looking across at James, before letting out a big, hearty, disapproving sigh.

'He's not my boyfriend!' I snap, as Roxy comes bouncing in the kitchen door.

'Oh, Heather, I love your boyfriend!' she says, smiling at me for the first time in days. 'He said he's heard all about me and you've said such nice things. I was *so* embarrassed. His friend is really nice too.'

Suddenly the volume of the music in the dining area inexplicably increases. I put my head in my hands, as I hear the sound of Damo roaring with laughter from the restaurant and a chorus of other diners joining in.

'Please, I can handle them,' I beg Irene, stepping closer to her and whispering into her ear. 'Please let me. I should get over there . . . now.'

Irene purses her lips, lifting one long finger to her temple. 'Very well,' she says. And so I brace myself, ignoring my desperate need to try and explain to James what the hell is going on, and push through the kitchen doors.

When I reach their table, Damo is on his knees serenading both ladies on table three, while holding the nearest lady's delicate, wrinkled alabaster hands in his. Tim is at the bar, leaning over to top up his own pint, and Brett is delivering a tray of tequila shots to the ladies in the Auxiliary Club, who are squirming and giddy.

I march over to Tim, flick the ale pump up and wrench the pint out of his hand.

'You have to stop this. At least, please go into the bar area.'

I reach round to the stereo and turn the volume down abruptly, interrupting Damo's rendition of 'Oh Danny Boy'.

'Sorry, everyone,' I say to the entire restaurant. 'Through to the bar, you two. Now!' I insist, to the audible disappointment of the ladies. 'Let's go,' I say again, and Tim is laughing as they both head through to the bar area where, mercifully, there is no one around for them to harass.

'Guys. Please,' I say. 'Tim, *please*. Can you guys call it a night soon? My boss is really pissed at me, and I need you to go back to your room or find a quiet corner in the library. Could you please do this for me? I can get you a free bottle of aged whisky to take to your room? Or a bottle each? Whatever it takes.'

Tim looks at Damo and shrugs. 'Fine. One more drink, then we'll go.'

'One more,' I repeat.

'One more,' Tim says, nodding.

One hour later, to the booming sounds of Beyoncé's 'Single Ladies', I am trying my best to drag Tim – who has smashed two crystal tumblers in less than thirty minutes, is wearing the silver deer antlers on his head and singing at top volume to whoops and cheers from all the extremely drunk dinner guests – out of the library. Damo has now gone missing, and I'm slightly worried he's upstairs with one or both of the ladies from table three.

'Best night ever!' says a regular, who dances past in a three old-person conga.

'You got to admit they've livened the place up,' says Bill as he struts past, hips jiggling, this time with a tray of Jägermeister. He's clearly been on the booze himself.

'Traitor!' I hiss.

I try to pull Tim down the hallway, to the protests of his fan club, pulling the stag horns off his head and pushing him towards the stairs.

'Bedtime, you fucker,' I say, trying to jolly him out.

As we reach the bottom of the stairs he suddenly seems to come to, and his eyes momentarily focus on mine. He smells of whisky, and he laughs as he makes out my pained expression. How did I ever like this man? I thought he was fun, but it turns out he was just a colossal shitbag.

'Baby bird,' he shouts over the noise. 'Look at you, all stressed.'

He tries to tuck my hair behind my ear, but kind of misses and ends up tugging out my hair grip.

'Ow! That fucking hurt,' I say as I scramble to readjust it. 'Come on, you have to go to bed now.'

He grins and turns round and makes his way out to the back entrance. 'Isn't your room this way?'

'No, Tim,' I say and actually stamp my foot, but he grabs me and pulls me out of the back doors and we spill onto the pebbled court-yard. I feel the evening chill and rub my arms. I consider smuggling him down to the cottage and into my bed to shut him up, but his bed is closer and I want him out of the public eye. As fast as possible.

'Birdy,' he says again, swaying. 'We should have gone out properly. I didn't treat you well enough.'

What a time to come to this conclusion. He leans in and opens his mouth, like he's trying to kiss me, but I'm too angry to let him invade even a single inch of my space.

'No,' I say, shoving my hands on his chest and pushing him back. 'And don't call me "Birdy".'

'Come on,' he says, putting his hand round my waist and trying to pull me closer.

He leans in to try and kiss me again and I turn my face away and step back, causing him to stumble forward a little. 'Seriously, fuck off!'

'Jeez. Sorry,' he says, looking sheepish. He knows this would have worked on me before.

'You shouldn't have come.'

'Don't you like me any more, Birdy?' he asks, with a grin.

'Tim, honestly. Look. You shouldn't have come,' I say, trying to remain calm and generous. I don't hate him. And in any other situation I would have found his own and Damo's drunken, boisterous antics hysterical. 'I really care about this job.'

'You've changed. What's gone on up here? Are you fucking the waiter?' he says, laughing.

'No. Which waiter?'

'The one that looks like a Scottish Jason Momoa?'

'Oh, Brett? No,' I say laughing.

'Built like a brick shithouse.'

'He's very handsome, but no.'

'It's got to be someone,' he says, trying to grab my hand again. 'You've found yourself a Scottish shag, Birdy. Is he ginger?'

'No. There's no one else,' I shout. 'Tim, please, what do you want to hear? There's no one else. And, honestly, why do you care? You've never been a proper boyfriend. We don't date or order fucking Deliveroo and watch TV together. We've *never* watched TV together. I've never met your parents. You only see me when you've got nothing better to do. You're off to a family wedding and after – what? – like eight months of whatever we are, or were, Damo is your plus one? I should have ended this months ago.'

'What? You made it pretty clear *you* didn't want to be serious.'

I fold my arms and step back again, when suddenly I hear footsteps behind me. I turn round and, to my horror, see that James has appeared outside the kitchen entrance. He's changed, probably heading back to our house. For a second we lock eyes and I will him, with every ounce of myself, to hear the apology that I'm screaming from inside me.

He looks protective, despite what he must have heard. I can see that his shoulders are stiff and his right hand is a little flexed.

'James,' I say, raising my hands to my face. I can't look at him.

'Everything okay?'

'Yes. Everything is fine. Tim here is just going up to his room.' My voice is shaking, and I want to say more, but I'm terrified of setting Tim off. I have no idea what he might say if he feels upset or humiliated. 'Sorry,' I say quietly to James, and he nods gently in return.

Then Tim looks over my shoulder to James and shouts, 'Be careful, my dude, this Birdy will up and fly. Right when you want to keep her around.'

I can only look at the floor as I hear the kitchen door shut and James heads back inside.

'Time for bed,' I say, as I feel the prickle of tears in my eyes. James must have heard me say there was no one else. At least he heard the rest – all of which was true. Tim was terrible for me, and terrible to me. He was never a true boyfriend; just someone I saw whenever he had time to see me. We were never close. He never really cared to know me. And that was understandable, because I didn't really know myself.

I cannot bear to look back as I push Tim into the house and drag him up the stairs. As he finally gains enough sobriety to climb into his linen bed sheets, he reaches a drunken hand out to me and I recoil.

'It's over, Tim,' I say, hoping it goes in.

'Fair enough,' he murmurs. And then he's snoring.

35.

Back in my room I've hauled my suitcase from under my bed and I'm tossing in clothes through a stream of tears. I have to get out of here. It's the only thing I know now. I shove all my clothes inside, try to force the zip closed, then remember I need to get my bathroom things. I toss my brand-new hiking boots in the cupboard in some kind of defiant act of self-sabotage, and slide the door shut so hard it comes off the rails and gets stuck.

I walk into the bathroom, flick on the light and stare hard at myself in the mirror. Red eyes, swollen underneath. I turn on the tap, splashing cold water on my face. My heart is pounding and my mouth is dry. I hold up my hands and I'm shaking. I need a cup of tea. Or something stronger.

I go to the kitchen, but there's nothing in the back of the cupboards, just a few empty wine bottles by the bin. But then I remember the cases of bottles in Bill's room and march upstairs. I fling open his room, stepping over a pair of boxers and a newspaper on the floor. It's *The Scotsman*, open at our review. I shake my head, flick open the lid and slide out a bottle of wine. It *is* the wine from that film night. *Oh, Bill.* I am suddenly thirsty for a glass of chilled water instead.

The door below slams heavily and then I hear slow, shuffling footsteps in the hallway.

I slip the bottle back into the case, creep out of the room and skip down the stairs, trying to be light-footed, as if I've been doing something totally normal upstairs. I find Bill with his arm on the hallway wall, holding himself for balance, checking his phone.

'Hi, Bill,' I say casually as I reach the bottom of the stairs.

'Heather,' he says, lifting his head. He's still lucid. 'Did you find what you were looking for?'

'Ah, no.'

'He's still in the kitchen,' says Bill with a rueful smile. 'Hiding, I guess.'

He thinks I was looking for James.

'I didn't ask Tim to come. He just turned up,' I say.

I head towards my room and decide tonight is not the night to get into any kind of conversation with Bill. I push my door open. 'Good-night, Bill.' But he moves towards me, and I can't get away without slamming the door in his face. 'Is there something else?'

'Are you going somewhere?' he says, looking over my shoulder into the room.

'Um.' My cheeks flush red, and I think quickly. 'Weekender in Inverness.'

'Are you taking everything with you? Including your wine book?' he says, and I spin round to see that my *Wine for Newbies* is sitting on the top of the clothes in the open case. Is Bill angry? I can't tell.

'Well,' I say, forcing a laugh, 'now you know my secret! Don't tell the Wine Society.'

'I do know your secret,' he says plainly. 'I've known since the first week.'

I stare at him in shock. He can't mean . . .

'It's Elizabeth, right? You're her friend. The real Heather's friend.'

I just blink, with my mouth open.

'You shouldn't leave,' he says.

I step backwards and collapse onto my bed, my head in my hands. *Fuck, fuck, fuck!*

'You have to do the Wine Society night.'

'What?' I say, shaking my head. 'No, Bill, no, no.'

'I've not told anyone, don't worry,' he says. 'I mean, I couldn't, could I? You've involved me as well, haven't you?'

I look up, expecting to be confronted with rage, but instead see a familiar look: self-loathing and sadness. My dad.

'I'm sorry, Bill,' I say. I feel a strange mix of shame and relief. *It's over.*

'It wasn't hard to figure you out,' he continues. 'By the second day I realized you knew practically nothing about wine.' Then he laughs.

'So then I did a bit of digging. Heather has many friends in hospitality, as you might imagine, so it wasn't hard to figure it out – if you thought to look. I mean, if you thought someone would pretend to be someone else. But who would do that?'

'Oh, Bill. I'm so sorry. I didn't expect the hotel to be so . . . It was supposed to be a lark, a jolly. If I'd known how important the role was.' I shake my head. 'It was a stupid thing that got out of hand.'

'What I'm unsure of, though, is if Heather knows. She's like a ghost on social media.'

'She doesn't know,' I say.

'Well, well,' he says grimly. 'Isn't that a pickle?'

'Please don't tell Irene,' I say pitifully. 'Just tell them that I lied to you, and I can go, and it can be over.'

'Well, I can't – even if I wanted to. Irene thinks Heather was properly vetted and that we had an in-depth Skype interview. I can't tell her I slept through the interview, can I? And then not to have told her, for all these weeks? She's given me so many chances, and I can't . . .'

'Oh God,' I say, feeling the air flush out of my lungs. He was hungover and missed Heather's interview.

'Anyway, there's no time to go over all this now,' he says more firmly. 'Time to get yourself together and finish what you started. The Wine Society Highland Fling. You have to do it.'

I look up and shake my head at him. 'I can't. I just can't. Tonight, with Tim, it was all too much.'

'You have to,' Bill says firmly. 'You're ready. And you will do a great job. You've worked really hard, and this can't come crashing down. I can't lose my job. I'm nearly seventy. Where am I going to go? What am I going to do?'

'Couldn't Russell find somewhere for you?' I start.

'No,' he says sharply. And I realize that Russell probably doesn't mind Bill being tucked up here out of the way at Loch Dorn, but at a top restaurant in Glasgow he would be seen as a severe liability.

'Bill, you're sick. You need to get help. You can't keep spinning plates,' I say, realizing at the same time how pointless my words are.

'Just finish the job, Birdy. Please.'

For a second we lock eyes.

'Bill. Look, I'll stay, okay? But only if you get help. My father didn't and . . .'

I pause for a moment, wondering if I should go there. I look at Bill swaying in the doorway and decide that I must.

'Mum kept covering and covering for my dad. She once found me choking on flour in the kitchen, blue lips and everything – with Dad passed out on the sofa. I was four. *Four!* And she covered for him at the hospital: *My naughty daughter got into the kitchen cupboard and pulled out the flour.* They were so obsessed with conspiracy theories and yet their whole life was a conspiracy. She chose to protect him, and I guess herself. Over my own fucking safety. It was never my dad's fault. It was always someone else's. And often, that someone else was me. I don't speak to either of them any more, because the fucking gaslighting was so extreme I drove myself crazy. You know what it's like having your mum shout at you for calling an ambulance when your dad has passed out in the shower? *Shout at you.* Tell you off for calling for help? Tell you there is nothing wrong, when you can smell the vomit and piss? Do you know what it's like to have to second-guess what you think you're seeing? You stop believing in yourself.'

I realize I'm crying, but I can't stop.

'And you know where it's got my parents? Nowhere. Fucking nowhere. I hate them. Covering and protecting – it's fucking wrong. You need help. You can still make a change, it's not too late. You've been stealing from the hotel. I've seen the wine in your wardrobe. I see the little shots of whisky you take during service. You can go about pretending you're fine, but you're not, and someone is going to get really fucking hurt. And, honestly, it's probably going to be you.'

Bill looks a little taken aback and leans into the door frame.

'You're wrong,' he says.

'I'm right,' I counter. 'You know it. You know, in your heart. I'll do the fucking wine evening, okay? I'll do it. But you? *You* have to get help.'

'Okay,' he says flatly, and I want to punch him. *It's a disease, Elizabeth Finch. Support him.* I breathe out slowly. I will stay. Just till after the Wine Society event.

'Heather called earlier, by the way,' he says. 'That's what I was coming to tell you.'

I stop in my tracks, wiping the tears from my cheeks.

'Wanted to speak to Irene,' he continues. 'But luckily I took the call.'

'She called here?'

'Yes, wanted to apologize for pulling out of the job, I suppose.'

My blood turns cold. 'What did you say to her?'

'I told her Irene was out and that she needn't worry, and that we'd found an adequate replacement. She was quite keen to speak to Irene anyway, but I think I dissuaded her.'

'Oh God,' I say, feeling myself begin to tremble again. 'Thank you.'

Then we both hear the door open and James appears. He's wet, and I realize it's been raining outside. He rubs his hands through his hair and shakes the excess drops away.

'Is everything okay here?' He looks between me and Bill.

'Heather has been feeling a bit embarrassed about her ex-boyfriend's behaviour up there,' says Bill. 'I've told her she needn't stress.'

James stares at me, studying my face. Blotchy, I suspect, and red. Obviously upset.

'You look terrible,' he says, frowning.

'I'm sorry,' I whisper, despite Bill still standing there. 'I'm sorry for all of it. Tim is going in the morning. I should have made it clearer that it was over. I thought I did, but . . . I guess I wasn't clear enough. Honestly, James, you don't have to believe me, but I really didn't think he'd care, or need to be broken up with. Tim never considered me a girlfriend. I'm as astonished as anyone that he actually turned up.'

'Well, it's all irrelevant in the end,' James says plainly. Like he's practised it in his head. 'You'll be moving on soon anyway. I guess we always knew that.'

'I'm sorry,' I say, feeling the tears coming again.

He looks at me, more softly now, and for a moment I think he might reach for me, pull me in, stroke my arm and tell me it will all be okay. But he doesn't. In a flash, his face shifts back to distant. Like he's been switched off.

'It's fine, Birdy,' he says, his shoulder brushing past me as he heads down the hall to the stairs. 'We've got the Wine Society pre-planning meeting in the morning, and there's still so much to get done. You should both get some sleep.'

And then he disappears up the stairs, two at a time.

I turn, eyes streaming, to Bill, who shrugs.

'Yes, I know,' I say. 'I have to finish what I started.'

'You won't rush off then, if I go to sleep?'

'No.'

'Good,' he says, looking relieved. 'Oh, don't look so upset. You did very well, all things considered. To learn that list the way you did, it was really quite something.'

I drop my head.

'You were dedicated, and quite brilliant. Anyway. Tomorrow. Up, dressed and back on the horse, eh?'

36.

August

It is the day of the Highland Wine Society event, and there has been a team from Fort William erecting a huge marquee outside all day, with sixteen round white-clothed tables of ten and a parquet dance-floor with disco lights hanging above. I glide through the space, the most important person of the moment. *If only they knew.* Lightning flashes, followed closely by a tremendous roll of thunder.

'Mind your head!' booms Brett, carrying a log on his shoulder.

'Shit, will this tent withstand the rain?'

'Oh aye,' he says, thumping his log to the ground and rolling it to the edge of the tent. 'We're weighing it down extra, like.'

It looks impressive, and I feel a little tingle in my stomach as I run over the speech in my head and wander towards the kitchen, bracing myself against the strengthening winds. I'm actually a bit excited.

One last night, I remind myself, then I'm out. My bag is packed and the taxi is booked for later.

James and I have been working with minimum interaction all week, only communicating about the prep we need to do for the event. Now I watch him wrap a surprisingly light black-pudding mixture around a quail's egg, while I discuss the final pairings with Russell.

Russell's appearance adds mystery to the future of the place. Why is he here, after a couple of weeks' absence? None of us have been told anything, and I've been too scared to ask Irene. It feels like the captain deciding to stay on a sinking ship, after assessing that the water is too cold to dive into willingly.

'So we have the Bolney Pinot Noir for the English suggestion, and the Saumur Champigny for the traditional pairing,' I say, holding both the bottles up so that Irene and Russell can inspect them.

'Good,' says Russell, nodding his head, his perfectly groomed hair so full of spray it looks like a Ken doll's. 'And for the dessert?'

Before anyone speaks, I jump in, all animated. 'Oh my God, wait till you see what Anis has done. It's this fabulous take on Eton mess.'

'It's really excellent,' James agrees, nodding. For the first time ever, Anis looks a little embarrassed and fetches her deconstructed Eton mess from the chiller.

'It obviously needs to be put together fresh,' she says, sliding over a plate that looks like it has a St George's cross made of raspberries, strawberry jelly, soft pillowy marshmallow and meringue, plus quenelles of whipped cream on it. I learned the word 'quenelle' from her earlier today, after I complimented her on the pretty 'blobs'. I have learned so much this summer, but not everything.

Irene and Russell both scrape a spoonful off the plate, and we wait for a moment while they taste.

'Welcome back to the Great English Menu,' I say. 'Anis, will you be cooking for the hundred-and-fiftieth anniversary of the Royal Marines in Blackpool? Have you pushed the boundaries of culinary achievement enough? Is it original? Have you responded to the brief? Side-note: women never make the final.'

James smiles. A small victory.

'I'd give it a solid nine, Anis,' I say quickly.

'Yes, very good, Anis,' says Russell. 'You'll make a good pastry chef one day.'

'One day? She already is a great pastry chef. She's amazing,' I say.

James looks across at me, and this time he smiles warmly, and Russell cocks his head sharply and furrows his brow. 'She is doing well in her training,' he concedes.

I sigh, loudly. 'Christ, she's not training to be a Jedi Knight. She's a great chef. And anyway, Russ, it's not like you're ever here to see what she does. She's brilliant. If she was a watch, she'd be that *Apollo 13* watch that saved Tom Hanks – she's that reliable.'

Anis gasps, but I don't care what Russell thinks of me any more. I'm a fake sommelier trying to do my best, but he is a *real* chef not trying at all. And, worse, not helping anyone else do better, either.

'She's only twenty-four,' says Russell, shaking his head as he drops his linen napkin in the bin.

'Twenty-five,' Anis and I say at the same time, and we both look at each other. Then she smiles slightly. *Smiles!*

'Didn't you run your first restaurant at twenty-six?' I say with a grin.

'Thank you, sweetheart, for your input,' Irene says, ensuring the conversation is shut down before I cause any more trouble. 'That plate is divine, Anis. I think this fun little experiment is going to work. Bill, have you finished the reception area? Are we ready to go?'

'Bunting is hung,' he says. 'And I've cued up Heather's playlist. It's certainly eclectic.'

'Well, thank God it's not your terrible music,' says Roxy, who has appeared in her waitressing uniform. 'He keeps playing me Roxy Music. He thinks it's hysterical.' She grins at me. In all the fallout from Tim's visit, my friendship with Roxy has almost recovered. Tim did a good job of repairing that for me, at least.

'James, are you nearly done?' Irene asks.

'Yep,' he says, rolling the last Scotch egg in panko crumbs and sitting it neatly in a tray with baking-paper lining.

'Well, dear,' she turns to me. 'This is *your* evening really and, as you know, it is customary to do a little introductory talk to the guests about the theme, and what they can expect from the wines. But we are all here in support. I would really love to see what you're planning to say,' she adds.

'I'm ready!' I say, pulling my now-recovered notebook out of my pocket. 'You can trust me, I've got this.'

'Very well,' says Irene, with a flicker of sadness in her eyes.

'Just quickly, though . . . um, James?' I say and he looks up, with his hands still covered in crumbs.

'Yes?'

'Can I see you? Two minutes?'

'Sure,' he replies slowly, then nods to the kitchen fridge. 'I have to get the endive.'

I follow him and the icy setting seems rather apt, but I bravely put a hand into my apron and pull out my little surprise. It's small, but completely perfect.

'Porcini?' he smiles.

'Well, I remembered in that first week, when we went foraging, Anis said they're your favourite . . . Are they?' I start to lose confidence immediately.

'They're out early this year,' he remarks. 'How did you know what to look for?'

'I've been reading your foraging book. I have been really worrying that I got it wrong, but it's that netting pattern on the stem, right?'

'That's right,' he says softly.

'I know it's been super-busy this week for you, so I went back to that oak grove near your house?'

'Really?'

'Well, in the book it says that you have to catch them right away, or the worms and slugs get to them. So, well. Sorry, I don't know what you're going to do with one mushroom . . .'

I can feel myself shrinking into my shirt. And I'm angry at myself. What did I think would happen? It's one fucking mushroom.

James heads to the left of the kitchen and lifts up the flap on a cardboard box, which I see with dismay is filled to the brim with porcini.

'You can put it there,' he says bluntly, and I oblige, placing my tiny little foraged mushroom next to the bulging specimens, which must have come up with the veg delivery that morning.

'I'm sorry,' I say flatly – meaning, for everything. For the stupid tiny single porcini and the boyfriend-not-boyfriend turning up. For all the lies.

I hear James breathe out and shake his head, and then it all comes tumbling from my mouth.

'I'm so sorry,' I say. 'You don't have to believe me – God knows why you would – but honestly, I thought I'd never see Tim again. But turning up like that? That's his kind of shtick. I should have been firmer with him.'

James looks up to the roof of the chiller, and I continue, because he's listening at least and I will never get another chance.

'I know you got a lot of mixed messages. I told you we weren't together, but in some technical fashion we *were*,' I say, my voice wavering a little as I continue. 'But it was nothing official. I didn't *feel* deeply about Tim. That was the whole point of it. To hang out and not stress about it ever getting serious.' *Ugh, that didn't sound good.*

He looks down at me, and I can see he's just waiting for me to finish, so I go for the final truth.

'It wasn't like how I felt when I was with you. Nothing like how it was with you. I'm sorry – I'm not always the most open person. I should have been clear about my feelings. My best friend says it's because I don't believe people are invested enough in me to care.'

He cocks his head slightly. 'Do you think that?' he says.

'I don't know. Maybe.'

'Either way, what you did was shit.'

'I know,' I say, trying to bury the rising anxiety. I can't fix all the lies, but I really want to fix this one. 'But on this one thing: Tim. On that, I want you to know that my feelings for you were a hundred per cent real. *Are* a hundred per cent real. And whatever shit I had with Tim is over. Really over.'

James looks at me, searches my eyes, and I summon all my strength to hold his gaze. I need him to see that part. That part is true. His face softens slightly. 'But, like you've been saying all along, you're leaving.'

The chiller swings open, and Anis is standing there, glaring at both of us.

'I've got to go and get changed. Good luck tonight,' I say, shooting one last apologetic smile, which he acknowledges with a smile in return. On the subject of Tim, there is some movement at least.

I slip into the staff toilets to check my make-up, brush my hair back into a tight low bun and attempt a look that says: *I've made an effort*. I reach across to the hanger with the long, black silk gown that Irene has generously loaned me. I slip it out from its dust cover and carefully – so as not to crease it – pull it over my head and let the light, voluminous fabric fall to just above my shoes. The cut is a simple V-neck: perhaps a little Twenties in style, with a bias skirt falling from the waist and a little touch of silver-thread detailing around the neckline. It fits pretty well and doesn't show the rolls around my back from the too-tight bra, but clings a little more than I would like to my belly. Nothing an apron won't cover, though, I guess.

270

I pull down my eyelid and run a brown pencil along the base, and flick on enough black mascara so that it's not clumpy. I use a nude lip-gloss I found at the back of the bathroom cupboard, take a deep breath and look into the mirror.

'You've come this far, Elizabeth Finch. *This* far. You can do it.'

I pull out my phone to check the time, and there's a message from Heather that simply says: *Catching up on some stuff. Let's talk early next week. I will have lots to tell you . . .*

I want to be with Heather. I understand now the work she puts in – knowing not only one list, but hundreds and thousands of wines, their origins, how they grow. She can tell a raspberry topnote from a gooseberry with a quick whiff, and although I didn't appreciate it before, I can now see that every time she pulled out a Chianti for our takeaway pizza, or a Sekt before we went out to party, she wasn't just offering me a drink, she was making everything better. It was love. I cannot wait to appreciate her in a hundred new ways.

I take one last look in the mirror and then head towards the bar area of the restaurant. Bill has done a spectacular job setting up. He looks well. And sober. I give him the thumbs up.

I am ready. *I'm going to fucking nail this*, I think, as the thunder claps once more overhead.

37.

'Heather, isn't it?'

I spin round and recognize Matthew Hunt, the sexy Bond-villain President of the Highland Wine Society, whom I met that very first week. He is handing his rain jacket to one of the many temporary staff I don't recognize, and sliding a large black umbrella into the basket by the door.

'You look a picture,' he says.

'Hi, Mr Hunt,' I say, rubbing my hands down my apron before I offer him one. He lifts my hand to his lips and kisses the back of it gently, and I blush.

'Call me Matthew,' he says and, when he smiles, I notice that his teeth are yellow and full of fillings, and I feel kind of grossed out, but also grateful the universe has handed me a leveller.

'Sir. How are you this afternoon?'

'Very well, my dear. Tonight should be interesting. I tasted a few of these at the British Wine Awards – were you there?'

'Yes, I was,' I reply.

'Well, I'm sure the Society will find this all very novel indeed. English wines at a Scottish wine event. What a hoot!'

'We have plenty of Old World wines to compare,' I assure him. 'I hope you'll find it fun, at least.'

'Oh, look – Nicol!' he says, waving to a tall, thin gentleman in a three-piece suit with a tartan waistcoat, who is rocking back and forth on his heels. 'See you later, my dear.'

I head to the restaurant to check everything is in order, as Roxy and another young woman appear with two trays of champagne glasses.

'Shall I start pouring?' Roxy says as she slides her tray onto the bar, and Bill puts two bottles of bubbles up on the counter.

'Yes. Let's get going, they're arriving in droves now.'

'Good luck,' she whispers at me, and the sweetness in her voice makes me almost tear up for a second. I'm going to miss her.

'Thanks. Who needs luck when you're wearing this dress, though?'

'You look great. But you should take the apron off,' she says as she glides away with a tray of a dozen glasses of sparkling English wine.

Roxy hands out the fizz, while another three young waiters circle around with large silver trays of iced oysters, placing them on the waiting silver stands that are dotted around the various tables.

Men in suits and kilts, with varying degrees of grey whiskers and wiry hair, chat in thick Scottish accents. The women wear gowns in various shades of bottle-green, navy and burgundy with sashes of tartan, and copious jewels. They drink and mingle animatedly, part of a club that for many years was closed to them.

As the volume of chatter in the bar area reaches a certain pitch, I look across to Irene, who nods my way as Bill rings a small bell.

'Please make your way through to the marquee, ladies and gentlemen,' she says.

We slowly follow her over what must have been a hastily erected walkway, across the pebbled path, to the marquee. Although it is still dark overhead, with the threat of more stormy weather, the rain has momentarily ceased.

Once the room is full, I grab a glass of fizz and brace myself. I take the step to the small podium at the top of the dance-floor, where everyone is assembled, and tap once on the microphone.

'Is this on?' I say, my voice booming around the marquee, and there is a gentle laughter from the room as more than a hundred people turn to see me speak. By the entrance the waiting staff are watching on, along with Roxy, Bill and Irene. Thankfully, James isn't here to see me make a tit of myself.

'We can hear you,' says a jolly-looking rotund man near the front.

I blush wildly and try to focus. This all went much more smoothly in my head.

'Well, then. Ladies and gentlemen,' I say, my voice trembling a little.

I look over towards the entrance to see that James has appeared. Of course he'd bloody turn up now, wouldn't he? I steel my nerves and carry on.

'Hello, and welcome to the Wine Society Highland Fling. And today on the menu it's the invasion of the English,' I say, and there are a few audible laughs. Shit, I was hoping that would get everyone going! I look at Matthew Hunt, who has his head cocked sideways as if deciding whether to take pity on me or be angry. I feel my cheeks blush a deep crimson, and down the glass of fizz in my hand.

'Oh, that's better,' I say, and there is a murmur akin to a giggle from a few at the back. I know I can do this. I know this speech is funny. I've worked so hard to get to this point. 'Today we take a tour, not of the ancient vines of the Loire or the fertile soils of Bordeaux. No, today we take the M20 from Croydon and drive bumper-to-bumper at a steady ten miles an hour through the Canterbury bottleneck to a completely forgettable part of Kent.'

Laughter. Real laughter. I look at Matthew, who is glancing across at his friend Nicol to share a chuckle.

'It is here we begin our journey with the cheeky little sparkling wine you are all suffering right now – from an estate called Hush, whose chalky slopes actually provide the same growing conditions as Champagne.'

A small gasp from a few, and others are nodding to confirm my little-known fact.

'But while the growing conditions may be the same – the name cannot be. As you know, only wines grown in the French region can claim the prestigious title of "champagne", and so therefore, not to be outdone, the English have gone for the very English name of "Blanc de Blancs".' I pronounce the last bit in my most Kentish accent.

This time there are actual bellows of laughter, and one old guy slaps his friend on the back. The room has warmed up, and I feel myself relax.

'But don't sniff at it until you've tried it. This Blanc de Blancs is rich, complex. It has aromas of apple and hints of strawberries, rhubarb and nectarines on the palate, along with brioche and nuts, with a fruitiness on its elegant finish.' *Thank you to Top Ten English sparkling-wines review I mostly copied that from.*

274

'Enjoy your glass, please, with our delectable Scottish oysters – because some things shouldn't come from south of the border . . .' I pause as the room erupts into throaty chortles once more. 'And find your places for our English-themed dinner: five delicious courses prepared by James and Anis in our kitchen, and a selection of wines chosen by me and my delightful co-sommelier, Roxy.' I smile at her, and she grins back. 'And I'm confident in the knowledge that if they do not provide you with libatory pleasure, you will certainly take great pleasure in hating them.'

Laughter. And then applause.

I grin broadly, looking from face to face around the room. Irene, Roxy and Bill are still standing near the back, and I can see pride across their faces. I glance across at Matthew, who is clapping and nodding in approval. I feel a warmth spreading through me as I soak up the sound of their adulation and feel a bittersweet sense of satisfaction. I allow myself a little look at James, who is clapping, though looking pensively at the floor. I need to talk to him again.

The music kicks in and the guests make their way to their tables, and suddenly I can feel the tremors in my body as I step down from the stage. I grab another glass of fizz from an abandoned silver tray and make a beeline for James, who looks like he's about to head back into the kitchen. But then, from out of nowhere, Russell blocks my path.

'Hello, Heather,' he says. 'I think there was someone you forgot to mention in your little speech. It's my restaurant, after all.' He says it jokingly, but I can tell he's pissed.

'Oh, of course – sorry, I totally blanked up there.' *No, I didn't.*

'I'd like to speak myself, so could we talk about an introduction before the dessert wines?'

'Ah, but the whole night is planned,' I say, trying to catch James's eye.

'Look, this is my restaurant and you'll do what I say,' says Russell sharply.

'Will I?' I snap back. I want to get to James before he goes back inside. 'I need to go.'

As I manoeuvre past Russell, I feel a tug on my apron and it unwinds and falls down to the floor. I nearly trip as the strings tangle around my legs in the process.

'Hey, what the fuck?' I say as I turn to Russell, grabbing my apron off the floor and holding it to my belly. 'What, are you like eight years old?'

'I'm still your boss. You *will* respect me.'

Forget it, Birdy, I say under my breath as I turn and walk straight into James, who has witnessed the event and is glaring at Russell. I quickly grab James by the hand and pull him away from the marquee to the safety of the kitchen.

'Arsehole.'

'Yes. He is,' I reply, grateful that there is still some caring for me inside James. 'What's going on with Russell? Why is he still here? I thought we were all dreadful and he wanted to bestow his talent elsewhere.'

'Mr MacDonald is here,' James whispers. 'So Russell wanted to come and oversee the event. Though I've told Mr MacDonald that Russell had nothing to do with tonight. And next week he won't have anything to do with Loch Dorn. He's been let go.'

I'm shocked. James has taken control and stood up for himself.

'So are you taking over then? Head chef?' I ask.

'Not quite,' he says, shaking his head. 'I do have some plans, though . . .'

But before he has a chance to continue, a line of waiters with large silver trays containing the starter stream past us towards the marquee.

'Let's go! Starters out, and come back straight away for your next tray!' barks Anis, who has never looked so in charge as she does now. The waiters take off in formation, like a military parade.

'You'd better go and introduce the first white,' James says, as I nod my head and bite my lip. 'You were great,' he adds, his eyes dropping to the floor again. 'I'm proud of you, if that's not too weird a thing to say.'

I shake my head, feeling the sting of tears in my eyes.

'James, I'm going to miss you so fucking much,' I blurt at a whisper. And then I turn away and rush back to my podium, my heart thumping. I can't bear to see his reaction.

I take a deep breath, then momentarily panic as I cannot fill my lungs. I try again and remind myself it is only anxiety.

Breathe in, breathe out.

After a moment I feel able to speak. The white wine, I explain to my now-captive and slightly lubricated audience, is from Norfolk. 'It's a stunning blended white with a punch of tropical aromas, which complements your lightly smoky fish to perfection,' I say. 'This little beauty has more cups than Norwich City Football Club. Though, frankly, that's not much of an achievement.'

As the evening wears on, my confidence grows and I find I am enjoying myself. As the cheese board and last wine are delivered to each table, and the band sets up for the post-dinner dancing, I take to the stage for the final time.

This is the last trick up my sleeve. I look around the room and watch the guests as they taste their final glass. I watch as they seem confused, then taste again. Their noses screw up and disappointment spreads across their faces, aghast at the wine in front of them. Perfect!

'Ladies and gentlemen, I hope you are all enjoying this last wine,' I begin. They try to be polite, and smile and nod my way. A gentleman at the back, showing no such grace, spits his back into his glass.

'I'd like to hand the floor over to one of you, to appraise and identify this final wine – as you can see, we've concealed the label on all the bottles. Do I have a volunteer?'

Almost immediately Mr Hunt raises his hand. 'I'll volunteer.' *Brilliant.*

A smatter of polite applause around the room, and then lightning. We all wait a moment for the thunder that follows and then, with great comic emphasis, Hunt stands and shakes his head. 'Heather, thank you for a fascinating tour of England, and I'll admit I have enjoyed some fantastic wines here tonight. But I'm afraid you've quite ruined yourself with this final choice, lass.'

I stick out my bottom lip and cock my head, playing along.

'It tastes like vinegar. Like blackcurrant juice left on a countertop for a month. Atrocious! Now this is what I would typically expect from an English wine.'

Around him faces nod: finally, an English wine they can rely on to disappoint.

'Well, that's a real shame, Mr Hunt,' I say into the microphone.

He stands with his hands out and shrugs.

'Why don't you take the sleeve off and reveal the estate please?'

'Very well,' says Mr Hunt, as he reaches across the table and plucks up the bottle, slipping the black paper sleeve off, and the rest of the tables follow, eager to see which dreadful English estate the wine is from.

'Mr Hunt?' I say.

'Well,' he replies as the room begins to bubble with laughter. 'It seems the joke is on us. The wine comes from Stirlingshire, right here in Scotland.'

The room erupts into gales of laughter. Applause follows, and a few people even rise from their seats. I glance across at the waiting team, who are also clapping. Roxy is red-cheeked and clapping enthusiastically, and even Irene is beaming.

'Thank you all for a wonderful evening, everyone. Now please welcome the Grant Fraser Band, and I hope you will enjoy yourselves well into the wee hours. Goodnight.'

I briefly close my eyes and soak up the final moments of success. And then my eyes open and catch on something familiar in the room. A face in the crowd that wasn't there a minute ago, standing by the flapping doors of the marquee. That curly hair pinned to the side, and the big blue eyes wide with shock. It takes a moment, but then it comes.

Heather. Heather is here.

38.

As the band kicks in, I half-fall off the stage and rush towards Heather.

Irene is the first to block my path. 'Dear, you were wonderful – congratulations.'

'Thank you,' I say, yanking up the hem of my gown so that I can move more freely. 'Sorry I have to—'

'Heather! Well done,' says a beaming Roxy. 'You were amazing. That was so funny! A Scottish wine. When did you order it?'

'I can't talk now, Roxy,' I say, pushing past her.

'Heather?' I shout, just as Bill tries to get to me. 'Not now, Bill.'

I reach her under the fairy lights in the walkway, the light of her phone shining against her face. She hangs up and shoves it into her coat pocket, and my first impulse is to rush across and hug her. I don't know where to begin. I don't know what to say.

'What are you doing here?' I blurt. My mind is racing. Who told her I was here? Why would she come?

She scoffs, and I want to get her away from the marquee so that we can talk, away from prying ears. Surely there must be some way I can . . .

'What am *I* doing here?' she repeats flatly.

'I can explain. This isn't as bad as it looks.'

'Oh, this is going to be good, Birdy. I can't wait,' she replies. 'Nice dress, by the way. Who did you steal it from?'

Behind me, waiters are struggling to remove cleared plates, and I want us to get out of the way.

'Can we talk, please,' I beg.

'I'm waiting for my taxi to return and take me back to Inverness.'

'You can't go in this weather,' I say, as a gust of wind blows us hard enough to make us both uneasy. I grasp at my dress, billowing wildly now, and look to the sky as lightning shoots across the dark clouds and brightens the valley for a moment. 'Come on.'

Thankfully, she follows me over to an awning by the side of the house – still outside, but further away from everyone. I wrap my arms around myself, and then the verbal diarrhoea begins.

'I know I lied. I know I did. I'm so sorry. It's just that I didn't know where to go. I couldn't go to my parents, and my cousin has a partner now and he wouldn't let me stay, and I didn't know what to do. I didn't want to worry you. And I went to the Wine Awards and I was wearing your name badge; and then Irene came up to me, and I couldn't tell her the truth and so she believed *I* was *you*, and it snowballed. Totally snowballed. And since you said you didn't want this job and that this place was an isolated shithole, I thought it wouldn't be a problem.'

'Well done, Birdy, you've already made it *my* fault.'

'That's not what I'm saying,' I reply, putting my hand on her folded arms, but she shrugs it away.

'I'm just saying you called it a dumb placement in a shithole, so when you pulled out, I thought I'd come and do it. I did some waitressing a million years ago, and it seemed easier to pretend I was you than reapply as myself.'

'I'm a fucking trained sommelier, Birdy. FUCK! What the hell? You wouldn't have got the fucking job yourself, and you know it. Don't minimize my years of hard fucking work.'

'Okay. Yes, I know. Look, I didn't let you down, Heather. I worked really hard. I learned as much as I could. Though I could never know as much as you, of course.'

I'm all over the place. I don't know how to explain my stupid actions, and I just want to say sorry. I want to hug Heather and scream *Sorry*, over and over and over until I'm forgiven.

'I loved learning about wine, but you must be so amazing to know what you do. It's so hard. Oh, Heather, you were in Italy, lying low. It seemed mostly harmless. I've been *you* before. You've let me pretend to be you heaps of times.'

'At parties I couldn't go to! At the odd concert. But, Jesus, this is outright fraud!' She's full-on shouting now, though the wind and rain are helping to conceal it from anyone within earshot.

'No. Not really. Irene paid me cash. Like, there's no legal issues here,' I say quickly, as though that could absolve me of some of my crime.

'I am so fucking angry, Birdy. This is the worst thing you've ever done, and you've done some crazy shit over the years.'

'Please, Heather,' I plead. 'If you could see it for what it was. It was a bit of harmless fun. No one has been hurt, really.'

'Oh, no one has been hurt,' she says, and now she's got glassy eyes. 'Why here, Birdy? Why did you have to do this here?'

Wait, am I missing something?

'What are you doing here?' I ask again.

She looks up at me, and then I see the wild rage in her eyes.

'Don't FUCKING worry about it, Birdy,' she shouts. 'Don't worry about me or anyone else. Just you fucking worry about you, okay?'

Right then we are blinded by the lights of a taxi pulling up, and I can see the rain starting to fall in the beams of its headlights.

'Taxi for Heather Jones?' booms a voice, and Heather turns to go.

'Don't go,' I beg. 'Please stay. We need to talk about this. What's going on? Please, Heather.'

She breathes out, tears in her eyes, and something in her softens. 'It's fucked, what you've done, but for more reasons than you know.'

'Tell me,' I say. 'I'm so fucking sorry.'

'*Please* don't interrupt,' she says as the rain turns heavy, and we crouch as far into the awning as we can.

'Okay, okay, sorry,' I reply, feeling a rising dread. *What is coming?*

Heather waves at the driver to tell him to wait, then reaches into her handbag and pulls out what looks like an old Polaroid.

'My stepmum sent me a box of stuff about a year ago. She was clearing out Dad's things and she thought I would want them. Just dumb photos. Old wine books. His watch. That sort of thing. And there was an old wine-cellar diary and, tucked in the back, under the flap, was this photo. I don't know if he meant for me to find it or forgot it was there, but I found it.'

She fiddles with the small picture.

'And I think this woman in the photo might be my aunt,' she says, her voice wavering. 'I have this memory of Mum talking about her sister. You know how you hear things when you're little? I didn't really think much about it for years. Then one day I asked my dad outright, and he said there was no one. Only him. So I thought I'd imagined it. But I didn't, Birdy. I know I didn't.' The rain is heavier now and her voice rises with it.

I realize I've not responded, but I'm confused. 'An aunt?'

'And, if I'm right, she has a kid too, so I might have a cousin. Dad never told me, and I have no idea why. Why wouldn't he fucking tell me my mum had a sister? I was worried there was a terrible reason – like they don't want to know me, or whatever – so I got scared. But while I was in Italy I realised I *have* to know.'

I turn the photo to the light and study it. I recognize Heather's mother from other old photos I've seen, and her dad in the middle. But the woman standing on the other side of Heather's dad: it's *Irene*. A young Irene. With dark, dead-straight hair, not the grey hair she has today – it was her. I look between Heather's mum and Irene. They were so alike. *So alike.*

'When I tracked her down, I thought if I took a job at Loch Dorn I could check her out and spend time with her, to see. You know? And then as the time came closer, I got scared. What if there was something really terrible that my dad was protecting me from? So when Cristian asked me to go to Italy, I ran.'

'Hang on,' I say, grabbing the photo to study it again.

My eyes scan across to Heather's dad this time, and I feel a sinking in the pit of my stomach. With the wild curls and those sideburns, he is unrecognizable as the man I knew in Plymouth, but he *is* recognizable from somewhere else.

Heather's dad is the same man as the one in the photo in James's cottage.

Heather's dad is also James's dad.

If Heather and James share the same father, that makes them siblings, not cousins.

Which means: what? Heather's dad had an affair with her mum's *sister*? With Irene?

'Christ!' I say as my chest tightens, and I feel the air suck out of me.

'There must be something terrible if my dad kept me away from them. But I have to know. And now you've fucking ruined it.' Heather's voice turns bitter as a tear rolls down her cheek, and the headlights of a second car pull up, lighting up the full anguish on her face.

'Uhh . . .' I don't know what to say to her, and now she has her hands up to her face and is crying properly.

My mind races. I hand the photo back to Heather. Why on earth didn't she tell me about this? She lied to me too! I thought she was my best friend. If I'd known, I'd *never* have done this. I can't look at it. I want to be sick.

I have to think fast. Should I tell her? Should it come from me?

Just then Bill appears with a large black umbrella, holding it fast against the prevailing winds. 'Heather?' he says gently. 'I'm so sorry, but there are two taxis here for you. Both are for Inverness, so I'm sure you can imagine that I don't want to send them home without a job, if I don't have to.'

Heather looks up at him, and for a moment the waves of sick in my stomach turn to dread. This is it. This is the beginning of the end.

'Ah, hello,' Bill says, in sudden recognition of the situation. 'Oh dear.'

Heather, ever polite, shakes the hand he offers.

'What should I tell the drivers, my dear?'

And then I remember. 'Um, one is for me.'

Bill nods to me. 'Are you off too, then?'

I don't speak, but sort of nod my head. I don't know what to do. Bill probably thinks it's best that we both leave now, in case he gets found out too. I've done my bit. But what about Heather? I glance across at her and want to hug her, but don't dare. She looks like she's in a daze.

'Bill, can you give us a moment? Tell the taxi I'll be there,' I say sharply.

'Yes,' he replies, before handing me the umbrella and slipping away.

'Can we get out of the rain?' I open the umbrella above us. We're both soaked through.

'I want to go.'

'Okay, we can do that,' I say.

'I want to go *alone*,' she says, sobbing into her hands.

'Okay, let's get out of this rain for a minute, and then you can go,' I reply, taking Heather by the hand and leading her into the bar area. I can't let her bump into Irene without warning her, and Irene is still in the tent, as far as I know.

'Can you get her a glass of whisky?' I say to Bill, who has returned and is hovering, looking panicked.

'Might it be better for you both just to leave?' he says.

'We're going,' I snap, turning to him. I'm frustrated. I don't have time for this now.

'I can't lose my job,' he says, sounding desperate. I could cover for him – tell Irene that I fooled Bill too. I could never mention the stolen wine, leave it all as it is.

'It'll be okay,' I say. 'Go back to the cottage, all right? I'll be there soon.'

Bill nods, looking utterly defeated.

I take in the bar area, and there are only a few guests milling around. Brett is behind the bar, mixing cocktails. Then the kitchen door swings open and I see James grabbing a bottled water from the fridge. He clocks me, sees I'm soaked, then sees Heather and looks quizzical. Suddenly the situation overwhelms me and I turn to her, grabbing both her hands.

'Let's go.'

She shakes her head. 'I don't want to go with you.'

'Fine. Fair enough. There are two taxis waiting, so we can go separately, okay?'

She nods, lifting her head for the first time since we came inside. Her curly hair hangs in wet links around her face, and her eyes are bloodshot and swollen.

I glance across at James, who is still standing there, concerned now, and I feel panicked. *We have to go.* I tug on Heather's coat.

But then Irene walks in. Her smile wide and her arms outstretched. 'Heather!'

I hear Heather sniff. She looks at me, and then to Irene.

But then Irene pulls *me* in for a massive hug. 'You were absolutely amazing! I've been looking everywhere for you. But you're quite frozen, and so are you, dear,' she says, turning to Heather. 'Brett, can you bring us some blankets? Or maybe a couple of towels? I'm so proud of you, Heather,' she says, pulling back to look at me, holding both my hands in hers.

'She's not Heather. I'm—'

No, no, I can't let her find out like this.

'Um, the thing is, Irene,' I say, taking a deep breath, 'I'm not Heather.'

Irene has shepherded us to a quiet table away from the guests. She is confused, though seemingly more concerned with towels and blankets and that everyone has a warming cup of tea than with what she's heard.

'What on earth do you mean – you're not Heather?' she says, as Brett arrives with two fresh dressing gowns, so that we're all surrounded by fluffy white cotton.

I look over at James, who has now moved from behind the bar to stand in front of it – not wanting to get so close as to interrupt, but close enough to listen in. I suppose that I may as well get this out in front of everyone.

'When I met you, Irene, at the Wine Awards,' I say, 'I wore Heather's name badge.'

'I don't follow, dear,' Irene says. 'And what is your name?' She directs this to Heather, who just sits there, watching in complete shock. Has she recognized Irene?

'What I'm trying to say,' I jump in, 'is that I was wearing Heather's badge.'

'I'm confused, Heather,' Irene replies.

'I'M NOT HEATHER!' I snap, my hands covering my face. And then I can hear it: the silence of unwanted attention. The room is looking at me. I pull my hands down from my face and I see that Anis has joined us. Okay, like a plaster, I have to rip this off. 'When I met you at the Wine Awards, I had gone in Heather's place. I was wearing her name badge.'

'So you're not Heather?' Irene repeats.

'No. I'm Birdy. Finch. Elizabeth Finch. My friends call me Birdy.'

'Birdy? What kind of a name is that,' Brett says.

'It's her nickname,' James says, and I can hear the anger rising in his voice.

'Yes,' I say, my heart breaking a little. I look at Heather, but she is staring down at her nails. 'It's my nickname. My best friend gave it to me when I was six.'

'And who is Heather?' asks Anis, trying to catch up as Roxy slides up next to her, removing her apron. I see her whisper to Anis, *What's going on?* and Anis lean over to fill her in.

I ignore her and keep going. 'I'd had a couple of wines when we spoke at the awards, and I didn't really think through what I was doing. You were so nice and warm, and . . .' I look at Irene and feel the prickle of tears in my eyes. 'I did some research. It seemed like a fairly old-fashioned rundown place. No offence. The online wine list was very small. There was no hint of the renovations. I didn't know exactly what I was walking into.'

'The website was very out of date,' interjects Anis, nodding.

I glance at Heather again and she has that look. The look that first drew me to her all those years ago, back in primary school. I want to hug her, but I also want to get this done, and then get the hell out of here. With Heather.

'I was between jobs. I couldn't afford a new house-share. And I . . . I thought it wasn't such a crazy idea,' I say, trying not to listen to how crazy I do indeed sound.

'It's fucking nuts,' says James loudly, pacing the length of the bar.

'Quite,' agrees Irene.

'I didn't think through the consequences properly. Irene, I didn't think Loch Dorn might be in trouble, or I would never have taken such a risk with your business. The only excuse I can give you is that I was stupid and thoughtless and selfish. I thought it would be a fun summer job, and no one would really care who I was.'

No one has ever really cared who I am. No one has cared, except Heather.

I look up at James, who has stopped pacing by this point, and see a flicker of compassion on his face, before the anger returns.

'I know there is no way I can be forgiven, but I want to tell you that I've loved every day that I was here. I've loved my job, in the end, and I gave it everything. I've loved the cooking lessons with James, and the walks around the loch . . .' I pause, feeling Heather's eyes on me once again. I can't look at her.

'How could you put the hotel at risk like that?' James says.

'I'm sorry. As I said, I just didn't think about it. I only thought of myself. To be someone else, for a while. To see how it felt to be as amazing and talented as Heather.'

The tears are streaming down my cheeks now, and great balls of snot appear in my nose every time I breathe out. Irene fishes a napkin out of her bag and hands it to me.

'Bill?' says Irene, as the information starts to sink in, and I feel the questions begin. 'He knew, didn't he? Where the hell is Bill?'

'He didn't know till too late.' And then I decide that now is as good a time as any. 'He's gone back to the cottage. He's really upset. And on that subject: please stop protecting him, because you're not helping him. You're making him worse. He's fucking up all the time with orders, and hiding stock for himself. He's sick. It's a disease. You can't simply hide it. He needs help. Protecting him doesn't help him. And it means other things get hurt. Other people. And your hotel.'

Irene looks at me and for a moment I think she might actually lose her temper, but she doesn't. She looks down at her hands and nods.

And then there is silence. Everyone sits quietly, unsure who is going to take control of this mess.

'Well,' Irene says, shaking her head in overwhelming disbelief. 'Well, this is a lot to take in.'

'Um, hello,' says Heather in barely a whisper. 'Could I speak to you for a moment, Irene?'

'And who are you, dear?'

'I'm the real Heather.'

My heart sinks. I look at Heather and realize there's nothing else I can do to delay the inevitable.

'Shall I stay?' I whisper to Heather, as Irene shoos the rest of the staff away.

'No,' says Heather, without looking at me.

39.

It is nearly 2 a.m. by the time I reach Inverness station hotel, alone, and ring for the night porter. The cheery sign says *Under new management*, which can only be read as a promise that things have improved since the last time I was here.

The night porter opens the door. He's short – maybe five foot two – with a goatee. I can smell him as soon as the door is ajar.

'Ms Finch?' he asks. I nod wearily.

'Come, come. You're a little later than we were expecting. No mind. No mind. I'll show ye to ye room.'

He pulls the door open and motions me through.

'Up those stairs ahead – can I take your bags?'

'I only have this one. I can take it.'

He opens the door to a little single room at the end of the second-floor hall and bids me goodnight. Exhausted, I perch on the end of the bed. The floral curtains are open enough to see the glassy shimmer of the Ness River.

I check my phone for the hundredth time. No notifications. Nothing from Heather. My last message, *Can you ever forgive me?*, sits unread.

I left Heather there with Irene. She told me to get my taxi and leave her be, and I finally gave up trying to stop the inevitable. Who was I, anyway, to interfere any more in Heather's life? When I tried to speak to James, he stormed through into the kitchen, and so I left.

I wonder what happened? Did Irene really have an affair with her sister's husband? I can't believe it, but I also can't think of another explanation. Poor, poor Heather. I hope that the truth of their family will bond them, rather than tear them apart – certainly Irene could do nothing but love an unexpected niece. I imagine the pain she will feel, knowing the years that have been missed. And I feel sick that I can't be there to help Heather when she finds out.

The train back to London the next day still brings nothing from Heather, although the distance does something to ease my ache. I check into a grotty hostel in King's Cross and lie in bed, listening to the sound of sirens and drunken arguments outside my window.

I text Heather again.

Are you still there?

Still nothing.

As I wander around the streets the next morning, with the late-summer heat wafting its putrid city-smells, I realize I will probably have to go back to Plymouth. The envelope of cash that Irene gave me will run out soon, and isn't enough for the deposit on a room anyway. I'll have to call my mum. It seems like apt punishment.

I feel so dreadfully empty, it is overwhelming. I want to go back to Loch Dorn. I felt something was beginning, like a little seed of who I am was finally starting to germinate. Who am I, now I'm not there?

I have come to appreciate wine, though I'll never be anything like a real sommelier. I have loved learning about food. I love what James does at the restaurant, and I love the care that goes into Irene's home cooking. But I could never cook for a living. Once again I'm Birdy: good at nothing, not even bullshitting, it turns out.

That night, at the hostel, there is an almighty fight between two Australian backpackers, which ends with a hair extension landing on my face.

40.

The next morning I find myself wandering around North London again, with nothing to do and nowhere to go. I know I'm putting off the inevitable, but I can't bear to make the call.

I spend thirty minutes in some awful coffee shop, drinking a latte that tastes of frothy nothing. Then I really need the loo, but the one there is dirtier than the stables at Loch Dorn, so I use the ones at the nearby Caffè Nero instead. The lady behind the counter scowls at me as I slip past the queue. By twelve I've been into Oasis, Waterstones and a retro sweet shop, where I treated myself to a bag of liquorice and then promptly ate all of it. Feeling deeply sorry for myself, I sit on a bench by a bus stop for a while, relentlessly checking my phone.

I notice a small shop, tucked in between a mobile-phone store and a betting shop, its inviting little window set out like a picnic, with a selection of rosé wines and glass tumblers laid out on a tartan blanket. The name is sweet – 'The Wine Library' – and it stirs a memory of Heather. I think this was somewhere she used to go.

I decide to have a perusal, and maybe a free tasting if they offer it. I push open the door and hear a little *Tring!* The sound immediately sends me back to Portree for a moment, and I close my eyes to enjoy the picture of the boats bobbing in the bay. James smiling freely at me, his hair blowing around his face in the sea breeze. The smile of beginnings.

'Morning,' says a voice, and a woman (I think French) comes up from a basement. 'Oh, or afternoon, I suppose. Can I 'elp you?'

There's all these bottles crammed onto every shelf, and a long fridge running the length of the back wall. 'I'm not sure. It's a hot morning,' I say, spotting a big sign that says, *British, organic & actually quite good.* I can't help but smile. 'That one *is* actually quite good,' I say, picking up the bottle and examining the label, though I know it by heart.

'Yes, it is made in almost identical conditions to champagne,' she says.

'Yeah. I know,' I say, smiling warmly at her.

'Ah, you know your English wines!' She claps her hands together, delighted. She must be in her fifties, I guess, with a full bohemian skirt that swishes along on the floor as she moves.

'A little,' I reply. 'I was a sommelier for a bit.'

'Oh yes?' she replies, immediately animated. 'I grew up surrounded by vineyards. My aunt and uncle even have a *petite maison* in the Loire.'

'That must have been fun,' I say, picking up a different bottle, this one with a pencil sketch of rows of vines along a deep valley.

'Well, it was very lucky for me, but of course I didn't appreciate it as much, when I was seventeen. Couldn't wait to get out.'

I nod, as my thumb runs back and forth along the row of vines. 'No one wants to live at home at seventeen. Try coming from Plymouth.'

She giggles and holds her hand out. 'Do you want a tasting?'

'I *did*,' I say. 'But I'm thinking I'd better keep a clear head.'

'At least let me offer you a taste of this rosé?' she says, wandering across to the fridge and plucking a bottle from the bottom shelf. She pours out a generous tasting glass and, when I frown at her, we both grin.

'Thanks,' I reply, thinking about her family vineyard, wondering what it would be like to have a home that you couldn't wait to return to. 'Can I ask you something?' I say, looking up at her.

'Of course.'

'How did you know you wanted to open this wine shop?'

'Well, wine is in my blood, as you know, and I think although time passes, you never lose the love for where you are from. It is who you are.'

'Hmm,' I say, downing the drink. 'But what if you don't have those roots. What if you moved around a lot? Or you had shitty parents. You know, not everyone wants to stay where they were. Lots of people want something better, right?'

'Tell me what you love,' she says.

'I love,' I say, running my fingers around the nearly-empty bowl of rosé, 'I love belonging. I mean, what the fuck does that even mean?'

'To a man?'

'No. No,' I say, shaking my head.

'A family?'

'Yes, I suppose, though not my own.'

'Perhaps you must find somewhere to put your roots into the earth? A little water, a little sunlight, a little time and space? Like the vine? You cannot hope to debut the perfect vintage if you do not take the time to grow and nurture and love.'

'I don't believe that,' I say, feeling my head become dizzy and suddenly wanting to leave. I down the rest of my glass.

'Don't you?' she says, taking a sip of her rosé.

My mind drifts back to the loch, the dark clouds thick overhead, the wind whistling across the grey water. I walk back through the woods, along the river. I pass the little stables where Brett is grooming the horses, and along to the cottages. Bill and James are making coffee in the kitchen. I head up the pebbled path to the main house and see Irene standing in the doorway, wearing something flamboyant and fabulous. Inside, Roxy is bobbing about in the restaurant; and in the kitchen Anis stands by the main counter, ordering the two rookie chefs about. And then I think of Heather, and I can see her there. Standing in the doorway, smiling easily, with a bottle of wine in one hand and two glasses in the other.

''ello? I lost you?'

'Oh, sorry, I was in my own little world,' I say, repeating those words back to myself. *My own little world*. I want to speak to Heather. 'Someone once asked me: if I could do anything in the world, what would it be?' I continue. 'And my answer was always: *fuck-all for twice as much.*'

'And now?'

'Well...' I say the words in my head – words that I would have crucified Heather for, something that I would have seen as being against my feminist ideals, something I thought was weak. 'I want to belong. I want to be loved.'

She gives one of those knowing smiles, with the eyebrows raised and a slight nod of the head. I would have found this condescending a few months ago. But now it feels warm and approving. Like I got the answer right at last.

'Thanks for listening,' I say, realizing this poor woman only wanted to sell a bottle of wine, not provide therapy for the most fucked-up woman in London.

'You sure you want to go?' she asks, holding the wine up to offer more.

'I have to make a call,' I reply.

Impulsively I hug the woman whose name I don't know, and head out into the early afternoon, half-cut. I find a bench seat outside the station and I try Heather again. Once again, she doesn't pick up.

I head into Angel Tube station, not completely sure where I'm going next, but just as I step onto the down escalator, my phone goes and it's Heather. I turn and start trying to run back up the escalator as I fumble with the answer button.

'Heather!' I say, as I bat aside incoming commuters with my huge bag. 'Sorry! Excuse me,' I pant, as I focus entirely on getting up the stairs.

'What are you doing?' Heather asks.

'Trying to get up the escalator! Fucking Angel. Massive fucking escalator,' I shout as I reach the top and almost stumble off. I rush to the window ledge by the ticket gates and toss my bag to the ground. 'I made it. I'm here. I can hear you,' I say breathlessly.

'Hi, Birdy,' she says, her voice soft, if not friendly. 'I'm glad you called. It's time to talk. Where are you going?'

'I was about to go – God fucking knows where. Home, maybe.'

'Plymouth?'

'Yes. Maybe.'

'Well, to cut to the chase, I'm heading back to London this afternoon and I thought we could meet and talk.'

'You're not staying at Loch Dorn?'

'I'll explain everything when I get there. I don't want to get into it now.'

'Is everything all right? Oh, Heather, will you ever forgive me?'

'It's only been three days.'

'Okay,' I reply feebly, feeling the slightest shred of hope. 'I'll see you at your house. What time?'

'Can you be there tomorrow around midday?'

'Yes. Of course.'

'Bring my paddle brush,' she snaps. 'And no more lies.'

'No more lies,' I say quietly. I want to ask about Irene and James, and Roxy and Bill, but I'm afraid to. All of my focus needs to be on Heather right now, and on repairing the damage I've caused.

She hangs up, and for the first time in a week I feel a little lighter. I look down at my bag, yank it back over my shoulder and head to my hostel for one more night.

41.

November

I'm looking down at a Friend request from Roxy on Facebook. She's in a pink bikini and a towel, with her arms outstretched on the edge of Loch Dorn, a huge smile on her face. It's been there for a few days and I've been too nervous to accept it.

It is November and the wind has turned cold in London, but I am tucked up in Heather's little flat – all mine for the next week, before I head off. I've ordered pizza and a six-pack of some lager from Uber Eats, and I'm planning a little party for one in the lounge with a crappy movie. I know, I know – but it's sourdough pizza and *local craft* lager.

The house feels different without all Heather's things around, but the memories remain, and the warmth and love I feel for her are stronger than they have ever been.

'I'm so sorry,' I said to Heather that day at her house. 'I can't pretend I didn't know what I was doing. I did. I did know the risk I was taking with your reputation, even before I learned about the renovations. It's just that the stakes got higher. It felt like there was no way out but to try to be a good enough version of you so that no one got hurt. But that's no excuse. In the end I made the decision to use you. Your hard work. Your dedication. Just to ride on the back of it. It was a terrible thing to do.'

'I do understand how it happened,' Heather said. 'Like, I get how you talked yourself into it being okay. And I do see how my evasiveness about the job, and my reasons for going and then not going to Scotland, contributed to the confusion.'

'Don't take any responsibility. It makes me feel worse,' I said. 'It was fucking stupid.'

'It was,' she said, shaking her head at me. But the tone had softened. She wasn't angry any more. Disappointed perhaps. 'Well, the one thing it did achieve was that I finally met my family.'

'Do you know the full story yet?'

'Oh yes,' she replied. 'And it's quite a lot to take in. I'm still not sure if I fully believe Irene's account. It means my dad was, well, an arsehole . . .'

'He wasn't to you,' I said quickly.

'Irene said she had an affair with Dad. One or two nights, very early on in Mum and Dad's relationship. Before me, obviously.'

'God, I just can't imagine Irene . . .'

'She said it was a mistake, but that she cannot regret it, because it gave her James.'

'But how did your mum not . . . ?'

'Listen, Birdy, for God's sake, and I'll explain.'

I zipped my mouth shut with my fingers.

'Dad and Irene worked at the same restaurant together in Edinburgh. That's how he met Mum, actually. Mum was a nurse, so they were all doing this kind of crazy shift work, and Dad and Irene had a couple of nights when . . . well, you know hospitality: late nights, drinking, whatever. It's a close business. Irene regretted it, and wanted to come clean to my mum.'

'God, imagine,' I said. 'Your mum must have been so hurt.'

'Sure, but in the end Irene says she never got to tell Mum. Dad insisted that he would be the one to come clean. But Irene doesn't know exactly what he said – just that Mum never spoke to her again. Never took a single call. Nothing. And then they abruptly moved to London. My dad made it clear they didn't want to hear from her. So Irene took off to the west coast.'

'So your parents flee to London, and Irene is what . . . pregnant?'

'Exactly. And she takes a job at Loch Dorn, and the owners look after her. Put her in her own cottage. Help keep her on her feet. I mean, she was only like twenty-five or something.'

'But why didn't she tell your dad about James?'

'She was ashamed at first. That would have totally devastated her sister. The nail in the coffin, I suppose. But then, when Irene finally did pick up the courage to reach out, Mum had died.'

'Oh God, that's devastating,' I said, aching for Irene.

'Irene was kind of careful about how she put this, to protect James's feelings, I suppose, but she said Dad made it clear he didn't want a relationship with James, and so that was that.'

'Shit! Poor Irene. Poor James.'

'My father turned out to be worse than yours,' Heather said, trying to make a joke of it.

'Maybe he didn't want you to think less of him. You were the apple of his eye,' I offered her.

'I guess so. He was a great dad to me, in every other way.'

'But why did you keep it secret from *me*?'

'Because it's always been you and me,' Heather said, looking directly at me, 'and I was scared of how you would feel.'

'I would have helped you. I'd like to think I would have been thrilled and excited for you . . .' But as I said it, my voice trailed off and I realized that if Heather had gone to Loch Dorn without me – if everything had unfolded as it should – I would definitely have felt left out too.

'I wanted to find out for myself first. Irene was pretty easy to locate. A quick google and she came up on a lot of hospitality sites, and then I saw the terrible Loch Dorn website.' There was a trace of a smile as Heather said this, but she continued, 'I was so scared there was something terrible behind my dad's decision to hide it from me. But these memories I have of Mum talking about a sister kept chipping away at me. They are so alike in that photo, aren't they? I feel so sad that perhaps Mum wanted to forgive Irene, but never got a chance. Like enough time didn't pass or – maybe worse – Dad didn't let her?'

'Maybe it's best to imagine there was a lot of pain on all sides?' I said. I just didn't want Heather to have to hate her father.

'Well, yes. Speaking of which, you really need to deal with your issues,' she said, without mentioning seeing a therapist, though that was what she meant. She clearly wasn't going to let me get away with my crime that easily. I'd still got a long way to go before she would trust me again.

'What about James?' I dared to ask eventually, my voice tight as I thought of him.

'James has his own plans in motion. He wants to go and work abroad for a bit.'

'He wants to leave?' I felt proud but sad.

'Yes. I think,' she said, and I didn't feel confident enough to probe further.

'Do you like him?' I asked, my eyes filling with tears.

'Yes, I like him very much. What's not to like? He's warm. Kind. Smart. Talented. What more could one ask for, in a new half-brother.'

I felt a tear fall down my cheek and for a moment I forgot myself. 'Will he ever forgive me?'

'I think they understand the whole picture now,' she said carefully, and I could tell from the way Heather wouldn't look at me that they had discussed it at length. I winced. 'Birdy. James will forgive you. I'm pretty sure he was in love with you. He probably still is.'

I took in a sharp breath. *In love with you.*

'Just give me some time there on my own,' Heather said. 'Then we'll see.'

A couple of days later she'd gone. To Loch Dorn, to work with Irene and get the place back up on its feet. Russell had left, and Mr MacDonald was working to put the building into a trust and hand over full running of the place to Irene.

And now I am readying myself to head back there too. I have spent ten weeks waiting for Heather to say I could come, and now she has. In that time I've done some work. Heather very generously agreed to let me house-sit for her, since the Airbnb high season was coming to a close. I begged for a job at The Wine Library, which Brigitte agreed to. I earned fuck-all an hour, but it was great to have something to do. I went to see a therapist, and it was actually pretty helpful. His name was Alexander Dumpf – obviously chosen for his comical name – and he looked a bit like a healthy version of my dad. He cost me everything I earned at The Wine Library, but we've made a bit of progress in the last two months and it turns out I'm a negative, sarcastic motherfucker because I never learned how to express joy without feeling ridiculed. It also turns out that having an alcoholic for a father, and a disengaged mother, has given me some kind of attachment issues, which means that I avoid honest, open relationships. Also, for the record, lying can be a trait of people with emotionally detached parents. Apparently I do it for approval.

I'm not sure if knowing that I've actually got some real problems to work through helps or makes me feel worse about myself, but for now I'll keep at it.

I look back down at the Facebook request, take a deep breath and hit Accept. For a second it feels like a bigger, more symbolic acceptance of myself. I look down a moment later and there is already a message.

Hello, Elizabeth? Or can I call you Birdy? OMG YOU'RE TERRIBLE!

I'm not 100 per cent sure if Roxy's angry or laughing at me, but I do owe her a sincere apology.

I'm so sorry, Roxy. It was a dumb, shit thing to do.

I couldn't believe it! No one could believe it!

I'm sorry. Really, I wish I'd never done it.

You're completely infamous now, you know. Matthew Hunt wants you to do the next wine-night.

What?

Yeah, Forgery and Fraudsters was the suggested theme. About counterfeit wine! You're something of a legend now. LOL. ☺

Oh dear God. Roxy, I'm so sorry.

It's okay. I forgive you. At least I know I wasn't going crazy now #gaslighter ☺

Sorry.

You should be ☺

What are you going to do next?

I'm sticking around, now there's a proper sommelier to learn from. ☺ ☺ ☺ No wonder you made me do all the ordering.

Okay, I deserve that.

Bill has gone to rehab.

REALLY?

Irene took him; he wasn't happy, but everyone says it's for the best and that they hope he will be back.

Well, I'm glad.

Anis and Brett are still pissed at you.

Well, I deserve that. And the others?

Do you mean James?

Maybe.

☺

Is he still around? I'm coming up.

The doorbell interrupts us and I realize I'm absolutely starving, so I press the buzzer and wait by the door for the Uber Eats guy. He hands over the piping-hot box and, as he heads back to the lift, I shut the door and feel a little sense of delight at snuggling down to a feast for one.

There is a sharp rap on the door, and I guess the Uber Eats guy has forgotten something – either that or the neighbours want to complain about the sound of the TV again – but when I fling it open, it's him. It's James.

He smiles and his cheeks flush red.

'The driver guy, he let me in. I should have buzzed, sorry.'

He looks different. His hair is longer, and his face is paler than when I left.

'James, hi, my God,' I say, feeling my heart start to quicken.

'I'm sorry I didn't call or write, or warn you in any way. It just seemed easier this way,' he says. 'And I was coming through London, and Heather told me how to get here, so . . .'

'I can't believe you're standing in front of me.'

'Can I come in?'

I drop my eyes to the floor and step to the side to make way. 'Of course.'

He looks like he's just come back from a walk around the loch, windswept and relaxed. He must have turned a few heads on the Tube with his green waxed sheepskin-lined coat and his big hiking boots.

'Come in, sit down.' I indicate the sofa.

'It's a nice place,' he says, looking round the apartment. 'It's weird thinking my dad left Heather money for this, but didn't want to know me.'

I realize that in all of this I hadn't thought enough about how Heather's news would affect James. For some reason I only focused on Heather's feelings. 'Are you okay? How do you feel about it all?'

'It's mostly great. I like Heather. She reminds me heaps of Mum, and it feels like I've known her for ever. But it's hard not to think of Dad when I look at her. Not that I ever knew him. Thinking of my dad is basically picturing that one photo, with a bunch of fantasies attached to it.'

'That photo . . .'

'You didn't recognize him?' he says, turning to me, his eyes narrowing a little.

'No. It felt familiar, but without a context I couldn't place it. I thought he reminded me of you. And he died when Heather and I were still kids. I mean, I hardly knew him really. Just that he was different from my parents. Older. Much older, and kind of refined and worldly – because of the wine business, I guess.'

'Right,' he says, nodding, like that's one thing checked off his list.

'Do you want some pizza?' James standing there is making me nervous. I want to know how long he's here for. Where is he going? What can I do to make him stay? But as my chest begins to tighten, I try to remember to breathe and *let go*.

Mercifully he sits down and flicks open the box of pizza.

'I've got some beers?' I say.

'That would be great,' he replies.

I head to the fridge and pull out two, then flick the tops off using the side of Heather's kitchen counter, before reminding myself I need to be more caring of her things. I hand a beer to James and cringe at my bitten fingernails, painted a silly pea-green, and quickly hide my hands under the table.

'What are you doing here?' I ask.

'I've got a flight tomorrow. I'm going to San Sebastian.'

'Oh,' I say, feeling immediately distraught. 'On holiday?' I'm hopeful. Hopeful it's only a holiday.

He shakes his head. 'No.'

'I was hoping to see you at the hotel when I got back. I'm heading up next week.'

'I know.'

'Damn!' I whisper, taking a quick swig on my beer.

'It's only for a few months,' he says. 'I'm doing a short placement at a new restaurant there. It's a barbecue seafood place, just south of the city, right up on the cliffs. A bit of a different set-up for me, but they do a really amazing local, foraged menu and I thought it was time to try something new for a bit. But only for a bit . . .'

'And then?'

'Well, I'll be trying to do something at the bay.'

'You mean . . . your house?'

'Yes, that's the plan. The second building, next door to the main one, do you remember it?'

'Of course I remember it,' I blurt out, wanting to grab his hand. *I'll never forget it.*

'Well,' he says, his eyes flicking to mine and then back to the safety of the pizza. 'Yes. I've spoken to the bank and they are going to lend me some money for the renovation. It's not going to be anything fancy . . .'

'It's going to be perfect.'

'Well, it's going to be all mine.'

'Won't you miss Loch Dorn?'

'Miss it? No. It's a drive away. Besides, we'll work together. Loch Dorn will hopefully offer horse treks with Brett to my place, for some kind of fancy brunch,' he says.

'Brett & Breakfast,' I say.

He laughs. A warm, spontaneous laugh, covering his mouth with his hand as he does so. I laugh too. We catch eyes, and it's all I can do not to throw myself across the table and into his lap.

'Oh, that's great,' I say instead. 'I'm happy for you. It seems right.'

'It's right,' James says, nodding his head like he's just accepting it himself, and then there is a silence again. I know he didn't come all the way to London – flight out or not – simply to tell me that. He stands up and begins to pace the short length between the door and the kitchen sink. 'Look, I need to know how much of *you* I knew.'

'Uh,' I put my head in my hands. 'I don't know how to answer that.'

'Heather talked to me about you a lot.' He stops by the fridge for a moment.

'Is this about Tim?'

'I don't care about him,' James says, waving his hand dismissively. 'But Heather – the way she talked about you, it sounded like the person I knew.'

'It was all me.'

'All of it?'

'Well, apart from the wine stuff. I had to work hard to pull that off,' I say. 'I mean, I worked *really hard* at that, and working really hard is definitely not something that I could have considered *me*, before. But all the rest – I mean, it was as much me as was possible.'

'The stuff when we went fishing, about wine not being your passion? That's why you were so evasive.'

'Yes.'

'What you did was so reckless. I find myself so angry at you a lot of the time. That you could put the hotel at risk like that. I mean, just thinking about it now, I feel angry. I don't think that anger will go away quickly.'

I don't speak. I don't say sorry again. I've worn the word out so much it feels threadbare on my lips.

'But I do kind of get it, on another level . . .' James continues, looking over at me, and I can't meet his eyes. 'Like I can see how it spiralled out of control. Heather has battled hard in your corner.'

My heart lurches for my friend once more.

'James, I loved spending time with you. I didn't want to be fake with you. That's why I kept saying it couldn't go anywhere . . . and then it did – *go somewhere* – and I kind of panicked. The more I liked you, the worse it felt.'

He nods. He doesn't look angry, or hurt. Just like he's processing information that he already knew.

'But, James, in case of any doubt: I really like you.'

His eyes flicker up to me and he studies my face.

'Do you think you could forgive me? I think you felt . . .'

'I'm working on it,' he says, before looking me in the eyes again, this time with a hint of the James from before. 'I definitely want to.'

'You want to?' I say, my breath catching in my throat.

'Yes.' He must sense my distress because he leans across the table and puts his hand on mine. The warm weight of it fills me with hope. I am fighting back tears when he says gently, 'I do. I just need time.' He sits back, takes a big gulp of his beer and looks pensively at the pizza and then up at me. 'What are you going to do?'

'Well, I'll go back to Loch Dorn and face the music.'

'And then?'

'And then, what?'

'What will you do?'

'I was hoping . . .' I trail off. *I was hoping they might ask me to stay.*

'If you want to, they need some help in the bar. Especially with Bill out of action now. He won't ever work the bar again, I don't think. Could you do that?'

'Really?'

'Yes, really. But could that sustain you?' he says.

'What?'

'Working at Loch Dorn?'

My heart lurches at the idea of it. 'Of course it could, James. What do you mean?'

'Well, you want a passion. Could that be it, or would you be off again in a year?'

I think of the cottage, the loch, Portree, the river, the craggy mountain range on Skye. I think of James's little house with the large window out onto the water, and watching the gulls dive into the sea. I think of Anis and Brett and Irene. I think of Roxy. And I also picture Heather.

'Yes. It would.'

'Well, Elizabeth Finch,' he says looking at me, then at the cheesy salami-thin crust in the brown cardboard box and back to me, 'there won't be any pizza.'

'I can live with that.'

42.

May

Spring has returned to Loch Dorn. It's cold and wet. But the promise of warm weather is in the air.

I pull back the curtains and stare out across the estate. The view from Bill's old room is the same as James's view was.

Eggs, says the message on my phone.

I yawn and stretch and make my way downstairs into the kitchen. The cottage is all mine, for now at least. Heather is staying with Irene, and James has moved permanently to his place by the sea.

I pull on my new waxed-canvas jacket, and the hiking boots that I reclaimed from my old wardrobe. I have never owned a pair of shoes that sit so perfectly around my feet. I pull a beanie down over my head, and go out to the little jeep parked by the back entrance, swinging the keys as I walk.

As I slide the key into the driver's door, I spot Anis heaving an ice-box full of salmon out of a white van.

'You need a hand?'

'Fuck off,' she replies. But she's smiling.

'Yes, Chef,' I reply as she pushes the door open with her bum and disappears back into the kitchen. *Her kitchen*.

Then I remember. *Eggs*.

I follow her into the kitchen and go to the chiller, grabbing a tray of eggs, then head back out. I glance into the restaurant, to see Roxy fussing over a full breakfast room and the new-season staff being put through their paces. With the entrance of the kitchen now blocked by another delivery van, I walk back through the reception area. The library looks much more stylish, with its heavy oak shelving and the books restored to upright and readable. I love that they've replaced some of the more deliberately mismatched furniture with antique leather. The 'help yourself' games cabinet has also proved a hit with the guests.

Once I'm out of the estate, I drive down the lane to the now properly cleared and sealed road that leads to James's house. I pull up next to one of the hotel's SUVs and make my way to the door of his cottage. When I come through the door, Irene and Heather are already there.

'Birdy,' Heather says, clasping her hands together, 'look at this!'

She thrusts an iPad under my nose, open at *The Guardian*'s food section.

'It's by the *Guardian* travel writer who visited last week,' she says. Heather knew him well from her days in London and convinced him to come by and review.

'It's a fabulous review,' says Irene.

'Awesome,' I say, grinning as I walk over to hand the eggs to James. He puts them on the countertop and places a kiss on my forehead, turning quickly back to the bacon frying on the stove top.

'Happy birthday,' I say.

'It feels very happy,' he says, threading his fingers through mine and leaning forward to kiss me first on the cheek and then on my lips, then he moves down my neck and I push him back.

'Not now. They're just there,' I whisper.

'I'm so glad you're here, Birdy,' he whispers back.

'Thank you,' I say, feeling the same old prickle of shame in my cheeks. 'I'm sorry.'

'No more *Sorrys* we said, remember?'

'Sorry,' I say, laughing this time.

'What are you doing with my brother?' Heather shouts and we both giggle, red-cheeked.

And then we are all sitting at James's walnut table and bench seats, eating breakfast in the completed cottage – modern, simple, stunning. Oak and stone form the bones of the house, with Scottish tweed and tartan soft furnishings used sparingly to finish the look. It's unmistakably Scottish. It's comfortable and authentic and humble. And it's 100 per cent James.

The huge window looks out onto the bay, with the morning sun sparkling on the water like a million tiny diamonds. A gull hovers in the air, riding the wind before plunging into the water for fish.

Heather and Irene are talking at a hundred miles an hour. There is work to be done on the annexe, and there is the Wine Society night to consider again.

'Well, Birdy should do it,' Heather says, nodding towards me.

'Oh no – I mean, it's your job,' I say. 'As the sommelier.'

'Nonsense. I'll help, but you should do the hosting. It's your thing.'

'Sure I can do it,' I say, blushing, 'but it's not, like, totally my thing.'

'What do you mean?'

'I mean it's not the one thing that makes me jazzed to get up in the morning. Not like you, James – and you, Heather. I still don't have that *thing*. The *calling*.'

'You can still find it,' says James.

'Maybe. But maybe I'm just happy being happy for a bit. Then we'll see what's next.'

'That makes sense,' says Heather.

'Maybe I don't even need a calling,' I say. 'Maybe I just need to be me for a while.'

'Well, that would make a change,' says Heather, and then everyone laughs and I blush. Heather reaches across the table and touches my hand, giving it a little squeeze. The tease is meant kindly. It's a kind ribbing – something Heather probably needs to do for a while. And I'll take it for as long as I have to.

And then they're off again and on to the next subject: the return of sherry. Artisan gins. Has Irene eaten at Arthur's in Glasgow? What about a trip to Provence in the autumn?

James pulls me in close and drops a small kiss on my shoulder. I still feel shy accepting his affection, especially in front of Heather.

I watch my best friend's face light up every time Irene speaks: like she's fallen in love. Heather has found the love she has spent her adult life looking for. The great, lonely hole that she had inside her when her father died. The pain I didn't understand, and which she tried not to burden me with. We wanted so much to be enough for each other, but it was too much of a burden for each of us to carry.

And I think about myself. The aimless wanderer. The directionless woman who didn't know what she was missing until she found it. Family. Community. Love. Did I need any more? Or was it okay to just be?

Just be *me*?

I think, for a while, it's exactly what I need. For now, being Birdy will be my calling.

And then we'll see.

Acknowledgements

This book is first and foremost a love letter to my time living and working in hospitality in Scotland. Thank you to the Manson family for taking me in and not only showing me how to eat a langoustine, but also the often stressful but wonderful and rewarding world of the hotel business. All my love, I am forever grateful.

The characters in this book are inspired by the many people I've worked with in Inverness, Edinburgh and Aberdeen, but also Queenstown in New Zealand and across several London restaurants and bars. It's the people who make hospitality so special; those who have made a career of it and those who are blowing through on their way to something else.

And so, a big debt of gratitude to the waiting staff, the kitchen staff, the managers and everyone across the hospitality supply line who take huge pride in their job to show us a good time. Thank you for keeping the beer cold and the pies hot while you risked your own safety in order to let us raise a glass during the pandemic. (If you can afford to, please tip!)

My unending gratitude to my beta readers, and plot-line support team: Kristie Frazier, Nicki Sunderland, Carolyn Burke, Kaite Welsh, Caroline Leech, Sarah Chambers-Tooner and Laura Gilbert.

Thanks to Ben the Forager, Edinburgh. To Fiona Melling for making sure I kept things Scottish. To my old bar manager in NZ who is part-inspiration for my Maitre D, Irene.

To Michael Smith at Lochbay for the tips on food delivery and crafting a local menu. Sorry for all the bits I got wrong – I so wanted to come to the West Coast to edit this book and make it as up-to-date and accurate as possible but 2020 was not the year for travel.

Thanks to Grant Manson for fielding panicked calls from me when I was at my most anxious, and for gently reminding me that he knows me and he understands.

To Rachael Johns for the writing inspiration, to The Maybies for picking me up when I was on my knees, and to all the dear friends and family who have listened to me moan and squeal and cheer as I rode this publishing rollercoaster.

To my Mum for not only letting me steal her name, but also for her unwavering belief in me, and endless loving support. And to my wonderful Dad who is also an author and understands the stress and the passion it takes to get through the last edits. Love. Gratitude. I miss you.

To everyone at Penguin Random House who has worked on this book, but obviously and most importantly Katy Loftus and Tara Singh Carlson. I have LOVED working with you both. Thanks for your advice, your enthusiasm and your brilliant ideas for how to bring out the best of my girl Birdy.

Katy, thanks so much for taking the leap of faith. I hope I do you proud.

Special thanks also to Victoria Moynes, Natalie Wall, my copy-editor Mandy Greenfield, and everyone else who has touched this book along the way.

And finally, to Hattie Grunewald for all the reasons she already knows, and a few I need to tell her over a wine when we can meet again in person.